For Doreen Wells and Mary Godwin.
With love and thanks for your friendship and
constant encouragement.

CHAPTER ONE

'What is this place?' Joseph pulled on his all-in-one protective suit and shivered.

'A selection shed. It's where they size and grade the potatoes before bagging them.' Nikki pulled up her zip and eased the hood over her head. 'Stan Ruddick and his family have been growing vegetables here on Carter's Fen for decades.' She looked across the big sorting machine with its rollers and hydraulics, towards the back of the gloomy wooden barn. 'I guess she's over there.'

Lights emanated from the far corner and dark figures moved to and fro.

The call had come in at around two in the morning, and DI Nikki Galena and DS Joseph Easter had responded. It was early October and although the weather had remained unseasonably warm, the nights were becoming chill and damp. And being out on a muddy Fenland farm at night did nothing to warm either their bodies or their spirits.

A phone call earlier to Greenborough police station had stated that a local lad, on the look-out for somewhere quiet to bring his girl, had entered the shed at the back of Ruddick's Farm, and found a body. As the station had been inundated with hoax calls recently, a lone bobby called PC Mick Manners had been dispatched to check it out, but as soon as he had stepped into the barn he had realised it was no hoax. He knew the "local lad" in question as the sort of little scrote that would sooner eat broken glass than talk to the Old Bill. If he said that he'd wandered into this stinking barn on the promise of a shag but found a dead body, then a dead body was exactly what Mick would find. He had rung it in immediately and now the long, sad process had begun.

'Is the pathologist here yet?' Nikki asked the young PC.

'Yes, ma'am. He arrived about fifteen minutes ago. The doctor has pronounced life extinct, and we've cordoned off the whole area.'

Nikki thanked him and moved towards a small gaggle of uniformed officers talking softly as they waited behind the blue and white tape.

Thick plastic duckboards had been placed on the soft ground to prevent policemen's boots contaminating the area and in the glare of a halogen lamp, Nikki could see the tall, thin form of Professor Rory Wilkinson, the Home Office pathologist.

'Good evening, uh, morning, uh, night, whatever it is, Detective Inspector. Ah, and Joseph too, I'm honoured.' Rory rubbed his eyes sleepily. 'But I believe this particular death does indeed warrant the presence of a full contingent.'

'That does not sound good, Rory.'

'Indeed it is not. I think you have a very unpleasant case on your hands.'

Nikki frowned. Rory's trademark high camp and black sense of humour for once seemed to be absent. 'Now you *are* worrying me. No wicked wit, no graveyard humour? Are you ill, my friend? Or are we dealing with something truly horrible?'

'I'm in the rudest of health, my dear Inspector, and you are quite correct about the horrible bit. I can't say much at this early stage, I'll need the PM to confirm it, of course, but if I were you I'd start checking on the Police National Computer for kidnap victims and hostages. This youngster's injuries have been inflicted over quite a long period of time.' He pushed his wire-rimmed glasses up onto the bridge of his nose. 'I think you'd better take a look.'

'Any idea how long she's been here?' asked Joseph quietly.

Nikki noticed that her sergeant was trying hard not to look at the young woman. Maybe it was because he had a daughter of his own, and it was almost impossible not to think of your nearest and dearest at a time like this.

Rory screwed up his face and puffed out his cheeks. 'Estimated time of death, damned difficult to nail until all the factors and decomposition changes are duly noted.'

Nikki glowered at him. 'We all know that you are the most accurate pathologist in the county, no, country, no, *the world*, so come on, give!'

He grinned sheepishly. 'Actually, I'm pretty sure she didn't die here. It's such a mess it's hard to tell, but the body has certainly been moved, and I'd say, considering the temperature, the gross swelling, and the discolouration and condition of the skin that she's been dead, oh, approximately three days.'

'Thank you, Professor! Now that wasn't too difficult, was it?'

'Not difficult at all, but you know how I enjoy making you ask. It's such fun.' His attempt at light-hearted humour was short-lived. A moment later his expression was once again sober. 'Anyway, I must get on. I have all my preliminary notes to make and she has yet to be photographed in situ. My SOCO has started a meticulous examination of the place for trace evidence, so as soon as

I've finished, I'll leave you to seal it up until the findings are known.'

Nikki nodded. 'And from the look on your face, I guess you are going to make this a priority?'

'When you know all the details, I think you'll be itching to get your hands on the bastard who did this. Never fear, she'll be first on my list in the morning.'

Outside, Nikki sighed. 'Better go talk to the Ruddick family.'

Joseph was slow in walking from the shed. 'Poor little devil. She can't be very old, can she?'

'Not long out of her teens, I'd say. How on earth did she come to be in that state?' Nikki frowned.

'Down to us to find out, isn't it? And we will.' Joseph's voice had a hard edge to it.

Nikki gave him a little nudge. 'Come on, Joseph, let's get this over with. After that, there's little more we can do here tonight. Uniform have it in hand. We'll speak to Stan and his family and head off home, okay?'

They found Stan, his wife Betty, and one of their sons, a tall, well-muscled lad called Ryan, all sitting round the kitchen table. Nikki glanced around. The old place had changed beyond recognition. She'd come here often as a child to collect vegetables with her dad, and then the kitchen had been a glorified scullery with a coal-hole attached, and water had to be brought in from the well. Now it was all granite worktops and gleaming stainless steel appliances, everything in a brasserie style with more features than a glossy magazine. Briefly she wondered how a few bags of taties could generate such luxury. Then she saw their shocked faces and fell back into police mode.

'Can you give us an account of what you know, Stan?' Nikki accepted a chair, but Joseph remained standing.

Stan Ruddick was a ruddy, muscular man in his early fifties. He was the image of his father and Nikki felt very much like a small child again.

'It was around midnight I s'pose, won't it, Bet?'

His wife nodded and wrung her hands in her lap.

'Lad came hammering on the door, screaming up at the bedroom winders.'

'I thought it was an accident,' said Ryan slowly. 'Some idiots use the fen lane here to cut out the village, offen finish up in the dykes.'

'I went down,' continued Stan, 'Asked him what were wrong and he kept babbling about a body. Couldn't make any sense of it, then he said about the shed, so I take Ryan, and we goes and looks for ourselves. And he were right.'

'Who rang the police?'

'Boy said he had already rung on his mobile, but he were in such a state that I rang too, in case they dint get the right address. Oh, that poor little kid, I keep seeing her in me mind's eye. I've seen some dreadful things, Nikki, working the land — accidents with farm machinery and the like, but I've nivver seen anything like that.'

'Like something off the late night Horror Channel,' added Ryan grimly.

'That's enough, son. Show some respect.' Betty spoke for the first time. 'Is she still out there?'

Joseph nodded. 'They need to follow a careful procedure, Mrs Ruddick, but she'll be taken away and looked after just as soon as they have finished.'

Nikki didn't expect a lot from her next question, but she didn't get anything at all. 'Did anyone hear anything out of the ordinary last evening?'

Stan shook his head. 'Wunt, would we? It's harvest. Machines are churning up the fields day and night. Denis and Clive are out now with the tatie harvester in the lower field. And anyway, that shed is a fair way from the farmhouse.'

'Any cars up and down the lane that you didn't recognise?'

'Plenty. The pickers are out all hours. Cars and transits all over the place.'

'Thought that would be the case,' said Nikki. 'Busiest time of the year, isn't it?'

Stan sighed. 'You can say that again. I don't think I'll ever go in that shed again without seeing that poor lass.' He paused. 'In fact . . .'

'Come on now, Stan. Let's not start that again, not now.' Betty sounded exhausted, she looked at Nikki and gave her a hopeless smile. 'He wants to sell up, move away.'

Nikki's mouth dropped. 'But your family has been here for generations, Stan! Surely things aren't that bad, are they?' She couldn't stop her eyes moving around the bespoke kitchen.

Betty had seen Nikki's glance. 'All this dint come from the farm, Nikki. My father died and left me his house in Norfolk. I sold it and used the money to renovate Ruddick Farm. Now this old fool wants to move. Can you believe it?'

Nikki shook her head. 'Carter's Fen would not be right without the Ruddicks.'

Stan threw an accusatory glance towards his son. 'Don't rightly think there will be any Ruddicks left here before long, if these here boys have their way.'

'Stan! This is not why Nikki and the sergeant are here. They don't want to hear our problems. Now concentrate on what has happened to that poor child and don't waste their time.'

Nikki decided that shock had a lot to do with all this. 'Don't worry. We'll get some officers to come back tomorrow and get written statements from you. You try to get some rest. I'm afraid our people will be out there for the duration.'

Betty stood up and went to fill the kettle. 'Then they'll be wanting some hot tea and biscuits, won't they?'

'You'll be very welcome out there, Betty. Coppers and their cuppas! Need their brew to keep them going. Thank you for your time. We'll be off now, and believe me, I'm really sorry for what has happened here.' Nikki stood up to leave.

The faces looking back at her told her that what had "happened" would stay with the Ruddick family for a very long while.

* * *

'First thoughts?' asked Joseph, as he manoeuvred the car through the dark fen lanes.

Nikki leaned back in her seat. 'Well, Rory is sure that she was not killed in the shed, and given that that part of Carter's Fen is in close proximity to the main Greenborough to Spilsby road, it probably isn't a local killing. Probably someone drove off the road, out onto the farmland, and dumped her in the first available deserted spot they came across.'

Joseph grunted. 'Like they do with their rubbish. Tip it in a lonely stretch of dyke, rather than drive it the same distance to the official landfill site.'

'I don't want to liken her to rubbish, but yes, exactly like that. And if it hadn't been for that young bloke and his girl, Stan probably wouldn't have found her immediately. That shed is no longer used. He said they are using the bigger, newer one that's just off the main farm entrance.'

'Mmm, so was she dumped by design? Or was it just a random choice?' He yawned.

'You were very quiet tonight, Joseph. Were you thinking of Tamsin?'

Joseph let out a long sigh, then gave her a weary smile. 'Of course I was. She's been on my mind constantly for the last few months, what with the engagement and all that. Then you see some lovely kid brutally murdered, and oh, I don't know, you just realise how fragile life is.' He paused, then groaned out loud. 'Oh God! Me and my big mouth! I've done it yet again, I'm so sorry, Nikki, I don't know what I was thinking!'

Nikki reached across and squeezed his arm. 'It's alright, you know. Every chance comment about daughters or children does not bring me crashing to the ground in spasms of uncontrollable grief. Well, not any more. My darling Hannah is where she belongs, in my heart. So don't walk on eggshells, okay?'

Nikki's only child had died as a teenager, and although the pain would never leave her, she had found a way to cope, and that was work, work and more work. Working to stop what happened to Hannah from happening to other young girls. And when inevitably it did, like the girl in the potato shed, she would move heaven and earth to find the killer.

* * *

As Nikki and Joseph drove away from Carter's Fen, not too far from them in a more remote area of the Fens, another girl lay awake and frightened.

She wished he would come back. He had forgotten to leave her any food again, and she was scared to eat her two last biscuits, the ones she had hidden under the mattress. At least he had remembered to leave her some water and her medication, so she could have a few hours with a little less pain. What if something happened to him? What if he had an accident? No one ever called. No one knew where she was. She shuddered and pushed the thought away. It was too awful to contemplate.

The room was full of shadows and the sound of rushing water was louder than usual, perhaps it was one of those exceptionally high tides tonight. Her stomach grumbled loudly, and as if in answer, somewhere out in the twilight, an owl screeched. Earlier, she thought that she had heard the sound of an engine, but as no one ever visited and it seemed as though he may have sold his car, perhaps it had just been an airplane. Then when the darkness seemed almost too much to bear, she heard the familiar squeak of his old bicycle, and with a sigh of relief, she gobbled down the two remaining biscuits.

CHAPTER TWO

Joseph sat in his tiny cramped office, drawing up the action programme for the team. Outside in the CID room the others were talking about the grim discovery of the night before. It never ceased to amaze Joseph how quickly news travelled in Greenborough police station.

'Everyone here?' Nikki called out.

He stood up and stretched as Nikki's voice echoed around the big room. For some reason he felt very low, an emotion he was neither used to nor comfortable with. Joseph was not just a glass half-full kind of man, he was a "Hey! What luck, we have a glass!" type. And with his only daughter getting engaged to one of the finest young police officers in Greenborough, he should have been feeling good.

'In your own time, Sergeant Easter! Don't worry about us, we have nothing to do.' Nikki tapped impatiently on the whiteboard beside her.

He grinned apologetically, gathered up the work rotas and hurried out. 'Sorry, ma'am.'

'Right, let's get started.' Nikki stood up straighter and folded her arms. 'Two items to deal with this morning, and I'll get the quickest one out of the way first. Although that's not to say that it isn't a very important piece of information. Superintendent Woodhall has received intelligence that Freddie Carver has been seen in this county.'

Joseph frowned. Carver hadn't been a particular problem to the Fenland Constabulary, but his dirty dealings had been plaguing the Met for years. Then a local case that he had been involved in had backfired, sending the filthy rich villain scurrying away to live in Spain. Word had got back that he hated it. He was a big city criminal, he liked the sun and sangria for holidays, not forever.

'Most of you won't recognise the name, but I urge you to do your homework on this man. He is utterly ruthless. I wouldn't like to count how many suspicious deaths and disappearances in London and the south-east can be attributed to him or his henchmen.'

'What is he doing in the Fens?' asked DC Dave Harris, the team's oldest and shrewdest detective. 'Surely we can't offer him more than the city does?'

Nikki shrugged. 'Your guess is as good as mine, Dave. We have no idea why he's here. But,' she ran her hand through her hair and looked at her team anxiously, 'When I mentioned his henchmen, you should know that I'm talking about two men we *have* had dealings with — two very unpleasant men who go by the names of Mr Fabian and Mr Venables.'

This time a low murmur of recognition rippled around the room.

'Mmm, I thought you'd know those names. And after the last murder case, we do not, under any circumstances, want that toxic pair on our patch. So we need to find out exactly why Freddie Carver is here, and what he's up to. Dave — I'd like you to put out an attention drawn to all the other stations in the area. We need to keep a close eye on his whereabouts and so far, we know SFA, okay?'

Dave nodded. 'Wilco, ma'am. And I'll get Niall and Yvonne to see what the word is on the street about him.'

Uniformed officers PC Niall Farrow, soon to be Joseph's son-in-law, and WPC Yvonne Collins were the team's eyes and ears on the ground. There was little that went on in the high streets, back alleys, the pubs, the clubs, and the homes of Greenborough, that Yvonne and Niall didn't know about.

'That's good, Dave. Keep me up to date on anything and everything you uncover.' Nikki took a deep breath. 'Now, as you will have heard, the body of a young woman was found last night out on Carter's Fen. The consensus is that she was held captive for a period of time before being murdered. She was white, a natural brunette in her early twenties, and Professor Rory Wilkinson, the pathologist, believes she has been dead for about three days. He has promised that we will have his preliminary findings later today.'

'Any form of identification on her, guv?' DC Cat Cullen interjected.

'The girl was wearing an anklet engraved with the name Lilli. Now, this could mean nothing. It could have been stolen, given as a token by a friend, belonged to a dead loved one, anything, but we can't ignore the fact that it might also be her name. The other important thing about her, until we get the forensic report, is that one finger had been removed.'

DC Jessie Nightingale shuddered slightly. 'While she was alive?'

'Most certainly. Professor Wilkinson's description was most unclinical. *Hacked off* were his words.'

'Lovely.' Cat absent-mindedly ran a finger down the long scar that stretched from her temple to her jawbone. 'She really got mixed up with some sweet people.'

'I want you to start checking the PNC for any missing females, especially ones suspected of being abducted. We think the finger was the usual token — cut off and sent to whoever was expected to pay the ransom. Cat, check everything local and national that involves missing women with the name of Lilli, Lily, Lilly, Lilian, Lili, you know the score. It's not a bog-standard spelling, so it may be a variant. Jessie, could you get onto the Missing Person's Register? I'd like a printout of all the women between the ages of nineteen and twenty-seven.'

Jessie groaned. 'I'll probably need a shopping trolley for all the paper that will throw up. Perhaps I should start locally then extend the range?'

'Sorry, I know the Misper list for that age group is horrendous, but it's not as bad as the teenagers. As you say, start local and concentrate on the hair colour and the name. I'll let you all know the minute the reports start to come in, both from the crime scene and from forensics, then you should have more to go on.' She gave them a cool smile. 'I know I don't have to ask this of you guys, because you always give one hundred per cent to everything you do, but I need a fast result on this. The super is shitting hot bricks over the news that Freddie Carver is back from the continent, and now we have this unfortunate girl to deal with. Joseph will pass around the action programme and what little info we already have, and then, pals, get off your arses and get to it.'

Nikki beckoned to Joseph. After handing out the sheets, he followed her back to her office and closed the door behind him.

'You don't think this could have something to do with Freddie Carver, do you?' he asked. 'No one's ever been able to get any hard evidence on him for anything, but we know from the Met that he's quite capable of torturing or topping someone.'

Nikki flopped down in her chair. 'As you say, he's certainly capable of it, and I'd dearly love to nail him for something like this, but Freddie's big league and way too clever to instantly shit on the doorstep of his new home.' Nikki pulled a face. 'This doesn't seem like a very professional job to me, it reeks of desperation. As in, get rid of the body, and fast. Carver's way would be to make her disappear without trace. Still, who knows? Let's get all the evidence on Lilli first, and if he fits the bill, then maybe we should run with it.'

Joseph bit his lip. 'You're right, of course, but it just seems a bit of a coincidence, doesn't it? Carver is seen in the locale, and a dead body turns up.'

Nikki nodded. 'Oh how I *hate* coincidences.'

* * *

True to his word, Rory Wilkinson had gone directly from the crime scene to the Greenborough Hospital morgue to await the arrival of his deceased guest. Something about the dead girl had touched a nerve and he needed to know that everything was in place for the following day.

By the time Matthew, his lab technician, arrived in the morning, Rory had already completed the external examination. He had carefully noted every feature, mark and scar. He had listed her hair and eye colour, her height, weight and general condition, checked her dental work, taken her fingerprints, and extracted material from under her fingernails. He had also photographed her in the remains of her clothes, and then again naked.

'Ah, Matt, my lifesaver! Before we start dissection, just pop down to the canteen and get me a bacon sandwich, would you?'

Matthew looked down at the mutilated body on the autopsy table, almost unidentifiable as human. 'With or without ketchup?'

'Brown sauce, please. And a strong coffee would be nice.'

As Rory waited for his breakfast to arrive, he sat on a high stool, tilted his head on one side, and stared at the naked woman. It was strange to think that this putrid, stinking heap of flesh and bone would soon begin to tell him the frightening story of what had happened to someone's daughter. He already knew a lot. He knew that she had been held prisoner, bound and unable to move freely, for a long time. He knew that she had been beaten and regularly abused. And although he did not know the exact manner of her death yet, the cheap, gold coloured identity bracelet round her ankle had given him a name. That made the whole thing much more personal. Of course the anklet could have belonged to anyone, but he liked to find some way of personalising his cadavers, so to him she was Lilli.

Mathew returned, and Rory took his food to his office, but left the door open so he could talk to his technician. He sat staring out — industriously munching on his sandwich, while his assistant began the top to bottom internal examination. As he began the Y-shaped thoracic-abdominal incision, he looked across to the professor. 'You know, the smell is making me want to puke.'

'You'll get used to it in time, my boy. A dab of Vicks under your nose always helps.'

'I don't mean this.' He jabbed his knife towards the corpse. 'It's that bacon!'

* * *

Three hours later Rory finished the prelim report, sat back and lifted his phone. Nikki answered almost immediately.

'Your place or mine, Inspector? I've cobbled together everything I have so far.'

In just under twenty minutes Nikki and Joseph were sitting opposite him in his office.

'This is the bare bones of my preliminary report, if you'll forgive the unintentional pun, without the lab and toxicology test results, of course. I'll get them to you as soon as they come back.' He laid the file on the desk in front of her and sighed. 'It makes grim reading, but before you begin, I can tell you what I know for certain, and give you my opinion on what has yet to be confirmed.'

'I'd appreciate it, Rory. Then we can immerse ourselves in this little lot.' She flicked swiftly through the series of appalling photographs.

'Okay. She is aged between twenty-three and twenty-five, has had no children, was five feet seven inches tall and her weight prior to being confined was probably in the region of eight stone. I believe, from the multiple injuries, and the degree of scarring and tissue damage, that she must have been some sort of prisoner for anything up to six months. Her condition was poor, almost emaciated, prior to death.'

'Do you know the actual cause of death?'

Rory frowned. 'Yeah, and here's the bummer, it's not what you'd expect. It was a pulmonary embolism, a fatal complication following a deep vein thrombosis in her calf.'

'So it's technically not a murder?' asked Joseph incredulously.

'Whatever, the poor kid was killed as surely as if they'd stuck a knife through her heart, just in a much slower and crueller manner. The clot in her leg occurred either because she had been injured, or because she had been tied up and was inactive for very long periods of time. Part of it broke off, travelled to her lung, and bang! Oh yes, and I suggest that whoever held her was mighty jarred off when she died. She is covered in post-mortem bruising.'

'Could that have occurred earlier, or maybe when she was moved?'

'Absolutely not. There is a very different presentation of contusions administered after death — the blood isn't flowing, you see. My findings will show that she was kicked, repeatedly, after she died. It's this part that disturbs me so much. I've never seen such a vicious attack post-mortem, and believe me, I've seen a lot.'

Nikki's eyes narrowed. 'You said her ring finger was cut off. At what point over her six month period of imprisonment did that occur?'

'Early on, it was not a new trauma.'

She drummed her fingers on the table. 'So it seems that she was abducted, the finger was sent to the family, or whoever, as a means of identification, but they didn't or couldn't pay up. So her kidnappers kept her for six months? That's ludicrous! They'd either top her or let her go, not hang onto her. Can you imagine trying to keep a secret like that for months on end? It's far too risky.'

'I agree, but that's what appears to have happened. Our Lilli must have been very important to them, alive that is. She must have been very well hidden too. Sorry I haven't been able to give you any positive help yet. I'm hoping some of the forensic tests will be able to place where she was held. She was covered in detritus. Soil, dirt, fibres, animal hair, that kind of thing, and although I have been able to distinguish their nature, their origins will take considerably longer, I'm afraid.'

Nikki glanced down at the report. 'I'll take what I can from this, Rory, if you can let me have the rest as soon as they come in. Until we know if this is a local crime, or whether we've just been the recipients of a kind donation from out of the area, it's going to be a bloody needle in the haystack job to know where to start.'

'If it helps, I've got a student of mine working on a facial reconstruction. It's one of our laboratory's new super-duper hi-tech gadgets. The laser beam scanner and a computer should give us a digital likeness in no time.'

'Great, that will make life easier. In the meantime, if we get a missing person that seems to fit the general description, I'll send you a photograph, so you can do one of your superimposing jobs, is that right?'

'Yes, no problem there. That's a simple procedure. We photograph Lilli's skull, superimpose the skull over the head of the Misper and hey presto, if it's our girl, we'll have an exact match.'

Nikki sighed and stood up. 'So all we have to do is find you a picture. Simple enough . . . I don't think.'

Rory looked up at her. 'Nil desperandum, Inspector, you've had much worse than this. A few more pieces and the puzzle will come together, it usually does.'

'I don't like the sound of that word, *usually*.'

With a grin, he said, 'Sorry, I forgot I was talking to the great DI Galena, naturally I meant, *always*.'

CHAPTER THREE

His jacket was worn and faded, and he noticed that the cuffs of his shirt sleeves had begun to fray, but it was not out of keeping with the other working men in the public bar. The only difference was that they sat in groups, conversing and sometimes laughing together, whereas he sat alone. He did nothing to encourage others to sit with him, and his small table was entirely taken up with a selection of daily papers, and a pint of local ale.

Maggie, the publican, looked across as she polished a beer glass, and threw a weak smile in his direction. He returned it, as he always did, with a nod, and then returned to scanning his newspapers. The foreign news, the weather, even the sport did not interest him. It was the national stuff, home affairs, that he read — every word.

An hour later, he carefully folded the papers, placed them on the bar for Maggie to use for fire-lighting, and without a word to anyone, buttoned up his jacket and went outside. It seemed as if the season had changed overnight, and today was the first day for months when he felt really cold.

He blinked quickly as he strode along the street. The sun was bright, but it was the east wind that brought tears to the eyes. He glanced at his watch. He had a job to do, and he wasn't looking forward to it. The only thing in its favour was that it paid his rent. He almost laughed aloud when he considered what he was paying for. It was hardly a dream home. Still, it would not be forever. He rubbed his eyes, smarting from the brisk wind, or were they real tears? He wasn't sure. Sometimes, he thought, you had to do things you detested, in order to have the things that you truly wanted. And there was something he desperately wanted. Something he would do *anything* for. The image of a woman's face floated into his mind and he swallowed hard. On to work.

* * *

Nikki sat in the comparative quiet of her office and steeled herself to go through the photographs of Lilli. As she stared at the images, a multitude of feelings flooded through her. The mutilated hand affected her most. The ring finger had been crudely excised, but the stump had managed to heal, after a fashion. It was clear that this girl had been given no medical attention of any sort, which led Nikki to assume that the amputation had been done without anaesthesia. She pushed the pictures away. They were very hard to look at, especially when you knew that the child, because she was little more than that, must have suffered beyond all comprehension. Suddenly she knew why Joseph was so affected by this case. It was the juxtaposition between the intense happiness of his daughter Tamsin and the awful suffering and sadness of Lilli. Two girls, both in their twenties, one on the brink of a bright new life, and the other lying mutilated in a mortuary. Fragile, he had said, life is so fragile. It's a game of chance, Nikki thought, it's win or lose. And poor Lilli had been dealt a rotten hand.

She looked again at the pictures and wondered where the girl had come from. Because if she was local, was someone out there going to be looking for a replacement? Would another young woman go missing? Or was it just Lilli who was so very important to him? There was little point in mulling this over, and she knew it, but it was hard not to. Waiting for forensics to come back was nail-biting stuff. Nikki Galena was no good at waiting. But until something found on Lilli's body could tell them roughly where she had been imprisoned, it was all guesswork, and she would just have to exercise patience.

Nikki gazed through the window and watched Joseph talking earnestly to Dave.

Maybe she should consider taking him off the case and let him work on the search for Freddie Carver. She pulled a face — as if he'd stand for that! And anyway, he'd still be seeing the photos on the evidence boards and hear the others discussing the case. Nikki exhaled. Oh well, he'd get through it, they always did. But she would be watching Joseph Easter very carefully over the next few days.

* * *

Jessie stood up and stretched her aching back. Hours over a computer did little for the posture, and made her shoulders ache like blazes.

'Cat? Fancy a coffee, and maybe a doughnut?'

'Someone say "doughnut?"' Dave's head jerked up.

'Yes, old mate, I'll get you one too, never fear.'

Cat rubbed hard at her own shoulder. 'Are you thinking about Café des Amis?'

'I certainly am.'

'Then I'll grab a few moments' break and walk round with you. I need to stretch my legs.' Due to an injury in the line of fire, Cat found sitting for long periods very uncomfortable. She pulled a black leather jacket from the back of her chair and slipped it on. 'What's yours, Davey-boy? A skinny latte?' Cat grinned at her partner.

'Full fat milk and three sugars, as if you didn't know, cheeky!'

The two women left the office and made their way down to the foyer.

'Is it my imagination or is everyone a bit subdued today?' Cat slipped her arm through Jessie's. 'Especially you, my friend.'

'It's nothing, really.' Jess didn't want to talk about what was bothering her. It would sound so trivial to anyone else, but to her it was an all-encompassing ache.

'Come on, this is Cat, remember? Your bestest friend in all the world?'

Jessie was forced to smile. Then she sighed. 'It's Graham's birthday.'

The three words hung in the air. They needed no explaining.

Cat stopped walking. 'Oh shit! I'm such a plank! I should have remembered! I'm sorry, Jess.'

'Why should you? It's ancient history now, isn't it?'

'Not for you it isn't.'

And it wasn't. Eighteen months ago she had been in a happy relationship with the man she loved. They had lived together and were verging on making the "big commitment," when she woke up one morning and found that her life had turned upside down. PC Graham Hildred, with his lopsided grin and big heart, had eaten breakfast with her, and as she snuggled back down to sleep after a night shift, he went off to work at Greenborough police station. But he never arrived, and Jessie never saw him again. The romantic, fairy-tale story came to an end.

'Silly isn't it? But there you go, I just can't forget him.'

'Why should you, Jess? You loved him. How long is it now?'

'One year, six months, and eight days. And for what it's worth, I still love him.' Her eyes had begun to well up. 'I just want some sort of closure, Cat, just to know if he's dead or alive, that's all. Then maybe I could cope better, accept things and get on with my life. It's the not knowing. I just can't move on.'

Cat put her arms around her and hugged her tightly. 'And anniversaries bring it all back, don't they?'

'Yeah, don't they just.' She pulled out of the embrace and wiped her eyes. 'And you're going to think I'm a total flake when I tell you that I bought him a birthday card and put it by his photo.'

Cat looked hard at her. 'I don't hear any laughter, do you?'

'No, but you should be laughing, it's bloody pathetic.'

'It's human, Jessie. If he'd buggered off with another woman, or been killed in an accident, or whatever — something tangible, then yes, I'd definitely report you to the force medical officer, but not the way he disappeared. Even I lie awake wondering what the hell happened, so how you cope, I have no idea.'

Jessie hung her head and whispered, 'I'm not coping well, Cat. If it wasn't for the job, I'd be a head case by now, or more of one than I am already.' She shook her head. 'Worst thing is, I'm *sure* he's alive, but if he is, then where? And why?' She spread her hands. 'But this isn't getting Dave his doughnut, is it?'

* * *

As the time for the four o'clock meeting drew closer, Nikki was starting to feel that nothing had been achieved at all. When she entered the murder room she saw that some of the PM photographs had been attached to the whiteboard. Other than those and the word LILLI, carefully written at the top, there was nothing more to say . . . yet.

Nikki scanned the faces in front of her. 'Where's Dave?'

'Just taking a call in the CID office, ma'am,' said Joseph. 'He won't be long.'

'So, in his absence, has anyone got anything concrete on Lilli?'

Cat stood up. 'No one locally of the same or similar name has been reported missing in the last two years, ma'am. I picked up two women with that name on the PNC but the photos don't match, not by a long stretch.'

'The Misper list, Jessie?'

'Nothing so far, ma'am, although I'm still working on it. I have pulled out the names of three young women that went missing within that time frame, but their descriptions don't quite match. I just thought I would check them out in case they'd changed their hair colour or appearance. I'll do it when I've finished with the list."

'Okay, Jess, I'll leave that with you. Joseph? Anything at all?'

Joseph shook his head. 'I've been tracing national reports of suspected kidnaps or abductions with ransom demands, but nothing pertains to anyone like Lilli. Sorry, ma'am.'

Nikki sighed. 'Can't be helped. We are dancing in the dark until we get some more forensic evidence.'

Dave hurried in and sat down. 'Sorry I'm late, ma'am. But I have got a few bits of news.'

'Thank heaven someone has! Go on then.'

'Well, I've had Yvonne and Niall make a few enquiries with their snouts, and they've hit on something interesting. Apparently Carver has dropped his multi-faceted criminal career in favour of drugs, and only drugs.' He opened his pocket book. 'He was into robbery, people trafficking and protection mainly, plus the odd contract to remove unwanted obstacles that got in his way. Now this nasty piece of work is aiming to be the biggest drugs baron this side of the Channel.'

'He is back for good, then?'

'That's what they're saying on the grapevine, although he has yet to set up a permanent base.'

'So where is he staying?' asked Joseph.

'No one knows, but Yvonne and Niall think they might be able to work on an old lag that sometimes coughs up some good intel. They'll report directly to you if they find anything tasty.'

Nikki chewed on the inside of her cheek. 'So he is back in this country, and he's been seen here in Lincolnshire. That's very bad news indeed.'

'The other thing they found out, ma'am, is that he travels a lot. They think they have a lead on someone who is acting as a driver for him. It seems he's been in and out of the county a lot, and he's only been back in England a few weeks.'

Nikki frowned. 'Setting up a network, no doubt. We need to keep our ears to the ground on anything drug-related around here. If he's planning on a takeover, there will be casualties.'

'I wonder if the Leonard family knows anything about Carver turning up here?' Joseph mused. The Leonards were an old-time criminal family who lived on the infamous Carborough Estate and controlled anything villainous in the local manor.

'Ask.' Nikki smiled at him. Joseph did not know the Leonards quite as well as she did, but he had taken one of the younger members of the family under his wing and got the boy out of trouble on several occasions.

'I'll ring Mickey, see what he's heard.'

'Good idea.' She looked around. 'Well, until we have some more reports back in, that's it. Keep chipping away, because someone is missing a daughter, a sister, a niece or a girlfriend, and we need to find that person.'

'How about releasing this to the press, ma'am?' suggested Cat.

'I want to get more info in before we do that. It might not even be our case.' She stepped away from the whiteboard. 'See you all tomorrow, nine sharp.'

As the team dispersed, Joseph walked with her to her office and waited in the doorway. 'At least I have some good news. Mario's has opened up again in his new premises. He'd like to see us when we can make it. So, fancy an Italian meal tonight? My treat.'

'I'll come if we go Dutch.' Nikki licked her lips. 'I've missed his potato and leek frittata, with that delicious cheese on top.'

Joseph smiled at her. 'Ah, the dreamy Taleggio. And I've missed his asparagus with four cheese sauce. Let's pig out, shall we?'

'It'll be my pleasure, believe me,' said Nikki with feeling. 'I get the feeling that as soon as this investigation gets underway, we will have precious little time left to even grab a sandwich, let alone dine out.'

'I'll ring him now.' Joseph took his phone from his pocket and was soon chatting happily with his old friend. After a few minutes he looked at Nikki and asked, 'Does Eve like Italian food?'

Nikki thought about it. Eve liked good food, and she was a great cook, but as to specifics, she didn't know. There was a lot she didn't know about Eve.

'I was thinking she is probably still trying to find her feet here in Greenborough. Shall we ask her if she'd like to tag along?'

'Sure. I'll call her. Ask Mario to add a provisional extra and we'll confirm as soon as I know.'

Nikki keyed in her mother's number and waited for an answer. Eve took a while to pick up.

'It's Nikki. Joseph and I are going to an Italian restaurant tonight after work. Can we interest you?'

Eve laughed. 'Oh you can indeed! I've just about had it with unpacking boxes. A glass of Italian wine is exactly what the doctor ordered. Shall I meet you there?'

'We'll pick you up on the way, now that you are a local.' It still felt weird to Nikki. Eve was her biological mother, who Nikki had known nothing about until eighteen months ago. As soon as it became clear that Nikki wanted Eve in her life, she had sold her big house in

Coningsby and bought a smaller property on the edge of the town. Nikki tried to see her at least once a week and was slowly finding out about the extraordinary woman that her father had loved.

Nikki ended the call and gave Joseph the thumbs up sign. 'Seven thirty at Eve's place, okay?'

He nodded. 'Perfect.'

* * *

The evening made a welcome contrast to the harrowing day. Because Eve was there, neither Nikki nor Joseph mentioned the investigation, and it did them good to free themselves, even if for a short time, of the sight of the murder room whiteboard and the pictures of Lilli.

Eve put down her glass. 'I cannot believe my luck with the new house having a garden office. It makes the perfect studio, so I can leave all my paints and artist's materials out ready to use. It's a real dream.'

'What are you working on now?' asked Nikki.

'I'm trying out pastel painting. It's mucky on the fingers, but you get such wonderful blends of colour, especially for dramatic skies. I think pastels are going to become my medium of choice.'

Joseph dabbed his mouth with a napkin. 'I tried that once. Sad to say, I made a right pig's ear of it.'

Nikki grinned. 'Because you don't like getting dirty, Mr Neat-and-Tidy?'

'Probably, but more to the point, I'm no artist. It was another therapeutic activity I tried when I left the army. For most people it is a great way to relax, but I found it quite stressful.'

'How so?' asked Eve with interest. 'It is the *only* thing that relaxes me.'

'Because one, what I wanted to see on the paper never seemed to materialise, and two, as you say, I hated the dusty pigment all over my hands.' He shivered and did a Lady Macbeth. 'Especially the black.'

Eve laughed. 'I'd try watercolours if I were you, much more genteel.'

'I think I'll leave the arty stuff to those of you who are good at it. I'll stick to catching villains, thanks.'

As he spoke, Nikki saw a shadow fall across his face, and she knew he was thinking once again about Lilli. At that moment she knew this was one case she wanted tied up very quickly, and not just for the sake of the girl and her family, but also for Joseph.

* * *

He had been in all day, although she had only seen him once, when he brought her some supper. He had seemed preoccupied and he hardly seemed to hear her when she told him that she thought her medication was not working, that the pains were getting worse. For a second, consternation had darkened his face, but then he had shrugged his shoulders and was suddenly telling her that this was the last day off he could take for a while, that they were short-staffed at work. She did not like to mention the tablets again.

Perhaps she needed different drugs? Perhaps her body was so used to her usual pills that they no longer had any effect. She stared through the dirty window up to the moonless sky. Its absence gave her some relief. She could sleep easier without the implacable moon regarding her all night. She lay down and pulled the old duvet tighter around her. His going to work was a great relief, but it did bring its own problems, and the worst of all was when he forgot to leave her food. Water was not an issue. If he forgot her flask of tea or coffee, or the jug of orange squash, she could always get water from the basin. It tasted horrible, of metal and of . . . well, she preferred not to think what it tasted of. But she needed her food. She had nothing much else in her life, and a meal was the one thing she looked forward to. For a while she had tried to stockpile dry foods, biscuits and the like, but he never really gave her that much in the first place and she had usually eaten them by evening time.

Food was not the only thing that made her anxious. She was constantly worrying that one day he would not come home. He might have an accident — a car might veer out of control and hit him, he might trip and hit his head. Or even something medical could happen, like a heart attack or a stroke. And then she would die, slowly.

Sometimes, when the pain was really bad, she would try to imagine what it would be like to starve to death. Would she try to eat the mouldy paper from the walls? Her bed linen? Dead flies? How long would it take? At her lowest ebb, she had considered taking her own life, to get it over before that fateful day when she was alone, permanently. But she had him to consider. She should not put him through the anguish of finding her, it wouldn't be fair on him. He loved her. It would finish him, apart from which, how could she achieve such a feat? He kept her drugs. He always took her cutlery away after her meals and there was nothing sharp in the room. She had no mirror and no pictures. And if, on one of the occasions when he did not use the restraints, she managed to smash a window, could she draw that fatal shard of glass across her own flesh? She doubted it. She was weak, in body and spirit. Please God, that day would never come.

She rocked backwards and forward and tried to think of her mother. Tried to remember her hair, her eyes, her face, the smell of her, the things that she would say, the poems that her mother had read to her. She tried and tried, but the image was hazy. She could only conjure up a few lines from the past, and they all seemed to revolve around death, the thing she was trying to forget.

Then, as the pain and sadness were reaching a crescendo, she saw a star. Just one diamond-bright spot shining through the clouds, and she heard her mother's voice:

"Do you wish they'd leave
Your bedroom door ajar
So you'd see a golden crack
Shine from afar?
Do you wish a fairy'd come
And light a fairy light,
To glimmer and to shine for
you
All through the night?
See, from heaven shine the
stars,
Silent, steadfast, true;
God is caring all the time,
Little one, for you.

For the first time in years she saw her mother's face clearly, smiling with a beautiful radiance. She felt loving arms tighten around her. The soft voice sang the familiar verses that told her frightened daughter that she would sleep in peace.

As a night wind gently moved the clouds away and a cascade of bright stars filled the sky, she closed her eyes and slept.

CHAPTER FOUR

While Superintendent Greg Woodhall finished a phone call, Nikki couldn't help staring at the untidy piles of files and folders, books, printouts and crisp packets that passed for a filing system in his office. When Woodhall had taken over from Nikki's old friend, Rick Bainbridge, the superintendent had been quiet, well-organised and calm in the face of chaos. Over the last year, Greenborough had changed him, evidently not for the better.

'Well, bloody find it, man! And this side of sodding Easter would be nice!' Woodhall slammed the phone back into its cradle, and let fly with a string of expletives.

'They run anger management courses at Greenborough Community Centre, Tuesday evenings at seven.'

'Very amusing, Inspector.' He flopped into his seat and rummaged haphazardly around in the jumble of papers on his desk. 'Right, what have we got so far?

'She was definitely not imprisoned somewhere local, sir. Professor Wilkinson has just rung me to say that the soil samples taken from her shoes and clothing are not from our area. He's isolated some pollen and other plant debris and is hoping this will show broadly where the girl was held. Apart from the entomology report that confirms she was only in the potato barn for twelve or so hours, we are no further forward in finding out who she was.'

Nikki pulled a computer-generated picture from an envelope. 'Rory has sent me this. It's not quite what I was hoping for, but it's not too bad. It's been circulated to all forces. What do you think about hitting the media with it?'

The superintendent took the picture from her and examined the face as if he might know her.

'Yes, we owe her that much. I'll try to get the earliest possible slot on the news if you'd send this to the nationals, and get copies to all the local papers too. She might be from out of the area, but it's worth a go.' He looked again at the slender features and the dark brown hair. 'She'd been held captive for six months, you say?'

Nikki nodded. 'And very badly treated, sir. Let's just hope someone recognises her.'

'That finger thing is odd, don't you think? I mean, that indicates someone trying for a ransom, doesn't it? So if her people couldn't pay, why haven't they reported her missing?' He shook his head and frowned. 'It really does not make sense.'

'Nor does holding her for all that time. It's not what kidnappers do.'

Woodhall shrugged. 'Oh well, keep digging, Nikki, and put some pressure on forensics for that geographical location.' He sat back. 'I think that's all for now, I'm sure you want to get on.'

Nikki looked at her watch. 'Mmm, I see it's time to take the morning meeting, not that I'm expecting much to have come in since last night. I'll get Sheila to make sure this photograph is circulated to the press.'

Nikki left the superintendent sorting through his rubbish heap of a desk and hurried downstairs to find Sheila Robins, her office manager. She handed over the photograph for distribution and made her way to the murder room, where she was met with eager smiles.

'Don't tell me we have made some headway?'

'Not absolutely sure, ma'am, but a definite *maybe*.' Cat sifted through some sheets of paper. 'We had a call from the Derbyshire Constabulary. They haven't got anything directly linked to Lilli, but they had a very similar case last year.'

'How similar?'

'Woman found dead. She was in a terrible condition, the post-mortem showed that she had been held for over six months. She also had the ring finger missing and an index finger too. It looks like she managed to ligature herself in the end, poor kid.'

Nikki looked up, alert. 'And where exactly did they find her?'

'Dumped in a disused quarry in the Dark Peak. I was wondering, ma'am, if I might drive over there to speak to the detective in charge of the case.'

'Good idea, Cat, and the sooner the better. Did they identify her?'

'No, and she was found nearly a year ago. The case is still ongoing, of course, but they have scaled it right down.'

Nikki nodded slowly. 'I see. And anything from our own enquiry?'

'The Missing Persons Register can't match Lilli, ma'am.' Jessie looked at her hopefully. 'Have we got *anything* more from forensics yet? Without more evidence, I'm a bit stuck on which way to go.'

Nikki passed her one of Rory's computer-generated likenesses. 'This is as close as they can get, but he thinks it's a fair representation of Lilli. And as we now know that it's not a local killing, it is going to be released to the media today.'

'And once we get some idea of where she was held, we can move the search into that particular area,' added Joseph.

'Ma'am, I've got another email in from Derbyshire. It's from the detective who was running the case.' Cat stared at her screen. 'He said that as both girls were tied up for long periods of time, we should know that their girl had a very distinctive kind of restraint, a kind of electrical flex.' She read from his report, "An old variety of electrical flex was used, in which the wires were encased by a rubber sleeve, then wrapped around with strands of coloured fibre (the kind used on electrical appliances such as irons, in the fifties). This particular flex left particles embedded in the skin and was identified as that used by a company called Sunbeam."

Nikki flicked quickly through the forensic report, then let out a small exclamation. 'Lilli has the same! Well, it's old-style flex, although we haven't got details of the exact type yet. Colour of thread is identical, so it looks as if the two cases *are* connected.' She looked excitedly at Cat. 'What do we know about the detective who was on this case?'

'His name is Ben Radley, ma'am, and it's been his obsession ever since. He's still digging around whenever he gets an opportunity. He thinks her kidnapping was related to drugs in some way.'

'For God's sake! What crime isn't? Not exactly a revelation, is it?'

'Whatever, he's happy to give us everything he has on the dead girl. Oh, he calls her Fern, by the way, because of where she was found — in a bed of bracken. I guess it might help us to make comparisons when the pathologist's report comes in.'

Nikki nodded. 'Dead right. You really do need to talk to this Ben Radley. It's only around two hours from here, are you up for it?'

'You bet, ma'am.' Cat grabbed her jacket.

Nikki looked at Joseph. 'Considering what we now know, I suggest we put a hold on looking for Lilli until Cat has got us more info from Derbyshire. Perhaps you and Jessie could give Dave a hand and concentrate on looking for Freddie Carver?'

'Good idea, definitely the best use of our time.'

Nikki watched him go. She thought she saw distinct relief in his face. She almost called him back, and then thought better of it. If something was really troubling him he would come to her, she knew he would. That was what they did. And yet. With a little shrug of uncertainty, she hurried off to see how Sheila was doing with the press releases.

* * *

The superintendent had managed to get a slot on the lunchtime news, and he asked the public to ring a designated number if they recognised Lilli from the photograph.

Jessie raised an eyebrow at Dave. 'The Strawbs are going to be busy this afternoon.'

He smiled. The Strawbs were the civilian staff who manned the phones. Strawberry Mivvies to rhyme with civvies. 'Always the same with something like this, how to sift the wheat from the chaff.' Dave had been on the other end of some weird calls in his time and knew that few people actually came forward with honest concerns and solid information, but the nutters and the time-wasters would be queuing up to bend some poor sod's ear.

'Rather them than me,' said Jessie. 'Now, what can I do to help?'

'Find Carver?'

'Of course, and after lunch?'

'Find Flight 19?'

'What?' Jessie looked puzzled.

Dave grinned. 'Five torpedo bombers that disappeared over the Bermuda Triangle in 1945.'

'Right, we'll just pop over to the States, shall we? We can barely afford petrol for the vehicles.'

'Then you better get to work on Carver, hadn't you?' He handed her a printout, 'This is from Spain. Ever since he bought a property there, the Spanish police have been keeping a close eye on him. This is a list of known associates with shady backgrounds. Check them out and see if there's anyone known to us in the Fenlands.'

Jessie took the paper and scanned the names. 'Okay, no one I actually know, but I'll do a search on them.'

Dave watched her as she walked to her desk. She always seemed to be on top of things, but he wondered what she was like when she went home, to an empty house inhabited by the ghost of Graham Hildred. Dave had worked with Graham for years, and his disappearance had hit him harder than he would ever have expected. It hadn't made the headlines, but it hurt like hell. Graham was a good copper, and he had loved Jessie. He and Dave had had many a heart-to-heart while stuck in a car on all night stakeouts. Dave was afraid that he would never see his old mucker again. He was pretty sure Graham had upset someone badly enough to warrant his permanent removal from the force, and he feared that the man Jessie waited for lay buried under a building site. He doubted PC Graham Hildred would ever be found. It was deeply sad, he had deserved better from his colleagues. And Jessie needed answers so that she could draw a line and move on.

Dave sighed. If they couldn't find their friend, it would be good for Jess to meet someone new. But she probably wouldn't even notice another man, even if he were right in front of her, offering diamonds and champagne. He sighed again, and turned back to his computer.

A uniformed officer called around the door, 'Is someone free to talk to some bloke about the Lilli case?'

'Some bloke? Doesn't he have a name, Constable?' Joseph was coming out of his office.

'Sorry, Sarge, yes, it's a Dominic Jarvis. He is a regular. Usually talks to DI Mercer, but she's out.'

'Regular?' Joseph pulled a face. 'As in . . . ?'

Jessie looked up. 'Dominic Jarvis's sister went missing a couple of years ago, remember? He haunts DI Mercer.'

She hunted through the paperwork on her desk. 'Look, this is his sister Dina. She is one of the three Mispers I wanted to double check.'

Joseph nodded to the constable. 'I'll come down. Give me a couple of minutes.'

Dave rubbed his chin. 'I'm not surprised it doesn't mean anything to you, Sarge. We never had dealings with that one. We were up to our necks with the Flaxton Mere killings, and to be honest, DI Mercer never saw it as abduction. She believed the girl had simply had enough and done a runner.'

'Okay. Still, I'd better see what he has to say. Want to come with me, Jessie?'

Jessie pushed back her chair and stood up. 'Sure.'

* * *

The young man was too thin. He had the haunted look of the obsessed. Immediately Joseph wished he had let someone else handle it. But here he was, so he'd better get it over with. 'Good afternoon, sir. I'm DS Easter and this is DC Nightingale, how can we help?'

Dominic Jarvis gave him a long, slightly disturbing stare. 'I saw the news earlier.' He folded his hands in his lap and looked into Joseph's eyes. 'You are asking for help to find the killer of that dead girl.'

'Yes, sir. Do you know anything about her?'

'Why didn't you put my sister's photograph on a news flash? Why didn't you fill the papers with her name? Why did you do nothing to help me find her?'

The man's eyes were bright, glinting with flashes of pure anger.

'Forgive me, Mr Jarvis, it wasn't a case I was involved in. I am working on the present investigation and you asked to see us because of that.'

'You were never working on my sister's case, as you laughingly called it, because it never was a *case*. You never took me seriously and you did nothing!'

'I'm truly sorry about your sister, Mr Jarvis. But from the little I do know she was not deemed to be at risk. She was not under age, she was not sick in mind or body and there were no suspicious circumstances about her leaving to warrant an investigation.' Joseph tried to keep his voice soft and even. He was very aware that Dominic Jarvis was either on something, or slightly deranged. Maybe both.

'I *know* my sister, Detective. She would never have left without talking to me first. No matter what happened, we always talked.' He clenched his fists into a tight knot. 'When we were teenagers our parents split up. They went their separate ways, neither wanted us, so we stayed at home together. Do you understand? We supported each other through everything. She would never, never just leave me.'

For a moment Joseph wondered if there might be a grain of truth there. 'So what do you think happened to her?'

His voice cracked with emotion. 'She met a man. He took her, he lured her away with empty promises. He got her drunk then abducted her. I wouldn't be surprised if it isn't the same man who took that Lilli.' His eyes narrowed to little more than slits.

Joseph exhaled, his sympathy for the man evaporating by the second. This was a waste of time. The man was clutching at straws and using Lilli as an excuse to rekindle the matter of his sister's disappearance. He was sure Dominic Jarvis was right. Dina had met a man, fallen in love and run away with him. End of. If her brother was this intense in his everyday life, then no wonder she had done a bunk.

'I'm really sorry, sir, but unless you have any proof . . .' He let the words fade out.

'If it were one of your own, you'd damn well find them! Well, wouldn't you? Wouldn't you pull out all the stops and not give up until the bitter end?'

Joseph felt Jessie tense beside him and he threw her a concerned glance. Sadly this was not missed by Dominic Jarvis.

'Ah, of course! I remember now! You lot can't even find a missing copper, can you? In which case my sister stands no chance at all.'

'DC Nightingale, could you please go and inform the desk sergeant we are finished here, and perhaps he would be kind enough to have an officer escort Mr Jarvis from the station.' Joseph stood up and bundled a seething Jess out of the room.

'Touched a nerve, did I, Sergeant?'

By now Joseph was wishing he were a 1950s copper. No one then would have batted an eyelid at the bruises this man might wear when he left the station.

Jarvis stood up. 'Okay, I'm going. But two things you should know, Detective Sergeant Easter. The first is that my sister did *not* run away. I would know because she's my twin. And second, I think I've seen Dina with that girl in the picture. It was years ago, and the girl was younger and much prettier, but I'm certain my sister knew her.'

'Why the hell didn't you say this before?'

'Why should I help you? You've done sod all for me.' Dominic shoved his chair under the table and pushed past Joseph. 'If you want to talk to me in future, you come to me, okay?' He walked out and slammed the door.

Before Joseph could find Jessie to see how she was, he saw Nikki almost running down the corridor to meet him.

'Joseph! We've just had a call from Derbyshire. They've picked up a girl wandering on the main A52 near Ashbourne. She's been badly beaten and her right index finger has been severed.'

'Jesus! When was this?'

'A couple of hours ago, thanks to that detective who has been fixated with the investigation. The moment he heard about it, he rang us. She's been taken to the Derby

Royal Infirmary. He reckons she's too traumatised to talk yet, but she probably holds the key to what happened to both Lilli and her predecessor, Fern.'

'Then we should be around when she *is* fit to talk, shouldn't we? I know Cat is probably halfway there by now, but this could be the breakthrough we need, so we should go too.' Joseph tried to sound enthusiastic, but the last thing he wanted was to sit with a young woman who had been tortured and probably imprisoned and abused.

Nikki gave him an odd look, and said, 'Actually, I'd rather you stay here and steer the ship, or possibly man the lifeboats, if Freddie Carver turns up. It doesn't take two of us to check this out when we already have Cat on scene.' She turned and started back towards the foyer. 'What was that Derbyshire detective's name?'

Joseph thought for a moment. 'DC Ben Radley, ma'am. Cat reckons he's a bit of an old terrier. He got really pissed off when they scaled down the Fern case. He can't let it go, even works on it in his own time.'

'Then I really need to talk to him, he'll know more than anyone. Okay, I'll grab my bag and hit the road. I'll keep you updated all the way, and Joseph, you do the same, won't you?'

Joseph touched her arm. She was leaving him behind for a reason, he knew, and he wondered why he had agreed to stay. Normally he would have insisted on going with her. 'Of course, and you drive carefully.'

Nikki threw him a withering look. 'Honestly, Joseph. I'll ring you when I get there.' Too impatient to wait for the lift, she ran up the stairs. 'Can you contact Cat and tell her what has happened? If she doesn't know already, that is, and I'll meet her at the hospital.'

Joseph watched her retreating figure, still wondering why he felt so relieved to be staying in Greenborough.

CHAPTER FIVE

The girl was in a private room, a little way from the main ward.

'The poor kid, she's in deep shock. She can't even tell us her name, Inspector Galena.' The detective held out his hand to her. 'I'm DC Ben Radley, ma'am.'

Cat had called Ben Radley a terrier, but Nikki thought pit bull would have been more accurate. The man was as broad as he was high, and seemed to possess no neck at all. His prematurely receding hair had been sensibly cropped, and his skin was weathered and creased.

With a smile she shook his hand, thinking that he would be a pretty terrifying adversary if he didn't have such soft, sympathetic eyes. At present he seemed almost distraught at the victim's condition.

Together they looked through the glass partition.

The young woman who lay in the bed was thin and pale — apart from the areas that had been kicked or beaten. Her hair was matted with dried blood, and a deep cut on her arm still oozed blood from between the sutures, even though the wound had been cleaned and treated. Her right hand was heavily bandaged and suspended above her head in a sling-like device. She lay perfectly still, nothing moving except her eyes. They darted around the room like those of a wounded animal.

'It may be some time until she talks, ma'am. You could be in for a long wait.'

'I have to get back to the Fens tonight. So, after we've had a talk, I'll be leaving Detective Constable Cullen, who you've already met. I assume you won't be going too far from this young lady's bedside?'

Ben's face said it all. 'No, you're right. I'll be here for the duration. He sighed. 'If I'd found the bastards who killed Fern, this child wouldn't be lying here. And your Lilli wouldn't be laid out on a mortuary slab either.'

'Not your fault, Detective.' She looked at him shrewdly. 'Now, are you certain she's a victim of the same people who held the other women? Is there any chance she just got caught up in some bizarre accident?'

'The finger was deliberately amputated, ma'am. The doctors think maybe by heavy-duty wire cutters, or something similar. Fern's finger was severed by a hacksaw, that's the only difference.' Ben's face contorted into a wrinkled, leathery mass of hatred. 'I wish I'd got my hands on them the first time around, I'd . . .' He smashed a balled up fist against the wall.

Nikki's piercing blue eyes narrowed. 'That's not helping, Ben. We are not responsible for the evil these people do. We just have to do the best we can to sort out the shit that they leave behind, and nail the bastards whenever possible. Now I suggest you start thinking in a more positive way if you really want to prevent this from happening again.' Nikki looked back through the glass. 'At least you now have something solid to work with.'

Ben stared at the floor. 'Sorry, ma'am. I just get so angry.' He looked up and matched her cool gaze with his. Nikki saw that he was sizing her up, trying to get a handle on what she was all about. Then he seemed to come to some sort of a decision and with an almost imperceptible nod said, 'I had a daughter once, took her abroad for the

42

holiday of a lifetime, and she picked up some godawful bug. She was only twelve.' He swallowed loudly. 'There was nothing anyone could do to save her, even the doctor told me how helpless, how powerless he felt.' He looked away. 'I couldn't help my own child, now I feel I'm letting these girls down too. I feel as helpless as that doctor did.'

Nikki stiffened and felt a chill sweep through her. She felt his pain deep in her heart. She wanted to blurt out about her daughter Hannah, to tell him what a lovely bright child she had been, to reach into her handbag and bring out a photograph, but she didn't. Instead she kept her voice steady and said, 'I'm so very sorry about your daughter, Detective, but that was something you had no control over. This is totally different. If you want to help her, or others like her,' Nikki indicated the pathetic figure beneath the white sheets, 'you are very welcome to work with us, but for God's sake, keep your cool.'

Ben nodded.

'So, if there's somewhere we can go? I see Cat is back now, so she will stay here. Perhaps you'd tell me what you know about Fern? On and off the record.'

Ben ran broad fingers over his short hair. 'There's a relatives' room just along the corridor. We've temporarily commandeered it.' He gave Nikki a wan smile. 'Sorry about my outburst, ma'am, it won't happen again. I've completely forgotten my manners. Can I get you both a drink before we get started?'

Ben went to get some coffees, and Cat moved to her side. 'This is a right turn up for the books, ma'am. Another victim?'

'Something of a shock, I must say.' Nikki stared after Ben and raised her eyebrows.

'Too involved?' Cat asked.

'I hope not, but I get the feeling he's making a crusade out of this rather than facing his personal grief.'

43

'He told me about that, but solving this case won't bring his daughter back.' Cat winced. 'Although you'd know all about that, ma'am, wouldn't you?'

'Exactly, and by the way, I'd rather you kept what happened to my daughter under wraps. It's not relevant at the moment and I'd rather he didn't know.' She watched Ben carefully take the beakers from the coffee machine. 'And if he's hurting that much, I wonder what he will do when it's all over?'

'Throw himself straight into another case, I guess, like you did.'

'Yes, like I did,' whispered Nikki.

Ben returned balancing three polystyrene cups. 'Strong coffees all round.' He passed one to Cat and said, 'Why don't you sit in the room with her? You've got a really nice friendly face. I'm sure it would make her feel safer to see you there.' Then he turned to Nikki and said, 'Ready when you are, ma'am.'

* * *

He steadied his shaking hand and finally unlocked his door.

He moved straight to his kitchen and stripped off all his clothes, leaving them in an untidy heap on the stone floor. He turned the tap on the water heater, and a splutter of hot water began to trickle into the sink. He filled a bowl to the brim, took a large bar of old-fashioned soap and began to wash. First he viciously scrubbed at his hands, making the skin red and sore, then he worked from top to toe, flannelling or scrubbing every inch of his naked body. It took him twenty minutes before he reached for the threadbare towel and carefully dried himself. Avoiding the dirty clothes as if they had belonged to a leper, he walked into his living quarters and selected some clean ones from his suitcase. Carrying them back to the kitchen, he paused at the work bench and stared down at the small cardboard box sitting beside the kettle. The woman's finger nestled inside it on a bed of white kitchen roll. There was very little blood, just a dark brown glutinous mess around the severed end where the bone protruded. He looked closer. The fingernail was torn and ragged. The nail varnish was a weird navy blue colour that youngsters seemed to favour these days. Not a colour he found particularly attractive, and it looked odd on that single finger sitting alone in the box. The others had been nicer, one a peachy shade, and the other a bubble-gum pink. He shivered, carefully placed his clean clothes on the workbench and went back to the sink, where he emptied the bowl, re-filled it with fresh, hot water, and began to wash again.

* * *

It was after ten in the evening when Nikki arrived back at Greenborough police station. Ben Radley had done some pretty impressive work during the hunt for the people who had held and tortured Fern. He might have become rather too deeply involved, but he had honestly investigated every avenue open to him, until there was none left to explore. Nikki had talked with him for over an hour, and had been sincerely impressed by his painstaking approach to the case. She in turn had volunteered to send him all the reports on Lilli. Together, and hopefully with the young unidentified woman's help, they would finally get a result.

Joseph met her in her office, yawning. 'I waited just to make sure you got back okay. Not that I've been slacking. I had Prof Wilkinson in here earlier and he says he'll have the botanical forensic report by tomorrow morning.' He looked around. 'No Cat?'

'She's going to hang on at the hospital until the girl is well enough to talk. DC Ben Radley has organised somewhere for them to crash out between shifts, then he's volunteered to come back with her and see if he can be of help.'

'And at the same time have a snoop to check out what we've come up with, no doubt.'

'He's welcome. This case should be a joint venture between Derbyshire and us, so I've said we'll pool all information.' She threw her jacket over the back of a chair. 'So what time did Rory come in?'

'Only about an hour ago. He says he's got a massive workload on and will be working late all week. He's not long returned to his beloved morgue.' Joseph yawned again. 'He sent you love and kisses and said he'll see you in the morning.' Joseph shook his head and smiled. 'You know, I wouldn't mind living on Planet Wilko. He's definitely a one-off, isn't he?'

Nikki nodded. 'Oh he's that alright, but I'm not sure about his world, it's a bit too ghoulish for me, thank you.' She sank onto her chair. 'Nothing else of interest come to light on Lilli? No leads from the picture we gave to the media?'

'Nothing yet. Loads of the usual calls that follow an appeal, but not a single lead worth chasing up . . . Wait. Except one.' He told Nikki about Dominic Jarvis.

'It sounds a bit like he threw that comment in at the end just to wind you up.'

'You may be right, but he's a weird one, for sure, seriously freaky. I thought I'd talk to DI Gill Mercer about him tomorrow.'

'Good idea, and now I hear Cloud Fen calling, don't you?'

'It's been crying out for hours now.'

Nikki looked at him fondly. 'You should have gone home, muppet! You really don't have to worry about me being out late.'

'I know, but I do.'

'Are you alright, Joseph? You don't seem your usual "get stuck into everything" self?'

Joseph shrugged and sat on the edge of her desk. 'I know, and I've got no answers, Nikki.' He gave her a half-hearted smile. 'All I can put it down to is worrying about Tamsin and the engagement.'

Nikki leant forward and patted his leg. 'Niall is the most honest and kind young man I've ever had the pleasure to work with. He knocks spots off most guys of his age, and he's a brilliant police officer. What more do you want for your girl?'

'Maybe you've hit the nail on the head. He's a police officer. Like you and me.'

Nikki stared up at her friend. 'He's nothing like you and me. I've said this before, but Tamsin and Niall are a completely different breed to us, and they have totally different goals in life. Plus, they are deeply in love and are young enough to adapt to each other.' She gave a little laugh. 'You *do* know that Niall, the station's number one Burger Boy, is now embracing healthy eating? Not quite a veggie, but heading that way.'

Joseph relaxed a little and smiled back. 'Tam told me. And in turn, she is testing the lad for his exams, and showing honest interest in how twenty-first century policing works. That is something I never believed I'd see in my lifetime.'

'So why the mardy face? Is it to do with this case we are on? With Lilli?'

Joseph nodded.

'She and the girl before her are affecting a lot of people, Joseph. That other detective from the Fern case, you know, Ben Radley? He's well screwed up over her . . . He lost a young daughter, which doesn't help at all.'

Joseph gave a little groan. 'And *that* didn't help you much either, did it?'

'One of those moments, I admit, but this time I kept it together. You'd have been proud of me. I didn't even mention Hannah.'

'I'm always proud of you, Nikki,' Joseph said softly. He stood up from his perch on the desk. 'Now let's go home. And if you care to call in at Knot Cottage, you can

47

help me polish off a nice little lasagne before you retire, because you haven't eaten, have you?'

'Two packets of crisps, a Mars bar and a sausage roll, actually.'

Joseph held up two crossed index fingers. 'Aargh! Go wash your mouth out immediately.'

* * *

Cat and Ben sat in silence, watching the sleeping girl in the bed next to them. Earlier, her panic had been so severe that the doctors had decided to sedate her rather than let her injure her mutilated hand any further. Now, as darkness fell outside, and the nurses came in and out occasionally to monitor her progress, a stillness settled over the two detectives and oddly, considering they were strangers, it wasn't uncomfortable. Once Cat had spent a bit of time talking to her Derbyshire colleague, she found him both interesting and sincere. It wasn't the usual way coppers behaved. Sometimes the bitching and backbiting in the mess room was as bad as a Miss World contest. And that was just the men.

Ben stretched his legs out in front of him and yawned. 'So what's she like, your guv'nor?'

'Top woman. No complaints.'

'You're lucky, Cat. The last thing I'd call our current DI would be "top man." I have a whole shedload of complaints.'

'Well, I suppose not everyone likes DI Galena, either.' Cat gave a little laugh. 'At one point a way back, *no one* liked DI Galena! She certainly doesn't carry passengers. If you're on her team, you work damned hard and you don't piss about! But she'd take your side against anyone, and at least you know exactly where you are with her.'

'Can't argue with that, can you? I'd rather have a strong boss and know where I stand, than some drippy university graduate that doesn't know his arse from his elbow where proper police procedure is concerned.' Ben screwed up his face.

Cat grinned. 'Can I assume your actual DI is one of those?'

'Dead bloody right, but I'll say no more because I need to look after my blood pressure.'

Their voices were hushed, although there was little chance of the girl waking. It just seemed appropriate.

'Greenborough sounds like a pretty good nick to work at,' said Ben.

'Yeah, very good.' Cat pulled a face. 'We had one arsehole who made my life hell, but he's moved on now, and funnily enough he actually helped the boss out of a sticky situation, so . . .' She shrugged. 'Apart from that one DC, they are a really solid crew.'

'Lucky you. There are a few good old boys that I'd miss here too, but I'm thinking of mov—'

A painful moan escaped the dry lips of the girl, interrupting Ben mid-sentence.

Cat leant forward, and in a soft voice introduced herself and Ben. The frightened eyes darted from one to the other, then they rested on Cat, and flooded with tears. Gently, Cat reassured her that she was safe from any more harm and that she would have a police officer with her constantly.

'Can you tell me your name?'

The girl swallowed, but remained silent.

Ben stood up. 'I'll go tell the nurse that you're awake, leave you two girls alone for a moment.'

Cat nodded to him, appreciating his tact.

'We really need to know your name, so we can help you.' She covered the girl's good hand with hers and squeezed it gently. 'We are on your side, I promise. We want to get whoever hurt you, before they do this to someone else. Do you understand?'

The girl seemed to hesitate. She looked at her bandaged hand and choked back a sob. 'Sophie. My name is Sophie.'

'Good girl, Sophie. Now first, can I contact someone for you? Family? A friend?'

Again the girl refused to answer.

'Listen, Sophie. We don't want to cause you any more pain, I promise, but we have to catch the people who did this. Now, if you'll just talk to me, tell me all you can, then I'll organise a victim support officer for you. You won't be alone in this. You'll have someone to be with you every step of the way. So will you help us?'

'I'll talk to you, but only you.'

There was an accent, but Cat wasn't sure what it was. Whatever, she decided to get straight to the point while she had the girl to herself. 'Do you know who did this to you, Sophie?'

'No. I'd never seen him before.'

'It was one man?'

'I only saw one man. He was big, and strong, very strong!' Her voice was rising and Cat feared more hysterics as she began to recall her experience.

'Sshh, it's alright, it's alright.' Before she could continue, the door opened and a doctor appeared. 'I'm sorry, Detective Constable, but I'm going to have to ask you to wait outside while I check my patient. I need to see that she is up to being questioned, before you upset her any further.'

There was no room for argument, and with an unspoken curse Cat stood away from the bed. She whispered to the girl that she would be right outside, on the other side of the window, and would not let her out of her sight for a minute.

CHAPTER SIX

Joseph knocked. On hearing, "Come!" he entered the office of DI Gill Mercer.

'Got a minute or two, ma'am? Before your morning meeting?'

'I know exactly who you want to talk about, Joseph, so come in and drag up a pew.'

'I had a visit from your nemesis.'

The DI snorted. 'I heard. I'm sorry you had to take an earful of Dominic. He's not the nicest young man, is he?'

'Bit full on, to say the least. The thing is, he suggested that his missing sister could have known the dead girl, Lilli. Is there a chance he's telling the truth?'

She brushed her hair back over her shoulder. 'Very little I should think. He's done the same kind of thing before, trying to tie in his sister's disappearance with current investigations. I really thought he would have backed off by now, but he never gives up.'

'It's his twin sister, isn't it? I guess you can understand it.'

'That's why I did everything I could to make quite sure that we were not missing something. The super was none too pleased about the hours I spent on what he always believed to be a runaway, but I honestly felt for the guy.'

Joseph sat back. 'What do you think happened to her?'

Gill Mercer took a deep breath. 'It's my belief that Dina Jarvis met a young man, fell in love with him, and didn't know how to tell her brother that she was leaving. They'd had a happy childhood, we know that for sure. When I asked Dominic for a photo of her, he produced an album of pictures from childhood onwards, all happy families stuff.'

'But he said his parents went off and left them?'

'Not exactly. Initially the Jarvis family, minus the obligatory Labrador, looked like the prototype for the Perfect British Family Unit. When the kids were in their teens, Mum and Dad went off the rails a bit, and suddenly — love don't live here anymore.'

'Ah, the split.'

'Yes, but the children were never meant to be abandoned. The daughter was the apple of the mother's eye, and likewise the son with the father. They could have gone on with their perfect life if they had chosen to, but they wanted to stay together. In the end the parents agreed to go their own ways, and let the siblings, by then eighteen years old, have the house.' She gave a dry laugh. 'Not too shabby a deal in my book.'

Joseph nodded. 'I see. That does rather support your theory about Dina's reluctance to tell Dominic that she wanted to leave. And I suppose he just couldn't accept that she'd up and go with no warning.'

Gill bit on the edge of her thumb nail. 'Look, this case has always bugged me. I've lain awake a lot of nights thinking, "Have I missed something?" Yet if I have, I sure as hell don't know what it is. If I get Sheila to copy my notes and reports, would you take a glance at them for me? See if anything stands out to you, maybe a lead I never followed, or a comment that I took the wrong way.' She looked at him hopefully. 'I'd appreciate it.'

'Of course I will, though with the Lilli case, and the hunt for Freddie Carver, I'm not sure how much time I'll have.'

'No rush. It's been hanging around like a bad smell for years now, but even so, I'd hate to think that Dina Jarvis really had been abducted and I did nothing because I didn't believe her crackpot brother's theories.'

Joseph stood up. 'I know what you mean, and I'll certainly go through it, ma'am. Thanks for your time.' At the door he stopped and turned back. 'Was there any absolute proof that Dina was actually seeing a man?'

'She was quite a gregarious girl, Joseph, and when we talked to her friends, they intimated that she had met someone she considered, and I quote, "Really special, and hot with it." So I think the answer is yes, although we never managed to identify him.'

'Thanks, ma'am. Leave it with me.'

* * *

'It's been a long, bloody uncomfortable night on this sodding chair!' Ben rubbed at the stubble on his chin. 'Any more luck with the lass, Cat?'

Cat closed the door behind her and smiled wearily at her dishevelled companion. She looked back through the window at Sophie. 'I'm not sure. She's hiding too much, and I don't know why. I'm guessing she's an illegal, but again I don't know.' She arched her back to ease the aching muscles. 'Whatever, she's still terrified of this man finding her. Even our presence here is doing little to ease her fears. In fact, from the way she looks at the doctor, and no offence intended, but you too, she's just terrified of men, full stop.'

'She still reckons it was just one man?'

'Yeah, but I don't buy that. Snatch her, drive the car, drag her to some place safe, torture her? All on his own?'

'She's not exactly an Amazon, Cat. If he stunned her, then bundled her into his boot, I think he could manage pretty easily.'

'What, and tell her to hold still while he took a pair of wire cutters to her finger?'

'She must have been unconscious for that bit.'

'She says she remembers it, and I believe her. Every time I get anywhere near that part, her eyes go the size of dinner plates.'

'What about a description of him?' Ben asked.

Cat looked down at her pocket book. 'Well, at least I've managed to prise that out of her, for what it's worth. Tall, rough-looking, badly cut dirty blond hair, and shabby clothes. Old denim jeans, a check shirt and some sort of weatherproof jacket, two-tone brown with a padded lining. Age, she's not sure. Maybe thirty something. Oh, and he smelled bad. Shall I ring this through to the station, or will you?'

Ben stood up and tried unsuccessfully to smooth the creases from his trousers. 'I'll do it. Seeing as she won't even tolerate me in the room with her, I'd better make myself useful somehow. And I'll get us some breakfast while I'm out. Any preferences? I'm told the cafeteria food is almost edible.'

'Coffee and a bun of some kind will be fine, Ben.' She took out her purse. 'My turn. You've been keeping me in coffees all night.'

Ben Radley reluctantly took the ten pound note. 'Get back in there, girl. If you can get enough out of her to nail this bastard, I promise I'll buy you the best slap-up dinner Derby has to offer, okay?'

'You're on, Detective. And be warned, I have expensive taste.' With another stretch, Cat walked back through the door and sat down once again beside the young woman.

* * *

In the CID room, Joseph had hung a map of Greenborough on the wall and was busy sticking coloured pins in it. 'I wish we had one of the new computer-generated screens.'

'Oh, fat chance. Rumour has it we are selling off this building. It's that, or go bankrupt next year.' Dave looked dejected at the thought. 'I cannot believe that the government cutbacks have made things this bad.'

'Well, in that case maybe I should be thankful for these little coloured markers, and I'll be very careful not to lose one,' replied Joseph sarcastically. 'Right, any more confirmed sightings of Carver?'

Dave scanned his list. 'Just one from a CCTV camera in Theobald Street, the Marina end. He was travelling in a silver grey Merc confirmed to be a taxi. He was with two unknown males and a female, heading out of town.'

Joseph added another pin to the map and stood back. 'Not exactly covered, is it? Ten sightings in three weeks.'

'And all somewhere in and around the west side of the town,' added Dave. 'Odd. It's neither high end posh, where you'd expect to find him, nor somewhere like the Carborough Estate.'

'What do we have of interest in the western area?' Joseph traced his finger in a circle on the map. 'The marina, and that is pretty low key. A few interesting redevelopments like the Grain Store and the Seed House. Other than that there is very little, other than some half-decent properties, and on the outskirts, the golf club.'

'The Leather Bottle is down by the river. It's not the most salubrious pub in town, but that and the Olde White Swan down Back Alley were the favourite haunts of many of our best clients, back in the day.'

'Like the Leonards?'

'Oh no, their watering hole was the Fisherman's Knot. Not that they hang out there anymore, although I reckon a few low-lifes still try the odd deal from the back room.'

Joseph rubbed at an aching shoulder. 'Greenborough isn't Freddie Carver's kind of place at all, is it? What's he up to?'

'I've got a horrible feeling we'll find out soon enough,' said Dave gloomily.

Sheila Robins waved to him from the doorway. 'Sergeant Easter? I've got some files for you from DI Mercer. Shall I put them on your desk?'

Joseph walked over to her. 'I'll take them, thank you, Sheila.'

'More work?' asked Dave.

'Bit of a favour actually.' He looked at Dave with interest. 'Did you ever know Dina Jarvis?'

'You are asking the wrong person, Sarge, but the right one just walked in the door.'

Joseph looked up to see Yvonne Collins and his soon to be son-in-law, Niall Farrow. 'Perfect timing, you guys. Dina Jarvis? What can you tell me?'

Yvonne narrowed her eyes, then nodded to herself. 'Yes, the girl that disappeared in January 2014. Pretty, dark-haired, around five foot three, blue eyes, one brother, Dominic. Lived with him at 53 Woolpack Lane, Eastside, Greenborough. Did a bit of temping then worked at the printing company on Main Road. Friendly, no run ins with us, although I seem to recall a report from her brother about her attracting a possible stalker, that was about six months before she disappeared.' Yvonne tilted her head to one side. 'And that is all I can remember off the top of my head.'

Joseph never ceased to be amazed by Yvonne's powers of recollection. 'That's plenty, thanks.' He scratched his head. 'Did you ever have any theories about what happened?'

'We did,' said Niall. 'Didn't we, Vonnie?'

Yvonne nodded. 'We didn't have any dealings with Dina, but we did have a few minor skirmishes with the brother.'

'Four to be precise,' chipped in Niall. 'We decided it was because he felt responsible for Dina, so he was, well, a bit overprotective.'

'We reckoned she was looking for a way out, and when she got an offer, she jumped at it. And she *was* seeing someone. We know that for sure, don't we, Niall?' Yvonne looked at her crew-mate.

'Oh yes, I saw her myself one night, round the back of the Golden Dragon restaurant. The clinch she was in was definitely more than just a friendly snog. But sorry to say, I didn't recognise him.'

Yvonne nodded. 'We had an influx of migrant workers and field hands from other areas at that time, and there were a lot of new faces around.'

'After she disappeared I tried my hardest to remember what he looked like, but they were in the dark, and I didn't exactly like to stare.'

Joseph shrugged. 'Seems almost cut and dried, doesn't it? And I suppose the brother was incandescent at us for not launching a major enquiry?'

'Yes and no,' said Yvonne. 'He's never stopped hounding us, it's true, but he never went to the extremes that some families do when a loved one goes missing. He never got the press involved in a big way.'

'He never got up petitions, like you would have thought he would.' Niall added.

'And he never used social media to accuse us of letting her down or not doing our job.'

Joseph made a face. 'Well, that's one blessing, but as you say, it is unusual.'

'We think that in his heart of hearts, he knows what happened to his sister. He just can't admit that she would move on and make a life away from him. Hence he makes waves every so often because it's expected of him, but *he* knows, Sarge, he knows.'

Niall suddenly looked older. He was so much more the capable adult now than when he first came to

Greenborough. Joseph had always loved the young policeman's enthusiasm but had wondered if he would ever grow up. Now it seemed he had, and Joseph was glad that he was going to join his family. 'Thanks for that, you two. Much appreciated. Now, any news on Fat Freddie?'

'Not much, I'm afraid,' said Yvonne. 'Just some rumours, nothing concrete. The thing that bothers everyone, straight and crooked, is that he doesn't seem to be doing *anything*. He's made no deals, no takeover bids, no threats and carried out no criminal activities that anyone knows of. His silent presence in the area is almost more worrying than if he was causing mayhem.'

'Why didn't he go back to his old hunting ground, the big smoke?' Dave asked.

'Because too many people are after him,' Niall answered immediately. 'And I don't mean just the Met, although they have numerous charges waiting for him. At the time he fled the country, he'd upset one or two big-time villains. He's not welcome down south.'

'He's not welcome here either,' growled Dave. 'Of all the other places he could have gone — big cities, small cities, towns with amenities — hell, why come to the Fens?'

'Well, we have *something* he wants, or he wouldn't be here. We've just got to dig deeper.' Yvonne glanced at her watch. 'And that reminds me, we are meeting Rancid in ten minutes.'

Joseph looked amused. 'Who?'

Yvonne grinned. 'He's a snout that I've been running for years — Rancid Reg Milner. Nosey little bugger, but a mine of information and happy to share it for a small remuneration.'

'None of which he spends on toiletries,' added Niall, wrinkling up his nose.

'Then good luck with that. Report back if your smelly snout gives you anything.'

'Other than fleas?' muttered Niall, as he closed the door.

Joseph smiled, then recalling what Yvonne had said about the crooks of Greenborough also being concerned, he pulled out his phone and keyed in Mickey Leonard's number.

'Hi, Joe! How goes it? Are you phoning with my invite to the wedding?'

Joseph laughed. 'Not much goes on around here without you hearing about it, does it?'

'How right you are.'

'Mickey, can I run something past you?'

'Sure, what's worrying you?'

Joseph still found it hard to equate this bright teenager with the troubled child that he had helped to get his life back. 'I'm sure your family is very aware of an unwanted visitor to the neighbourhood?'

Mickey went quiet for a moment. 'Yes, we seem to have a nasty outbreak of vermin around here, don't we?'

'It's King Rat I'm interested in.'

'Aren't we all?'

'I'm very keen that there are enough traps on the ground to make him seek pastures new, if you catch my drift?' Joseph waited a few seconds.

'I think we're going to need the Pied Piper for this one, Joe. But I suggest you and Inspector Nik talk to Uncle Raymond. He is pretty keen on exterminating this pest problem too. I think he'll be prepared to pass on info, if you'd do the same?'

Joseph had been here before. 'I'll talk to the inspector and if she agrees, we'll contact Raymond and set up a meeting. Thanks, my friend. How is life treating you these days?'

'Good, Joe, very good. I've got a girlfriend, how about that?'

'Hey! That's great news. What's her name?'

'Millie, and she's so cool! Can't believe my luck.'

'Then hang on to her, kid, and treat her well. You're not such a bad catch yourself, you know.'

'Aw, Joe, come on! I'm hardly Justin Bieber.'

'That's a relief! You're a brave kid with a good heart, cling to that, okay?'

'See you, Joe. And don't forget the wedding invite.'

'Should I send it to Mickey Leonard and guest?'

'Why not? Let's live a little!'

Joseph ended the call smiling. If ever there was a story to make you believe in the power of good over evil, then it was that of young Mickey and his climb up from the gutter. Some things about this job sucked, like finding dead girls, but some things, like Mickey, made everything worthwhile.

* * *

He was acting strangely. He seemed so charged up with energy that it was impossible for him to keep still for a minute. She watched him pace the room, waving his hands as he talked. He even offered to take her out into the garden for a while. She smiled at that, but decided not to act as if it were important to her. She had to be careful — too much enthusiasm and he would change his mind.

Her whole being screamed to be allowed to sit under the sun, to feel cool grass beneath her feet and to breathe fresh air. She begged silently to be free of the stuffy cottage and the dark, oppressive rooms, even if just for a while.

As he left, pulling the door closed behind him, her heart sank. He had already forgotten his suggestion. She shifted in the easy chair. The pain was almost unbearable today. But then, when wasn't it? And this time she could not blame him for forgetting her medication. He had been better than usual of late, and now he seemed positively on top of the world. She wanted to be happy for him, but it worried her. She loved him, but he was impossible to understand. She was sure that if she knew the cause of his recent high spirits, it would not fill her with similar transports of delight.

The door opened and he came back in, his smile wider than ever. To her surprise, he gently helped her to stand. A jolt of pain seared through her, and he waited while she caught her breath. Slowly he walked her out to the old wooden garden seat and sat her in the middle of a heap of cushions that he had made ready for her. He flustered around her solicitously, danced off and returned with a blanket for her legs and a glass of lemonade. He was talking fast, babbling. He was telling her to enjoy the fresh air, it was a beautiful day and she must make the most of the sunshine before autumn turned to winter. He said he had to get back to work later, but there was a little time for her to relax outside, although she must call him if she was tired or wanted to return to her bed.

As if! She couldn't even answer him. She felt a lump in her throat, and she knew that tears were not far away. She smiled again, and he was gone. He glanced back at her once before entering the cottage, then grinned, pushed the long fringe from his eyes, and disappeared inside.

The smell of the overgrown garden and the clean, crisp morning air were like champagne to her. She felt drunk with pleasure. She had not been outside for two years.

* * *

'Cat? Is that you?'

'Line's bad, ma'am, I'm walking around outside. Is that better?'

'That's fine. How are things there?'

'Apart from the fact that I've probably got piles from sitting on a hospital chair for hours on end, I finally have some good news!'

Nikki sighed with relief. 'At last! Go on, spill the beans.'

'Sophie is Sophia Kraja, an Albanian illegal immigrant. She had been working for a gang master somewhere outside Greenborough. You know the score, ma'am, bloody hard graft, shipped around the fields cutting cabbages or picking daffs, wherever the work is. Then she and another girl got offered a job in a big nursery somewhere in Derbyshire.'

'Don't tell me, when she got there . . . ?'

'Yup, no nursery, but surprise, surprise, if they wanted to earn enough money to feed themselves, there did just happen to be two vacancies at a seedy nightclub.'

'Poor kids! And I'm guessing it didn't end there?'

'Far from it. The bastards that owned the club weren't looking for glam hostesses or pretty pole dancers, just sex workers. And whoever picked those two girls up did a really good job of scaring the shit out of them. They were threatened with jail or deportation, and they were told that their families would suffer too. That's what really put the fear of God in them.'

'How did you prise all this out of her?'

'She's not a bad kid, ma'am. After farting around for far too long, I decided that considering the kind of life she'd led, she was probably a damned sight tougher than I'd given her credit for, certainly tough enough to be told the truth. So I told her exactly what happened to her two predecessors, and what would certainly happen to the next young woman who fell prey to those animals. When she understood how close she'd come to being tortured for months and ending up dead, her conscience kicked in. Oh, and the fact that I had a long chat with immigration. In light of what she's suffered, they are going to try to help her.'

'Nice one, Cat! Good for you.'

'Wait for the rest. We've just sat with a map and Ben Radley's stop watch and tried to work out roughly where she was taken. From the length of time she was on the road, and then dragged through woods and such, we place it somewhere south of Buxton. She was blindfolded, but she said the place she was held in stank of animals and manure. We reckon it must have been a barn or some old farm building. Then she gets very vague. A tox screen showed faint traces of some kind of rohypnol type drug, so we think she was given something prior to her finger being amputated.'

'Thankfully, I suppose.' Nikki winced at the thought of the wire cutters.

'From the beating she took, I don't think it was out of kindness, ma'am, more like a way to keep her still while he mutilated her.' Nikki imagined Cat shuddering. 'Well, we've passed it all on to the Derby lads, and if you think that's all I can do here, I guess I can head back?'

'And Sophie?'

'Derby is taking her into care, just as soon as she's discharged from hospital. They know how serious this is, they'll watch her day and night and she'll be well looked after.' Cat yawned down the phone.

'You sound like you need some rest, are you okay to drive?'

'I'm okay, and Ben is coming back with me, so he can drive if I get sleepy.'

'Cat, before you go, how did Sophie get away from this man, or men?'

'She's still adamant it was a single male who hurt her, but she thought she heard other voices at the barn, or wherever she was held. Whatever, this bloke had some kind of an attack. He couldn't breathe. From the way she described it, I'd say it was asthma. As soon as she realised what was happening, she took off and ran like the hounds of hell were after her. She had no idea where she was going, it was just pure luck that she wandered onto the main A52.'

'Phew! Lucky kid! How about the friend? Is she still at the nightclub?'

'No. Sophie said the girl had a boyfriend in Kings Lynn. She managed to ring him and he came for her. They are probably a hundred miles away by now.'

'Hopefully. Now you take great care driving back. And Cat? Excellent work with that girl.'

Nikki replaced the receiver and not for the first time, thought how lucky she was to have such a good team.

CHAPTER SEVEN

Greg Woodhall seemed to have made an attempt to clear his desk. Nikki noticed at least two areas where the veneer surface was actually visible.

'Regarding Sophia Kraja,' she stated, 'Uniform has already paid a visit to the gang master that employed Sophia and her friend. He's showed us copies of their documents, they are fake but apparently pretty good, and as the rest of his Eastern European workers are kosher, we are more or less certain he's not involved. He did see a man hanging around Sophia on a few occasions, just before she told him she had been offered a better job out of the county. The description fits one or two local villains, and the chap is willing to come in and look at some mug shots.' She turned to the next sheet. 'Derby has sent us the preliminary forensic report on evidence retrieved from Sophia's clothing, and they tally exactly with debris found on the skin and clothes of both Fern and Lilli. Professor Wilkinson is coming over shortly to explain his final botanical results, and he's pretty certain the pollen will give the precise location of the place where the girls were imprisoned. I don't know how the hell he's going to do that, but I have great faith in him.'

'Likewise. If I can, I'll come and listen in to what he says. Let me know when he gets here, will you, Nikki?'

'Certainly, sir, and I'd just like to mention that DC Cat Cullen's handling of Sophia was exemplary. She has extracted a massive amount of information without traumatising the girl further, and offered her all the right support. It can't have been easy to get someone who had been so badly treated to cooperate so well.'

'Duly noted, Inspector Galena.' Greg looked quietly pleased.

'Thank you, sir.'

* * *

While Nikki was leaving Greg Woodhall's office, three men sat on a threadbare sofa and fumed over the whereabouts of a fourth.

'I got better things to do than hang around here waiting. Where the fuck is he?'

'Dead right. I'm giving him ten more minutes, then I'm off.'

'Oh really, Lenny? You gonna stand the boss up? I don't think so.'

'Yeah, well, I don't like it out here. The quiet gives me the jitters. Gimme a bit of traffic noise, a few air brakes and a factory whistle any day. All these trees and darkness, not my cuppa tea at all.'

'So you won't be buying yourself a nice little peaceful retreat in the country when you retire then, Len?' That was Ezra's dream. Country life, far away from the city.

'Bollocks to that! When I've made enough dough, the missus and me are off to the sun. My kind of peace comes with the sound of jangling coins in the casino and rattle of anchor chains from them flash yachts in the marina. Ah yes, and people with money to spend and special requirements, and me so happy to supply them.' The little man leant back on the sofa and showed a row of uneven, mustard-coloured teeth. 'How about you, Vic? I know you're still young, but you got plans?'

The younger man's teeth were whiter, but the voracious gleam in his eyes was the same. 'Oh yeah, I got plans.' He coughed and spat on the floor.

'Come on then, share 'em with us, Vic.'

'Nope.'

'What's so special about you and your screwball ideas that you can't tell us? We're your mates.' Ezra sounded affronted.

'I ain't got no mates, and you wouldn't understand, what with you having shit for brains.'

'Why, you little punk! I'll fu—'

'Pack it in you two! I hear a car coming. He's here. He's not gonna be happy, so cool it.'

Freddie Carver, leaning heavily on a silver-topped cane, limped into the room and glared angrily at the three serious faces in front of him. There were no pleasantries. The deep voice was low and full of menace. 'I expected better. You've let me and my family down, and you know how much I love my family.' He carefully dusted one of the plastic chairs that faced the sofa, sat down and leant forward. 'Now, one at a time, I'd like to know exactly what went wrong. It was a perfectly simple job. You first, Lenny.'

* * *

Freddie Carver sat for almost half an hour, listening to nothing but bleating and excuses. True these three were the dregs of his organisation, but he still expected results, not a bungled mess. Between them they had caused him a problem, and not one he could easily rectify.

He peered at the men and wondered if it would be safer all round to waste the lot of them, recruit some new blood, and start again. He would probably be doing the world a favour. Let's face it, Lenny was loyal but he was past it now, he should have given up years ago. Ezra's heart wasn't in it anymore, and that could lead to sloppiness, and Freddie hated sloppiness. Then there was Vic. Vic belonged in a cage. He was volatile, dangerous and devoid of all feeling, which was exactly why Freddie had employed him. Sadly, that was also the problem. The fox-faced son-of-a-bitch psycho was perfectly suited to the work he'd been given. Unless he was willing to spend an inordinate amount of money, finding someone else with Vic's skills would not be easy.

He struck the floor with his cane. 'Okay. I've heard enough. Your excuses are a joke. If you want to keep on working for me, I'm going to give the three of you one last chance to make good.' He smiled lethally. 'And I do mean "last" chance. Just one more mistake, do I make myself crystal clear?' He looked at each white face in turn, and decided they were taking this seriously. 'Now listen carefully. This is what I want you to do.'

* * *

'A report from my friend the palynologist.' Rory waved a printout in the air.

'Come again?' Nikki looked puzzled.

'A specialist in pollen.' Rory adjusted his glasses and adopted his best pedagogic stance. 'Did you know that every one of us will die with pollen up our hooters? It is virtually indestructible, and will remain long after the nasal membranes have turned to dust.' He did a little sprinkling motion with his fingers.

'Really?' Even Greg Woodhall looked surprised.

'Absolutely. In fact, archaeologists and geologists have used pollen to reconstruct the vegetation of prehistoric eras, which tells you how invasive and hardy those pesky little grains really are.'

'And what does your report tell us exactly?' Nikki was already impatient.

The pathologist waxed lyrical. 'It tells me that Fern and Lilli were held and tortured in a place of great beauty.

There were limestone cliffs, carpets of bluebells, dog's mercury and ransoms, patches of yellow kidney vetch, all sheltered by the Venus of the forest, the ash tree, and the cloudy white blossom of the bird cherry. The hedges surrounding this place are hawthorn and of even more significance, there is a tulip tree with a magnolia close by, which indicates cultivation — a garden or an estate. Our other findings indicate the presence of Jacob's ladder and the close proximity of animals — horses to be exact. So, I think my report has given you quite a bit to go on, don't you?'

* * *

Nikki walked into the CID room and saw that Cat was back, talking to a vaguely familiar figure. She looked harder, and realised it was Ben Radley, the detective from Derbyshire. He had said he would like to come back with Cat, but she thought he might well have decided to pound across the White Peak with his colleagues, in pursuit of Fern's killer.

She had already sent a copy of Rory's report to Derbyshire and had spoken to the officer in charge. From the man's keen interest in what she told him, she was pretty sure that half his force would be out hunting for a magnolia and a tulip tree close to a hawthorn hedge. She smiled to herself, wondering how many police officers would recognise a tulip tree if they fell over it. She had suggested, with a wry smile, that the search teams be issued with photographs.

Judging by the coat and overnight bag over his shoulder, it looked as if he was planning to stay.

'Hello, DC Radley. Hope our Cat was of help to you?'

The man beamed at her and nodded furiously. 'Thank you, ma'am. She was fantastic, did a brilliant job with young Sophia Kraja.'

Nikki wondered what deep and meaningful conversations had taken place between the two of them as they whiled away the night hours beside the girl's bed.

'You look a little less stressed than when we last spoke, Detective.'

'Ah yes, well, we are finally getting somewhere, ma'am. It was the frustration, knowing some animal was still out there, and the case all but closed.' He hung his head. 'I'm still embarrassed about my outburst. I do apologise.'

'Forget it, Ben. Now I suggest you get Cat to show you everything we have at this end. There might be some little nugget of information from the reports on Lilli that would help your team. Oh, and I'm going to free up DC Cullen to act as liaison for the rest of this investigation.'

'Thank you, ma'am, I appreciate that. I'll be going back in the morning. I have a friend en route from Grimsby who is picking me up, so I'll get done all I can tonight.' He gave her an almost shy smile. 'And I *will* see you again. I owe Cat here a slap-up meal.'

Cat grinned. 'Dead right! And you better not forget.'

He briefly touched Cat's shoulder. 'As if! Now, if there is somewhere I could freshen up? Then we can get down to work.'

'I'll take you,' Dave offered, and the two men left the room.

Nikki wondered if she was the only one who knew that Ben could easily have accessed all the information that they had on Lilli directly to his computer. There had to be another reason for his trip to Greenborough, and Nikki was pretty sure she was looking at her now.

As the door closed, Nikki turned to Cat. 'Is there anything going on here that I should know about, Caitlin?'

'Ma'am?'

'Cat?'

'Absolutely not! He's twice my age!'

'Wrong. He can't be more than ten years older, and age is irrelevant anyway. Is he still married?'

'Ma'am! Honestly!'

'Well?'

'Divorced, actually. His marriage fell to bits after his daughter died.'

'Mmm.' Nikki saw Cat's cheeks begin to redden, and decided she'd had enough fun for now. 'Right. Now I'd like to discuss tulip trees with you.'

* * *

Joseph has closed the door to his office, something he rarely did, but he wanted a few quiet moments to look over Gill Mercer's files on the disappearance of Dina Jarvis. He knew that he should be chasing Freddie Carver, and the last thing he wanted to find in this folder was another dead girl, but even so, something drew him to it like a magnet.

He read for a while, then sat back and considered the things that Yvonne and Niall had told him. Dina was apparently gregarious, friendly, and had been seen in a steamy clinch with a man. That could describe hundreds of girls in Greenborough, but it did give him an insight into what her naturally exuberant personality might lead to.

'Sarge! That Jarvis bloke is back downstairs, and DI Mercer is in court today. Would you see him, please?' The young PC was almost begging.

'Playing up again, is he?' Joseph closed the file and stood up. Perfect timing, even if it did mean taking a load of flak. 'On my way.'

In the interview room, Dominic Jarvis had either run out of steam, or decided to take a completely different approach with Joseph.

'Thank you for talking to me, Sergeant.'

Joseph narrowed his eyes. 'No problem. In fact I was thinking of calling on you tomorrow.'

'Please do. Come anyway, I do have a pretty comprehensive file on what I suspect happened to Dina.'

I bet you do, thought Joseph and envisioned boxes of paperwork, newspaper cuttings and computer printouts. 'So how can I help you today, Mr Jarvis?'

'Well, because you never followed up my information about Dina knowing that Lilli girl, I did a little investigating of my own, and I think I know where they met.'

Joseph tried not to show it, but he felt a tiny thrill of excitement.

'I think it was when Dina did some temping for a vegetable produce company called Dewflex. She and one or two of the other girls would go to a cocktail bar after work some nights. It was called the Hot Sox. Do you know it?'

'It's closed now, but yes, it was down Herring Alley.' Joseph would have called it a sleazy dive rather than a cocktail bar, but who was he to judge? 'Did Lilli work at Dewflex too?'

'I think so. Dina had a picture taken at a birthday party at the bar, and that's where I recognised her from.'

'Have you got that picture?'

'Sadly no. I went through all her things last night, but it wasn't there.'

'Have you kept a lot of Dina's possessions?'

'Oh, everything, officer. Her room is exactly as she left it. Her clothes are still in her wardrobe and her cupboards. Nothing is touched. It wouldn't be right, not when . . .' He stopped.

Joseph understood. Jessie Nightingale had said the same thing. How could she get rid of his precious things when she didn't know what had happened to him? Joseph exhaled. 'Look, Mr Jarvis, this is rather off the record, but I will come and see you tomorrow, and I will look into her disappearance again. Just do me one favour, and keep this to yourself for the time being, okay?'

Relief suffused the man's face, and he nodded fast. 'Yes, of course.' He stood up. 'I knew you were different, Sergeant. You know how to listen.'

You hardly give anyone much opportunity to do anything else, thought Joseph. He thanked Jarvis and showed him out.

As he walked back up to the CID room, Joseph wondered if he had made a mistake by encouraging Jarvis, but even if he had, he knew he would go anyway. He wanted to see Dina Jarvis's room.

CHAPTER EIGHT

The man sat at the same table, reading his usual pile of newspapers. The comings and goings in the pub did not interest him, they never did. As he paid for his beer, Maggie flashed him that smile, the one that said, "You're welcome, because you spend money here, but frankly I wish you didn't because I don't like you and I don't trust you."

He didn't blame her. Although he tried to keep himself clean, he knew that his worn clothes and unfriendly demeanour didn't make him the best advert for her cosy public house. He looked towards her, and saw she was chatting with a couple of the regulars. Her conspiratorial manner, leaning forward over the damp surface of the bar and half whispering, made him pay attention.

'The police are swarming all over Ashwood Manor. Heaven knows what they are looking for. Bob said they were arriving by the dozen!'

'That's odd. They were up at the Old Hall at first light this morning. Didn't stay long, but I saw at least twenty men there.' The old man, wearing an even older wax jacket, looked puzzled. 'Can't have found what they were looking for though, if they've moved on to Ashwood Manor.'

The man's gut tightened, as if he had been punched hard. The police? Here? His mouth was dry, and he fought back the impulse to run from the bar. They mustn't find him! Whatever happened, they must *not* see him. But where could he go? He certainly didn't dare run away. He took a deep breath, steadied his hand and lifted his glass. He couldn't let this lot know how worried he was. He needed to think, but he couldn't do it here. He had to get back and check his lodgings. He had been thorough, but had he been thorough enough? There might be something the police could find. No fingers, that was for sure, but something else maybe?

He waited five long minutes, then carefully folded the papers and took them to the bar. 'All yours, Maggie.'

'Thank you, sir. See you tomorrow.' Her smile was forced.

Maybe, Maggie, or maybe not.

* * *

Just as Joseph was planning on going home, Yvonne and Niall knocked on his office door.

'Sarge? Got a minute?'

Joseph thought Yvonne looked much too bright for the end of a long shift.

'We've got something we think you'll like.'

That explained it. 'Come in, if you can both get into this cupboard.'

'Freddie Carver.'

'Wouldn't say he was something I liked, but . . . ?'

'We've finally got a snout that has inside knowledge of Freddie's comings and goings.'

'Really? Nice one, you two.'

'The first thing he tells us is that Freddie made a little trip to Derbyshire last week.'

'Where?'

'He was too smart to let anyone know exactly what he was up to, but our snout says he drove him to Ashbourne, then Freddie left him there and went on alone. Returned about two hours later, then our guy drove him home.'

'Ashbourne was where Sophia was found! I'm bloody sure he's involved with those dead girls.'

'Wouldn't surprise me at all, Sarge, but proving it could be difficult. Have the Derby lot found that geographical location yet?'

'Not to my knowledge, it must be like looking for a needle in a haystack. How many coppers do you know who could identify a tulip tree?'

'None,' said Niall, 'and I include myself among them. Oh yes, there is something Vonnie and I have only just unearthed. It may be nothing, but twice a year, regular as clockwork, Freddie leaves his beloved third wife and assorted kids, goes off alone, and stays away overnight. No one knows where he goes, and he has made it very clear that they are never to ask about it.' Niall stared at Joseph. 'What does that sound like to you?'

'An anniversary? A duty visit?'

'Yeah, that's exactly what we thought.' Niall gave Yvonne a little nudge and she took over.

'We've been trying to trace Freddie's family history. His mother has been brown bread since the late seventies, but I'll be damned if we can trace his father.'

'Daddy Carver is probably holed up in a nursing home under another name, hence the occasional visit from his loving son,' said Niall.

'That, or he doesn't have a father,' added Yvonne.

'Meaning that he truly was spawned by the Devil?' Joseph asked, a small smile spreading across his face.

'Meaning any father that begat Freddie would do a runner as soon as he knew what the little bastard was like.'

Joseph smiled, grateful for the light relief. 'Fair enough, but I still think my idea's the correct one.'

Yvonne raised her eyebrows. 'Most likely, Sarge, but I haven't got to the good bit yet. Freddie has been gathering some of his old workforce, bringing them up from London and settling them in temporary billets all over the place. Now, some of Freddie's men, not the higher echelon of course, but some of the jobbers have had a standing bet on who can find out where he goes, without him knowing. My snout says they took the mileage off his car on his last trip, and it was 238 miles there and back. 119 miles from Greenborough could mean Derbyshire.'

Joseph looked unconvinced. 'It could also mean he drove to Holland Fen and took Daddy out on some scenic tea-shop drives around the waterways.'

'The car comes back in a mess.'

'My car gets in a mess driving to Knot Cottage if I'm following a tractor!'

'Whatever, our snout reckons one of the lads is going to follow him next time.'

'Risky! Freddie would stick them under ten foot of concrete if he found out.'

'Very true, but who are we to stop them, especially as it's rumoured to be happening quite soon.'

'This could be just what we need. Let me know what you find out.'

Yvonne and Niall nodded.

'So, Carver's gathering his soldiers together,' Joseph mused. 'But why? What is he planning?'

Niall, too, looked serious. 'We have eyes and ears everywhere. If anyone lets anything slip, we'll be onto it, Sarge, and that's a promise.'

Joseph hurried over to Nikki's office and filled her in on what they'd just told him.

'It's certainly worrying.' Nikki rubbed her eyes. 'But I'm going to worry tomorrow, not now. I'm bushed. Let's call it a day, shall we?'

Joseph pulled a face. 'Tamsin is coming over this evening. More wedding stuff, I suppose. I think she's worried about this engagement party next week.'

'It's a big thing. Some couples only get married once, you know.' Nikki gave a little laugh.

'Want to join us? I could do with a feminine take on her suggestions. Half the time I don't even know what she's talking about.'

Nikki laughed again. 'And you think I would? I know more about blood spatter patterns than wedding dresses. I've spent so much time either in this place chasing villains, or fighting the gender wars to get promoted, that I probably know less than you! Sorry, but I'll take a rain check.'

'There's a homemade vegetable Korma with samosas and all the extras.'

'I love weddings. What time?'

'Seven, seven thirty?'

'See you then. Now off you go. I've just got to tie up a couple of loose ends and I'll be closing up shop.'

* * *

Nikki had never seen Tamsin so happy.

When they'd first met, all she had seen was a rather bitter and confused young woman. Sometimes Tamsin's anger came out in caustic comments and other times she spoke about her father in such negative terms that it made Nikki want to shake her. But she had mellowed. It had happened prior to meeting Niall, and getting together with him had made things even better. Niall was good for her, and she was turning Niall into a responsible young man.

'You will be there for the engagement party, Nikki, won't you? We've hired the function hall at the Sports Club. It's just a drop in, drop out thing from two p.m. until ten. First drink on us and then it's up to you. There'll be lots of faces from the station.'

'I'm sure there will, your lad is a popular guy.' Nikki didn't add that very few police officers would turn down the chance of a free drink. 'So when is the big day? Have you set a date for it?'

'We are thinking of this coming spring, if we can afford it.' She glanced towards her father, who stuck his tongue out at her.

'Don't look at me! I still favour Gretna Green.' Joseph placed a steaming serving dish in the centre of the table. 'Dig in. There's plenty.'

Tonight was the first time Nikki had seen father and daughter completely at ease with each other. They laughed, joked and teased each other in the most natural and heartwarming way. Nikki felt like crying. This was all Joseph had ever wanted — to have his daughter back. Now he finally had his wish. Nikki knew she had been right about the reason for his reluctance to look at the dead girl in the potato shed. He could not bear to think of losing her again. And Nikki understood that so well. The ghost of Hannah had drifted into the room, threatening to bring tears to her eyes. How she would have loved to have seen her girl sitting at the table with them, laughing with Tamsin and making plans for the wedding of the century.

'You're quiet.'

'Food, Joseph. You know how I love your food. Too good to waste time talking, I'm afraid.' She waved a forkful of veggie samosa at him and they smiled at each other. She hadn't fooled him, she knew that, but Tamsin laughed and agreed with her.

Nikki turned to Tamsin. 'So where are you two going to live when you are married?'

'Good point.' Tamsin laid her fork down and drew in a long breath. 'Bit of a story, but here goes. Niall's brother broke his leg, and Niall has been walking his dog for him. I was down for the weekend and went with him, and we saw this cottage.' She nibbled on her bottom lip. 'It needs a lot of work, and it's well out of the way, but, oh Nikki, I just loved it.'

'Where is it?'

'Jacob's Mere. It's on the lane that winds out towards the old mill. It's called Herondene. Niall is trying to get the price down, because of its condition, but he's having a bit of a fight.'

'It is a lovely spot, surrounded by fields,' said Joseph, 'but pretty remote.'

'You can talk, Dad! Cloud Fen is hardly urban, is it? And you love the place.'

'Touché. But I was just thinking about you being there alone when Niall is on shifts.'

'I love the city, and I love my friends, but I've grown to love the tranquillity of the Fens more.'

'I think I'm losing the battle.'

'I think you are.' Nikki sat back and stared at her empty plate. 'Tell me to butt out if I'm being rude, but what are they asking for the cottage?'

'A hundred and fifty thousand. It does have a large plot around it. Three bedrooms, a big kitchen — but as I said, it needs work. A lot of work.'

'If that's the case, they are taking the proverbial. Who is dealing with it?'

'Arden and Collett, the estate agent in the square.'

'Ah. Geoff Arden isn't a bad bloke, actually. I went to school with him.' Nikki rubbed her hands together. 'Maybe it's time I renewed our acquaintance. One hundred and fifty for a dump in the back of beyond! Joke! I'll see if I can make him see things a little more realistically, shall I?'

Tamsin's face lit up. 'Would you?'

'It's what she does best, Tam, terrorising innocent estate agents.'

'There's no such thing as an innocent estate agent.'

'Note she didn't deny the other part.' Joseph stage-whispered to his daughter.

When Nikki was alone in Cloud Cottage Farm she thought again about Lilli, Fern and Sophie. Lovely girls like Tamsin, but their futures had been taken away, or were deeply scarred. This might be a beautiful world, but there were some evil souls residing in it.

* * *

Her mother came to her almost every night now. It was a relief to have someone to talk to. He was rarely home, and when he was, he was more preoccupied than ever. His mind was definitely on other things besides her and her well-being.

She shivered and drew the old duvet tighter around her. A rasping cough tore at her raw and tender throat. A few days ago she had made a terrible mistake and now she was paying for it. The day had been bright and as he was at home for a while, she mentioned that it might do her good to go outside again. He had scowled at her, thrown the book he was reading to the floor, and practically frog-marched her out to the garden seat.

This time there were no cushions, and the wood hurt her back. After a while she had been so uncomfortable that she had called for him to get her back inside. He had not heard her. She had cried out in pain and exasperation for over an hour. Then the sky had clouded over and heavy spots of rain had begun to fall. It was nightfall when he remembered her.

Another cough sent a bolt of pain through her chest. He had been distraught when he realised, and had changed her wet clothes and towelled her shaking body. He had made her hot drinks and put her to bed with an old hot water bottle and an extra blanket. But the next day he was off out, not returning until late in the evening.

She turned on her side. At least this chill had helped her in one way. She had lost her appetite, which was a good thing, as her meals were getting fewer and further apart.

From her bed she looked out through the window, across the wild overgrown landscape. The sky tonight was overcast and cloudy. No moon, no stars. She smiled in the darkness. Things weren't all bad. Apart from her mother's visits, she'd had one amazing piece of luck. Earlier that afternoon, weak from hunger and coughing violently, she had fallen on her way to the toilet. In doing so she had hit her hip hard on the corner of the heavy oak dressing chest. As she lay on the floor, gasping for breath and wracked with pain, she had heard a clattering noise and had seen the glint of something metallic lying just beneath the chest. When the hurt had passed a little, she had crawled, inching her bony body across the filthy floor, until she could reach whatever it was that had fallen down.

She smiled again. It was an old knife. Maybe it had once been a wartime bayonet kept as a memento and used as a paperknife. It must have been caught up at the back of one of the heavy wooden drawers for years. Her fall had freed it, and now it was hers and she would make sure he didn't find it. Not that he cleaned her room anymore.

It had taken her the rest of the afternoon to get up from the floor and hide her trophy. But it had been worth it. She now had choices, and even although her mother kept telling her to hold on, to be brave, that she would go home again soon, she knew now that *she* would be the one to decide when she left this place for good.

CHAPTER NINE

Ben Radley rubbed his eyes. They were sore as hell and felt like someone had thrown a handful of sand into them. After a late night, he had left Greenborough just before six in the morning, and then gone straight out with his colleagues, trudging over miles of ground, hunting for those two special trees that would lead them to Fern and Lilli's killers.

It would help if they knew what they were bloody looking for, he thought to himself. Botanical identification did not come easy to a bunch of flatfoots. The magnolia was easiest, even most of his dumb mates knew a magnolia, although it was too late in the year for the tell-tale white or pink flowers, but a tulip tree? No chance.

He sat at his desk and looked around the office. Perhaps he should go back out there, but they had a full complement battering their way through parks, gardens, woods and fields. He was more use here. He could feel that they were close, and when he looked again at the note from Nikki Galena in Greenborough, he felt they were almost there. This guy, Freddie Carver, seemed like just the type to have animals working for him, the kind of animals that were capable of abusing kids like Fern, Lilli and

Sophie. Cat had said she'd let him know if Freddie's last trip had really been to Derbyshire. Meantime, he'd do a bit of checking up on this unpleasant piece of shit himself. He switched on his computer and logged in.

As he tried to decide how best to get the information he wanted, he found his mind wandering to the other night in the hospital. He had felt . . . well, he wasn't quite sure how he felt. Untangled was the word that came to him. His chaotic, twisted thoughts had miraculously unravelled themselves as he sat in the hospital with Cat and Sophie. And now he wasn't sure if it was because they were finally upping the ante on Fern's case, or being with Cat Cullen.

There was no doubt that he liked her. He would have dearly loved to work with her as his partner. They had gelled from the word go. And she seemed totally at ease in his company. But maybe Cat was like that with everyone. He sighed. She was very easy to talk to, and she had opened up to him as they passed the midnight hour, told him about what happened to her and how she was injured. Poor Cat! It was remarkable that she had stayed in the job, let alone remaining so capable and on top of things. He straightened his back. There would be time to think about this later, when they had caught Fern's killer.

* * *

He sat on the edge of his bed in his stable home, and stared at the stone floor. He had seen the police himself now, out at a big house up on the main road to Buxton.

It looked as though they were moving their search away from his area. He chewed at the inside of his cheek. He could not rest, though, dare not assume that it was safe. They might have some kind of plan, maybe they were covering certain areas at certain times, and they could easily circle back. No, he could not afford to relax yet. Not that he ever did. He stood up and stretched. He had sat there all night, frightened because he had heard a car draw up just before midnight. Now, tired as he was, he should get ready for work. The thought disgusted him, but there was nothing new about that.

In his kitchenette, he put a slice of anaemic white bread into the toaster. He could never eat much before going out, but he had to have something to keep his strength up. He never knew when he might need it next. He rolled up his sleeve and stared at the long, dark welts on his forearm. The scratches were deep, but they were healing, thank God. He had poured neat antiseptic over them, fearful they would become infected after the long nails had gouged furiously into his flesh.

He winced, rolled down his sleeve, and threw a tea bag into his mug. He had another ten minutes yet. He'd do what he always did before going to work, have a cup of tea and think of better times, times past.

* * *

Nikki was on her second coffee when Joseph knocked on the door.

'Can I run something past you?'

'Sure, come in and sit down.'

'I could be going off at a tangent here, but a whole load of seemingly separate occurrences are obscuring the picture.'

'Are we talking about the picture of Fat Freddie?'

Joseph ran a hand slowly through his hair. 'I think so. It concerns missing girls, the ones we had down as Mispers and runaways. Jessie gave me some photos and their details, and I could be wrong, but from their age and general appearance, I don't think they just ran away. I think they could have been taken for use in the sex trade. Like Sophie, they were fed some story about getting big money to dance in clubs, or being a model, you know the kind of lies these men dish out, then they get taken to some sleazy dive miles away and used and abused. We know he was involved in that racket when he was in London.'

'But Sophie was an illegal. These kids are local. He couldn't hold the threat of deportation over them. Why would they not just run away and come home?' Nikki stared at the pictures that Joseph had laid on the desk.

'Shame? Guilt? Threats against their families?'

'Mmm, could be. And you think Carver is behind it? Surely he was down his Iberian rat-hole while this was going on?'

Joseph nodded. 'He was, but Yvonne and Niall's informants say that all the time he was away, he was planning his comeback. He had his organisation ticking over in Britain while he was in exile.'

'And now he's home. Oh, great!' Nikki put her head in her hands. 'But why here?'

'Our foot soldiers are working on that as we speak.' Joseph picked up one of the photos. 'Would you mind if I go and talk to Dominic Jarvis? His sister is one of the girls on Jessie's list. She's similar to Lilli but strangely, I think something different happened to her, and I'd like to check out her home.'

Nikki looked interested. 'Want me to come?'

'No offence, but I seem to have made something of an impression on him. If it's alright with you, I'll go alone and informally this time, and if I think it needs an official visit, I'll tell you.'

Nikki would rather Joseph had concentrated on something other than missing young women, but he seemed quite fired up about this Jarvis girl. 'Okay, but why do you think she is different to the others?'

'I've read Gill Mercer's files. It was not a full investigation because the super thought she was just a missing person. No vulnerability and not our business, but Gill felt sorry for Dina's twin brother, Dominic, and delved as far as she dare.'

'And what have you sifted from the ashes?'

'I talked to a couple of her old friends and some workmates, and I've formed an as yet unsubstantiated theory.'

His eyes were bright, and Nikki thought of a hound dog on the scent.

'Dominic swears she was abducted, and I think he's kind of right, after a fashion.'

'Don't talk in riddles, Joseph! Get to the point and tell me what you think.'

'I think she *did* meet someone. After all, Niall saw them together, and I'm certain she thought he was the love of her life. I'm pretty sure she either ran off with him, or maybe chased after him if he left Greenborough. I really need to know who that man was.'

Nikki nodded. '*And* what happened to Dina. Then you go and chat with Dominic, but don't tell him of your suspicions. Gill told me he's volatile.'

'He certainly is. And don't worry, I'll be more than diplomatic.'

As Joseph left the office, Nikki wondered why they had been chosen to host the next episode of the Carver Saga. With a grunt of disgust at his choice of location, she picked up the phone and dialled a number that she'd scribbled on her memo pad.

'Geoff! Long time, no see! Nikki Galena here.' She smiled and doodled pound signs on the pad as her old school friend asked how things were with her. 'Pretty good, but can I ask a favour? If I said, Herondene, Jacob's Mere, what would you say?'

She listened for a while as the estate agent extolled the beauties of living in the "gloriously secluded spot" and how "a little sympathetic updating" would restore the cottage to its original beauty.

'Geoff, this is me, Nikki, the girl who tipped frogspawn in your lunchbox because you nicked my peanut butter sandwiches. Let's use real speak, shall we? For *secluded spot*, read *lonely with no amenities and no bus service*, and for *a sympathetic updating*, read *spend a bleeding fortune on a money pit*. It's a dump, my friend, and you know it. But sadly a couple of kids that I happen to care about have fallen in love with it. I know what the asking price is, but I'm asking you for a reasonable one. How about you ring the owners and then get back to me?'

Then Nikki sat back and began to formulate stage two of her cunning plan.

* * *

'We're just off out, Radley! Going to join us for a jolly country hike?'

Ben looked up from the pile of printouts and photographs that covered his desk, and was astounded to realise that he had been sitting there for over three hours.

'I'll give it a miss, Andy. I want to finish up here.'

'Fed up with the great outdoors?' The booted and waterproofed copper grinned at his friend. 'I reckon you could do with some fresh air. You look like shit!'

'I only got three hours' sleep last night, so at least I have an excuse, bum-face.'

'Love you too, Ben. See you.'

As his colleague moved away, Ben looked up. 'Andy? What area are you on today?'

'Er, villages around Lower Buckley, I think. Why?'

'Just wondered. I'll join you after I've finished what I'm doing.'

'Sarge said we are making our way west towards Hillcote End.'

'Thanks, I'll catch up with you later.'

Ben looked down at the information he had compiled over the last couple of hours. Perhaps he should ring Greenborough. He was pretty damned sure that although Freddie Carver had no known or documented activities in Derbyshire, he had a very definite presence here. He was like a ghost floating through at least half a dozen cases that Ben had examined. No mention of the name Carver, but there were dozens of references to an unidentified individual who provided enormous amounts of cash when required, and seemed to be able to magic witnesses away.

Ben turned a page. He could be wrong, but he thought he'd found a link. A man named Rosewood always seemed to turn up when the anonymous mystery man was mentioned. Ben had worked on several cases since Fern's was scaled down. He had often wondered where some of the new dealers and villains had suddenly managed to get their filthy hands on so much cash when they needed it, especially if it was intended to undercut the local drugs baron. Maybe Freddie was silently building a powerful new empire. Ben scratched his head. All this was being achieved when Freddie Carver was safely out of the picture, sipping Rioja in his villa in Spain. Ben's eyes narrowed. If Carver was working this area, albeit incognito, then he might well have something to do with Fern, Lilli and Sophie.

'DC Radley! Phone call in the outer office. It's Sergeant Morris, he wants you urgently.'

Ben rubbed a stiff knee and hopped out of the CID room. 'Sarge? Ben Radley here.'

'Get yourself over to the Royal, fast as you can. A&E department. There's a girl there, name of Zoë Wallace. There are two WPCs with her, you'll need one of them present for the interview, but don't let anyone else talk to her, understand? No one.'

'I'm on my way, Sarge, but what's the story?' Ben fumbled through his pockets for his car keys.

'She was attacked while walking her dog somewhere around that stone circle near Lyton Peak. Just get over there and talk to her yourself. I think it's connected to your Fern case.'

* * *

Anger and outrage were holding Zoë Wallace together. Considering her harrowing ordeal, Ben thought it odd that her main concern seemed to be the whereabouts and state of her pet Labrador.

Her doctor took Ben aside. 'I think it's a case of trying to dissociate herself from what happened to her. Make something else more important, then it makes the main issue less so.'

Ben nodded bitterly. He understood perfectly. He'd been doing it for years, ever since his daughter died and his wife left him. 'Do we know about the dog?'

'Not yet. We hope it's on its way home.'

'Can I talk to her now, Doctor? It is vital I find out about her attacker. We believe this is connected to three other cases.' He paused for effect, 'And as two of the girls are dead . . . ?'

The doctor nodded solemnly. 'Of course. Just be as gentle as you can. She's been very badly assaulted.'

'Sexually?'

'Afraid so. The attacker undoubtedly intended to rape her, Detective. But he picked a strong, feisty girl who was not easily overpowered. Together with her dog, she might have inflicted some half-decent wounds on him. I damned well hope so. The evil bastard.'

Ben sat beside Zoë, and felt an awful sensation of déjà vu sweep over him. He wished Cat Cullen were with him instead of a WPC that he hardly knew. Cat's manner was perfect for both obtaining information and offering compassion at the same time. And anyway, he just wished she was with him.

'I hate to have to question you like this, Zoë, but it's really important that I do. Are you okay with that?'

The woman could have been beautiful, but there was no way of knowing. Her eyes were half closed, swollen and discoloured. Her lips were split and still oozed tiny droplets of blood. One cheekbone was clearly cracked, and a graze had pebble-dashed the skin down the whole left-hand side of her face. All superficial. No doubt they would heal, and later, she would be grateful for that. He looked at her hands and saw why the sergeant had decided there was a connection with Fern and the others. A deep, jagged laceration scored an uneven line across her ring finger.

'How did that happen, Zoë?' He pointed to the finger.

'The bastard tried to hack it off! That's what happened!' The tone was very different to Sophie's, but then she was a very different woman.

'What did he use?'

'A saw of some kind. One of those DIY tools like a Stanley knife with a long serrated blade.' She tried to laugh, then held her good hand over her damaged mouth and muttered, 'He came prepared alright.' She looked at him hopefully. 'Have you found Barney yet?'

Ben smiled. 'They are out looking for him now. They think he's making his own way home.'

'I hope so. Without him, and the two squaddies that heard me scream, I shudder to think what he'd have done to me.'

'Two army lads?' Ben glanced at the WPC.

'Orienteering exercise on the Peak. God certainly must have been looking out for me. They chased him, but said he was gone like a rat down a hole.'

'Can you give me a description of your attacker?'

'Sure as hell I can! All the time I was fighting him off, I was thinking — remember!' She shifted uncomfortably. 'Look, I'll do my best to tell you all I can, but would you check on my dog for me? Just see if they've picked him up yet?'

Ben walked to the door and beckoned to the other constable. 'It would really help to get an update on her dog. It's not helping her, knowing he's still missing.'

The officer nodded and walked down off down the corridor.

'Okay, Zoë, are you ready?'

She nodded vehemently, 'Yeah. Tallish, maybe five foot ten or taller, white, bad skin, five o'clock shadow, dirty brown, shaggy hair, smelt horrible.'

Ben wrote down everything as she spoke, then remembered that Sophie had said the same thing, and asked, 'Smelt bad? How so? Body odour?'

'That, and something else, something sort of sickly sweet. It was vile!' She retched.

'Go on.'

Zoë took several deep breaths. 'Right. Dirty brown trousers, a thick jacket, dark, yes, navy blue, with a paler lining. Red check shirt, thick like a lumberjack's, muddy engineers' boots in tan.' She shivered. 'And I think he may have a chipped front tooth.' Her voice had dropped almost to a whisper and she was visibly shaking. 'Well, that was the intention, if I kicked him hard enough.'

Ben realised that shock was setting in. He smiled reassuringly and said that he would leave her with the WPC for a few minutes while he went to get news of Barney. To his relief, as soon as he mentioned her dog she began to calm down.

'Oh please, if you would.'

Outside he called a nurse, and explained about Zoë's condition. She beckoned to the doctor who was still reading her files, and the two went in to check their patient.

'DC Radley!' The young constable called to him from the door. 'I've just heard that they have found the dog. He's been taken in by the next door neighbour.'

'Great! Is he hurt?'

'A bit shocked, torn pads and filthy dirty, other than that, he's fine.'

The doctor called him back into the room. 'Another five minutes, Detective, then I must ask you to leave. She's a very brave lady, but she really needs to rest, okay?'

That was fine by Ben. This woman had practically painted a picture of the man who had hurt her, and he couldn't wait to get it onto the police computer.

'First thing, your Barney is safe and he's fine. He's being looked after by your neighbour.'

Tears coursed down her face. 'Thank you, Ben. Thank you very much.'

'I've just got a couple more questions. Then I promise I'll leave you to get some sleep.'

'I doubt I'll ever sleep again, well, not until you've caught him. But yes, ask away.'

'Did he speak?'

Zoë nodded. 'I can't remember what he said, obscenities mostly, but he was English.'

'Regional accent?'

'Sort of. Not well spoken. Rough, harsh tone, not exactly local, but close.'

'One last question, Zoë. Would you recognise him again?'

'Absolutely anywhere.' She pressed her hand to her bruised eyes and sobbed. 'His horrible face is imprinted on my brain forever.'

* * *

After reporting everything Zoë Wallace had told him, Ben drove out to the scene of the attack. A uniformed officer checked his identity, and lifted the blue and white cordon tape for him to enter.

'Hello, Ben. Thought you'd be here before long.' A petite, dark-haired detective approached him, a smile on her angular, attractive face.

'Got anything yet?'

'Oh, we don't hang around here, Detective! We've already got the blade, and the SOCO seems to think we have just about every kind of bodily fluid going.'

'Lovely, and I've not even had dinner yet.'

'Well, maybe you should get yourself a nice greasy burger and chips on the way back to the station. That'll help.'

Ben pulled a face. 'Thanks. Still, it means that if we get our hands on someone, we'll have no problem doing a DNA test and nailing him. That's good.'

'Yeah, we've talked to the two squaddies as well. If they'd not arrived when they did, I believe Zoë would have been dead. She was far too fiery to leave alive. As it is, I'll bet he's shitting himself right now.'

'I sincerely hope so.'

'Me too.'

Ben went back to his car and sat for a while before driving home. This attack was very different from the others, but the injury to the finger and the man's distinctive bad smell were evidence that it was the same man. He pushed the key into the ignition. He'd have to wait for the lab reports to see if they tied in officially with the other girls. He started the car. What the hell was the man up to? Why break the pattern? Why attack a different sort of woman, and one with a dog? He'd always believed there was more than one man, but the squaddies had made it clear that this was definitely a loner.

He moved forward and bumped down the rugged track. This did not feel quite right, but surely the injured finger said it had to be the same man? Or did it? He pulled the car off the track, parked it beneath a huge beech tree and sat looking across the valley. He needed to talk to someone. After a moment, he pulled out his mobile and found Cat Cullen's number.

CHAPTER TEN

Joseph sat on a rather old-fashioned, but very comfortable, sofa and looked down at the glass-topped coffee table. It was strewn with folders, printouts, statistics on runaways, newspaper articles and every kind of memo pad known to man.

As Dominic made him a coffee, Joseph took a look around. The house was neat and clean, although the décor was dated and the furnishings quite basic. Still, it was a surprise. Joseph had expected either a messy pit, or something rather modern and male. This looked like the home of a couple in late middle age, not the bachelor pad of a twenty-six-year-old man.

Jarvis returned with cups and saucers on a tray, and Joseph could smell proper ground coffee.

'Sugar?' There was demerara sugar in a white bone china bowl with a small silver spoon. 'I think it's sacrilege to put sugar in real coffee, but,' he gave Joseph a tired smile, 'guests are allowed whatever they prefer. Not that I have many guests now. It used to be open house when my sister was here but to be honest, I think even my friends are fed up with me going on about Dina being abducted.'

'You truly believe that, don't you?'

'Completely, Joseph. Can I call you Joseph?'

'Of course you can.' Joseph sipped the sugarless coffee and wondered why he had not taken his usual two spoons. He sighed in appreciation. 'That's beautiful coffee, Dominic.'

'My one big vice. I spend quite a lot of money on the very best beans.'

Joseph looked at the piles of paperwork. 'You've done a lot of research on runaways and missing persons. What are your conclusions?'

'That the law is an ass.'

Joseph grinned. 'Tell me something I don't know.'

'You have no idea what I went through when she first disappeared. The definition of a missing person is, "Anyone whose whereabouts is unknown whatever the circumstances of disappearance. They will be considered missing until located and their well-being or otherwise established." That gave me hope,' he frowned, 'until it was pointed out to me that the level of risk for Dina did not meet the requirements for taking action. She was not a child, not a vulnerable adult, had no mental health issues or drug/drink problems, she was not under any form of threat, and frankly could not be considered "at risk" at all.' He exhaled. 'They fobbed me off with the Missing Persons Bureau at the National Crime Agency, and a charity called Missing People. They did what they could, but they found nothing either. They asked me if I realised that adults have a legal right to disappear. After a while, I didn't know whether to grieve or live in hope. I still don't. I'm in limbo.'

'250,000 people go missing every year in the UK,' said Joseph softly. 'And almost all of them have someone, or sometimes a whole family, torn apart by the not knowing.'

Dominic hung his head. 'Until it happens to you, it is impossible to describe. I told you that I don't get visitors anymore, but I don't want them. I don't want anyone around me. I used to be pretty gregarious — okay, not like

Dina — but I was no shrinking violet. Now I'm bad-tempered, I have no patience with anyone or anything, I'm almost violent sometimes, and I'm moody to the point where I even hate myself.'

'Who do you think took her?'

'A month before she disappeared, she changed. She became secretive and she stopped seeing so many of her usual friends. I knew that she had met a man, but every time I asked her who he was, she shut me out.' He rubbed at his forehead. 'She'd never done that before. We were close. We talked about everything, and she even used to get me to vet her boyfriends, you know, get my opinion? We are twins, we . . . I guess we had a sort of connection. It was almost a game, and up until then we had been a really good, cohesive family unit. We were friends, Joseph, and I loved my sister.' He passed the back of his hand across his eyes. 'I miss her and I want to know if she's dead or alive.'

Jessie Nightingale's words came back to Joseph. They were exactly the same as those spoken by Dominic. They *needed* to know what had happened to their loved one. 'Did you ever see this man?'

'Never, although he picked her up once in his car. She ran out and jumped in and they were gone before I had a chance to look at him.'

'What sort of car was it?'

'Something expensive, like an Audi or a Merc. As I say, it was there one minute and then gone. He didn't come to the house again, well, not while I was here.'

'And Dina took nothing with her?'

He stood up. 'Come and see her room.'

He led the way up the stairs and threw open the door to a big, light room. It had pretty bed linen on the double bed, a thick rich carpet and fitted cupboards and wardrobes. It was tidy, and obviously regularly cleaned, and there was a scattering of feminine things around, magazines, fashion trainers, makeup and bottles of perfume.

Joseph took it all in with a feeling of dismay. It was as if Dina Jarvis had just popped down to the corner shop for a new magazine or a bar of chocolate.

Beside her bed, with her alarm clock, box of tissues and a little bowl with some bead bracelets in, was a small posy bowl of fresh flowers.

As Joseph's eyes lingered on the blossoms, Dominic said, 'I guess *live in hope* comes into play more than anything.'

'And nothing was gone?'

'Not to my knowledge. Only what she was wearing.'

Joseph made a sudden decision. 'I'm going to try to trace this mystery man.'

Dominic stepped back as if Joseph had struck him. 'Really?'

'Yes, but I want you to listen to me. You mentioned every adult's right to run away, didn't you?'

He nodded silently, his eyes not leaving Joseph's.

'Be prepared for that scenario to become real. And if that should be the case, it will be heartrending for you to know that she has stayed away voluntarily, and with full knowledge that you will have been frantic with worry. Can you deal with that?'

'Do you know something, Joseph? Something that you are not telling me?

'No, Dominic, I don't, but I've seen what it can cause, and I just want you to prepare yourself.'

Dominic drew himself up. 'If it gives me a final answer, then so be it. At least I'll know, one way or the other.'

'Good man. Now I have to get back, but leave this with me, and let me come to you if I have anything, okay? No haunting the police station, understood?'

'Understood, but can I have your number, in case I remember something that could help you?'

Joseph hesitated for a moment, then took a gamble. 'This is my direct line at the station, and below it is a mobile number. But that one is for emergencies only, and I mean that.'

'You have my word, Joseph. Just find out what happened to my sister — please.'

* * *

Freddie Carver stared over the top of his glass at the man sitting opposite him. Mr Fabian was tall and well-built, with a head so closely shaved it almost looked varnished.

'I wanted to thank you for the excellent work you did while I was away, and to assure you that when my organisation is fully up and running, there will be work for you on a regular basis.'

'That is good to know.' Fabian sat ramrod straight and looked directly into Freddie's eyes, his face a lump of granite. 'We aim to please.'

My friend, thought Freddie, nothing about you could be called pleasing. Fabian and Mr Venables made even him shudder. They were the coldest pair he had ever had the misfortune to meet. But . . . they got the job done.

'At the moment, the job that is causing me most grief is an insignificant one, nothing you would undertake.'

'Tell me about this "insignificant" problem.'

Freddie placed his glass on a coaster. 'Alright. I hire three men on a two-year contract. I pay top rates. The work is simple, a little messy maybe, but straightforward enough given their capabilities. They've managed to louse it up.'

'Replace them.'

'We are only a month or so away from changing everything in the area where they are based. It'll be a takeover on a grand scale. If they can hold it together for a little longer, they will be history, well, as far as my organisation is concerned.' He glanced at his watch. 'I have put them on a very short leash. In fact I expect an update from Lenny any time now.'

'I could finish off whatever it is that they find so difficult.'

'You are in a different league, Mr Fabian. This is work for the dross, and it's something personal, not a part of the bigger operation.'

Fabian shrugged. 'But they clearly can't handle it.' His eyes narrowed to slits. 'I *hate* sloppy work. Listen, you have given me a lot of lucrative jobs in the past. I'm happy to slum it for a while, if it helps.'

Before Carver could answer, the telephone rang.

'Can I get that for you, Mr Carver?'

'Thank you, but no.' Freddie eased himself painfully from the leather sofa and limped slowly towards the ringing phone. 'But you can pour me another drink, Mr Fabian. I might need it.'

The voice on the other end was high-pitched and clearly disturbed about something. Freddie put a hand over the receiver and whispered to his guest, 'Better make that a large one.'

'Mr Carver, sir?'

He remained silent.

'Boss? It's Lenny. I'm afraid we've got a problem.' There was a long pause. 'Er, Vic's gone missing, Mr Carver.'

'What the hell do you mean *missing*? The job isn't finished.'

'The thing is, Mr Carver, he's been in a right state since we saw you last. I think it has something to do with those women. The girls, you know? The fingers?'

'Of course I know, you fool.'

'He's been acting really weird. Well, more weird than usual, ever since that foreign one got away.'

'He was never supposed to keep her in the first place, was he? He knew exactly what he was supposed to do with her.'

'I know, sir, but me and Ezra, we never knew anything about that, I swear to God. Anyway, earlier on we went out to that place of his, and all his stuff was packed up, ready to go, but he was nowhere to be found.' The voice stuttered to a halt. 'I'm really sorry, Mr Carver, but we've looked everywhere.'

'I see.' Freddie's voice was soft and sibilant. 'Now what kind of trouble do you think he got himself into?'

'I really dunno, Mr Carver, sir. Vic isn't all there. He's an animal, you know that, but from the way he's been acting . . . let's just say if I was a woman on my own, I wouldn't want to bump into him.'

Freddie seethed. For years, even while he was in Spain, everything had ticked along smoothly. Now, because that cretin Vic couldn't keep his dick in his pants, Freddie was going to have to lose a lot of money, do something very distasteful, and no doubt shed a lot of unnecessary blood. He gritted his teeth. 'Carry on as normal, Lenny. It will be sorted from this end. Vic never existed, understand? And you'll have to do his job as well as your own.'

The caller gave a muffled gasp. 'But, Mr Carver, I can't! I . . .'

'Business as usual, Lenny. Or you and Ezra get nothing. No cut, no money, no nothing, and if it gets to that point, I'd start looking over my shoulder if I was you. Do I make myself clear?'

'Yes, sir. Perfectly.' The line went dead.

Freddie accepted the tall glass Fabian handed him. Looking him full in the face, he said, 'Well, Mr Fabian, it seems I do have a job for you after all. Do you by any chance remember someone called Vic?'

'Tall, shabby clothes, sly-looking, rat-faced, with a serious personality disorder? Smells like rotting meat?'

'That's the one. Well, I'd like you to find him and explain that he is no longer in my employ.'

'Terminate his employment permanently?'

'Well, I'm not asking you to give him a P45, am I?' He gave an evil grin. 'So, if you'd be so kind?'

'Oh, it'll be my pleasure, Mr Carver, my pleasure. And rest assured, there will be no mistakes.'

* * *

Nikki had mixed emotions about all the activity in the Derbyshire area. Naturally she wanted the killer caught, but she had kind of adopted Lilli as theirs and felt a little miffed that the Fens had no part in the action.

Ben Radley seemed to be acting like some kind of super cop. He was trying to connect Freddie Carver to shady deals in his area, trace the magic tulip tree, interview recently attacked young women and find lost dogs. Nikki smiled to herself. The man had risen again, like a phoenix. She wondered if it was because Fern's case was well and truly out of the filing cabinet at last, or was it down to the entry of a certain Cat Cullen into his life.

Nikki would dearly love to see Cat happy with someone special. The girl had been to hell and back, and apart from a few meaningless flings, she had allowed no one to get close to her since had been hurt. Now Nikki sensed a change in her young detective, and she wondered if there was anything she could do to help things along a little. She had to admit that there was something very likeable about Ben Radley — maybe it was those wonderfully expressive eyes.

She checked the time. Almost three o'clock, and after the late afternoon meeting she had planned to go out and do a little terrorising of a certain estate agent. She had never approved or indulged in matchmaking. Now, however, she thought she'd give it a go.

'Cat! My office, please,' she yelled out of the door.

'Ma'am?' Cat hurried in.

'I've got a little job for you, if you want?'

Cat's face lit up. 'You know me, ma'am. I love a challenge.'

'I'd like you to get hold of DC Radley and see if he needs a hand. I'd really like to have some eyes and ears in the Derby camp right now, especially since this recent attack. I'm sure he can square it with his boss, and if not I'll give him a ring myself.'

Cat nodded. 'Good idea, ma'am. There's a lot going on over there right now, and it is all connected to us really, isn't it?'

'Absolutely. So go ring him and keep me up to date, okay?'

As Cat hurried out of the office, Nikki allowed a smile to creep across her face. 'Two birds with one perfectly aimed stone! Nice one, Nikki Galena!'

Joseph stood behind her looking somewhat puzzled. 'Talking to yourself is not a good sign. And where is Cat going in such a hurry?'

'On a quest, and I hope she finds treasure.'

'Now I am worried. Have you been sniffing something from the evidence store?'

'No, but I do feel a little high,' Nikki frowned, 'and, do you know, I quite like it.'

'Should I take the four o'clock meeting for you, while you pop in to see the FMO?'

'No, I'm good, thank you, Joseph.' She flashed him a wild smile, and he left shaking his head.

* * *

Nikki stood in front of her depleted team. 'Right, now, I want to make this quick. In the light of recent events in Derby, I've asked Cat to go back there to offer assistance, and also to keep us updated on progress after this recent attack on the woman named Zoë Wallace. We have drawn a blank with our attempts to identify Lilli and we have to assume that she is not local, and was possibly a runaway or a missing person, and that will make identification very hard indeed.' She looked at Joseph. 'Now I'm going to ask Joseph to fill you in on his theory about some of the girls on the Misper list being used in the sex trade, and how Freddie Carver may be behind it.' She sat down and waved Joseph to the front of the room.

The whole team agreed that his scenario was indeed probable.

'It is highly likely, given what we have found out about Carver working under cover,' Yvonne said. 'That was one of his old games — putting young girls in his clubs. And, according to our sources he has been accruing money hand over fist. He was clearly planning something.'

'Why can't we find where he is staying?' asked Dave. 'This is not exactly downtown Manhattan, is it?'

Niall raised his hand. 'We think he moves around, Dave. Even the guy who sometimes drives for him picks him up at different locations every day. He really does not want anyone to get a fix on him.'

'And he's doing a rather good job of it,' grumbled Jessie. 'It's really frustrating.'

Nikki looked at Joseph. 'What about your visit earlier, regarding one of the missing women from Jessie's list? Er, Dina someone? Does it need the team's input?'

'Not at this stage, ma'am. I need to do some more background research first, then I'll let you decide if it's worth a follow-up.'

'Okay. Any other matters?'

Yvonne stood up. 'We think Freddie is going out tonight, ma'am, and one of his men is going to try to follow him. My snout will let us know tomorrow if he was successful.'

'Excellent. Let's hope he heads west.'

Joseph was looking thoughtful. 'I was wondering about us having a word with Raymond Leonard, as Mickey suggested? The Leonards could be helpful in tracing Carver.'

Nikki shook her head. 'I think that should be a last resort. Things seem very different since Archie Leonard died, and I'm not so comfortable talking to his son.'

'Fair enough, and anyway, I'm sure Mickey would pass on anything interesting.'

She stood up. 'Okay, if there's nothing else, off you go.'

Back in her office, Joseph frowned at her. 'You didn't hang about with that, did you?'

Nikki pulled on her jacket. 'Got an appointment. Can I leave you in charge?'

'I'm intrigued.'

She grinned at him. 'I'll bet you are. See you later.'

Nikki left the station.

Jacob's Mere was a twenty-minute drive, and Nikki, pleased to be alone for a while, began to unwind and enjoy the familiar countryside that she so loved. The town soon gave way to a scattering of houses and then to acres of fertile farmland. A line of pylons stretched into infinity across the miles of carefully farmland. To her they always looked like giant metal men, marching ever onward towards the horizon.

Geoff Arden was already there when she arrived, and she saw immediately why Tamsin and Niall were so enamoured of the cottage. But she also saw the enormous amount of work that would have to be done.

Geoff held out his hand. 'Good to see you, Nikki.'

'You too, and thanks for coming out at short notice.'

'It does have promise, doesn't it?' Geoff stared up at the peeling paintwork.

'Yes, if you have enormous visionary powers, and a small fortune to spend.'

'Let's go inside.'

The door opened directly into the front room, as was the case with so many fen cottages. Nikki knew at once that this was where Joseph's daughter was going to live when she was married. It was in a state, no denying that, but it would be a challenge worth taking on. 'Geoff? Who is the owner?'

'Remember Patricia Lombard, that was? In the year above us?'

'Odd eyes and big dandruff?'

Geoff nodded, 'That's the one. She still has those eyes, but fortunately the dandruff's gone. She married one of the Benton boys. This was his grandmother's house.'

'Did you speak to her about the price?'

'Yes. She's a bit sticky, but I think she'll drop a little.'

'She'd better, if she wants a sale. This place is in need of serious attention.'

'Most of it is cosmetic.'

Nikki snorted. 'Bollocks! It'll take more than a coat of magnolia and a nice lampshade to make this liveable. And I haven't even seen the bathroom yet.'

'Ah, well . . .'

'It does have a bathroom, doesn't it?'

'Oh yes.'

'Show me.'

They went up the stairs and along a short landing.

'Originally it didn't have a bathroom, but the smallest bedroom was converted into one, back in the fifties.' Geoff opened the door.

'Damn! Talk about pink!' Nikki's eyes widened as she took in the pink tiles, pink flooring, pink bath, basin and ah yes, a pink toilet. 'So this is at least fifty-five years old?'

'At least. Very retro, isn't it?'

'That's one way of putting it.' Nikki tried and failed to imagine Niall doing his morning ablutions in this candy-floss nightmare.

They checked the bedrooms and then went back downstairs.

'It has around half an acre of land, and there are two outbuildings — a garage and a small workshop.'

Nikki looked across the fields to where the tower of a ruined windmill still stood. All around was arable land interspersed with drainage ditches. Right now the soil was rich brown, ploughed in deep furrows. There were small clusters of trees, brambles and wild briar roses along the lanes. Idyllic, thought Nikki. She pictured what it would be like at dawn, or when the sun was setting against the big Lincolnshire sky. Not everyone would like it, some would see a lonely and inhospitable place with no near neighbours, no transport and no shops.

'What's her best price, Geoff?'

'She's looking for a hundred and forty, nothing less.'

'And did Niall Farrow say what he had in mind?'

'Lower than that, I'm afraid.'

Nikki stared at the old property thoughtfully. 'It needs rewiring, the damp course attended to, that chimney needs rebuilding and the roof wants attention. Even if the bathroom didn't give you a migraine, it is worn and damp, the tiles are lifting and the bath is stained to the point where I wouldn't bath a mangy dog in it. And it will have to be redecorated, both inside and out. I think Patricia needs a reality check, don't you?'

'She sees it as an ideal opportunity for someone to do a restoration job, and given the size of the plot, I think she'll hold out.'

'Then this place will sit here until it rots. If it was a bequest, then she's not reliant on this to buy a property of her own, and the Bentons aren't short of money. Isn't it better to have money in the bank, even if it is a bit less than you planned?'

'I totally agree, and believe me, I don't want to see it festering on my books forever.' Geoff smiled at her. 'I'll see what I can do, Nikki. No promises, because she's not the sort of woman who'll be moved by a sob story. The old, "newly-wed young couple and their dream cottage, if *only* they could afford it," wouldn't wash with her.'

'Then try her with first-time buyers, good jobs and the main earner being a police officer with a guaranteed good credit rating. If she's that money-orientated she should realise she's onto a winner.'

'She's a shrewd business woman.'

'Or a greedy bitch?'

Geoff laughed. 'Possibly. No — more like probably.'

They walked back to their cars. Nikki bade farewell to her old school friend. 'Give it your best shot, won't you? This is for the daughter of my closest friend. She's marrying a lad who works with me, and I happen to think a lot of him.'

'Of course I will. I'll ring you later and tell you what she says.'

'I appreciate it. Now I'd better get back to murder and mayhem.'

Geoff grinned. 'Me too. The estate agent business can be pretty cut-throat sometimes.'

Nikki drove back to the station and spent the rest of her shift in her office, writing up reports and checking on incoming updates. Just as she was thinking about going home, the phone rang.

'How does this sound, Nikki?' Geoff rattled off a price.

'It sounds like music to my ears, my friend. However did you get her to agree?'

'To be honest, I simply put it exactly as you said, and added that with the market as it is, she could wait a very long while to get another buyer in such a good position. So, shall I ring Mr Farrow with the good news?'

'Please do. And Geoff? Don't tell him that we met out there. I told them I'd have a word with you, but no more than that. I really don't want to steal the lad's thunder. Just let him think that you have negotiated a damn good deal for him, and that you are a stellar estate agent, which of course you are.'

'Have it your way, Nikki. As I recall, you generally did.'

'Now, now.'

'I never got over that frogspawn, you know. I was scared to open my lunchbox for weeks after that. I could have starved.'

Nikki laughed. 'Thanks for what you've done. I really do appreciate it.'

'Pleasure. Any time. And if it all goes well, your young friends will be happy, and I'll have got Herondene off my books. Win-win, Nikki.'

'Indeed, and now I can go home and sleep the sleep of the just, for once.'

CHAPTER ELEVEN

There was something terribly wrong with her new medication. He had told her he had called in at the surgery because he was so worried about her, and the doctor had prescribed some stronger pain relief. He had been warned that it would make her drowsy at first, and some people took longer than others to get used to them.

She understood all that, but the effects had been terrifying. She had certainly felt far from drowsy. In fact, she had felt capable of anything. For a time she had been pain-free, but she had paid dearly for that short period of relief.

Even this morning she was still confused, and she had the worst headache she could ever remember. She sat in her chair and listened out for him. She had heard nothing since she woke up, but she sensed that he was somewhere in the house. Somehow she had washed herself and managed to get dressed. She seemed to recall that he had been with her last night, but she wasn't certain. There was a vague memory of him standing over her, his head tilted and his arms outstretched, like Jesus on the cross, and his body had shone and glistened in the candlelight. But of course that couldn't have happened. Because then he would have been naked, wouldn't he? So it had to be the drugs.

And the drugs must have been responsible for her mother dancing around her room, dressed in rainbow-coloured taffeta and showering her with bright, silvery stars. She could remember trying to catch the shining, twinkling lights. She had been light as air, and had danced with her mother. She looked down at her swollen legs and sighed. Had she ever danced? She had been in this room for so long that she really couldn't remember much else, although the thought of dancing seemed to kindle some sort of emotion inside her, so maybe she had once. Well, she had wanted new painkillers, but she would not be taking those again.

She was almost embarrassed at the thought of seeing him again, after what she had imagined in her hallucinatory state. And worst of all, she must have pulled her own clothes off in the night. They were on the floor beside the bed when she awoke.

A wave of nausea washed over her. Should she tell him? She would be mortified, but he really should know that they had affected her so badly. She could have hurt herself, or even hurt him if he came to check on her.

She moved stiffly in the chair, then stretched her arms out in front of her, carefully turning them, palms up, then palms down, then bringing them into her body and out again. There was still some freedom from her usual morning agonies. And hadn't she managed to get herself out of bed unaided? Perhaps she should risk it and continue with the pills? Some tablets did affect you to start with but you got used to them, didn't you?

She would do as she always did, and be guided by him. He knew best, and he always did the very best for her, even when she didn't deserve it. She sighed. She was so lucky to have him.

* * *

After the morning meeting, Joseph took everything he had managed to find on Dina Jarvis into Nikki's office and spread it out on her desk. He had been up half the night trying to piece together what might have occurred in the time leading up to her disappearance. He had accessed the files from the National Crime Agency's missing persons bureau, and had had a long conversation with a very helpful man from the charity organisation that Dominic had contacted.

Joseph scratched his head. 'I have a distinctly unsettling feeling about this girl, Nikki. I hate to say this, but I'm starting to agree with the brother. I think her disappearance is suspicious.'

'Isn't that a bit of an about-turn? I thought you believed she had run off with, or after, a man?'

'I still do. It's what happened to her after that that worries me.' Joseph looked anxiously at Nikki. 'Think about it. And look at these.' He pulled some photos from an envelope and laid them on the desk. 'I got them from her bedroom.'

Nikki flashed him a warning look. 'Was that wise?'

'It's alright. Dominic let me take them and copy them.' He pointed to one in particular. It showed brother and sister together on a ride at the big travelling fair in Hull. They were not identical twins, but there was a close resemblance. Both were slender and fine-boned with fair hair and blue-grey eyes. They were obviously enjoying themselves. 'There are dozens like this. When Dominic said they were close, he was right. They were really good friends. These photos go back to early childhood, and they are all happy and smiling. I know I thought he was weird and intense, but now I think that's a by-product of his grief. Even he admits he's changed for the worse since she went. I cannot get my head around the fact that she has never once contacted her brother, not personally or through a third party, just to let him know that she's safe.'

Nikki drew in a deep breath. 'The thing is, we can't be sure there wasn't a rift between them. Sometimes family breakups are catastrophic, they can lead to decades of ill-feeling within the family unit. What if they argued and she ran off to pour out her heart to her mystery man? What if he said, "Leave him, come with me," and she did?

'Two nights before she disappeared, Dominic took her to a local restaurant and they had dinner together. The waiter that served them that night said they left together. They were in good spirits, and they left a decent tip. What could happen in twenty-four hours to make her upset or angry enough, not to just up and leave, but to abandon everything she owned? Nothing has gone from her room. It's all ready and waiting for her return. It's creepy.'

'I've seen that so many times before.'

'Me too, but . . . oh, I don't know, Nikki, it just doesn't feel right to me.'

'Okay. Since the Derby lot seem to be galloping ahead with our murder case, take the time to look a bit deeper. Get Jessie to help you.'

'Do you think she should, Nikki? Another missing person case?'

'Jessie knows that if she continues to work, she'll have to deal with things like this, Joseph. I can't treat her with kid gloves. If she's up to the job, then she has to be prepared to handle whatever she's given.'

Joseph knew that she was right. He would have been happier with Cat, but Cat was not available.

'So, do you know anything about this elusive boyfriend?'

'Only that he had an expensive car, and one of Dina's friends said he was pretty well off.' Joseph gave a little smile. 'Niall caught them out at the back of the Golden Dragon, and I think they were doing more than just discussing the weather.'

'So Niall actually saw him?'

'Unfortunately he admits to averting his eyes in embarrassment.' Joseph was silent for a moment. 'But talking of Niall, I'm forgetting something important! Guess what? The owner of the cottage out at Jacob's Mere has dropped the price. They are going to put in their offer today! Good news or what!'

Nikki gave him what could only be described as a smug look, and then she broke into a delighted smile. 'But that's great! They must be over the moon.'

'And back again!' He peered at her suspiciously. 'That's not got anything to do with you by any chance?'

'Me? No. I just rang up yesterday and had a quiet word with Geoff, like I told Tam I would. It must be all down to the estate agent.'

'You did say he was a good bloke. Well, he's certainly come up trumps for them. Okay, I have to admit I'll worry about Tam being so isolated out there, but they both drive, and it's only fifteen minutes from Cloud Fen.'

'More to the point, they both love it and it's what they want. And they'll have their feet on the property ladder.'

'I'm going to help with the deposit. I've got a bit of money that I put aside after I sold my flat in Fenchester. It will give them a bit of a platform to kick off from.'

'And the wedding? Who is going to pay for that? The mother of the bride?'

Joseph pulled a face. 'Somehow I don't think so. I don't think everything is going particularly well in Laura's neck of the woods right now.'

'What about the high-powered job in Switzerland?'

'I don't know the full facts, but it seems she was an expert witness at a trial involving one of the big drugs companies, and they weren't too pleased at the evidence she gave. Suddenly she is not very popular, her workload is drying up, and Tamsin seems to think that she might be returning to Edinburgh in the near future.' He paused. 'And to make things worse, her partner, the great and gorgeous Gavin, has done a runner and taken a large part of their bank account with him.'

'Oh dear. I see what you mean.'

'Ma'am? Sorry to interrupt, but the Sarge here asked to be told when we had something on Freddie Carver.' Yvonne stood in the doorway.

'And?'

'He did go to Derbyshire last night, Sarge, to Ashbourne.'

Joseph punched a fist into his cupped hand. 'I knew it! He does have something to do with the dead girls! Where did he go exactly?'

'That I can't tell you. My snout said that one of his men followed Freddie's car. When he got to Ashbourne, he left his driver in a McDonald's and went off alone. At that point the guy who was following him lost his bottle and thought better of tailing him any further, but he waited to see how long he was away for. Apparently he was gone for more than two hours.'

'Damn! He could have driven anywhere in that time. Did this man of Freddie's follow him home?'

'I know what you are thinking, ma'am,' said Yvonne. 'Did he find out where he's staying? No, he lost him before he got to Greenborough.'

'At least it places him in the area where Lilli and Fern died and Sophie was held and tortured. That makes him top of my list.' Joseph looked at Yvonne. 'Well done for that, Vonnie. Keep your snout on the listen-out for any more info, won't you?'

'Oh, he knows what to do. I've asked him if there is anyone who might be prepared to talk to us about where Carver may be staying, but he clammed up, said they valued their lives too much. It's going to be down to us to find him, I'm afraid.'

'What about tracing the car?' Nikki asked.

'He keeps swapping them, ma'am. He seems to have a fleet of vehicles at his disposal. I'm thinking that's one of the things that were being set up while he was out of the country.'

'Well, good work, keep at it.' Nikki turned to Joseph. 'I need to tell Cat and Ben about this, and then let the super know.'

'And I'll go back to trying to get an ID on Dina's mystery man. Maybe I'll take a walk round to the Golden Dragon, see if any of the staff were working there back when Dina was around.'

'Okay. Keep in touch, won't you?'

'Wilco.'

* * *

Cat took the call from Nikki, and relayed the information to Ben Radley.

'So he *is* the man behind all these deals!'

'We don't know that for sure, Ben. There could be other reasons for him visiting this beautiful county of yours.' Cat sat opposite Ben at his desk.

'Oh, a holiday perhaps? Or maybe he just likes original Bakewell pudding?'

'Don't be facetious, it doesn't suit you.'

'Ben! Got some news!' A slim, crater-faced detective, grinning from ear to ear, called out from the doorway to the CID room. 'We've got Rosewood downstairs. Only this time, *he's* the one being interviewed.'

Ben frowned. 'Lewis Rosewood, the brief? How come?'

'That drugs case involving the strip clubs? Operation Rainbow? The one we've been working on for almost a year? We've had a bouncer in our pockets for a month or two now, and he's finally come through for us. Rosewood's been helping to launder the proceeds for the owners, among other things. We've got the lot on him, including photographic evidence placing him with all the bad guys, and we picked him up in possession of the biggest stash of marked notes you've ever seen! He's going to be going down for a very long while.'

Ben walked over and slapped his colleague on the shoulder. 'Nice one, Gaz. Really well done.'

As Gary went off to crow to more of his mates, Ben returned to his desk and stared thoughtfully at Cat. 'I'm really not sure if I'm pleased or disappointed about Rosewood. I'm absolutely certain he has something to do with Freddie Carver, probably a lot to do with him, and if Rosewood is banged up, it could be another bloody hold-up on the road to finding Fern's killer.' He bit hard on his thumbnail. Just as Cat was wondering what to say to him, she saw she had mail to pick up. One message stood out like a beacon — a memo from Dave. On Cat's instruction he had unearthed some old surveillance pictures of Freddie Carver. One picture showed him shaking hands with an unknown associate, another having dinner with the same man, and there was an image of the two of them coming out of a club. Cat had asked for the pictures in the hope that Ben might be able to identify the anonymous man. She clicked on the JPEG and there was Freddie, looking every inch the fat-cat business magnate, proffering a tanned hand to an overweight and rather sleazy-looking man with a comb-over and a thin moustache.

'Is this anyone you've met on your travels?'

Ben almost fell off his chair. Before Cat knew what was happening, he'd leaned across and planted a kiss on her cheek. 'You wonderful· woman! This is Lewis Rosewood. You've just made the connection! He's the link between the dodgy deals and the mystery man with all the money! This is abso-fucking-lutely great . . . Sorry, Cat, I forgot myself for a moment there.'

'Feel free.' Cat smiled broadly and wondered if he meant the swearing or the kiss. She didn't know which one she was referring to either.

'Now, how to go about using this information? We need to think this through.' Ben leant back in his chair, rubbed his temples and noticed a new email message. It came from one of his colleagues who was helping him out, and scouring Derbyshire for Fern and Lilli's place of imprisonment.

> *Ben get in touch, asap. Either your phone is off, you plonker, or there's no signal and I've got something for you. Jace.*

Ben keyed in his friend's number, and turned on the loudspeaker for Cat to hear. 'Jace? It's Ben. Where are you?'

'At bloody last! I'm at home, trying to grab some sleep. But, listen, this may be nothing, or it may be exactly what you're looking for. I don't rightly know.'

'Spit it out then, and I'll tell you.' Ben raised his eyebrows at Cat.

'Okay, okay. Well, my girl's been working at a little pub over near Appleton Dale. The other night everyone was talking about us searching all the estates in the area, and trying to guess what we're looking for. She keeps shtum naturally, but keeps her ears open. Then she hears some bloke say we should forget the big estates and go check out the Cavacini place. He had no idea what we are looking for, but he reckoned there were an awful lot of comings and goings there, both day and night.'

'Cavacini place? Should I know it?'

They heard Jace yawn. 'Well, I didn't, but I've made some enquiries and I think you might like to take them a step further. It's a large private house, not big enough to be called an estate, and years back it used to be a livery stables. It's called "Woodlands," and it's owned by someone called Rick Cavacini. He doesn't live there himself, but someone does. Rumour says it's a madman.'

Ben gave Cat bemused look. 'Madman? What do you mean?'

'Well, he's certainly a recluse, but most of the stories about him are made up. A Chinese whisper would be more reliable than some of what the locals told me.'

'Did you speak to him?'

'No time, so I have left that to you, *if* you can get past his staff.'

'Staff?'

'Gardener, cook and general dogsbody. A right bunch of weirdos, if you ask me.'

'He's rich, then?'

'Must be, but where the money comes from, heaven knows. Actually, Ben, I can't trace a damn thing about him. It's like he doesn't exist.'

'Okay, Jace. Thanks for all that. Leave it with me now, and I'll keep you posted if it's a bona fide lead. Get back to sleep. You've earned it.'

Jace yawned again. 'Dead bloody right, mate.'

Ben ended the call and turned to Cat, 'What did you make of that?'

'More than you, I'm willing to bet. I know the name Cavacini, but not in connection with any of this, and it's most likely a completely different family. A few years back one of our officers risked his life to pull a child from a flooded river. The girl's name was Susie Cavacini.'

Ben's mouth dropped open. 'That was PC Hildred, wasn't it? He got a medal for saving her. We were at police driving school together, doing our advanced driving course. Really nice bloke, Graham. I often wonder what happened to him.'

'Don't we all, especially his partner, Jessie Nightingale.' Cat exhaled. 'That child is the only Cavacini I've ever heard of.'

'So we need to check for a connection, don't we?'

'Mmm, we do. But before that, how do you intend to make the connection between Rosewood and Freddie Carver?'

Ben looked unsure. 'It's difficult. Rosewood's a really slippery customer, and I don't want to rock the boat by confusing the issue. My colleagues won't thank me for muddying the waters, not after it's taken a year to bring the whole thing together.'

Cat took a deep breath. 'I wonder, do you think your boss might be open to the suggestion of offering Rosewood a carrot? Easing his present and rather unpleasant situation if he grasses up Carver?'

Ben wrinkled up his brow. 'A deal? I don't know about the DI, but Rosewood would be a dead man if he went for it. Everyone knows Carver's a ruthless brute. Rosewood would be signing his own death warrant.'

'From what you say, Rosewood could go to prison for a very, very long time if he's convicted. Ben, if you could only see the dossier that Greenborough, the Met and the Spanish police already have on Freddie Carver. It's frightening. I think they only need one bit of help and everything will fall into place, and then that bastard will go away for life. I think that one bit is sitting downstairs in your custody suite.'

'I suppose if Rosewood could supply certain information that would allow us to "find" some evidence, then Freddie need never know who squealed?'

'It's something to consider.'

'It is, and so is finding where Freddie goes. If we could do that, we could nail him legitimately, then everyone gets their man. So let's first check out the Cavacinis, and Rick's posh house filled with mad people, shall we?'

'Sounds like a great way to spend a day. Let's do it.'

* * *

Joseph and Jessie had no luck at the Golden Dragon but as they were leaving, a waitress called them back. 'I'd try to speak to Cassie Hedges at Tino Vino in Carter's

Lane. She worked here at that time and I'm sure she knew Dina Jarvis.'

They thanked her and headed for the wine bar tucked away down a cobbled lane between Greenborough's only department store and a mobile phone shop.

They found Cassie busy cleaning the coffee maker. Obviously pleased to have an excuse to stop working for a while, she showed them to a table and they all sat down.

Joseph thought Cassie resembled a cheeky French Gendarme, in her rather military style uniform and peaked pillbox hat. She certainly looked smarter than her place of work. Tino Vino was not just dated, it was tired and rundown. Everything about it looked jaded except Cassie.

'Oh yes, I knew Dina well.' She tried unsuccessfully to push a cloud of blonde hair under her hat. 'We were good friends for ages.'

'Did anyone speak to you about her when she went missing?'

'No, although I was sent to help out at the Dragon's sister shop in Spalding around then, so maybe I just wasn't in Greenborough.'

'What do you think happened to her?' asked Jessie.

Cassie pursed her lips and made a little whistling noise. 'It's a mystery to me. I really have no idea. It made no sense then, and it still doesn't.'

'She gave you no impression of being unhappy, or of anything worrying her?'

She shook her head slowly from side to side. 'She was exactly the same as always, bright, cheerful and great fun to be with.'

Joseph sighed. They were going to get nothing more here.

Jessie leaned forward. 'Tell me, was her brother as controlling as he seems?'

'Dominic? No way. He was sweet with her. They had a really good relationship, and it must have been hard, having to look after themselves in their teens. He looked out for her, but not in a dominating sort of way. I liked him.'

'Are you still in touch with him?'

'No. Dominic was distraught when no one could find her. He changed, he was almost hostile to their old friends. I tried for a while, but he became quite unpleasant, and I'm sorry to say that I gave up.'

'Boyfriends? Dina was very pretty, wasn't she?'

'Lots of men liked her. She'd dance with them, have fun, but she never had a regular bloke.' Cassie paused. 'Or I didn't think she had, but the last time I saw her she was really excited about something. I know it involved a man, but she wouldn't tell me anything.'

'What was your impression? Was it like, "Oh, this new guy I've met is *so* hot!" or "This rich, good-looking guy says he fancies me." You know what I mean.' Jessie looked at her.

Cassie screwed up her forehead, bit her lip, then said, 'It was more . . . more like he'd suggested something really important to her, something exciting.'

'Like promising her a brilliant new career?' Joseph knew how villains groomed youngsters with promises of fame and fortune.

'Yes! That's just what it seemed like. As if she was on the brink of something special. But then she was still talking about ordinary things too. I don't believe she was planning to run away with someone, if that's what you think.'

'One of our officers saw her making out with a man out at the back of the Golden Dragon. Would this be one of the guys that you spoke about, the ones she danced with and so on?' Joseph asked.

'Dina? She wouldn't do that!'

'It's a fact. He saw her.'

Cassie sniffed. 'Then your officer is ly—, mistaken. Dina didn't *get off* with men. She . . .' Cassie looked uncomfortably from one to the other. 'She never . . . I mean, she hadn't . . .'

Jessie sounded amazed. 'Are you trying to tell us that Dina Jarvis was a virgin?'

'Exactly. They do exist, you know.'

'Sorry, Cassie,' Joseph chipped in, 'but we have been told by so many people that she was gregarious and sociable, a real party animal, so it's just a bit surprising that's all.'

'Dina just loved fun and dancing. She was no good-time girl in the sexual sense.'

'And these men who you say liked her, I suppose they were locals?'

Cassie nodded. 'There were three that I can remember, always pestering her to go out with them, but she never led them on. She was friendly, because that's the way she was, but she always told them exactly where they stood.'

'Their names?' Jessie took out her pocket book.

'Well, there was Arthur. What was his surname? Ah, Arthur Kirkby, that's right. He was a nurse of some kind I think, although I'm not sure where.' She paused. 'And Robbie Lyons. Now he really liked her, he used to eat more Indian food than was good for him, just because he needed an excuse to see her.'

'What do you know about him?'

'He worked the land, I think, on his father's farm, somewhere not far from town.'

'And the third man?'

'Keel Chandler. Now I actually felt sorry for him, because he was, well, I think the polite term they use now is "challenged." He was a cute guy in some ways, but he was more like an adoring puppy than a prospective boyfriend. And he never understood why she didn't want to go out with him.'

'What does he do for a living?'

'Nothing. I've been told he's not employable. He lives on the fen somewhere with his grandmother, looks after her and does chores and runs errands for his keep.'

'How old is he?'

Cassie exhaled. 'He's hard to gauge. Maybe twenty-five, thirty?' She looked up as her manager beckoned to her. 'Duty calls, I'm afraid. I have a strong feeling that no one else here is capable of cleaning that coffee machine. I have to go.'

Joseph stood up. 'Thank you for talking to us, Cassie. We may be back.'

'Any time, and if you find her, tell her to contact me. I miss her.'

As they walked back towards the police station, Joseph and Jessie decided that they had learned more about Dina than they had expected to.

'I don't suppose there's any chance that Niall got it wrong, do you?' Jessie said cautiously. 'You did say he looked away quickly.'

'No, he was certain, and he's too astute to get it wrong.' Then Joseph added, 'But I'll ask him again.'

Jessie grinned. 'He is rather . . . naïve is probably not a word you want to hear about your future son-in-law, but he is easily embarrassed. The other WPCs think he's quite adorable.'

'Yuk! I don't think our young action hero would like to be thought of as adorable. For heaven sake, don't tell *him* that!'

'Actually, when you think about the stick some of our women police officers have to take, believe me, it's a big compliment.'

'Even so, keep that one to yourself.' Joseph actually felt rather proud that the man who wanted to marry his only daughter had a squeaky clean reputation.

'Where next, Sarge?'

'I think we'll see what we can find out about Dina's three suitors, and maybe do a few house calls, how say you?'

'Lead on, Macduff.'

CHAPTER TWELVE

Cat and Ben had drawn a blank. They were unable to find any Cavacini other than the family of the little girl who had been pulled from the river, and there was nothing to be found after that.

'How about we take a break and I show you a bit of the Peak District?'

'We have time for a picnic?'

'I was thinking more of a nature ramble, one that involves tree spotting.'

Cat was getting square eyes from searching the computer, and her leg was beginning to ache. A walk would be very welcome. 'Ah, yes. Luckily I have my hiking boots in the car. Oh, I've just had a thought. Before we go, I'll pass this Cavacini search on to Dave. He's rubbish with computers, but if he ties up with Yvonne Collins, they could just come up with some info for us.'

'Go for it. I'll meet you down in the yard.'

* * *

Appleton Dale was a quiet village. It was pretty, but not pretty enough to attract a mass of tourists, which meant that it was still inhabited by locals, not relocated southerners looking for rural bliss.

Ben drew up outside the pub nearest to Woodlands. He and Cat got out of the car and went inside. A few people looked up, but hearing him order a half of bitter and a sparkling water in his Derbyshire accent, they paid him no further attention.

'I've been in here before,' he murmured to Cat, 'but I don't see anyone I recognise.' Which was disappointing. Ben knew that they could have marched straight to the Cavacini house and asked to search the grounds, but he had a very funny feeling about it. He felt it would be better to use the softly-softly approach.

'We need some general background information, and although once you get them going, the regulars usually tell you far more than you need, we want reliable info, not gossip.'

'Agreed.' Cat took a sip of her water and looked around the bar. 'How about him?'

Ben took a mouthful of beer and followed her gaze.

The man sat alone at the bar. He was perched on a bar stool, openly watching the barmaid as she poured a brightly coloured drink into a long glass. The man was well-dressed in casual clothes and was drinking the local brew. A muddy spaniel lay at his feet, one eye closed, and the other keeping an unblinking watch on his master.

'You're right, just what we need,' he whispered, 'a well-bred local. Come on.' They moved down the bar and Ben smiled at the man. 'Hello. Excuse me for asking, but are you from around here?'

The man looked at them, and after taking a moment to size them up, he grinned back. 'Three doors up, for the last twenty years. Why?'

Ben held out his hand, instantly liking him. 'Ben Radley, and this is Cat Cullen. Pleased to meet you.'

Changing his mind about spinning a yarn about house-hunting, he slipped his warrant card from his pocket and discreetly showed it to the man. 'DC Radley and DC Cullen actually. We need some help.'

If the man was surprised he certainly did not show it. He looked around and seeing an empty table in a corner, indicated for them to join him and his dog.

'My name is Harry Watson. How can I help?'

'I need to know about a house called Woodlands. Do you know it?'

The man looked intrigued. 'Yes, it's just across the way, Detective.'

'Call me Ben. I'm not keen on attracting too much attention.' He took a sip of his drink. 'Do you know the owners?'

The man shrugged. 'Can't say I do. They keep themselves to themselves.'

After Jace's information about the place being a hotbed of activity, Ben had hoped for more.

'We've been told there are a lot of comings and goings, day and night. Any idea why?' asked Cat.

'If I listened to the local gossips, I'd be able to offer you a dozen reasons, each one more fantastic than the one before.' Harry Watson smiled. 'I'm afraid I'm more a facts and figures sort of guy. All I know for sure is that it belongs to incomers, not locals.' He lifted his glass and half emptied it. 'And someone who lives there isn't in the best of health.'

'Who would that be?'

'I believe his name is Mr Cavacini.'

'Rick Cavacini?'

'I have no idea of his first name, and I've never really seen him, but I believe he suffers from something like Alzheimer's.'

'Then he must have a local doctor?'

Harry Watson smiled. *'I'm* the local doctor, and Mr Cavacini is certainly not registered with me.'

Ben frowned. 'So who looks after him?'

'A private doctor visits every week. I only know that because I bumped into him recently and recognised him as one of the founders of a private psychiatric hospital just outside Derby. Pricey place it is too, caters very discreetly for the rich and famous. Cavacini must have money to be that well looked after. He has a cook, who I understand doubles up as his nurse, and there are two others who help out as well.'

'And they all live in?'

'The nurse certainly does, but there are outbuildings, part of the old stable block. I think the men live there.'

'Do you know them? Speak to them?'

'When I said they keep to themselves, I meant it. I probably see at least one of them every single day and apart from a nod, that's it. One of the men drinks in here, too, but I still have no idea of their names, or anything about them.'

Ben stared into his glass and slowly swirled the golden liquid around, 'And the local gossips? Anything actually plausible?'

'What a question!' The doctor leant down and stroked the dog's silky head. 'I'm not a betting man, but I'd go for the theory that he's an embarrassment to someone, someone well-known, a celebrity or a politician maybe. Someone very high up. So rather than bung him in a home where he might be recognised, and be condemned as an uncaring son or daughter, they've set him up, way out here in the sticks, with his own private entourage of health professionals and carers. Hence the comings and goings. And no doubt they are now simply waiting for him to die.'

Ben felt a shiver of déjà vu and glanced at Cat. From her expression, she had the same thoughts as him. He remembered the conversation about Freddie Carver's annual trips. Duty visits to a relative? Cavacini? Carver? He tried to stop his mind from racing ahead. 'Does he have any visitors?'

Harry raised his eyebrows. 'Well, I don't make a point of watching the place, but he did have one last night. It was very late. I was on my way back from an emergency at the hospital when I saw a big, dark car pull in. It was gone by this morning.'

The very night Freddie Carver had been seen crossing the county border line into Derbyshire. Now, if Fern, Lilli and Sophie were to find justice, all they needed was a magnolia and a tulip tree. His heart leapt. 'How's your knowledge of trees?'

The doctor looked blank. 'Well, I can recognise a Christmas tree, and that's only because I come across one in the corner of my sitting room once a year. Oh, and maybe a conker? That boyhood thing, you know? Why?'

'How about a magnolia?'

'Ah yes, the pinky-white jobs that get clobbered by the frost, just when they are really starting to look good. We've got one of those.'

'Does the Woodlands garden have one?'

'No, I don't think so, although it's a few years since I've been in there.'

Ben's excitement began to ebb.

Harry rubbed his chin thoughtfully. 'Although, come to think of it, there may be one out beyond the paddock, not actually in Woodlands grounds, but quite close. There are lots of mature trees out there.'

'Who owns that land?'

'No one's too sure anymore. Donkey's years ago it was all part of a TB sanatorium. It was so badly bombed in the war that they pulled it down. A few old cottages and outbuildings are still standing. Attracts the occasional tramp or squatter, but the land is well overgrown. It runs from just behind Woodlands right down the river at Dalesmeet.'

Ben felt a shiver of excitement. 'Thank you, Doctor. You've been very helpful.' He handed the man a card. 'My number, in case you think of anything else. Now we've really got to go, but please, will you allow us to buy you another drink?'

* * *

As she had rather expected, he had pressed her to have patience and to continue with the medication. He had explained that the new drugs were very strong and it would take a bit of time for her system to adjust to them. She had to agree that her pain was less, but the confusion and the strange visions were still very worrying. Last night she believed that she had been out on the fen, walking barefoot on the path across the marsh. She had been surrounded by fuzzy, dancing, patches of light, weird jack-o'-lantern type shapes that had twisted and bobbed ahead of her. In the darkness, out over the fen, her mother called anxiously to her, telling her to watch her step and not forget the treacherous tides.

Next day she had found that her feet were mud-caked and scratched. There was no way she could have stepped lightly through the boggy ground as she'd imagined she had, but she had certainly not got plastered in mud here in her bedroom.

She moved slowly across to the table and broke off another piece of the delicious chocolate he had left for her. She'd had no dinner, and it looked as if supper had been forgotten, but she did have the chocolate. It would see her through till morning, and at least he had recently managed to remember her breakfast, not that she had been in any fit state to eat it. The medication left her sleepy, nauseous and with a ferocious thirst. He said it would ease, and she was sure it would. Her pain had been terrible and her chest still rattled when she coughed, so it was no surprise that the doctor had prescribed something so powerful.

With a bony finger, she cleaned a tiny circle in the greasy dirt on her window. The evening was still. No wind stirred the black reed grass that grew near the cottage, and she could hear very few bird calls. She wondered if he would return in time to give her the medication. She didn't want to miss it, and then have to begin again with those awful side effects.

For the twentieth time that day, she checked the hiding place of the old knife. She would probably never have the courage to use it, but it was there if this dreadful existence became intolerable. It was her insurance, her provision against an even darker night. With considerable tenderness she kissed it, and laid it back to rest.

* * *

All three of the men who had been interested in Dina Jarvis still lived in the area. Joseph had managed to contact two of them, but the third, Keel Chandler, was proving more difficult to track down.

'We need "Amazing Yvonne" to get the lowdown on this one,' Jessie grumbled, 'And she's out on a shout.' She turned to Dave. 'You don't know of a family called Chandler, do you? Live out on the fen somewhere?'

Dave seemed totally engrossed in checking his computer for something, and didn't reply.

'Earth calling Dave!' Jessie yelled.

'Sorry. Cat asked me for a trace on someone, and it's not turning out to be straightforward.' He stared at the computer accusingly.

'I asked if you knew a fen family by the name of Chandler.'

'Bryn Chandler is the secretary of the bowls club. Fred Chandler is in charge of the allotment society. Alma and Fred Chandler live over the chip shop in Corley Eaudyke. Then there's—'

'Whoa! I don't need you to recite the telephone directory. How about a man named Keel Chandler?'

'Never heard of him.'

'Great. You know thousands of Chandlers but not the one I need.'

'Why not ask—'

'I know, ask Yvonne. Sadly I can't, she's attending to a traffic accident on the High Road.'

Jessie went over to Joseph and told him.

'Okay, well, I suggest we go visit the other two, and continue the hunt for number three when Yvonne is free to join us.' Joseph stood up and glanced at the memo he had just written. 'Robbie Lyons first, then Arthur Kirkby.' He indicated the door. 'Shall we?'

Jessie gathered up her jacket and bag. 'I'm ready.' She glanced back at a worried-looking Dave, and added, 'Good luck with that search of yours.'

* * *

Dave muttered a goodbye and returned to his screen. He was glad that Jessie had left the office. He had not wanted her to see what he was researching.

Susie Cavacini. He remembered the whole affair well. Mind you, he ought to — he was there when Graham had ripped off his uniform jacket and dived into the water to rescue the child. He had never seen anyone act so quickly.

But he needed to know considerably more than what he remembered. With an exasperated sigh, and wishing that Cat were here to help him, he tapped the name Cavacini into Google.

His sigh became a loud groan when he saw the quarter of a million hits that came up. The first ones were all about football or tennis, and he refined his search. After a while he found a mention of Susie Cavacini and wondered why he hadn't started the search with her full name in the first place. 'Getting old, mate.' He double-clicked the site and found a blog about the young swimmer, who after nearly drowning, had gone on to swim for her school and was a hopeful to represent the county. 'Well done, Graham,' he whispered. 'Without you, I might be reading an obituary.' Under news about PC Graham Hildred's dramatic rescue, he found several newspaper archive reports. Finally he arrived at what he wanted, and opened it. It was a whole section of photographs. He smiled. 'That's our Graham, one seriously good bloke.' He shook his head, downloaded one of the pictures and moved on to the next. Susie with her parents, shaking hands with a smiling, uniformed Graham, a really poignant photo, and one the papers used frequently after the police officer had gone missing.

Dave suddenly froze. He leaned closer to the screen, then pulled out his desk drawer and snatched up the photographs that he had emailed to Cat earlier. Throwing several to one side, he grabbed one of them and held it up against the picture on the screen.

The girl's father! He had very similar features to the well-heeled entrepreneur shaking hands with the bent brief, Lewis Rosewood. Yes, this man was younger for sure, and certainly better looking, but there was a marked resemblance to Freddie Carver.

Dave printed off the picture and pushed back his chair. He needed to talk to the boss.

He hurried through to her office and showed her what he had found. 'A relative, ma'am?'

She scrutinised the picture. 'I'd say so, wouldn't you? Good for you, Dave. This could be the reason Carver is in this area. Family, but living under a different name, so we would never know.'

'Can I go and have a word with them?' Dave asked, 'Casual like, see if I can check if we are on the right track, but not alarm them.'

'If they still live in the same place.' She tapped out a staccato tattoo on the desk. 'And you'd need to think up a really plausible excuse for being there.'

'I don't think they would recognise me. On the day it happened, as soon as the child was on dry ground I was sent to look out for the ambulance, then I was busy keeping the crowd back. The family never saw me, and even if they did, it's been years now. They'll think I'm just some old codger, not a detective.'

Nikki sat back. 'You're far from being an old codger, my friend. But okay, think of something believable, and don't go alone. Take another plain-clothed officer with you.'

'And if Freddie Carver opens the door, I leg it, right?'

Nikki smiled at him grimly. 'Somehow I don't think that will happen. Have you let Cat know about this yet?'

'I came straight to you.'

'Then I'll ring her and bring her up to speed. And, Dave? I want an update immediately you are back.'

'You got it, ma'am.'

* * *

Robbie Lyons was not exactly ecstatic about receiving a visit from the police. Joseph could see from his body language that he was far from comfortable.

'I can barely remember her. Anyway, she left the area years ago, so why talk to me now?'

Lyons was tall and well-built, not in an athletic way, but he was obviously strong from working the farm. Joseph didn't like his defensive tone.

'I'm surprised about that, sir. We have met several people who thought you were very fond of her,' Jessie said.

'Well, they are wrong.' He sniffed. 'I did fancy her a bit at one time, but she wasn't interested so,' he shrugged, 'end of story.'

He stood close to the side of the tractor and fidgeted. Joseph guessed that Lyons was probably wishing it was a fast car, because he showed every sign of doing a runner.

'We are trying to build a picture of Dina, sir. What was she like?'

Lyons looked at him with narrowed eyes. 'Has something happened?'

'No, sir, not that we know of. Do you know anything?'

'No!' He almost shouted the word. 'I haven't seen her since she ran away. Okay, I did ask her to go out with me, and once, just once, we went to a club and had a good time, but then, well, I . . .'

Jessie glowered at him. 'You tried it on, and she told you where to stick it. And probably quite literally.'

He sighed. 'Something like that. Well, alright, it was *just* like that. I tried to talk her round, to apologise, but she didn't want to know.'

'So, I ask you again, what was she like?'

Lyons kicked at some dried mud. 'Lovely. She was so bright and full of life. I really thought she'd run off with some rich git.'

'You know that for sure?' Joseph asked.

'I saw him. I was following her. No, not stalking her! I just wanted to try one more time, say I was sorry, that's all.'

'Where was that, and more to the point, when was it?'

'At the Marina. It must have been only a day or two before she left. I had almost caught up with her when suddenly she waved, and ran over to this bloody great shiny car. The driver opened the door for her and she jumped in.'

'Did you see him?'

Lyons puffed out his cheeks. 'I've asked myself that a lot since she left. He looked familiar, that's all I can say. Then he drove off. Sadly it had tinted windows, so no chance of a second look.'

'Familiar?'

'I just thought I recognised him in that fleeting moment, but I guess I was mistaken, because it's never come back to me.' He looked suddenly sad. 'And after all this time, I guess it never will.'

Back in the vehicle, Joseph looked across at Jessie. 'That expensive car again. And now it's been seen by two witnesses, Lyons and Dominic Jarvis. This man existed, didn't he?'

'Oh yes. Hell, I wish we could see CCTV footage from the marina, but as we are going back a while, that's definitely out.' Jessie frowned. 'He was well twitchy, wasn't he?'

'Some people are like that around the police though, aren't they?'

'Only if they have something to hide.'

'You didn't like him, did you?'

'Not much, but I guess that doesn't make him an abductor.'

'Okay, so let's go see if you like Arthur Kirkby any better.'

* * *

It didn't take long to reach Cannon Vale Nursing Home, where they soon located Kirkby. They sat in a staff room at the back of the big house. Kirkby immediately began to make them tea.

'I've timed my break to fit in with your visit, officers. After your call I was most concerned that you'd found out some bad news about Dina. Is that the case?'

'How well did you know Dina Jarvis?' asked Joseph.

'Not as well as I would have liked, to be frank.' Kirkby gave a little laugh. 'Not for want of trying, it has to be said.'

Jessie's look said chalk and cheese. And Joseph agreed. The two men could not be more different.

'But she turned you down?'

Kirkby laughed. 'Oh yes, on a regular basis! She was really cool, that one.'

'Do you have any theories about her disappearance, sir?' asked Jessie, gratefully accepting a steaming mug of tea.

Kirkby was silent for a while. 'No, not really, although at the time I was shocked to the core.' He handed Joseph his tea and sat down heavily on one of the tatty plastic chairs. 'All I know is that one day she was on top of the world, then the next she had vanished off the face of it.'

'Do you think she was abducted?' Joseph asked.

Kirkby pulled a face. 'No.' He leaned forward, closer to Joseph. 'Did you know Dina could sing? And I mean *really* sing.'

Joseph frowned. 'No. No one has mentioned that to us, even her brother.'

'Ha! Dominic! Well, I'm not surprised there. He didn't exactly approve of her singing in public, and by heck, she had the voice of an angel.' His grin widened. 'And dance! She could have been a pro, you know. She was that good.'

Joseph felt a thrill of excitement. It was almost a passing comment, but he had a feeling that this was the key to her disappearance.

'Back then, I was well into music,' Kirkby volunteered. 'Dina used to come round to my place and we'd play stuff I'd downloaded. She wanted to make a demo, and I told her I had a mate who could arrange it for her. He had a sound studio and after I told him what a great voice she had, he was well up for it.'

'Did she do it?' asked Jessie.

He shook his head sadly. 'No, she decided against it. She told me that she knew Dom wouldn't want her to, and she didn't want to hurt him. They were very close, you know.'

Jessie placed her mug on the table. 'Surely you have some idea of what might have happened to her? You seem to have been pretty close, even if you never made it past go.'

'There were rumours. I tried not to listen, because to tell you the truth, I was gutted. For a time I wondered if it was to do with me, because I tried to push her too hard to make the demo, but—'

'What rumours?'

'There was a crazy kid. He used to follow her everywhere. He was harmless, but he was besotted with her.'

'Keel Chandler?'

'You know him?'

'We know *of* him.'

'Maybe you should talk to him, if you can get any sense out of him. He said he saw Dina the night before she went missing. If the story he told has any truth in it, then you might have the answer to where she went.'

'What did he say?'

Kirkby seemed to shrink into himself. 'It would be hearsay. Not only that — Keel, poor kid, is far from reliable. He has learning difficulties and a multitude of other problems. I'd rather not pass on what is probably a load of rubbish. If he tells you, then make what you will of it, but that's all I want to say.'

'One last thing, and you have been really helpful, Mr Kirkby, you said you didn't think she had been abducted, so what did you think?'

'That maybe she had been offered a chance for an audition. She had been seen with a man in a flash car, and she had mentioned something about a gorgeous guy making her an offer. I never thought it was anything to do with sex, because Dina, well, she . . .'

'We know about Dina, sir.'

'Ah, well, I thought he'd offered her an audition or a chance to try out for something like a musical.' He shrugged, 'I still do. But as I say, talk to Keel, he was obsessed with her. If anyone knows something, it's him.'

'Where can we find him?'

'Somewhere near Rainer's Gowt. His grandmother has an ancient old cottage out there somewhere. He lives with her.'

Back in the car, Jessie said, 'We are only two minutes from the Post Office main sorting office, and they would know where the Chandler cottage is.'

'Good thinking, Batman.' Joseph pulled out onto the main road into town, 'So did you like Arthur better than Robbie?'

'Considerably, although I'm slightly apprehensive about what Crazy Keel is going to tell us when we find him.'

'*If* we find him. Have you ever been to Rainer's Gowt?'

'On a tributary of the river, isn't it? On the flatland approaching the marsh?'

'It's an odd spot alright. I've only been there once and I didn't know how the hell to get back to the road. The lanes and tracks all twist and turn until you have no idea which direction you are heading in.'

They turned into the drive-in area outside the sorting office and parked.

Jessie spoke with the woman on the front desk, and she asked them to wait while she made some enquiries.

In just a few minutes a tall, tanned, smiling postman came out to them. 'Hello, I'm Nigel. I hear you're looking for the Chandler cottage?'

Jessie looked at his shorts. Judging from how tanned his legs were, he probably wore them all year round.

'We are,' said Joseph. 'Can you give us directions?'

'I could, but there's a good chance you'll be calling for your mates to come and find you.' The smile faded. 'There's nothing wrong with the old duck, is there? She's a smashing old girl, bit of a jingle-brain, but she must be near ninety.'

'No, nothing like that. We just need a word with Keel Chandler.'

Nigel looked at his watch. 'Tell you what, I've got a special delivery for an address only about half a mile from their place. If you follow me, I'll take you there, then you'll see what a devil it is to find.'

They thanked him and returned to the car. In a few moments they heard the tooting of a horn and saw Nigel waving to them from his bright red Post Office van.

'Oh well, into the unknown,' Jessie said.

'Here goes nothing,' Joseph replied.

CHAPTER THIRTEEN

Dave stood on the doorstep of a rather pleasant house in Station Road and waited while a young boy of around eight went to fetch his father. He had decided to stick as closely to the truth as he could, so as not to trip himself up.

'Mr Cavacini? I'm Dave Harris and I'm so sorry to bother you, but I'm doing an editorial for the local police magazine. My colleague here and I are trying to find some background stories about some of the Fenland officers who were awarded medals for bravery.'

The man was something of a disappointment. For one thing he didn't look nearly as much like Freddie as Dave had first believed, and then when he spoke, he seemed rather weak and ineffectual, nothing at all like Fat Man Carver.

'I'm sure everything that could have been said about the officer who saved our Susie has already been said. The papers were full of it for so long.'

'And how is the young lady? Doing well, I hope?'

'Oh yes, she's a star. Of course she's a teenager now, but every day we give thanks that we still have her with us.'

The man sounded almost like a religious convert, not a villain's close relative, and Dave started to have doubts.

'Look, it's not a very good time right now, I have to get my boy to football practice, but if you ring me and make an appointment, I'd be happy to help you if I can.'

Dave took out a pen and fished around in his pocket for something to write on. He didn't want to produce his official pocket book because he was anxious to appear retired or at the very least, a civilian. Finally he found a petrol receipt and scribbled the Cavacinis' number on the back. 'Thank you, sir, that's much appreciated.' He held out his hand and was surprised at the strength in the man's grip. 'I'll ring you, maybe next week.'

As he made his way down the path, he glanced back, and saw the man watching them go. Dave drew in a breath and continued walking. The expression on Cavacini's face was pure poison. And in that flash of a second, he looked exactly like Carver.

* * *

In the Derbyshire office, Ben Radley and Cat Cullen waited impatiently for orders. Cat had just finished a long call from DI Nikki Galena in Greenborough and had passed all the information on to Ben. He in turn had told his inspector, and had got the go-ahead to search the Cavacini property in Appleton Dale.

Cat looked at her watch again. The warrant seemed to be taking an eternity, and the waiting was killing them both.

'Not long now.' Ben pulled on his stab-proof vest and thick jacket.

Cat's stomach fizzed. It was the feeling she got whenever she was sent to a particularly dangerous or high priority shout. She looked again at the photocopied pictures of the two trees. She, like most of the others, knew nothing about them, but she was sure today was the day when she would be introduced to the famous yellow poplar.

A uniformed sergeant and a group of men and women entered the office. 'Ready when you are, Ben. We've got the paperwork. Shall we go?'

Ben took a deep breath, and looked from Cat to the group around him. 'Okay, you all know the score. There's the house called Woodlands, and to the back of it, some overgrown parkland, the remains of an old hospital with derelict buildings. We take them at the same time. I'll have four officers with me to check out Woodlands and its residents. The rest of you take the hospital grounds. So if you're all clear on that, let's do it.'

The drive to Appleton Dale took about twenty minutes, and Cat was acutely aware that dusk would be upon them in two hours. That wasn't long to do everything that they had to. She looked out of the window. The late afternoon sun over the craggy limestone of the peak was strangely uplifting.

She and Ben were accompanied by a young detective, DC Murphy, known as Spud, and a team of ten uniformed officers, along with the dog handler. On Ben's instruction, the three vehicles parked in a lay-by some two hundred yards before the house, and they approached on foot.

A narrow lane, apparently only ever used by dog walkers, ran along the side of the property and led through to the hospital grounds. DC Murphy and his team slipped silently into the muddy alleyway, and disappeared.

She, Ben and their group took careful stock of Woodlands.

Nothing stirred. No screams or cries of the kind the locals whispered about. In fact, nothing at all.

'Go round the back and take a look.' Ben's eyes glinted.

Two constables moved off in opposite directions to the rear of the old property, and Cat and her new colleagues pushed through the front gate.

The woman who finally opened the door was in carpet slippers. 'What the hell do you want?' she said with a suspicious frown.

Cat noted the chain firmly in place.

'Sorry to bother you, miss. I'm DC Ben Radley.' He pushed his warrant card almost into her face. 'May we come in? It's urgent.'

'No you bloody can't! I've got a sick man here.' She made to close the door, and found Ben's size ten in her way. She raised wide eyes from his boot, and her expression turned from anger to fear. 'You *can't* come in! I'm sorry. I'm not allowed.'

'I have a warrant, miss. So I'm afraid I'll have to ask you to step aside. If you won't grant us admittance, then the door will have to go.' He indicated the officer beside him, who was holding a heavy metal enforcer. He raised his eyebrows. 'Your choice.'

'No! No . . . please! Don't do that. I'll let you in, but you have to be quiet. My employer is very ill.'

Ben nodded. 'Mr Cavacini?'

She opened the door with shaking hands. 'That's right.'

'And you are?'

'I look after him.'

'Not quite what I meant, miss. Your name, please?'

Before the woman could answer, the old house rang with a piercing, blood-thinning scream.

Cat and another officer immediately ran towards the stairs.

'No! You can't go up there!' The woman was almost screaming herself.

Other noises, like muffled gurgles, were now coming from the upper floor. Ben placed his hand on Cat's arm. 'Why? What exactly is wrong with Mr Cavacini?'

'He has advanced dementia, if you must know! And if he gets frightened or disturbed, his medication wears off too soon.' She climbed a step and looked beseechingly at

Ben. 'Please! Leave him to me and my helper. It takes two of us when he's like this.'

'Who is your helper? Where is he?'

She wrung her hands. 'He should be here by now. Mr Cavacini will settle again if it's quiet. He must have heard you and got scared.'

'Not one for giving names, are you, miss?'

'Call me Janet. And my helper is John.'

Ben gave her a withering look. 'Janet and John, huh? Nice one. Well, *Janet*, I'm afraid we have to search the house and garden.'

'What for? There's nothing here, I promise you. Just John and I. Oh, and the gardener, Keith.' She pointed up the stairs. 'Oh yes, and one barmy old man!'

'What, Freddie Carver's father, you mean?' Cat said.

Her gamble paid off. Janet's mouth went slack, and her frightened eyes told them everything, even though her mouth asked, 'Who? I've never heard of any Freddie Carver.'

Ben called to one of the other policemen. 'Get outside and find the other two, bring them in, then we'll have to go up and see the old man.' He turned back to the woman and tilted his head towards the first floor. 'Is Cavacini locked in?'

Janet gave a dry bark of a laugh. 'Damn right he is!' Then her face softened. 'The poor old sod, he has about one or two lucid moments every day, and that's all. For the rest of the time, if he's not sedated . . . well . . .'

'Then he belongs in a proper facility.'

'Really! You don't say.'

Something clicked. Cat thought, that's it! Freddie Carver hadn't stuck his father out here in the sticks because he was ashamed of the poor old man. He was afraid of him! Because of those one or two very dangerous lucid moments! Moments when he could talk about his dear son and what he got up to.

'I need the telephone number of Mr Cavacini's son, please,' Cat asked urgently.

'I don't have it.'

Ben butted in. 'Oh right! Come on, Janet! You look after this sick old man and you don't have a number for his son?'

The woman bit her lip. 'I mean it. He rings us, twice a day.'

Cat looked at her. 'And you don't think that's just a teensy bit odd? Or maybe he pays you so well you don't care.'

Janet glared at her venomously.

'Ben! We've got the gardener, but can't find the other one.'

'Okay, one of you stay here with these two. Keep them together in the kitchen. Cat, Dino, come with me, we're going visiting the sick.'

Janet's hands flew to her mouth. 'No! Please! Don't go up there.'

The three officers turned their backs on her and headed for the stairs.

Only one door was locked, and from behind it, Cat could hear a scuffling noise.

Screwed into the doorframe was a small hook. Ben took the key from it, and unlocked the door. Knocking firmly, he said, 'Please don't be alarmed, Mr Cavacini. It's the police, sir. If it's alright with you, we're coming in now.'

There was no answer. They all heard a sort of scampering, then silence.

'Okay, sir. Stand away from the door.'

The smell hit them first.

'Jesus Christ!' The constable called Dino put his hand to his nose and mouth before moving forward into the room. 'Is that what I think it is?' He pointed to the brown stains smeared across the walls.

'I'd say so.' Cat tried unsuccessfully not to breathe in too much. 'Does anything else smell quite like that?'

Ben looked around. 'Mr Cavacini?'

The room was sparsely furnished, although an effort had been made to make it comfortable. A television screen flickered mutely in one corner. The single bed was a mess, the sheets wet and screwed into a ball on the floor, pyjamas tangled among them.

'Where the hell . . . ? Oh shit, I think we need help.' Ben looked at Cat, then said to Dino, 'Get an ambulance out here. We can't cope with this.'

Cat looked towards the window. An elderly man, who had to be Cavacini, crouched on the wide sill like an animal. He was naked. His white, hairless legs, a mass of scrawny, leathery skin, were drawn up to his unshaven chin, bony arms wrapped around them. He rocked backwards and forward, and shivered every time his bare backbone touched the cold glass behind him. His face was fixed in a broad, snaggle-toothed smile and the rheumy unfocused eyes seemed fixed somewhere between Cat and the end of his own nose.

Without a word to each other, they left the room and locked the door.

'Ambulance and a doctor on its way. What are we going to do with the woman and the gardener?'

Before Ben could answer, his radio crackled into life. 'This is DC Murphy, we've got a situation here, we need back up! Over.'

'Ben here, Spud. What's occurring?'

'We've found your bloody trees all right! Along with three men, one dead. Shot at point blank range.'

'Accidentally?'

'Hardly. Unless he could reach the back of his own neck with his hands tied. More like an execution.'

'Have you got the other two apprehended?'

'Affirmative.'

'Are they the killers?'

'Doubtful. They deny it. They are shit-scared, and they look shocked enough to be telling the truth. And, Ben, there's an old storeroom, near the trees, it's full of filthy old blood-stained bedding, torn clothes, and some tools, including wire cutters. I think we've found where the girls were held.'

Cat looked at Ben's face. He looked elated and emotional.

'At last! Okay, good work. Now, report all this to the super and get the SOCOs down here. Secure the whole area, understand? All of it. Our situation here is still active, so Roger and out.'

The other policemen were staring at him, waiting for orders. Cat knew that he was near to tears. After all this time, they'd finally found the place where little Fern and the others had been imprisoned. Now they really could nail the bastards that had hurt them.

'This is it, guys! We've finally found it.' Ben spun round and glared at the man and the woman. 'Radio in for more men, and get these two back for questioning. We just need the missing man.'

He marched over to Janet and stuck his face close to hers. 'Okay. Where is he? Where's he hiding? Your bloody *John*?'

She was shaking. 'I don't know. He must have heard you and run off.'

'What does he look like?'

She shrugged. 'Er, tallish, dirty fair hair. He wears an old weatherproof jacket — brown it is.'

'And he lives here?'

'No, he lives in the old stable block.'

Ben looked at the constable who had gone after him.

The man nodded. 'Found the place, but it was empty, Ben.'

'Right. You two, look after this pair and wait for the ambulance. Cat, you come with me. He'll be around here somewhere, hiding probably, if he's seen the others. We'll get him.'

Ben turned tail and ran from the house, with Cat at his heels.

By now, the sun was sinking, and shadows were beginning to spread across the ground. Everything glistened, as the fading golden sunlight shone through the evening dew. Cat's boots were sodden from the wet grass, and she heard Ben mutter, 'Footprints . . . there should be footprints where he ran across the long grass.' He ran to the old stable and searched around it for the path the fugitive had taken.

Then Cat spotted it, and began to run. 'Over here, Ben! I think he's gone this way, towards the river.'

Faint tread marks led off along a narrow track of mainly gravel and mud. Ben caught her up, and they ran together for about two or three hundred metres, then came to a fork.

They hesitated. 'It's difficult to see which way he went, it's just moss and short grass here.' Ben looked around. 'Okay, you go one way, I'll go the other. And yell like hell if you eyeball him.'

The ground was slippery and the track sloped down quite steeply towards the river. Several times Cat skidded and almost fell. The rush of water grew louder, and then she heard a different noise. Cat stopped her headlong dash, clutched at a low branch to steady herself, and stood silently, listening for the sound to come again.

There it was! A soft crunching. The sound of someone attempting to move silently through dying bracken.

Cat crouched down, hardly daring to breathe, and strained her ears to try to make out exactly where the noise was coming from. Cat had never been one to pussyfoot around. As soon as she thought she had it sussed, she charged headlong towards it.

The man gave a small gasp of surprise, and continued his wild race down to the river.

'Police! Come back here! There's nowhere to go! Ben! He's here!' Cat swore and cursed and crashed along behind the man.

Suddenly, her quarry slipped and lost his balance. Cat grasped at the waxy material of his sleeve.

'Oh shit!' The wet jacket slipped from her grip, and after a swift backwards glance at her, the man lurched on down the hill.

Cat stopped. In that craggy, unshaven face, she had seen an expression of pure terror. And something else. Her mind felt like a combination lock. All the numbers were there, none of them in the right place. She screwed up her face and closed her eyes, desperately trying to make sense of what her brain had told her.

The fleeing man had now made it to the riverbank, and was preparing to wade out into the fast-flowing water.

The numbers clicked into place.

Slowly she followed the terrified man down the incline and stopped, watching the water darken the man's trousers and creep up towards his calves

'Graham! Graham Hildred! It's alright! It's over!'

Her voice rang across the glistening frothy waters of the river, and the man froze.

'Graham! We've got the others! We know all about Freddie Carver. I mean it, it's all over. You can come home, Graham.'

The man turned, disbelief on his face, and then his jaw slackened and his body went limp. With an almost animal cry, Graham Hildred pitched forward into the shallow waters of the river's edge.

* * *

Graham sat in the back of the ambulance with a thermal blanket wrapped around him. Cat and Ben sat beside him.

Graham's eyes were still wide with fear. 'Before you do anything else, you have to listen to me. You must get Jessie to a place of safety! Carver will go after her now. It's not your fault, but you don't know what you've done in coming here! She's in terrible danger.' Tears mingled with the river water running down his cheeks.

'It's okay. She's safe at Greenborough nick, mate,' said Ben softly.

'No, she isn't! Carver has someone on the inside! He has someone in his pocket. She must not stay at Greenborough police station! Believe me, that's the last place she should be. Get her to a safe house, *now*, before all the shit hits the fan and Carver finds out — if he hasn't already.' Graham began to shake. 'You have no idea what that man has in mind for Jessie.'

Cat hopped down from the ambulance and called Nikki Galena. She told her boss the incredible news — that amazingly they had Graham Hildred safe with them. Then Cat passed on his exact words of warning.

'Oh no! Oh fuck!'

'I know, ma'am. But you have to do as he says. He knows what he's talking about. You wouldn't believe what we've seen here — dead men, mad men — oh God, I can't tell you!'

'Cat, I *will* get her to safety, promise Graham that, but she isn't here right now, and that is worrying me a lot.'

Cat heard an intake of breath and a groan.

'At least she is with Joseph, so that is a blessing, but they are heading out to a remote spot on the fen, and you know what our bloody county is like for radio and mobile signals, you can be damned sure there will be no contact. I'm going to go after them myself, right now, okay? And don't tell Graham she is not here. He's been through enough, I'm sure.'

'Go careful, ma'am, won't you?'

'Of course, but I'm not having that monster threaten one of our own, not on my watch!' She paused then added,

'And Cat, you've done a brilliant job, but now it's time to come home, okay?'

Call ended.

* * *

For possibly the first time in his life, Freddie Carver did not know what to do.

In the last ten minutes Carver had experienced anger, pain, confusion and fear. Now he felt nothing but pure fury.

Everything he had been working towards was slipping away from him. From the calls he made that had gone unanswered, he knew that rats were jumping from the sinking ship.

His father was God knows where. His brief was banged up, albeit nothing to do with him for once, and he had no idea how many of his operatives had been taken into police custody. On top of that, and possibly worst of all, one of his spies had seen the police leading his tame policeman prisoner to an ambulance. For the filth to have found his father's house, it had to have come from Hildred in the first place. The man must have found a way to get a message through. Well, he had been warned. Now the gloves were off. Freddie owed him nothing now.

One thing was for sure, he would keep his promise to Graham Hildred. Vic was no longer available, but he knew a man who could do the job.

Carver picked up his phone and called Mr Fabian.

CHAPTER FOURTEEN

Unaware of the drama unfolding in Derbyshire, Joseph and Jessie were chasing the little red van across the fen lanes. Jessie let out a low whistle. 'I had no idea this place was so confusing.'

'I know. It's one of the few places sat nav can't find, and right now I'm very grateful for our postie friend, Nigel. I'd hate to be out here at night.' Joseph peered out at the winding lane and the increasing number of potholes.

'And an old lady and a daffy lad actually live out here! What if she needed help — an ambulance or a doctor?'

'Well, they do have a landline phone, so I'm told. Otherwise the "daffy lad" jumps on his bike and rides like the clappers, I guess.'

The lanes twisted and turned alongside deep drainage ditches and fields that bled into the far horizon in a blur of green and grey.

'How much further?' Jessie queried.

'Not far, I think. See that cluster of trees in the corner of that field? I'm pretty sure the lane branches off there and down to Rainer's Gowt.'

'What is a gowt?'

'An old term for a water pipe that runs underground, like a sewer.'

'Lovely. Fancy living in a classy address like Rainer's Sewer!'

'When they use it as a place name, it generally comes after a flood-gate — the marsh-water runs from the reens into the sea.'

'What's a reen?'

'What county do you come from, Jessie?'

'Dorset, and I'm sure there's no reens there.'

'It's a ditch, a drainage channel.' He smiled. 'I love all the traditional stuff about the Fenlands. You're always learning something new.'

'I'll take your word for it.'

'See this stand of trees?' He drove past a lone cluster of windblown trees and straggly undergrowth into an even narrower track. 'They call them Devil's Holts.'

Jessie was half turned towards him. She seemed genuinely interested. 'Okay, tell me why.'

'Old-fashioned insurance, actually. Farmers planted them in the corner of the field to give Satan somewhere to play. The hope was that he would leave their crops alone if he had somewhere to amuse himself. There are usually three of them in a triangle, and that's not because they're in a corner. They formed a trinity, which would keep the Devil in check.'

Jessie chuckled. 'You should give lectures at the local museum in your spare time.'

'What spare time?'

'Ah yes, I forgot about that.' She pointed. 'Nigel is slowing down, I see brake lights.'

Joseph drew alongside the Royal Mail van and wound down his window. 'Thank you, Nigel, much appreciated.'

The man grinned. 'Cottage is a couple of hundred yards down the lane, behind all that scrubby hedging. Do you think you can find your way off this fen? It is the back of beyond.'

'Yes, I think so. I took care to note a few landmarks on the way in.'

'Don't leave it too late. It'll be dark soon, and I've seen quite a few cars winched out of these ditches in my time.' Nigel waved but before he drove away, he called back, 'And don't rely on your mobile or your radio, reception out here is rubbish.'

* * *

Joseph had thought his beloved Knot Cottage was full of charm and character, but the Chandler home was like a tiny piece of the old Fenlands, left untouched by the passing of time.

They found Keel turning the handle to winch water up from the well. He looked at them with evident delight — Joseph guessed that visitors were something of a pleasant novelty.

Joseph showed him their warrant cards, told him who they were and briefly why they were there.

'Better come in and take the weight, looks a bit backend-ish out here this evening.'

Jessie glanced at Joseph and spread out her hands.

'He means autumnal — misty and a chill in the air.'

A fire was lit in the iron grate and the small, snug kitchen was warm and welcoming. Keel pulled out three wooden chairs from under an old scrubbed oak table and they sat down.

'I loved her, you know.'

Joseph nodded. 'We had heard.' He looked at the young man. It was difficult to guess his age, he could have been in his mid-to-late twenties, or even much younger. He was as skinny as a beanpole and had sharp, rather feminine features framed by a shock of wavy fair hair. He had a ready smile and was altogether rather likeable.

'Do you want tea? I make Gran's at five sharp, every day. She's having her nap now but she'll be up soon.'

'We're fine, Keel. We don't have too long, but we need to know if there is anything you can tell us about Dina Jarvis.'

'Why?'

It wasn't so much rude, as very direct.

'We are looking at the circumstances surrounding her disappearance, Keel. We believed she had just gone away, but now we are rather worried about her.'

'She didn't run away. She's still here. Well, she was until a while ago.' He looked sad enough to cry.

'Oh dear.' A tall, rotund woman was standing in the doorway that led through to the stairs, leaning heavily on a walking frame. 'Is he telling you all that rubbish about his lost love again?' She smiled. 'I'm Mary Chandler, and who are you?'

Joseph jumped up and introduced Jessie and himself. 'It's our fault, Mrs Chandler. We came to ask Keel what he can tell us about Dina.'

She eased herself into a winged armchair close to the fire. 'Then prepare yourself for a long night. He goes on a bit.'

Joseph turned to Keel. 'You said she never left. What do you think happened to her?'

'I don't like to say in front of my gran.' He hung his head and twisted his hands in his lap.

'Don't mind me. I've been on this earth long enough that nothing shocks me.' Mary picked up a ball of crochet yarn and a hook and began to work.

'She was beautiful, and she could sing and she could dance, and then that city man in the big car did something to her, and then she didn't laugh anymore.'

Jessie frowned. 'When was this, Keel?'

'The day before.'

'Before what? Before she disappeared?'

'She didn't disappear.'

'So where is she?'

He gave a little shrug. 'I don't know. I still look for her though.'

Joseph liked riddles, but not at the moment. 'Okay, tell us when you last saw her.'

Keel stared at the floor, then looked up and grinned. 'I need my diary. You can read it if you want. That will tell you everything.' He jumped up, ran out, and they heard him pounding up the steep wooden staircase.

The old lady put her crochet down and looked at them intently. 'He saw something.' She rubbed her gnarled hands in front of the fire. 'I'm just not sure what exactly. He came home one evening in such a state. He was fair messed up he was. And cry! Like a baby! I do know that somewhere in that mixed-up brain of his is the answer to all your questions.' She raised her eyebrows. 'He's just a bit difficult to fathom though.'

'Did you know Dina?'

'Oh no, me duck, I don't go out. I've never slept one night away from my bed right here.' She smiled again, showing more gaps than teeth. 'But even out here you get to hear things from those who come and go.'

'What do you think happened?'

'I think someone took something precious from Dina Jarvis, something she would never have given them. And afterwards, they killed her and took her to the marsh.'

Joseph glanced at Jessie and saw her face turn pale.

'I've got it!' Keel raced into the room like an excited five-year-old. 'As you are the police, you *can* borrow it. I want it back though. Should I get you to sign something to say you have it?'

'No, we'll be very careful with it, and it's very kind of you, Keel. It's a very responsible thing to do, to help the police with their enquiries.'

The man-boy instantly grew in stature.

'We should go, Sarge.' Jessie was looking out of the window.

'Aye, soon be darklings. Better get off the fen lanes, as you're not used to them.' The old lady nodded to herself. 'The twilight plays games with your eyes out here. So take care, you young people.'

'We'll see you again when we bring your diary back, and thank you for your help.'

In the car, Joseph flicked open the dog-eared book and gasped.

It was a mass of words and pictures, sketches and cartoons. Each page was crammed with intricate writings and drawings. He turned it towards Jessie, and exhaled. 'We really need to look at this very carefully indeed.'

'Mr Policeman!'

Joseph wound down his window and saw Keel's face close to his own.

'I used to hear her singing, out close to the marsh, somewhere near Carter's Fen. Then a few months ago, she stopped.' He flashed that oddly sweet smile. 'I just thought you should know.' Then he ran back into the cottage and slammed the door.

* * *

While Cat was speaking to her boss, Ben asked the paramedic if he could give them a minute alone. He pulled the door to, and looked at the weary, haggard expression of the missing policeman. He wanted to be excited — after all, this man was practically a legend, but the empty look in Hildred's eyes worried him. So he placed a hand on his shoulder and squeezed. 'Freddie must have threatened you with something pretty damned awful for you to stay in hiding all this time.' He paused. 'You had some serious evidence on him, didn't you?'

'Right on both counts.'

The voice was dull and tired. Ben desperately wanted to fire question after question at him, but he knew it was too soon. 'Graham? You do know I have to get you checked over at the hospital, then when we get the all-clear, you'll be taken to a safe place for debriefing?'

Wearily he nodded his shaggy unkempt head. 'And psychiatrically evaluated. I know the drill. But I also need to be somewhere other than Greenborough or here. Carver will be coming after me as well as Jessie.'

He was exhausted, so Ben decided to leave him. He patted his shoulder again, and stood up. 'I'll give you some space, man. We'll talk later.'

Graham's hand shot out and gripped his wrist. Ben was taken back by the strength of it.

'No! Stay. I need you to do something for me. Please?'

Ben sat back down.

Graham pushed a lock of wet hair from his forehead. 'You seem to have worked it all out about Freddie. If you found this place, when it was supposed to be a closely guarded secret even from his own men, then you must know a lot.'

Ben pulled a face. 'Not really. Just the basics, but there's one hell of a lot I don't understand, that's for sure.'

'Like what?'

'Why you're alive for one thing. Has it got something to do with the little girl that you saved from drowning? Susie Cavacini?'

Graham smiled bitterly. 'Funny, isn't it? I saved her life, and in a weird way, she saved mine.'

'Is she Freddie's niece?'

'Yes. He's got a twisted set of values, that man. He can kill, torture, and maim, but where his own family is concerned, he plays strictly by the rules.'

'And that means not killing the man who saved his brother's kid?'

'Right. He's a real Godfather.' The voice was stronger. Ben guessed that the original shock was wearing off and the realisation that he was no longer a prisoner was slowly dawning on him. 'Alright, I'll give you the story in brief, just so that you can tell the powers that be, and I'll keep the details for later. First though, can you assure me that WPC Jessie Nightingale will be given round-the-clock protection somewhere safe?'

'Cat's just arranging that with DI Nikki Galena. She understands the situation fully, so you can rest assured that she'll do all she needs to.'

'I can't think of anyone I'd rather have than that Rottweiler on my case.' Graham gave a weak smile. 'And could you ask them not to just blurt it out to Jessie that I'm alive. It'll be one hell of a shock for her. Ask them to get my old mate Dave Harris to tell her, would you?' He looked pained. 'I . . . I don't even know her situation, if you know what I mean, it's been a very long time. Maybe she's got someone else . . . ?'

Ben stuck his head out of the ambulance. He was surprised that the sun was already down. 'Cat? Graham wants you to contact your partner, Dave. He'd like him to be the one to break the news to Jessie, and to do it somewhere quiet.'

To his surprise, Cat looked anxious, and whispered, 'It's not as easy as that, Ben. Jessie is out of the station at present. The DI has personally gone to find her.'

Ben's heart sank. That was not something he would be sharing with Graham just yet.

'But I'll ring Dave anyway, okay?'

Ben nodded and ducked back inside the ambulance. 'Cat is ringing him now. And for what it's worth, I spent some time at Greenborough recently, and your Jessie was really cut up over some newspaper article about you. Her mates told me that there is certainly not another man in her life.'

'Let's just hope that's true, shall we?'

Ben sat back and tried not to think about the fact that Jessie Nightingale was far from safe right now. 'So what happened, Graham?'

Graham took a deep breath and began. 'I was on my way to work when I got a call from an old snout of mine.

He was one of Freddie's men, not high up, but pretty much in the know about Freddie's drug deals. It seemed Carver had badly hurt a mate of his, and it really pissed him off, so he'd decided to pay Carver back. He'd kept a diary on Freddie, details of his dealers, with times and dates, and he was ready to hand it over. I went to meet him, but someone had grassed him up. Freddie's men were there. They shot my snout, killed him right in front of me, and took me with them.'

'And brought you here?'

'Not immediately. They kept me prisoner for a while. Destroyed everything I had on me — my warrant card, phone, wallet, credit cards, the lot. They had my car crushed at some scrapyard Carver owned. They made me into a non-person.' He frowned. 'Then I had a visit from the big bastard himself. Seemed I'd been something of a problem to him, but he'd had this *wonderful* idea.' He shuddered. 'His father was becoming a serious threat to him.'

'Daddy had dementia, but occasionally took pleasure in telling colourful stories about his boy?'

Graham nodded. 'He said I had to help take care of his father.'

Ben tipped his head on one side. 'And?'

'If I ever tried to contact anyone from my previous life, he would take Jessie and give her to one of his goons, a man called Vic, to play with long-term. Vic is a psycho who does his really dirty jobs for him.'

'*Did*. We found him out back. According to two more of Carver's "employees," Freddie had him terminated earlier today.'

'So there is a God!' Graham gave a grim smile.

'But that wasn't all, was it?'

'No. He'd regularly send me photos of Jess, just to let me know that he was really watching her and to remind me of the danger she was in. Some were taken inside the police station, so that's how I know he has an insider.

Then he'd send me severed fingers, to prove he was in deadly earnest, and that if I ever tried to shop him, Jessie would also have her fingers chopped off and then she'd be turned over to Vic.' He gave another shudder. 'I knew he was hurting other girls, maybe even killing them, but I love Jessie! How could I . . . ? What could I do?' His eyes filled with tears. 'Ben? What could I have done?' His chest heaved with sobs.

'Exactly what you did, man. You protected her. That's all you could do.'

Graham hugged himself and stared down at the floor. His voice broke when he said, 'Even that wasn't enough for him. As extra insurance, Freddie set me up as having been on his payroll for years. Put a lot of money into an offshore account in my name. He promised to send anonymous "inside" information to the tabloid press about the dirty rogue copper that everyone had called a hero. He promised to destroy me and tarnish the character of every serving police officer in one go.' He looked up, his eyes red and sore. 'He could have done it, too. He still could!' Graham drew the blanket tighter around him and rocked backwards and forward. 'Then there was his father. That poor old man! It was alright at first, then he got really sick. He was like an animal, he smeared us with faeces, he attacked us, and then he'd cry like a baby. You'd scrub and scrub your skin, but you'd always smell the shit. It was horrible . . . horrible!'

'I think it's time we went, Officer. Our patient looks pretty upset. We need to get him to hospital.' The paramedic climbed in.

'Yes, of course, but an officer has to ride with you.' He turned to Graham and gave him a hug. 'You're one brave guy. I'll see you very soon.'

'Just tell DI Galena to catch that monster and never let him go, okay?'

'She won't need telling twice, believe me! Good luck, mate.'

'And, Ben?' Graham managed a small smile. 'Don't be too hard on Janet. She's a good woman.'

'Freddie had something over her too?'

'Oh yes. But Janet was brilliant with the old guy. She taught me a lot.' He forced a grin. 'And if they don't want me back in the force, at least I can get a job as a psychiatric carer, can't I?'

Ben shook his head as the ambulance moved away. He tried to imagine how Jessie Nightingale would react to the news, when they got hold of her. Her whole world would change all over again, that was for sure. He hoped it would be for the better, but two years was a long time. They would both be very different people now. Particularly Graham. He would be mentally scarred for life.

He walked across to Cat. They had work to do. Whatever happened, Freddie Carver had to be caught, and he must not be allowed to use any of his bent lawyers or friends in high places to get him off. If there was any justice, this time the murdering slimeball would go down for good.

CHAPTER FIFTEEN

Mr Fabian ended the call and put his phone back in his pocket. He stared out of the car window and thought how much he hated this flat land with its monotonous miles of ploughed fields and meandering lanes that led nowhere.

And the news that Fat Man Carver had just imparted did nothing to lift his spirits either. Still, he had always been an optimist and when one door closed . . . Carver paid very well, he always had, but if his brave new empire was sinking before he had even launched it, then it was time to abandon ship. No way was he going to go down with it. And he knew without asking that Mr Venables would feel the same.

He idly scratched at his chin. Considering all the jobs that Carver had put their way in the past, he felt that they owed Freddie one more favour before they took their leave of this appallingly bleak county. He would honour that debt.

Carver usually paid him in cash, but for the occasions when this wasn't possible they had set up a complex system of transferring money safely. It was untraceable, and Mr Fabian knew that as soon as he had agreed to accept this job, Carver would have made a payment into one of his many offshore accounts.

Fabian reached across to the passenger seat, picked up his briefcase and withdrew an opaque plastic folder. He had not expected to ever have to open it. Carver had said that it was a failsafe and would most likely never be activated, but since the Fat Man's best laid plans seemed to have gone awry, Mr Fabian's extraordinary expertise was now called for.

Inside the envelope was a series of photographs, a set of telephone numbers, a code name, and a short dossier of personal details. He took the first photo and contemplated it seriously. The woman was blonde, petite and looked about as far from the stereotype police officer as you could get. He looked closer and decided that she was considerably older than the ponytail and fresh face showed at first. He checked her date of birth and gave a little nod. She was probably one of the prettiest marks he had ever had the pleasure of dealing with. A lascivious smile spread across his face. So, the last job that he would ever do for Freddie Carver would be a labour of love. How nice. He knew what the Fat Man expected of him but the fact was, Mr Fabian was a great deal more inventive than dear Freddie. And just in case his remuneration didn't materialise, he would take his reward another way. Every job had its perks.

He ran a finger lightly over the slim body in the photograph and sighed. Up until now, all of his work had been purely clinical. It had to be for him to remain at the top of his game. He was a professional, with no emotions to hinder him. He and Mr Venables were little more than machines — killing machines. Only once in their whole career had they failed to complete an assignment, and that would never happen again. But this time Mr Fabian realised that he wanted more, something different. After all, it was going to be the last time that he and Carver ever crossed paths. Yes, he would concoct something a little more adventurous for his swansong, and then he and Venables would disappear, like a swirl of fragile marsh mist.

He sat back, took out his phone, and keyed in one of the numbers on the sheet. As soon as it was answered, he gave the code word. After a few moments a guarded voice said, 'What do you need?'

'Her duty rota times for the next two days and her whereabouts at present.'

'I'll text you.'

The phone went dead.

Fabian flicked through the other pictures while he waited for the text. They were mostly taken at the police station but others showed her at her home, at the local gym and out jogging on the river towpath. Fabian licked his lips. This was a new game for him. He just hoped he didn't enjoy it too much. He didn't want the pleasure to distract him.

A sharp buzz indicated an incoming message. He read the short text, then shut off the phone. It seemed he needed to act fast to secure his mark, and then, well then he would have all the time in the world to indulge himself. He quickly checked what he had been given with his ordnance survey map and nodded slowly. It was a little way away and in a very wild spot on the edge of the marsh, which was in his favour. He had already reconnoitred the area when he first came to this godforsaken spot. He made a very swift call to Mr Venables while he still had a mobile signal, then allowed a smile to spread across his face. They had work to do. He jammed the seatbelt home, turned on the engine and revved hard out onto the empty road.

* * *

As Mr Fabian sped along the main road to the marsh, Nikki was travelling even faster toward Rainer's Gowt. As she drove, she sifted through the information that had been thrown at her earlier. Her eyes narrowed. Cat and

Ben had done a brilliant job in Derbyshire, but they had also caused a chain reaction, one that had put Jessie Nightingale and Graham Hildred in a very bad place indeed. And Jessie was still blissfully unaware of it all. The poor kid didn't even know that her lovely Graham was alive and at least physically unharmed.

And Freddie Carver? Nikki knew that there was no loyalty within the kind of criminal fraternity he belonged to. He was a vicious, greedy, cold-blooded hoodlum, and he treated his "personnel" like dirt. If they saw him going down they would not throw him a line. But that meant that right now, with years of planning swirling down the plughole, Freddie would be hurting badly, and like a cornered animal, he could be very dangerous indeed.

Nikki eased the big Land Rover around a deceptive bend and tried to put herself in Carver's place. After a while she shuddered and thought better of it. What worried her now was the fact that Carver probably blamed Graham for this calamitous situation, and that meant retribution. And that in turn meant hurting the one thing that Graham truly cared about. Jessie.

And something else, something she hoped that the Derbyshire detectives had cottoned on to — Carver had *two* professional assassins in his pocket. That could mean one for Jessie and one for Graham.

Nikki swallowed and pressed down on the accelerator. She had one thing in her favour. She knew this part of the marsh like she knew the layout of Greenborough nick. Her great aunt had been born in a farm cottage in a hamlet that lay between Rainer's Gowt and Carter's Fen, and these dangerous lanes were etched on her memory from childhood. And as twilight lengthened the shadows across the darkening fen, she considered it to be pretty damned lucky that she did.

* * *

In another part of the misty water-world, far out near the marsh edge, a barn owl hooted and swooped past an old, decaying cottage. Inside, the person whose cries had disturbed the owl's flight, lay back on the filthy bed. She was hungry and in pain. He had told her he might be held up, and had left her food and drink. And he had, but last night he never came home. She had become confused, and had eaten it all. Now she was left with nothing but a couple of dry biscuits.

He had left her a mixture of different pills, and she wanted her other more powerful medication. Some of these had no more effect than an aspirin.

She pulled the cover up over her, drew her knees up to her chest and closed her eyes to the hateful, agonising place that had become her world. Vaguely she remembered a fun-loving girl who one day had jumped into a beautiful car. Had that been her? That girl had been full of hope. She had been promised an amazing chance to alter her life, and was standing on the brink of something special. She seemed to think that the girl could sing, and dance too. And there was a man as well, a man who excited her and opened forbidden doors for her. Surely that girl could not have been her?

She tried to sleep. At least she still had the knife, and now the thought of it sliding through pale skin seemed almost comforting.

* * *

In Greenborough police station, Dave Harris was still trying to come to terms with what Cat had told him.

Graham had been found. It was like a fairy story, one in which a terrible ogre had imprisoned the brave prince, and the knights had ridden in to rescue him and return him to his princess. Although in reality, things were not that simple. The princess was out on the fen at nightfall, and right now, the ogre's henchmen were possibly stalking the brave prince.

Dave rubbed his eyes. It was a lot to take in. And it would be a whole lot more for Jessie to try to absorb. He smiled ruefully. Jessie had always believed that Graham was still alive, but Dave had not. He had thought that Graham was dead, murdered because of something he knew. The body of one of Graham's snouts had been found around the same time, so if the informant has been killed, then surely the policeman had too?

Back then, Dave had had no idea of the Carver/Cavacini connection. He had just supposed it was a whisper about a drug deal that Graham had been following up, and had been taken out for his trouble. But now he felt guilty, as if he had let his old friend down by not keeping the faith.

He stretched. He was tired and wanted to go home, but no way was he going to leave the nick until he saw that Jessie, Joseph and Nikki were back safe. He worried more these days. Maybe he was getting old. He knew that each one of them was strong and canny enough to look after themselves, and he knew that they were all dedicated and prepared to take on anything. But he also knew that there were some evil people out there.

Suddenly Dave realised that the phone was ringing in Joseph's office. He hurried over and picked it up.

'DS Easter, please.'

'I'm sorry, he's out at present. Can I take your number and he'll call you back?'

There was a grunt of irritation. 'Will he be long? I've tried his mobile but he's not answering.'

'Look, I'm DC Harris. Is this something I can help with?'

After a short pause the man said, 'He came to see me earlier this afternoon. My name is Robbie Lyons and it was to do with the disappearance of Dina Jarvis.'

'I am involved with that investigation, Mr Lyons. Please go on.'

The man drew in a breath, then blurted out, 'I've seen the man she went away with!' He gave an exasperated sigh, then went on, 'Thing is, I was a bit of a prat when your colleague and this other officer came to see me. In truth I was really cut up over Dina and this other rich bloke, but I couldn't let anyone know. I would have looked like a right wuss.'

'And who is this man?' Dave asked patiently.

'I told Sergeant Easter that I thought I recognised him when I saw him with Dina just before she went, but I could never place him. Well, after work I went down to the pub for a drink. I was pretty rattled by their visit. It stirred up all the old feelings about Dina. I went to the Leather Bottle but there was a bit of a scrap going on, so I walked to the Olde White Swan, and that's where I saw him. He was drinking with two hard-looking men in expensive suits.' He took a breath then went on. 'Then it all came back to me. That's where I'd seen him before. He and a group of flash-looking city blokes used to drink there years ago. A mate of mine reckoned that they were entrepreneurs of some kind. I just thought they were crooks.'

'And it never dawned on you at the time that this was the same man you saw with Dina?'

'It was a fleeting glance as she got into his car, and apart from that, he was just a face in a pub I rarely used, no more.'

'How long ago was it you saw him?'

'Half an hour or so. But that isn't all. I was just thinking that I'd wait until he left and get his car number, or follow him if he was on foot, when this other guy comes charging in and speaks to the three of them, all intense-like. Whatever he said, they jumped up and hightailed it outside. Didn't even down their drinks, just left them. I ran after them down the alley to the marina, but by the time I got there they had thrown themselves into the back of a big black car and it was already moving.'

'Did you get the number?'

'I would have done, but it had been covered up. I don't even know the make of the car. It was really big, not quite like one of these limos you see pulling up at film premieres, but not far off.'

Dave drew in a breath. 'Look, I'll relay all of this to Sergeant Easter and our boss. Can you come in and make a formal statement, or can we come to you?'

'I'll come now, if it helps.'

'I'll go and inform the desk sergeant that you'll be here shortly, and I'll also get an officer down to the pub to see if anyone knows the identity of your man. Thank you, Mr Lyons. You've been a great help.'

Dave hung up and tried to contact Joseph. When he had no luck, he called Nikki, but she had no signal either. It was not uncommon in that remote area, but Dave felt a shiver of concern trickle down his spine and he cursed the appalling lack of radio coverage. He hated to think that his closest friends were out of contact. Then he thought, well, all but one. He rang Cat, and this time he got a reply. 'Hello, old mate, I'm already on my way back. I'll see you in around an hour and a half. Have you missed me?'

'You'll probably never know how much, my little Catkin. Drive safely, okay?'

She threw him a retort worthy of Nikki Galena herself, and Dave felt a very unusual emotion well up in him. For the first time in years, he wanted to cry. He supposed it was the shock of the news about Graham, but suddenly his work colleagues, who doubled up as dearest friends, had become very precious to him.

Precious and vulnerable. He swallowed. He wanted them back.

CHAPTER SIXTEEN

'Is this the right road?' Jessie stared into the gloom, totally lost.

Joseph nodded. 'Yup. We turn left at the next junction to Carter's Fen and then we follow the road all the way back to the main road into Greenborough.'

'Isn't Carter's Fen where Lilli's body was found?'

'That's right. At Ruddick's Farm.'

Jessie thought for a while. 'Keel said he'd heard Dina singing out near Carter's Fen. Do you think there might be a grain of truth in his ramblings?'

'Maybe when we've taken a good look at that diary of his, we'll know more.' Joseph slowed down at a junction and checked the weathered signpost. 'I don't think Keel is a liar. In fact I'm sure of that, but his view of the world and his way of conveying it to others is not exactly easy to decode.'

Jessie looked up at the darkening sky, then across, along the straight stretch of lane. She pointed. 'Look at that! Someone is driving this way like a bat out of hell!'

Joseph cursed softly. 'Not the way to drive on these back lanes. I just hope he sees our headlights and doesn't think we're parked up. There's nowhere to get away from him on this bit. There are ditches either side of us and no passing places until much further down.'

Jessie felt a jolt of fear. 'Oh shit! He's showing no signs of slowing!'

'Get out, Jess! If that bastard doesn't stop we'll be shunted right off the road!'

Jessie released her seat belt and was just about to leap from the car when she heard Joseph exclaim, 'Hold up, it's Nikki! That's her new Land Rover.'

They both climbed out of the car and watched as the big 4x4 skidded to a halt a few yards in front of them. Nikki climbed out, her face drawn and worried.

'What on earth has happened?' asked Joseph.

Nikki threw up her hands. 'Where do I start? But first, we have to find somewhere we can talk. And no questions yet, okay? I'm just very glad I've found you.'

Jessie frowned. Whatever was wrong, it was serious. She had never seen the boss act like this. 'Why can't we go back to the station, ma'am? Surely that's the safest place to talk?'

'Not right now it isn't, and I said no questions.' Nikki looked around as if searching for inspiration. Then she drew herself up and said, 'I'm going to reverse back to the nearest passing place. I'll turn round and I want you to follow me, and by that I mean tailgate me. Understand this, I want you to be so close that if you sneeze I'll feel the draught on the back of my neck.'

Joseph nodded and beckoned Jessie to get back in their car. 'Wilco.'

Jessie could never have backed along that lane in the dark. She was a good driver but she didn't have a death wish. Nikki, however, threw her vehicle into reverse and shot backwards as if she were on elastic. In what felt like seconds, Nikki had spun the Land Rover around and was flashing them to get behind her.

Joseph positioned himself a few feet from her bumper.

'What in heaven's name is going on?' Jessie asked.

'Ssh, hush,' Joseph whispered to her. 'No questions, remember?'

'I didn't know that went for you as well.'

'If I do anything right now other than concentrate on the arse of that Land Rover, we'll be in deep doo-doo.'

'Point taken.' Jessie sank down in her seat and tried not to let her mind go into overdrive. 'I just wish I knew where we were going.'

'Maybe *that* has got something to do with it.' Joseph's tone was grave, and he was pointing to the horizon, close to where the main road would be.

Jessie saw a set of headlights pull onto the marsh road. As she watched, they were joined by a second set, then both were dimmed and went out.

Suddenly her phone rang and she jumped. With shaking hands she pressed receive. It was Nikki. The patchy signal was back.

'Hang on tight, guys. We are going off-road, just trust me.'

The next five minutes were some of the most hair-raising that Jessie could remember. She had never been a fan of white-knuckle rides, and this was about as scary as it got.

They finally came to a halt at the rear of an old pumping station, a place the river authority probably checked once a month, if that. They were tucked well off the lane on a small area of concrete parking. To get there they had bounced down a field track and a grassy section of a farmer's field before picking up a footpath that led to the waterways pump house. Jessie felt as if she had been trapped in the spin cycle of a washing machine.

The rear door opened and the boss climbed in. 'Sorry about that. Are you both okay?'

'I've checked my dental fillings, and they're still there,' said Joseph with a grin. 'I'm assuming you are rather well acquainted with this part of the fen?'

'True, but right now, there are things you both need to know. You saw that we almost had company?' They both nodded.

'Who was it?' Jessie asked.

'Unless I'm wrong, it was some people who do not wish you well, Jess.'

'Me? Why?' Shockwaves travelled through her mind, and then she felt a hand on her shoulder.

'There's no easy way to do this, Jessie, so I think the best thing I can do is just tell you outright. Are you ready for this?'

Jessie froze. They had found Graham's body! It had to be that, or why would the boss be so guarded?

'Graham is safe. He was in Derbyshire, held by Freddie Carver. He's safe and he's unhurt, okay?'

Nikki's words made no sense to her. Then Jessie's heart began hammering in her chest. 'Safe? Alive?'

Nikki gripped her shoulder. 'He's been taken to hospital for a check-over, but yes, he's not been hurt physically.'

'I have to go to him! Please, can we go now?' She tried to control her breathing. 'Where is he? Where have they taken him?' She rubbed at her temples. 'And who was that out on the fen? Why are they looking for me? I don't understand!' Panic was setting in.

'Steady, steady,' Joseph gently reassured her. 'One thing at a time, Jess, but the main thing is that he is still alive. You always said he was, didn't you?'

'And you said I'd have my answer one day.' Tears began to course down her cheeks. 'My Graham! He's safe.'

'Now, Jess. I know this is a lot to ask, but you need to put your police officer's hat back on and listen to what I have to tell you. You will see Graham, I promise, but not right now.' The hand on her shoulder tightened its grip. 'You are both in great danger and we need to make sure that you are taken somewhere safe. There has been a major breakthrough regarding Freddie Carver, but we think he believes that the leak came from Graham. It didn't, but that is irrelevant. The main thing is that Freddie thinks it did, and he means to get back at Graham through you.'

The gravity of the situation suddenly became clear to her, and Jessie dried her eyes. Her joy at having her prayers answered would have to wait. For now she would be content to know that he was simply alive. 'I understand,' she said slowly. 'And I'll do whatever you tell me, ma'am.'

'Good girl!' Nikki squeezed her shoulder. 'First, we have to find somewhere to hide you. And no one must know, Jess. Not even your friends back at the nick. Sadly, *especially* your colleagues at the nick.' Her voice fell to a whisper. 'Carver has someone spying for him at Greenborough, and whoever it is has been monitoring your comings and goings ever since Graham went missing.'

Initially Jessie felt shock, which soon became anger, and then outrage. 'The slimeball! How dare they?'

'For money. What else? And if he has someone in our station, he could have eyes and ears in any of the other local nicks.'

Jessie puffed out her cheeks and exhaled. 'Where can I go, ma'am? Where is truly safe from a villain like Carver?'

'I think we have a few options, although they are all far from perfect.' Nikki sat back. 'Hear me out and tell me what you think.'

* * *

Cat sipped her tea and looked over the top of her mug at Dave. 'I can't begin to describe that place, it was like something out of a Victorian asylum. That poor old man! I mean, his carers did their best, but he should have been in a proper home that specialised in dementia. And when I saw Graham! He looked just awful! Haunted, would be a good word. He had a thousand mile stare.' She looked down into her tea, then brightened, 'But . . . with what we found out at Appleton Dale, plus Graham's evidence, we

176

have more than enough to charge Carver when we catch him. And get this,' she leaned closer to Dave, 'Graham saw and heard a lot while he was in Derbyshire, and because he knew it was too dangerous to keep a diary, he made sure to remember dates and times and all manner of stuff about Carver. He said he would lie awake at night and repeat what he had learned over and over, like a mantra. He is a walking dossier on Freddie's movements.'

'And if Carver has any inkling of that, he will be sure to want to silence him.'

'I think he'll want to do that anyway, Dave. But Ben says that he's got round-the-clock protection and is in a safe place. Oh, and Ben also said that Carver's remaining two stooges, Lenny and Ezra, are singing like birds.'

Dave looked perplexed. 'I'm not up to speed on this yet. What exactly was their part in this shambles?'

'Gofers, mainly. Carver employed the three of them to act as messengers between Greenborough and his newly established set-up in the Peak District. They fetched and carried — information, drugs, sex workers, money for laundering, anything. Lenny and Ezra lived a few miles away from Appleton, on a small mobile home park. The third man, an evil psycho called Vic, couldn't hack being cooped up and found himself a derelict cottage in the grounds of the old sanatorium, at the back of the Cavacini house.'

'And that's where the girls, Fern, Lilli and Sophie were kept and tortured?'

Cat nodded. 'Vic was supposed to hack off a finger, send it to Graham Hildred as a warning of what would happen to Jessie if he crossed Carver, then dispose of the girl in whatever way he chose. They were expendable, mostly illegal immigrants who weren't, for one reason or another, pulling their weight, or more likely, pulling the punters in the nightclubs.'

'But Vic didn't dispose of them?' Dave felt slightly nauseous.

'Vic was a predator. Deranged would be too kind a word for him. The others had no idea he had imprisoned the girls. They knew about them alright, and what was going to happen to them, but they believed he had killed and disposed of them, as per Freddie's instruction. Then Vic had an asthma attack and let Sophie get away.'

'Then they realised that he was working off the books, so to speak?'

'Yes, and when Vic found himself with no woman to use and abuse, his urges got the better of him and he attempted to abduct and rape Zoë Wallace, the woman walking her dog. As soon as he realised he'd gone too far, he went to ground. Lenny found out, told Freddie, and Freddie sent another one of his deadly associates to sort the problem, permanently.' Cat frowned. 'We don't know anything for sure but Fabian and Venables are the favourites for that. It had all the hallmarks of a professional hit.'

Dave massaged his temples. 'You said Vic had done a runner? How come he was found right where he'd been squatting?'

'That was Lenny and Ezra's fault. Vic was killed and dumped outside their caravan at dawn, a warning to keep them on their toes. They panicked, put the body in the car before it got too light, and took it out to the old hospital. No one ever went there. The idea was to wait in Vic's cottage until nightfall and bury him in the woods.'

'Except that you and Ben Radley and his team went calling. Nice one.'

'It was a brilliant result, but I can't feel pleased about it because of Jessie and Graham. If anything happens to them I'll never forgive myself.'

'Lord! It's not your fault, Cat. I'm sure the boss will find somewhere to magic her away to, until the dust settles.' Dave sighed. 'We can't use one of our safe houses because of the threat of a mole right here among us. So it's down to Nikki right now.'

'You've heard from her?'

'Yes, thank heavens, although it was just a brief message before the signal broke up again. She'd located Joseph and Jessie but told me no more than that. Where they are exactly, I have no idea.'

'Best that way, my friend.'

'I just don't like it. Carver is ruthless.'

'So is Nikki Galena. And Carver is threatening one of her little lambs.' Cat finished her tea. 'And I'll place my money on the detective inspector.'

Dave yawned loudly. 'We should get home and get some rest. But I want to see the boss back safe.'

'You go, Davey. I'll hang out here and ring you when she gets in, I promise.'

'You need sleep too, Cat.'

'I'm not sure I'll ever sleep again after seeing that awful house in Appleton Dale.' She stretched. 'And I want to call Ben and see how things have gone down in the Peaks.'

'You like him, don't you?'

Cat smiled almost shyly, 'You can't help but like him. He comes over so tough, the kind of guy that you'd cross the street to avoid on a dark night, but he's a really lovely man.' The smile widened, 'And I could be wrong, but I'm pretty certain that the boss sent me over there because . . . no, cancel my last. No way would Nikki Galena do a thing like that.'

'Thing like what?'

'Oh, nothing. You're right, I'm tired. I can't see the boss as a matchmaker, can you?'

'Our rough-tough boss? Perish the thought!'

CHAPTER SEVENTEEN

Nikki sounded rattled. 'As I see it, we are between a rock and a hard place. I'm certain those headlights turning onto the marsh lane were those of Carver's men. Now, for someone to know their way about on this stretch of the Fens, he has to have done his homework. That means he might also know that we are pretty well holed up here, as there is only one recognised way out of this maze.'

'So they'll be watching and waiting?'

'Exactly, although I'm not one hundred per cent certain that the second vehicle actually stayed with the first one. As they dimmed their lights, I thought I saw it turn back onto the main road. But I can't be sure, so it would still be very risky indeed to drive back up to that junction. I know that only one car would have Jessie in it, and we could conceal her under blankets in the back, but there might be two of them and two of us. Not particularly good odds.'

'Although as advanced police pursuit drivers we do have the edge in a road race,' murmured Joseph. 'Even so, we can't risk it.'

'What were the other ideas?' asked Jessie.

'This would be my third choice, simply because we do not know who we can and can't trust at the station.' Nikki nibbled on her bottom lip. 'We could request back up and bring the blues and twos out here in force. Carver's men certainly wouldn't want to get involved in chasing police cars around the county, and as his men are jumping ship, I doubt there will be any local assistance for them.'

Joseph nodded. 'That would be my first choice, if it weren't for the fact that there's a cuckoo in the nest. And possibly more of his people at other local police stations, so again, we really can't risk it, can we?'

'Which brings me to the last option, and even that isn't looking too clever.' Nikki sighed. 'There are five cottages out here on the edge of Carter's Fen, and I'm willing to bet even old farmer Ruddick, who has lived here all his life, doesn't know where two of them are. Three are inhabited, and two are derelict. One of those two belonged to my great aunt. We tried to sell it years ago, but had no luck. Apart from being a wreck, it's too remote to be even a hideaway retreat, and the ground is soft silt, so you could never build there. We left it to the elements.'

'You think we should camp there?' Jessie did not feel at all happy about that.

'You and Joseph, yes. Just for the night. But you'd be completely cut off, that's my worst fear, no phones, no radios, no contact.'

'So what about you?'

'You may have noticed that I said there was only one *recognised* way out of here. Well, there is another, but it would be foolhardy to attempt it at night with no lights.' She paused. 'Although I am considering giving it a try. I *have* to get back to set things up, and it's not easy when you can't rely on your fellow officers for support.'

'What about going back to that spot where we had phone signal coverage and ringing in,' Jessie suggested. 'We'd worry ourselves sick if you were going cross-country in the dark.'

181

'I wouldn't even attempt that off-road trek now that night has set in. We got here okay, but it's much darker now. No, I need to get to the station, and Joseph needs to keep you safe and hidden until I get back. I'm going to go back to the main road and take my chances. I can drive that stretch blindfold. When I get closer I can evaluate whether we are still being watched, then decide how to play it.' In the darkness, Jessie sensed her boss grinning. 'I'm good at games, especially when they involve fast cars.'

Jessie believed her, but was still unhappy about being left on the fen. 'Can't we come with you, ma'am? I'm willing to take the chance too.'

'But I'm not. If you fell into the hands of a man like Fabian, or his wicked sidekick, Venables . . .' Nikki shivered. 'It just doesn't bear thinking about.'

'If you say so.'

'I do. My idea is to come back at first light, with a small group of people we *know* we can trust, meaning Cat, Dave, Niall and Yvonne, maybe the superintendent. By then I will have sorted a safe house and we'll make sure that Carver and his cohorts *can't* find you.'

'So where is this cottage?' asked Joseph.

'About half a mile away and heading towards the marsh. This path will take us close, then we'll conceal your car in an old barn on the edge of the property and go on foot.' She drew in a breath. 'My hopes are that Carver's men did split up, and also that they don't know this area as well as I do. Hopefully they will suspect that one car took another route off the fen, and then I'll make a big thing about driving off onto the main road.'

'So they will believe that we have all left the area under cover of darkness and have no reason to hunt for us.' Jessie considered the idea. 'That's possible.'

'She'll be safe with me,' Joseph said solemnly to Nikki.

'I'd not leave her with anyone else, that's for sure.' Nikki touched his arm. 'Shall we give it a try?'

'I don't think we have much choice, do you?'

Nikki opened the car door. 'Then follow me, and no lights, okay? It's not nearly as bad as the route we took to get here, but, Joseph? Be careful.'

'Oh, I will!'

* * *

Ben Radley had half an hour before he needed to go. Initially he had been surprised that his chief superintendent had asked him to debrief Graham Hildred. Then he thought about it and understood the reasoning. When someone had undergone such a traumatic event in their lives, a friendly, familiar face, along with a psychiatrist, were considered optimum. Normally it would have been someone he trusted from his own station, but knowing that Greenborough had been infiltrated by Carver, that was considered unsuitable. And Ben had known Graham from their advanced driving courses. He guessed that his close involvement in the wrecking of Freddie Carver's new empire also made him a safe bet to be privy to the inside info that Graham had to impart. He just hoped that he was capable of juggling efficiency with compassion. Graham Hildred had suffered so much, the last thing Ben wanted to do was make him relive the nightmare.

The phone ringing brought him out of his reverie. He was delighted to hear Cat's cheerful voice.

'Home safe. Just thought I'd touch base with you.'

Ben felt ridiculously happy that she cared enough to consider phoning him. He was pretty sure that their private phones were safe from inquisitive ears, but did not dare risk telling her that he was just off to the private clinic where Graham was being cared for. Instead, they chatted for several minutes and he promised to get across to Greenborough as soon as things calmed down. He still owed her a meal and wasn't going to forget that.

When Ben reluctantly ended the call, he felt confused. The euphoria was wearing off, and he was feeling a strange sense of dislocation. Hunting for Fern's killer had occupied his life. It had been his reason for getting up in the morning and for going to work. It had filled his days and haunted his nights. It had been food and drink to him. Now it was almost over, and he wasn't sure how to cope with the void that was slowly opening up in front of him.

Suddenly his view of the police force had altered. And he was pretty sure that it was because he had met Cat Cullen and her boss, DI Nikki Galena. They had something he did not have, and he was pretty certain there was nothing like it where he was right now.

Apathy and resentment were spreading through his station like a cancer eating up healthy tissue. He realised that Greenborough would be fighting the same battle, but somehow they seemed to be handling it better. Cat's team were still just that — a proper team. DI Galena was clearly steering a steady course through the rough seas of political change, and he wanted to be part of something like that.

Ben looked around his spartan home and saw very little to warm his heart. So much had gone after he separated from his wife. Anything she had wanted, he'd let her have. Now, as he looked around, it seemed she had wanted quite a lot. And as for his lovely dead daughter, he couldn't even bear to look at a photo of her, so the place had no pictures and no decorations. He could be living in a monk's cell, and the only thing missing was a crucifix on the wall.

Then there were his feelings for Cat. During his crusade to bring Fern's killer to justice, he had allowed nothing and no one near him. In all that time, his only emotion had been anger — and frustration by the cartload. Then he had sat down with Cat in that hospital, and experienced something quite alien to him. He had been at peace. And when he'd spoken to her just now, he'd had the same feeling of calm. It had seemed to flow like a meandering stream, pooling in his head and his heart.

He looked around again. He would miss nothing here. There was nothing at work that was important to him anymore, apart from a few mates he respected. He could walk out tomorrow. He liked the area, but then he liked walking, and you could walk anywhere.

Ben drew in a deep breath. As he exhaled, he knew that there were only two things he truly wanted. To be rid of Freddie Carver, and to be with Cat Cullen.

* * *

As Ben contemplated his future, Graham Hildred was doing the same. From the grapevine he gathered that Jessie had held a torch for him all the time he had been missing. He had prayed that would be the case, simply because he loved her, but the thought of her being lonely and anxious had been very hard to bear. It had been so long!

All the time they had been apart he had fretted over her safety. He knew that Carver had her under observation, and he had been terrified that one of Freddie's psycho helpers would one day do something terrible to her. And he was still worried now. He had tried to get a message to her, but had received no answer. He knew that strict protocol had to be observed, and he would comply with it. It was just so hard not to be able to see her again. His heart ached to just be with her, somewhere quiet, peaceful. Just to *be*.

Graham looked down at the open notebook in front of him. He had been methodically writing down all his memories. Dates, times, personnel activity, telephone conversations, visitors and overheard conversations. His memory wasn't photographic, but it was good. He had trained himself to recall dates using a system of mnemonics he devised himself. There hadn't been much else to occupy his mind during that awful time. There had been no friends, no phone, no television and no radio. All he had were a few paperback novels and his imagination.

He looked around the room and wondered how long he would be here, wherever *here* was. As soon as he had been declared physically sound, he had been removed from the hospital and driven at breakneck speed to this place. It was evidently some sort of private clinic, with tasteful décor and an extremely comfortable room. He was watched around the clock by two police officers and he had seen a private security guard further down the corridor, close to the lifts. They were taking no chances. He just hoped that they were doing the same for Jessie.

'How are we this evening?' This was a new face. The man showed Graham his hospital ID. 'My name is Doug Cramer. I'm with the psych evaluation team. Are we looking after you okay?'

Graham nodded. 'Very well, thank you.'

'Good.' The young man slid a finger across the screen of his tablet and nodded. 'I see your physical health check was pretty impressive, all things considered. Blood pressure is fine and general health good, although your blood tests show some mineral and vitamin deficiencies. The food here is ace. I'd take full advantage of it if I were you. And we'll get you some supplements.'

'Well, you don't get much in the way of fine cuisine in a rundown, stinking stable.' He sounded bitter and angry.

'Are you up to discussing the findings of your initial assessment, Graham?'

'I am.' He wasn't actually sure, but there seemed little point in postponing it.

Doug gave Graham an encouraging grin. 'I'm glad to say that you did better than we had expected. But I'm guessing that some of your answers came from the psych screening for your job with the police. Am I right?'

Graham shrugged and gave a sheepish smile. 'The test was similar.'

'You know you will have to be monitored for some time?'

Graham nodded again. 'And attend counselling sessions.'

'That's right. You will be introduced to the psychiatric team in your area and you will have a dedicated one-to-one counsellor.' Doug sat back. 'There are indications of post-traumatic stress disorder, and we are anxious to try to limit the effect that could have on your life, so I do urge you to attend your sessions regularly and take whatever help is offered to you.'

Graham frowned. 'Like drugs?'

'Maybe, but more likely cognitive behavioural therapy. That's widely used and very effective.'

'I don't want drugs.'

'Good, but don't try to cope with this on your own. You have a whole team of people behind you who want to help. Remember that, okay? They are going to be looking out for you and your well-being. They are on your side all the way.' Doug glanced at the notebook. 'This is very impressive stuff, Graham. It must have been very important to you.'

'It kept me going when I believed all hope had gone. It was like keeping a fire burning through the night.'

'Was it a good fire? A healing, warming one?'

'No, it was burning hate. It was the hope of revenge on an evil man who hurt and killed innocent people.'

'Then I think I'd call it a cleansing fire, wouldn't you?'

Graham thought for a moment. 'Yes, cleansing.'

'So maybe it was a healing fire after all.'

'Maybe it was.' He gazed at the pages full of careful handwriting. 'I just know all this will help to seal his fate.'

Doug stood up. 'Then I'll leave you to your records, but do get some rest and watch some TV or a movie. Don't work all the time.'

Graham picked up the pen. 'I need to get this down, as soon as possible.'

'Because?'

'If I could, I would burn it, but the police will need it. But when this book is finished, it is *over* and I'll *never* go back there again.'

'You will need to talk it out. It's part of the healing process.'

'I will heal when I am home with the woman I love.'

'I wish you well, but don't underestimate what you have been through.' Doug paused. 'I understand your debriefing officer is on his way.'

Graham nodded. 'DC Ben Radley. He's a good guy. I trust him.'

Doug nodded. 'That is a help. But look, I realise there is a lot they need to know, and I know it's very important that you tell them all you can, but don't let anyone bully you. You are fragile, Graham. Do what you can, but don't overdo it. Doctor's orders.'

'I'll tell Ben you said that, shall I?'

'Do, and if things get tricky, give me a shout and I'll tell him myself.'

Graham gave a little laugh. 'I want to help the police, Doug. I know things about a very bad man that probably no one else does. I spent a lot of time with his old father, who had dementia, but when he was having a good day, he told a lot of stories about his son. I need to make sure that the authorities know everything.'

'Okay, but remember what I told you. I'll be around if you need back up.'

With a cheery wave, Doug made for the door. 'When your friend has gone, try to get some sleep and don't work on your memoirs all night! You need plenty of rest.'

CHAPTER EIGHTEEN

Nikki was almost disappointed that she had not seen Carver's hitman on the main road, but even so she had been dogged by the uncomfortable sensation that she was being watched. The rest of the journey was uneventful, but when she finally walked into the station she was accompanied by a deep sense of dread. It was truly chilling to think that one of their number had been spying on a detective for two years. Freddie Carver, a man she had never even met, had insidiously infiltrated her police station. It had tainted the whole place. It didn't have to be a police officer of course. Greenborough now used civilians for a large percentage of their tasks. It could be a call controller, a maintenance operative, an IT consultant, a secretary, front counter personnel, an evidence handler, ad infinitum. But it could also be a bent officer, and the thought of that sickened her.

She walked into her office. Something moved in a corner, and Nikki almost screamed.

'Sorry, ma'am. I took advantage of your futon.' Cat sat up, stretched and pulled her jacket around her.

'You should be at home in bed after all you've done in the last few days. You've earned a proper rest, not a doss on my couch.'

'I wanted to know you were all safe.' She looked around, 'Where's the Sarge? And Jessie?'

'Joseph is with her. We ran into trouble out on the fen.' Nikki threw herself down next to Cat. 'Jesus! This is a mess!'

'How can I help?'

Nikki smiled at her. 'By going home, sleeping, then getting back at dawn. I need to get a small handpicked team together to go and collect Jessie and take her to a place of safety.'

'I'll be there.' Cat's eyes were bright, all trace of sleep gone. 'Shall I ring Dave?'

'Do it from home. Walls have ears, it seems.'

'Ah, yes. And unless my info is flawed, I'm afraid it's the same in a couple of other stations in this area. Ben tells me that a little bird told him it was all part of Freddie's master plan to have several sleepers on the inside, so to speak. People he could activate at will.'

Nikki let out a low whistle. 'He had quite some plan, didn't he?'

'But luckily he also had a rotten apple, and it infected the whole barrel before he took it out.' Cat rubbed her hands together. 'Oh, I must tell you before I go, Niall and Yvonne have gathered up a couple of informants who tell us they are prepared to assist us in our hunt for Freddie.'

'In return for what?'

'Anonymity, and a small backhander. Yvonne said she was ready to cough up her own money to get Carver. She thought it was a bloody good deal. And Niall, bless him, offered to organise a whip-round.'

Nikki smiled. 'He'd probably raise a fortune if everyone knew it was to get that bastard behind bars. Are those two still on duty?'

'Don't think so, ma'am. Are you thinking about them for your elite team?'

'I am.'

'I've got their numbers. I'll ring them after I've spoken to Dave and get them to come in early.'

'Excellent. Now, get off home.'

Alone in her office, Nikki closed the door and rang the superintendent on her private mobile. Greg Woodhall, too, would be with her at dawn.

Nikki pulled a car blanket and a pillow from beneath the futon. She couldn't face going home, knowing that Joseph and Jessie were out on Carter's Fen in the rundown, leaking old cottage that used to be her favourite place as a child.

Happy to be going nowhere tonight, she went out to the CID room, where a couple of lone DCs were still working.

'Anyone going out for food? If they are, it's on me.'

'Thanks, ma'am, but I'm off soon. I'm happy to go get you something though.'

'Me too, ma'am. I'm done here for today.'

'No, forget it. You guys get home. I'll ring for a pizza.'

'Are you sure?'

'Absolutely.'

Joseph hated pizza. Mind you, if she could cook like he did, she'd probably feel the same. No she wouldn't, she loved pizza. But she had a feeling that tonight, without any of the team to share it with, it wouldn't taste the same.

She got herself a coffee from the machine and walked back to her office. It felt all wrong without her team gathered around her.

'Ma'am?' A uniformed WPC handed her a memo. 'From the desk sergeant, ma'am. DC Harris asked if we could check out a man seen in the Olde White Swan earlier today.'

'Thank you.' Nikki looked at the note and then noticed a long memo from Dave sitting on her desk. She sipped her coffee and read them both. So, Dina Jarvis's mystery boyfriend had been seen and identified here in Greenborough. And uniform, bless them, had got a name for him from the bar staff at the pub. Gibson Ash. Not one she recognised.

Nikki logged on to her computer and entered the name, then she pursed her lips and made a little noise of surprise. 'Oh dear! Gibson Ash, you are a naughty boy, aren't you? And even worse, your known associates are men who work or worked for a certain Freddie Carver.' She puffed out her cheeks and let out a long breath. 'So, Mr Ash, what on earth did you do to Dina Jarvis?'

Nikki began to dredge up every tiny piece of information she could find on him, then she circulated the details to all forces. As "wanted."

Nikki took Gibson Ash's photo from the printer and stared at it. 'I'll find you, you cocky little git. Then you are going to tell me exactly what happened to that lovely girl.'

* * *

Ben Radley sat opposite Graham Hildred and prayed silently for guidance.

The room was comfortable and warm with good quality furniture, and pictures on the walls. A jug of coffee and china cups sat on a tray on the table, and there were attractive biscuits and even proper brown sugar. It was certainly the perfect venue for a friendly chat. What worried Ben was the topic of conversation.

'You can go ahead whenever you are ready.' Graham's voice was steady. 'I won't break or crack up and run screaming around the room, I promise. I've already done that, only I was in a stable at the time.' He gave Ben a weak smile. 'Sadly, I'm not joking. There were bad days, and the nights were even worse.'

'I would say I can imagine, but I can't. You would have to have lived through it to truly appreciate what it was like.'

192

'The main thing is, I did live through it. I have to hang on to that. If I'm strong enough to withstand that kind of torture, I can see this through, can't I?'

Ben grinned at him. 'If you got through all that, man, I'd say you can face anything.'

'I hope you are right.' Graham sat forward, 'So. Where do we begin?'

'You know what they say, "Let's start at the very beginning, it's a very good place . . ."'

'Oh great! They've sent bloody Julie Andrews to do my debriefing. Just my luck!'

'Okay, I promise not to sing. Shall we start? Oh, and you know I have to record this?'

They talked for about an hour. As well as the recording, Ben made notes of issues to check out. Then Graham began to recall some of the things that Freddie Carver's father, Rick Cavacini, had told him.

'There was one day, not that long ago, when the old man was really disturbed. Janet gave him something to calm him down and I suggested that maybe we could download some old songs for him. We had no idea of what he liked, but we took a punt on some sixties stuff. For a while it worked like magic. The poor old guy started to sing along, Janet made us all some tea and he was about as relaxed as I'd seen him for months.' Graham scratched his head. 'I don't know if it was the words to one of the songs, but suddenly he grabbed my hand and started telling me not to trust his son. I wanted to tell him just what I thought of his evil son, but I shut up and listened.' Graham paused for a moment. 'Hang on while I order some more coffee. I wish I had something stronger, but the doc isn't keen on me keeping a bottle of Laphroaig under the bed.'

'Understandable, I suppose.' Ben switched off the recorder. He knew this wasn't easy for Graham, and he probably needed a break. It was three or four minutes before the coffee arrived and Ben was on tenterhooks by the time Graham was ready to begin again.

'I'd make a note of this if I were you, because this could just put Carver away for a very long time,' he bit his lip, 'or it could cost the force a fortune and produce zilch, I don't know.' He took a sip of coffee. 'Rick told me that his son had murdered his first wife. He said Freddie believed she was having an affair, and that was enough to have her terminated. Rick said he had really liked his daughter-in-law, he didn't believe she had been unfaithful. He had argued with Freddie, but the idiot was seeing red mist. Rick told me that one day someone would have some work done on Freddie's old house in Hackney in London, and find her body.'

'Hell-fire! That could be the very thing that puts him in the dock — *if* it isn't just a fairy story!'

'I believed him. He was about as lucid as I've ever seen him. He even asked if I would play a game of chess with him, and he managed a good fifteen minutes of careful strategic play before the lights went out again.'

'Well, that should be very straightforward to check out.'

'Especially as he told me her name. It was Glynis, and he even gave me the name of the house — Sheldonhurst. Carver had owned the house for years so, yes, it shouldn't be difficult to find.'

'I suppose he didn't tell you where she was buried?'

Graham grinned. 'You'd think that was too much to hope for, wouldn't you? But that was the first thing I thought to ask. If she is there, she is under the garden room extension.'

Ben let out a little whoop of surprise. 'Good work!'

'There is a lot of other smaller stuff, including details of telephone conversations I overheard while Freddie was visiting, but it will all be in this.' He pointed to the notebook on the table. 'Then it's over to you.' Graham sat back, exhausted. 'Are we done?'

'Yes, Graham. It's more than enough.' Ben switched off the recorder and put it in his jacket pocket. 'Although I'll come back and visit you.'

'I hope I won't need to be here too long. It's very comfortable, but I feel as if I've just swapped one prison for another.'

Ben squeezed his arm. 'We'll do everything we can to make it safe for you to get home where you belong, I promise you that.'

'And Jessie? When can I speak to her?'

Ben had been waiting for that question, and prayed that he wouldn't let the true situation show. 'Oh, you know what this red tape is like, Gray. Just as soon as we can guarantee that you are both out of harm's way, we'll get you back together.'

'You promise that too?'

'Solemnly.'

'I'll hold you to it.' He gave Ben a sad look. 'Things won't ever be the same again, I know that. I just hope I can make it work, if that's what Jessie wants.'

'I'd put good money on that being exactly what she wants, but you know what they say, take it one step at a time.'

Ben left, hoping he hadn't thrown Graham too many platitudes and empty promises. He had no training in victim support or post trauma situations. He had just relied on being a human being who cared.

CHAPTER NINETEEN

Joseph went over the old property from top to toe. He moved around the deserted, derelict rooms with the stealth of a soldier. Of course, that is just what he had been, and he'd never lost that heightened sense of alertness to danger.

'I thought it would be worse than this.' Jessie dragged thick, matted curtains across the window. Dust billowed up around her and she coughed loudly. 'Apart from all this mould and dust!'

'I suggest we make camp here in the front room.' Joseph looked around. 'Upstairs is a real mess. I think the roof has blown in one place, and the tank has leaked. This isn't too bad.'

'If this place were nearer civilisation, it would have sold straightaway. It reminds me of Keel's grandmother's cottage.'

'Probably built at the same time. It's solid, just neglected and abandoned.'

'I wish we could light a fire.' Jessie looked longingly at the old open hearth. 'There are even logs in the basket.'

'No chance. I'm afraid it's car blankets, and an emergency foil blanket if it gets too cold.'

'At least they left a couple of old armchairs.' Jessie prodded one suspiciously and waited to see if any mice ran out. 'I'll give them a good shake. They'll be better than nothing.'

'With those curtains, and the fact that this room only has one window facing away from the lane, I think we can light a candle, if we can find one. I'll go look in the kitchen.'

He returned a few moments later grasping a handful of bent and grubby household candles. 'Essential if you live in a place like this. The old lady had dozens in the kitchen drawer.' He lit one and placed it on the table. 'This cottage is so well hidden that no one would ever find it at night. We are safe with this tiny light.'

Jessie finished beating the dust from the old cushions and put them back on the chairs. 'They don't even feel damp.' She wrapped one of the car blankets around her and sat down. 'It's going to be a long night.'

Joseph placed a box on the floor between them. 'We won't starve. I always keep emergency rations in the car. I've been caught out too many times, on obo for half the night and shop handy.' He bent down and poked around in the box. 'Water, Diet coke, Mars bars, a packet of Hobnobs, some Jaffa Cakes and some salted rice crackers.'

'A banquet, no less.'

'Not what I would have liked to provide for you on such a special occasion.'

Jessie sighed. 'It really hasn't sunk in yet. I mean, I know he's alive and he's been taken somewhere safe, but until I see him for myself, well . . .' She gave a little shudder. 'I keep thinking he will be skin and bone, haggard and sick. I'm almost scared to see him.'

'That's natural, Jess. And you are in shock too. It's a big thing to take in. And this isn't exactly helping, is it?'

'Could be worse. If the boss hadn't driven here to find us like something out of *Dune*, we could be dead right now.' She frowned. 'Why didn't they follow her onto the fen?'

'I think they are too savvy for that. If they'd checked out this area, they would know that there was a good chance of getting lost or finishing up in a dyke. And if Carver is losing his grip on his men, they might think the risk wasn't worth it.'

'Plus, I suppose they had no way of knowing if the driver of the Land Rover was alone, or had a full complement of tooled up SCO19 armed response officers on board.'

'True. Whatever, I'm pretty sure that they bailed out after a while. They will either regroup, or quit.'

'So we sit it out until dawn, when the boss comes back with the cavalry?'

'Yes, petal. You have the pleasure of my company all night long.'

'I could do worse.'

'How are you at word games?'

'As I was probably nine when I last played one, total crap.'

'Good, I hoped as much. I'm a bad loser.'

'How about the Two Truths and a Lie game?'

'Oh yes, I like that.' He grinned broadly. 'Let's save that one until the early hours when you are at your most vulnerable.'

'Perfect. Same goes for you.' She looked down at the box. 'Can I have a biscuit?'

'Help yourself. Let me guess? Jaffa cake?'

'Got it.'

They talked for a while, then Jessie asked, 'The boss has a pretty unusual surname, doesn't she? I've never heard it before.'

'Galena? Yes, I knew it as a kind of rock or mineral, mined for its silver content. But she said it had nothing to do with that. Apparently it's a place name. Her ex-husband's great grandparents came from the town of Galena, Illinois, in the USA.'

'She kept the name after the divorce?'

'By now she couldn't change it if she wanted to. She simply *is* Nikki Galena. But I still think her name came from the grey rock with a silver thread running through it.'

'A silver lining? I think it should be a heart of gold. She's something special, and I'm proud to work with her.'

'Well said, Detective.' Joseph swallowed.

'And even the Christian name. "Nikki" isn't exactly traditional, is it?'

'I googled that when I was bored one day. It's quite weird, because they say that people with the name Nikki tend to follow professions that serve humanity. And it stems from Nike, the Greek goddess of Victory. Another site said that people with NK in their names are unimpressed by status or symbols of success. All they need is loyalty, and they will return the favour by being a faithful and dependable friend.'

'That's spookily accurate, isn't it?'

'I'd say.'

'Do you think you and the boss will ever get together?'

Joseph choked on his Hobnob. 'Whatever made you say that?'

'Oh, just nosiness.' Jessie eyes had a mischievous sparkle.

'We are friends, okay? Really good friends.'

'You two are so well suited. You like each other, and you trust each other, and—'

'Whoa! I was like that with my spaniel, but I didn't think about marrying him.' He took a swig of water. 'To be honest, Jess, even if it had crossed my mind, it would ruin everything we already have.'

'How?'

'We wouldn't be able to work together for a start. It would split up the team, and,' he looked at her seriously, 'we both had bad marriages. Now we have friendship and companionship, plus a damned good working relationship in a job we both love. There is simply too much to lose.'

'So you *do* love her.'

Joseph didn't think he needed to answer that.

'*She* loves you. I saw it the first day I came to work with the team.' Jessie nibbled on her biscuit. 'But I hear what you say. And I understand. I've seen what this job does to marriages. I've seen more domestic trouble and strife, separation and divorce than I've had hot dinners.'

'But you still want to marry Graham.'

'For some reason I always thought we were different. I knew I could make our marriage work. I never doubted it for a minute.'

'And now? If Graham still wants to marry you, will you say, *I do*?'

'I think we are going to have to start all over again. Like it or not, we are two different people now. No one could go through whatever Graham has and come out of it unscathed. I'll just be there for him and we'll see what happens. It's all I can do.'

'You are an astute and wise person, Jessica Nightingale.'

'Thanks, Sarge. Now, how about that game of two truths and a lie?'

* * *

Nikki glanced at her wall clock. Almost ten o'clock. With none of her team around her, she felt cut adrift, and anxiety about Joseph and Jessie had her pacing the floor. She had left them in one of the most inhospitable and inaccessible places in the entire Fenlands, which made it one of the safest too, but still she worried.

It was late, but she knew that Eve was a late bird, and she was sure that she wouldn't mind getting an unexpected call from her daughter.

'Eve Anderson.'

'It's me, Nikki. How are you?'

'I've just got in from the studio actually. Just finished another masterpiece.' She laughed. 'Or not, as is probably the case.'

Nikki had a flash of inspiration. 'Fancy a coffee?'

Eve didn't hesitate. 'Shall I put the kettle on?'

'No, meet me in Mario's. He makes wonderful coffee and he won't mind a couple of late stragglers.'

Eve asked no questions. 'Fifteen minutes?'

'Perfect.' Nikki grabbed her coat from the back of the door and hurried from the office.

In a quarter of an hour exactly, she and Eve were ensconced in a small booth at the back of Mario's restaurant. The waiter had placed the tray of coffees on the table in front of them and to Nikki's delight there was also a large plate of delicious Italian snacks and appetisers.

'I rang ahead,' Eve said. 'Because you haven't eaten, have you?'

'I meant to, but I sort of got waylaid.'

'As I suspected. It's only Bruschetta and mini pizza and some dips, but it will keep you going. Tuck in.'

Nikki did. 'Lifesaver.'

'So, what do you need to talk about that needs to be said "undercover?"' Eve looked at her knowingly.

'Apart from being in the RAF, you spent a lot of time working for the MOD, didn't you?'

Eve nodded.

Nikki kept her voice low even though there was no one left but a scattering of diners and one or two waiters. 'I need a favour. I'm looking for a safe house.'

'How soon?'

'Dawn tomorrow.'

'Just time to make up the spare bed. Blue or pink duvet cover?'

'Pink.'

'And will she have chaperones?'

'Two, around the clock, eight hour shifts.'

'Put them in workman's clothing, give them some decorators' tools and equipment, and find them a battered van — if you have the time.'

'*All* the vans in the station pool are battered,' Nikki said, 'but I'll need to get hold of one that isn't registered to us.'

'Good, and I'll go directly from here to Tesco and get some food in for my "niece" and the nice men who are going to redecorate the dining room. Duration of stay?'

'Unknown. Are you sure you're okay with this?'

'Dead right, I am. Art is fine, but there are only so many pictures you can stick on the wall. I'll get bored if I don't do something constructive soon.' She touched her lips with a finger. 'And I know not to ask questions.'

'I can tell you the basics. You've probably had more use out of signing the Official Secrets Act than I have.'

'Maybe.'

'She's a police officer, a detective, and she is under immediate threat from a trained killer. We suspect a mole in the station, so we can't use our usual places of safety. Other than a few trusted colleagues, no one knows you are my mother, and only Joseph knows your new address. I want to hide her in plain sight, right here in Greenborough.'

'Smart thinking.'

'Take this.' Nikki handed her mother a cheap pay-as-you-go mobile phone and a charger. 'Joseph and I use them for this kind of thing. You'll find all the names and numbers that you might need logged into the Contacts.'

Eve slipped the phone into her handbag. 'Give me a code word, in case anything,' she paused, 'anything *unplanned* happens.'

Nikki thought for a moment. 'Pizza. If I see or hear that, either in a message or in a conversation, I'll be round with a herd of policemen and big guns.'

'How many extra toppings for a helicopter?'

Nikki laughed out loud. 'You really are up for this, aren't you?'

'I miss my job more than I can ever tell you, Nikki. So don't worry about your little flower, she'll be safe with me. By the way, what's her name? My niece?'

'Er, um, Michelle. We'll call her Michelle Anderson, okay? And she's from Loughborough. I happen to know she's familiar with that area, so it'll keep things simple. Not that I'm expecting her to speak to anyone while she's with you.'

'I know the drill, Nikki. I'll be ready and we'll take it from there. Your officers on protection will explain what's expected of me.' She sat back. 'Now finish up this food before it gets cold.'

'Thanks, Eve. I know this is over and above, but I really do appreciate it.'

'And I appreciate you thinking of me, and your trust.'

'If I can't trust my mother, who can I trust?'

CHAPTER TWENTY

Nikki had arrived at the station just before midnight, and the call on her mobile made her jump.

'Inspector Nik?

'Mickey! Can't you sleep?'

'No one is sleeping on the Carborough tonight, Nikki.'

She stiffened. 'Why? What's happening?'

'I tried to get hold of Joe. Is he okay? His phone was dead.'

'He's out on an investigation, it's probably switched off.' She didn't like lying to Mickey. 'But what's going down on the Carborough?'

'Joe wanted news on King Rat. Well, it appears that he doesn't like the Fens anymore. Everything he's involved in is closing down.'

'Our colleagues in Derbyshire did light a blue touchpaper, although we weren't sure how badly the fire would affect him.'

'It affected him badly, Inspector Nik, because his army has disbanded. No one wants to be connected to him anymore, and I've heard that some of his boys are already looking for deals from you guys. He's turned from being King Rat to an outcast overnight.'

'It couldn't happen to a more deserving man.'

'I agree with you, and so does Raymond. He's well pleased the man has done a runner.'

Nikki paused then asked, 'Do you know a man called Gibson Ash?'

'He's one of Freddie's men,' said Mickey without hesitation. 'He hasn't been on the scene for quite a while but he's back now. He was involved in finding women for Ratman's sex clubs. Bit of a charmer, or so I'm told.'

'You know him?'

'Not personally. He's not my kind of person, Nikki, not anymore,' Mickey chuckled. 'But I still keep my eyes open and my ear to the ground.'

'I want to talk to him, urgently.'

'I'll do what I can.' Mickey gave a little yawn. 'Give my love to Sergeant Joe, won't you?'

'Of course. And thank you, Mickey.'

'No worries. Oh, and one other thing before I go, one of Freddie's men who has come over to Raymond's side, has it on good authority that Mr Venables is on his way to the East Midlands Airport. They run regular flights to Holland from there, and as he has a nice little flat in Amsterdam . . .'

'Music to my ears, Mickey. You are a star.'

'I am, aren't I?'

One down, thought Nikki as she ended the call. And if Mr Fabian were to do the same, she'd feel a whole lot better.

* * *

Joseph walked around the old cottage, leaving Jessie dozing in her chair. She looked exhausted. Joseph knew that the shock of today's news had caught up with her. He tried his mobile, then pushed it back into his pocket. Dead spots on the Fens were just that — dead.

He wanted to phone Tamsin, just to hear her voice. Since they had put aside their differences, she had become immensely precious to him. She always had been, but now that he was able to share that lovely, happy side of her, he was the closest he'd ever come to being totally content with his life. And now his girl was going to marry. He shook his head, marvelling at the fact that he was going to be part of her future life. He had always believed that one day he would learn about her forthcoming marriage from a notice in the paper or a terse message from Laura. The fact that she would be on his arm as they walked up that aisle filled him with delight.

He opened the back door and looked out onto the silent fen. He loved remote, he loved Knot Cottage, but he did not love this place. It might have been idyllic once, when Nikki was a small child, but not now.

He listened for a few minutes. The marsh wilderness was far from silent. Mainly he heard water — dripping, trickling, splashing. It came from the river close by, from the pools in the marshy ground, and it moved slowly along the myriad ditches, drains and dykes. Small animals scurried through the undergrowth. A soft wind rustled the leaves in the overgrown garden. And then there were those noises that were hard to explain. The creaks and groans of rotting fence posts and barn timbers could sound like wheels turning slowly on rutted ground, and he knew exactly why some of the old locals were superstitious. Owls and other night birds could freeze the blood with their screams.

There was one sound he could not identify. A strange keening noise that wasn't part of the fen. It had to be animal, maybe a feral cat or a fox, although they were not prevalent on the marsh. He shivered and ducked back inside, locking the door behind him. He went over to where Jessie slept.

'I'm only resting my eyes.'

'And I'm the Duke of Marlborough.'

Jessie yawned and stretched, then drew the blanket tighter around her. 'Shall we try to have a look at Keel's diary?'

'Sure. It'll pass some time.' He fetched the book, dragged his old chair next to Jessie's and picked up the candle. 'Once upon a time . . .'

Jessie shook her head. 'Oh my! How on earth are we supposed to make sense of all this?'

Each page was filled from margin to margin, almost covering the paper beneath. There were sketches, cut-out pictures, writing and some odd art work that was a cross between graffiti and doodling.

'He's actually quite talented,' whispered Joseph. 'These drawings are very good.'

'I'm sure you're right, if you could tell what they represented.'

'I don't think we are going to decipher this by candlelight. We need a bright light and a clear brain for this lot.'

Jessie leaned closer. 'What is this? It looks familiar somehow.'

Joseph stared at a sketch of an old ramshackle building. It appeared on several of the final pages, and in each case had a list of dates and times printed clearly down one side of it. Jessie was right, it did look familiar. 'And this? It's a drawing of the headlights and radiator grill of a car.'

'The mystery boyfriend's posh car?'

'I'd say so. It's an Audi A6, an executive saloon.' He turned a page. 'Oh, this is very dark indeed.'

The page featured twisted trees, and black-robed figures with slanted red eyes, long, pointed fingers and elongated legs. 'It's going to be hard to sort fantasy from fact.' He flipped back to the beginning. 'It starts more like an ordinary scrapbook type of diary, but as time goes on, Keel's artwork changes dramatically. The final pages look almost psychotic.'

'And scary. I've seen books like this before, in the bedrooms of stalkers, obsessive freaks and predators.'

'I don't think it's meant to be like that. Some of his sketches are beautiful, and he's written little poems beside Dina's name. It's more an ode to love than a threat to her.'

'Those black creatures didn't look too loving.'

'I think that's his fear for her. Something happened to her, and I think it scared him, so he has portrayed that person as a night creature.'

'I'm going to leave this to you, Professor Freud. I'll wait until we have some nice high wattage lamps.' Jessie snuggled into her blanket. 'I'd kill for a cuppa, wouldn't you?'

'Would you settle for a Mars bar?'

'Not my usual night-time snack, but thank you, I'd love one.'

As Jessie slept, Joseph sat until the early hours of the morning reading Keel's extraordinary diary by candlelight. Occasionally a night bird would call or screech outside and Jessie would stir, but she slept on.

Joseph stayed awake. He knew what could happen if he let his guard down. There were some very bad people out there.

He closed the book and thought about some of the things that had stood out, mainly the drawings of the building. Where had he seen it before? For the life of him he could not remember. But he had gained a little insight into Keel Chandler, and was even more certain that the young man had witnessed something that would tell them what had happened to Dina Jarvis.

* * *

In a hotel room, not far from what was supposed to have been the hub of his new dominion, Freddie Carver sat staring into space. After his nasty experience with the police a few years ago, he had prepared for possible failure. His exit strategy had been set up even before he left Spain.

He had ring-fenced a considerable quantity of his assets and protected his most profitable investments, but this was going to cost him dearly. He had poured more money than he cared to think about into planning and establishing a workforce, and he had already kissed goodbye to that. And why? Because, just for the sake of keeping his father quiet, he had been stupid enough to trust a sexual predator like Vic, and generous enough to keep a copper alive. Well, Vic had paid the price, and if everything went according to plan, the copper would suffer too. And this time he wasn't paying peanuts and using second-rate old lags. He had picked the best, and the best would deliver. It would do his finances no favours, but it would help ease the anger that was eating away inside him.

He heaved in a rasping breath and held it, then exhaled loudly. He was Freddie Carver. He'd rise from the ashes. He'd done it before and he would do it again. But not in Spain. This time he would choose somewhere sophisticated and elegant. His spirits lifted, then sank again. Could he afford it?

CHAPTER TWENTY-ONE

With vivid spears of orange and crimson light, dawn tore the grey-black clouds into strips. Nikki Galena was making her way onto Carter's Fen. With her were three other vehicles. Nikki was at the head of the convoy, with Dave sitting silently beside her. Behind her was Superintendent Greg Woodhall, accompanied by two trusted officers from the armed response team. Next came Niall Farrow and Yvonne Collins, with Cat bringing up the rear.

Nikki had kept her eyes firmly on the fen lane, while Dave scanned the surrounding area for signs of trouble. Thankfully all seemed quiet.

They pulled up outside the old cottage, and Nikki felt a stab of nostalgia along with her ever-present nagging concern for Jessie. She really should have done something to save her old aunt's home from rotting, but there had probably been too many drug dealers on her mind at the time. And now? Not when so much else of importance was going on.

Joseph opened the door. Jessie was close behind him, and Nikki felt relief wash over her. It was all she could do to stop herself rushing over and hugging him.

'Everyone inside please, except SCO19. If you would keep a close watch on the lane that we came in on, please?'

The two officers nodded and took up position outside the door.

Nikki grinned at Joseph and his ward. 'Both okay?'

Jessie smiled grimly. 'Tickety-boo, ma'am. Except for the absence of room service, the accommodation was five-star.'

Nikki turned to Cat. 'Have you brought what I asked you to?'

Cat nodded and opened a shopping bag that was hanging off her arm. 'Got the perfect thing, ma'am, from my undercover days.' She looked around and spotted a dusty, tarnished mirror in the hall. 'Give me a minute.'

'First, get these on.' Nikki handed out bulletproof vests. 'Then the plan is to drive back to the main road, then at the first roundabout we split up. I'd like the super to take the main Greenborough exit, Joseph and Niall will take the Spalding Road, and Cat the Castor village exit. I'll have Jessie with me, concealed in the back of the Land Rover, and be assured, there's a place all set up to receive her. We'll rendezvous back at the station, as and when. You can all take the longest, prettiest scenic route you fancy, okay?'

'I'm assuming you saw nothing on your way in?' asked Joseph.

'Roads are almost empty, and there was no one out there that we could see,' Dave said. 'Although that doesn't mean to say that someone wasn't observing us from a concealed position.'

'We have to assume that they were,' Nikki chipped in. 'We drive as if we are being followed and take evasive action to lose them, just as a precaution. With Carver's depleted forces, he won't be able to follow us all, that's for sure.'

'How's this?' Cat appeared from the hallway, the tension broke and everyone laughed.

Her old talent for disguise had not deserted her. 'Jessie? Meet Jessie!'

Cat wore a long blonde wig that she had carefully fashioned into an exact replica of Jessie's style of ponytail. She had caught it back with a similar tie and was sporting a short navy jacket, slightly different in design, but the same colour as the one Jessie was wearing. 'Through a car window, I'm pretty sure I'd fool them.'

'I'll say,' said Jessie. 'That's amazing!'

'Well, we aren't quite finished yet. It's your turn now.' Cat threw Jessie another wig, this time in a dark brown, shoulder length, bob style.

'For you, when you reach your destination,' Nikki said seriously. 'You are no longer Jessie Nightingale, your name is Michelle, okay?'

'I'm a brunette? That'll make a change.'

'And you wear my parka,' added Cat. 'It will cover up your vest and you'll look completely different.'

'Right, Cat, you go with Joseph, and Yvonne will drive your vehicle. If nothing else, if we do have company, our cavalcade should confuse them.' Anyway, Nikki hoped that would be the case. 'So, if we are all set, let's get off this fen before it's fully daylight. And good luck everyone. I'll see you all later.'

* * *

As Nikki's team set out across the Fens, a lonely woman sobbed into her stained pillow. He had not come home at all, and this time she knew he had deserted her. She had always known that one day this would happen. He had sworn he loved her, but he was a man, and she still had just enough sanity left to know that she was a hopeless, unkempt and vile creature that didn't deserve love from anyone, especially him.

She had once done something terrible, she knew, but couldn't remember exactly what it was. But he had stood by her. He had done everything he could to make things right again. He had protected her and hidden her. But now . . . ? She curled into a tight ball and wondered how long it took to starve to death.

* * *

When Nikki finally stepped back into Greenborough police station, she was almost on a high. The "special delivery" of her precious charge had been textbook, and she knew that Jessie was in the very best of hands. Eve had been the perfect choice. The highly experienced officers who were now "decorating" Eve's house had been drafted in from a different area and were tried and tested according to the super, which was good enough for Nikki. For the first time in days, she felt as if she could breathe again. She went to grab a coffee before going into the CID office, and found Joseph already at the machine.

'Thank you for what you did last night.'

'No problem, and the time wasn't exactly wasted.' He put down his coffee and took a notebook from his pocket. 'Keel Chandler's rather obscure diary of events surrounding the disappearance of Dina Jarvis.'

'Really?' Nikki took the notebook from him and flipped through it. 'Oh my! Am I supposed to understand any of this?'

'I did say it was obscure. But funnily enough, given a little more time and a quick word with Yvonne Collins, I think I might just have found a way into this young man's thought processes.'

'Now that is worrying. This is very weird stuff.'

'Then maybe I have a weird mind too.'

'Let's not go there on an empty stomach. I need breakfast. I'm starving.'

'You have a meeting in fifteen minutes.'

Nikki grinned. 'Perfect. That leaves just enough time for *someone* to go out and get me a croissant, or a nice big pain au chocolat.'

Joseph pulled a face. 'Okay, ma'am, on my way.'

'They are on me.'

'I should think so too. I missed dinner *and* breakfast, you know.'

'Ah, the policeman's lot is not a happy one.'

'Shut up, Nikki.'

* * *

The CID room was full of officers waiting for the nine o'clock meeting, and Joseph was anxious. Someone here was not who he or she seemed, so they would have to be extremely careful about everything they said and did until the bastard was routed out. Nikki had told him that the best they could do was concentrate on hunting down Carver as if nothing were amiss, and keep up the Dina Jarvis investigation, concentrating mainly on searching for Gibson Ash. She did not want the mole to know that she was aware of their existence. Hence, anything pertaining to Jessie was to be spoken about only in private or off the premises. Even Joseph didn't yet know her location, but he could tell from Nikki's mood that she was happy with it. He smiled to himself. If Nikki was satisfied, then he would be too.

'Is everyone here?'

There was a murmur of assent.

Nikki stood in front of them, her manner casual and easy.

Nice one, thought Joseph. *Keep them relaxed.*

'As you will have heard . . .' Nikki proceeded to elaborate on the collapse of Freddie Carver's claim on the Derbyshire underworld. Then, for the benefit of anyone who had not been present yesterday, she announced the discovery and rescue of PC Graham Hildred.

As she spoke, Joseph watched his fellow officers carefully. There was a chance someone would act out of character or display discomfort. He hoped and prayed that it wasn't someone they knew and trusted, but there was always that small chance. As it was, the lost policeman's miraculous reappearance was met with huge delight and utter amazement.

When things had calmed down, Nikki went on to talk about Dina Jarvis's disappearance. 'We have decided that she is now considered to be at risk. We believe that she was abducted, possibly by a man named Gibson Ash.' She told them what she had discovered about the man, including his involvement with Freddie Carver. 'As we now know that Carver was responsible for the abduction of Fern, Lilli and Sophie, we can assume that he was probably behind Dina vanishing from Greenborough. I have issued an *attention drawn*, so hopefully Ash will cross someone's radar in the not too distant future.'

Joseph stood up. 'Ma'am? I have unearthed a few more facts about Dina Jarvis. May I explain?'

'Please do. Go ahead, Joseph.'

'It has been confirmed that she had an excellent singing voice, and was also a very good dancer. We also know that her brother Dominic was never keen on her exploiting this talent in public. Now we know that Gibson Ash was a "scout" for Freddie's clubs, so I suggest he did exactly what we originally believed, and promised Dina a sparkling career in showbiz.'

'And the poor kid didn't want to upset her brother, so she attended these "auditions" without Dominic's knowledge,' added Yvonne.

'She fell in love with Gibson Ash en route?' asked Niall. 'After what I witnessed, I'd say she was more than smitten.'

'Well, you'd know, wouldn't you, Romeo?' called out a voice from the back. There was a ripple of laughter and Niall blushed.

'Okay, joke over,' Nikki interrupted. 'I think Niall is correct. Indications are that Dina fell for her baby-faced entrepreneur — hook, line and sinker.'

'So what happened to her then?' asked Dave. 'Why kidnap her when she would have gone willingly?'

Joseph answered as best he could. 'We don't know exactly, but I think Gibson Ash fell for her too. Possibly things went a little too far? Whatever, I suspect something else happened, and I also believe that a young man with learning difficulties, a man called Keel Chandler who had a big crush on Dina, was a witness to it, or some of it. One thing is for sure, he knows more about Dina Jarvis than we do. And given his poor mental health, it's going to be the devil's own job getting to the bottom of it.'

'But you will try?' asked Nikki.

'Oh yes, ma'am.' He looked over to Yvonne, 'And with your local knowledge and help, we'll fathom it, one way or another.'

'The oracle is at your disposal, Sergeant.' Yvonne grinned.

'Thank you. Now, we have two other men who were also very attracted to Dina, and we cannot rule them out as having been involved in some way. We have a care-worker male nurse called Arthur Kirkby and a farmer called Robbie Lyons.' He passed around memos with their details. 'I haven't had time to do any background checks on these guys, so perhaps someone would take that on.' Joseph looked around the room and in a sombre voice said. 'Our biggest concern right now seems to be, are we looking for Dina Jarvis, or her body?'

A low murmur echoed around the room. Joseph felt sure he knew what most of his colleagues were thinking, and he sincerely hoped they were wrong.

* * *

At exactly eleven o'clock Nikki received the call she had been hoping for.

'As quick as you can, Inspector Nik! He's in a hotel called the Alma on Station Approach, and he's packing up to leave.'

'You little angel!'

'I think I preferred being a star, but you need to hurry! See you.'

Nikki grabbed the photo of Gibson Ash and ran out to the CID room, where Cat and Dave were working away on their computers. 'Both of you! With me!'

The Alma was a seedy, rather tired-looking small hotel. Dead summer plants still hung over the edges of window boxes and hanging baskets, and the signage had begun to peel away.

The lobby was no better, and as no one was at the desk Nikki leaned over the counter and leafed through the visitor's book. 'Can you *believe* he used his own name?' she asked Dave. 'Room twenty-three, let's go visit!'

As it was they met Gibson Ash, suitcase in hand, at the top of the stairs. Before he knew what was happening he was wearing handcuffs and heading towards their waiting car.

'Was that too simple, or what?' muttered Cat.

'We deserve a bit of good luck, don't we?' replied Dave.

'True.'

As Nikki drove back to the station she glanced in the rear-view mirror and tried to read the expression on Ash's face. He was scared, that was for sure. In fact, he looked terrified, and that wasn't generally the case for a nicked villain. Usually the least you could expect was a stream of abuse, sometimes referring to you and sometimes to your parentage, but always accompanied by colourful and sometimes quite creative bad language. Gibson Ash had not spoken, and he looked more likely to cry than to hurl verbal abuse at them. Did he realise that he was about to be unmasked as an abductor, maybe the killer, of a young woman who had loved him? Nikki wasn't sure, but she couldn't wait to get him into an interview room.

* * *

At the same time as Nikki was checking out the décor at the Alma, Ben Radley was thumbing through reams of information on Lewis Rosewood, the bent lawyer. Ben's boss had categorically refused to cut a deal with the man, but Ben had seen another way to use him. After scrutinising one or two interesting pieces of info that Graham had supplied, Ben decided to have a quiet word with Rosewood. His idea was to let Rosewood think that other members of Carver's gang had admitted to having taken part in certain jobs, all ones that Ben already knew Rosewood had played a part in. Then Ben would intimate that if he denied his involvement, he could be taking the blame alone.

He walked down to the custody suite and arranged with the sergeant to have a few moments with the prisoner in an interview room.

Rosewood looked gaunt. Getting caught was something he had clearly never considered.

'Sorry to hear you were refused bail.' Ben kept his voice free of sarcasm. 'That's tough.' He sat down opposite the brief. 'Look, I wish this could be just between you and me, but as you well know, I'm obliged to record it.'

Ben activated the recorder and raced through the introductions.

'Lewis, if I may call you that? I need to tell you that after Freddie Carver's father, Rick Cavacini, was taken to a specialist hospital for care and his minders taken into custody, we have had several men and women come forward, all prepared to testify against Carver for a whole variety of jobs.'

Rosewood sounded sharp and mocking. 'I wasn't born yesterday, Detective. Men don't just drop Carver in it. Well, not if they want to live a long life and keep their looks.'

'So far I have spoken with five witnesses, and between them we have discussed the robbery in that Mayfair jeweller back in March, the drugs shipment that came in on the Zeebrugge ferry last month, the blackmailing of a high profile politician in the Peterborough area, oh yes, and the murder of two women and the unlawful imprisonment and rape of a third.' He raised his eyebrows. 'Together we have linked Carver to all of these, and I should mention that they not only talked about Carver, your name cropped up in dispatches on a regular basis.'

'Along with Santa Claus and the Grinch, no doubt.'

'I can't say I recall those names, but Lewis Rosewood . . . now that's one I do remember.' Ben leaned closer to the man and said, 'I have proof that Carver called you on the night of September the tenth at eleven seventeen hours, and you discussed how you would provide an alibi for him for the Zeebrugge incident. I have all the details. Phone records, and unfortunately for you, someone else heard it too and they are very willing to testify to it in court. My advice to you is to cooperate with us. Freddie Carver is no longer your best friend. He no longer has any clout anywhere or with anyone. He will not save you. But you could save yourself from the harshest sentence.' Ben stood up abruptly. 'I need to go. While I'm away, take some time to consider this.' He stared straight at Rosewood. 'If you confirm some information that has come into my possession, I will make sure that Carver does not know that you were involved. We have enough grasses around here right now to sow a lawn, but he does not have to think that you are one of them. Your cooperation would be noted and recompensed.'

Ben terminated the interview and walked to the door. He glanced back at Rosewood's pale face, and noted with satisfaction that the sardonic grin had faded.

Ben's superintendent met him outside the room. 'Good work last night with Hildred, Radley. I thought you should know that the Met have agreed to look at the house called Sheldonhurst in Hackney. As I understand it they are taking in some specialist equipment with a GPR analyst.'

'Ground penetrating radar? That scans concrete to find embedded objects beneath, doesn't it?'

'It's a state-of-the-art, non-invasive investigative tool, and it could save the force a fortune if it shows nothing.'

'And if it shows something?'

'I go buy you a bottle of champagne and we sort out a nice cell to accommodate Mr Carver.'

'I think it's Graham who deserves the champagne, sir.'

'Too right. That man deserves a medal.'

'He's already got one of those, and I do believe it saved his life.'

The super gave Ben a concerned look. 'I just hope he comes back from all this, Radley. So called "normal" life, after what he's been through, could be very hard on the man.'

'He'll come through.' Ben was surprised at how confident he felt about that. But he was sure he was right. As long as Jessie Nightingale stayed safe, and wanted her man back, Graham would survive.

CHAPTER TWENTY-TWO

Yvonne sat with Joseph and stared at Keel Chandler's notebook, in particular the sketch of the wooden building. After a while she closed her eyes and Joseph wondered if she'd been doing too many double shifts.

'Got it!' Her eyes flew open. 'It's Ruddick's Farm — the old potato grading shed.'

'Of course!' Joseph smacked the side of his head with his hand. 'I *knew* I'd seen it before, when we found Lilli, but I suppose it was dark when I went there.'

'So why is our young artist sketching a potato shed cum murder scene?' asked Yvonne thoughtfully.

'And what do those dates mean?' Joseph traced his finger over the carefully inscribed figures.

'The last one is only a few days prior to Dina's disappearance. Do you think he saw her there?'

Joseph scratched his nose. 'But why? If she were going out with that Gibson Ash guy, he had money. If he wanted to get his leg over, pardon the crudity, but if he did, he could take her back to his hotel or wherever he was staying, or even rent a room somewhere. Not take her to a remote part of the fen and seduce her in a bloody potato shed. It doesn't make sense.'

'The boss will be interviewing Ash as soon as he's been processed. Maybe you should ask him if he has a fixation on root vegetable storage facilities.'

'I will, don't you worry.' He smiled at her and held up the notebook, 'Have you got time to go through this for me? Just to see if anything makes sense to you. I have a couple of theories about Keel, but I'd value your input.'

'Of course, Sarge. Niall is out somewhere talking to one of our snouts, so until he's back, I'm all yours.'

Joseph passed the book to her, then realised that his mobile was ringing. It was an unknown number. 'DS Easter, can I help you?'

The voice on the other end was garbled and almost unintelligible.

'Calm down, sir. Let's start again, shall we? Who is this?'

'You said I shouldn't call you, I know, but I have to talk to you! I have to.' The voice broke into a sob. 'Something is going on, and I know it has to do with my sister. You must tell me, Sergeant. Have you found her?'

Joseph almost groaned. Dominic. 'No, I'm sorry. I don't know what you think is going on, but we have not found Dina.' He paused, then added, 'You know that I promised to tell you the moment I knew something concrete, don't you? And I meant that, Dominic.'

'They are talking, all around the town. I've heard them, they are talking!'

Joseph placed his hand over the receiver and whispered to Yvonne, 'I don't like the sound of this. I think he's having some sort of breakdown.'

'Want me to get a crew around there?'

He shook his head. 'No, I'll go.'

'Alone?'

'I'll be fine, he's okay with me. I'll assess his state and maybe give his doctor a call.'

'What about the interview with Ash?'

'Tell Nikki where I've gone, and ask her if you can sit in. And ask him about the barn at Ruddick's Farm.'

Joseph picked up his jacket and pulled it on. 'I shouldn't be too long. He's probably just a bit overwrought.'

'Go careful, Sarge.'

* * *

Joseph arrived at the house to find the front door open. He called out, but receiving no answer he went inside.

Dominic Jarvis was sitting on his sofa with his head in his hands. His fingers were wet with escaping tears.

Joseph knelt down beside him and tried to comfort him. 'We really are doing our best, Dominic, and we do have some leads now. We are following them up, and when I get some answers, I promise I'll tell you straightaway.' He put an arm around the shaking shoulders. 'I wouldn't lie to you, so I can't say we are close to finding out what happened, but we do know a lot more than we did.'

'If you'd done this a long while ago,' Dominic choked out the words, 'Then maybe she'd be back here with me now.'

'I'm sorry, really I am, but I can't change the past. I can only tell you that we have a full investigation in progress now, and we *will* find out what happened, I know we will.'

'Too late, too late for Dina, and for me.'

Joseph didn't like the way Dominic's voice slurred. 'Dominic? Have you taken something?'

'Too late. I'm sorry, but I don't believe you will find her after all this time, and I . . . well, I can't wait any longer, it's just too painful. I can't do this anymore.' Dominic looked straight at Joseph and very clearly said, 'You really should have found her by now.' Then he slumped across the sofa.

'Dominic! Dominic! Speak to me! Stay with me, come on, man.' Joseph tried to stand him up and get him walking, but he was too far gone, a dead weight. Even Joseph could not support him, and he laid him on the floor and turned him on his side. He checked Dominic's air passage with one hand and pulled his phone from his pocket with the other.

'Ambulance! Emergency! Category A! Overdose, patient not responding.' Joseph rattled off the address and answered the usual questions, then stood up and hunted around to see if he could find what Dominic had taken. He found nothing and he couldn't leave him, so he pulled a rug from the sofa and wrapped it around the unconscious form. Dominic was breathing, but it was shallow and laboured. 'Come on! Come on!'

After what seemed an eternity, but in reality only around six minutes, a green-clad first responder arrived, carrying bags and medical equipment. Joseph told him what he knew then left the paramedic working on Dominic while he went to search for whatever drugs he had taken.

In the bathroom, Joseph found a plastic bag and several tablet boxes, all empty.

He showed the paramedic. The boxes had contained anti-depressants and Paracetamol, but they had no way of knowing what had been in the bag, or how many tablets had been taken.

'I suppose you have no idea how long ago he took these?'

'He rang me about twenty minutes ago and he sounded weird then. That's why I came to check on him. He gets pretty manic sometimes. I just thought he was upset.'

'The ambulance is two minutes from here, but he's not in a good way, mate.' The paramedic had done all he could. 'I reckon he took most of this stuff some while ago. Any idea what brought this on?'

Joseph nodded sadly. 'Oh yes. I know exactly why he's done it. His twin sister went missing two years ago, and he blames us for not finding her.'

'Ah shame, that's seriously shitty.'

'Could be said.'

The paramedic stood up. 'Good, the crew are here. We'll rush him to Greenborough Hospital. Are you going with him?'

'No, but I'll get someone over there straightaway. Thanks for what you've done.'

'Sorry to say this, but I think it was too little, too late.'

'That's what he thought about our investigation.'

'You can't save them all, mate. I wish we could, but . . .' He shrugged and stood back for his colleagues to take over. 'You can only do your best.'

As Dominic Jarvis was placed on the stretcher, Joseph wondered why he so often felt that his best was just not good enough.

* * *

'Vonnie! Vonnie!' Niall entered the CID room at a gallop.

'She's with the boss in interview room 2. They are grilling Gibson Ash. What's so important?' asked Cat.

'I've been talking to one of Carver's drivers.' Niall was almost babbling with excitement. 'My snout set up a meeting. This guy is due to collect Carver later today, and then take him to an as yet undisclosed address. If I can get a tracker to him, he will put it in the car! We could have Carver behind bars by tonight!'

'Jeez! The boss needs to hear this.'

Dave looked up. 'Just caught the tail end of that. I'll go interrupt the interview. Cat, you get up to IT and see if you can get clearance for a tracking device.' He gave Niall a hearty pat on the back. 'Well done, lad! That's the best thing I've heard in years.'

Dave hurried downstairs to the interview rooms and spoke to Nikki. She didn't look pleased at the interruption, but when she realised what he was saying, a triumphant grin spread across her face. She suspended the interview and she and Yvonne followed him back upstairs.

'You are sure he can be trusted?' she asked Niall.

'Sure as I can be, ma'am. But believe me, Carver's men have lived under a reign of terror with that man. Most of them were only working for him because he had some kind of hold over them or their families. Now they want out, and they want to see Carver behind bars'

'Good enough.' Nikki turned to Dave. 'As soon as Cat's back with the tracker, get it sorted and go see uniform. They'll want cars on full alert to take him down when he arrives at his final destination. I'll notify the super. Any idea of the time of this pick up, Niall?'

'He thought it would be around four p.m., give or take, but he can't be sure. Things sometimes change, and whenever he gets the call he has to go.'

'Can he notify you when he's mobile?'

'He will, then he'll break contact and it will be down to us and the tracker.'

Dave glanced at the clock. It was just after midday. 'What about Gibson Ash, ma'am? The clock will be ticking for how long we can hold him.'

'I'll go straight back down as soon as I've seen Greg Woodhall.' She looked around. 'Joseph not back yet?'

'Haven't heard from him, ma'am. Maybe Mr Jarvis has thrown another wobbly and the sarge is doing his social worker bit.'

'Almost right. He was doing his first responder bit.' Joseph walked into the office and flopped down in the nearest chair. 'Dominic Jarvis overdosed earlier. I've been trying to keep him alive until the medics could work on him.'

'Successfully?' asked Nikki.

'He was still alive when they got him into the ambulance, but they weren't hopeful.'

'Just when we are getting close to finding what happened to his sister,' murmured Nikki. 'Silly, silly man.'

'And Gibson Ash?' Joseph asked.

'I'd only just started with him when we got the news.'

'What news?'

'Ah, of course, you won't know.' She smiled broadly. 'Come with me to see Mr Ash and as we go, I'll fill you in on some very exciting news indeed.'

* * *

'Interview resumed at 12.18 hours. Present are . . .' Nikki completed the formalities and sat down opposite Ash and James Dooley, the duty solicitor. 'So far you have confirmed that you knew Dina Jarvis, but insist that you never knew what happened to her, is that correct?'

'She just disappeared. I had no idea where she went. I still don't.'

'But you worked for Freddie Carver procuring women for his sleazy clubs?'

'No! Well, I represented a lot of people. I am an entrepreneur, so I was scouting for talented artists, not prostitutes.'

'Come on, Gibson! Carver wouldn't know a talented artist if he tripped over one. He wanted girls, any kind, as long as they could pull the punters.'

'I had nothing to do with that! Carver has a couple of legit clubs too, and he does have some half-decent cabaret artists. That's what he paid me to look for.'

'And the lovely Dina was one of those?'

'Yes. I was bowled over by her. She was the complete package, good looks, voice of an angel, and she could dance too. She was a real keeper.'

Nikki glared at him. 'So what happened? Started handling the merchandise, did you?'

Gibson Ash stared at her balefully. 'You've got this so wrong, Detective.'

'Then why don't you shine a light in my darkness, Mr Ash?'

'DI Galena.' The weary tones of James Dooley interrupted them. 'My client has volunteered to help you in any way he can, if you wouldn't mind at least being civil to him?'

Nikki gritted her teeth. The man clearly did not know her. By her standards, she *was* being civil.

Joseph stepped in, saying politely, 'What car did you drive when you were "negotiating" for Dina to audition, Mr Ash?'

'The same car I have now, an Audi.'

'Model?'

'A saloon, an A6.'

'Nice car.'

'I like it.'

'Did Dina like it too?'

'She said it was really posh, and yes, she loved it. Why?'

'Did you spend a lot of time with Dina Jarvis?'

Gibson Ash paused. 'A fair bit. I heard her sing a couple of times, then I took her to a hotel that has a dance floor, just to see how good her dancing was, and I probably saw her about six or seven times while I was setting up her proper audition in London.'

'Did you take her to London?'

'We were due to go, but that was when she disappeared.' He sat back. 'To be honest, Detective, I wanted to find a proper agency to represent her. She was worth more than Freddie's clubs. I wanted her to really *make* it, you know, musicals, recordings, maybe the West End? She was that good.'

Nikki stared at him, trying to read his open and rather too innocent face. 'Did you have sex with her?'

Gibson Ash tensed.

'You don't have to answer that,' said Dooley.

'I think he does.' Nikki pinned him with her icy stare.

'We got quite close. She was a sweet girl, nothing like the others that I'd had dealings with.' He clasped his hands together and stared down at them. 'She wasn't chasing fame. I don't think she had any idea just how good she was. She had a naivety about her, and it was pretty refreshing after some of the women that . . .' His voice trailed off. 'Anyway, no, we never got to sleep together. We kissed, but no more than that. I think,' he paused, 'I think there might have been someone else.'

'Did she say that?'

'Not in as many words.'

'Did you want to take things further?'

He looked up, but at Joseph not Nikki. 'Yes, I did. She was gorgeous. I'd have to have been some kind of eunuch not to.'

'And you didn't push your luck?'

'No, I did not.' He gave her that infuriatingly innocent look again. 'I think she wanted to, but something stopped her, so what could it be, except another man?' He shrugged. 'Maybe it was for the best, because I don't think my employer would have been too happy about it.'

'Freddie Carver?'

The man mutely nodded.

'I think you should know that there is a very good chance that later today, your "employer" could be sitting in that very same chair, only he'll be answering some rather different questions.'

'I wouldn't bank on that,' he said bleakly.

'We'll see, shall we?'

'You might think you know where he is, but you won't get him. He still has allies, even though some of his men have sold him out.'

'And you?'

'We, that is, me and the group of men I work with, were told to get away from this area. We would be contacted at a later date.'

Joseph looked at Nikki and nodded towards Keel's notebook.

Nikki went on. 'Thank you for that. Now back to the disappearance of Dina Jarvis. For the benefit of the recording, DS Easter is showing Mr Ash a diary.'

Joseph opened it at the sketch of the wooden barn. 'Do you recognise this place?'

Ash looked at it blankly. 'No.'

'You never took Miss Jarvis there?'

'I don't know what it is, or where it is. How could I take her there?'

Joseph turned a page. 'Would you say this is a good likeness of the front of your car?'

Ash sat back and frowned. 'It is an Audi A6, yes, but it doesn't have to be mine. What is this crazy book?'

'Not too many A6 saloons in these parts,' Joseph murmured almost to himself. 'Far too good for travelling across muddy lanes and byroads. Must cost around £60,000 new, so more a city car, wouldn't you say?'

Nikki nodded.

'What is all this?' Gibson Ash looked scared again. 'I had nothing to do with her going AWOL, I promise you that. Think about it. She was my golden goose, my ticket to get away from Carver. I was devastated when she disappeared. Why the hell would I kill her?'

'I don't recall mentioning that she was dead?'

'It's a figure of speech, DI Galena,' said Dooley slowly, 'as you well know. "Why kill the goose that lays the golden egg?" And I have to ask the same question, because it seems to me that my client had a very good reason to keep her safe, don't you think?'

Nikki glowered, but was forced to agree. She didn't for one moment think that Ash was snowy white. In fact he probably had two strings to his bow — looking for real talent, and finding girls for Freddie's sex work. But she wasn't convinced that he had abducted Dina, and although the thought of going back to the drawing board was a depressing one, it looked like that was where they were heading.

'Okay, you are free to go. But do not leave Greenborough. I want you to book straight back into the Alma and stay there until I say you can go. Is that clear?'

Ash nodded furiously. 'Yes, I'll do that.'

'You'd better, Mr Ash. This is not a polite request, it's an order.'

Outside, Joseph asked, 'You trust him to stay?'

'No, but he might surprise us. And there's something about his story that rings true, isn't there?'

'I think he did want out from Carver's clutches, and what better way to go than on the arm of a beautiful girl who could make him rich.'

Nikki leaned back against the corridor wall. 'So, they *were* planning a trip to London for an audition, they *did* hang out together, and he did ferry her around in his car. Mmm, and he did fancy her.'

'But he came to a grinding halt at the suggestion of anything more than a kiss.' Joseph pulled a face. 'Because she already had someone else?'

'Or more likely because she was a virgin.' Nikki raised an eyebrow. 'She'd held out for all this time, maybe she wanted to be absolutely sure that this young Lothario was not just going to have his wicked way and then bugger off.'

'But what if someone else *was* lurking in the background? Someone who was not happy about her hanging around with a well-heeled and charming villain with a flash car? Someone who maybe wanted her for himself?'

'Perhaps we should talk to her three suitors again — Robby Lyons, Arthur Kirkby and the diarist himself, Keel Chandler.'

Together they walked back up the stairs to Nikki's office.

'Let's see what the team have found out about those three guys, shall we? Then maybe we'll pay them another visit.'

'I should ring and check on Dominic Jarvis. I guess the officer watching him would have rung if he didn't make it, but I'd like to know what the score is.'

'Definitely, and I'll see how arrangements are going for apprehending Carver.'

'I hope Ash wasn't right about not knowing what Freddie is up to. This grass of a chauffeur with a tracker thing does seem a bit *convenient*, doesn't it?'

'I know, but we have to go along with it. Freddie's men are falling like flies, and the driver could be kosher. We'll soon see, and the worst that could happen is that while we are chasing one car, Freddie does a bunk in another one.'

'Any news from Jessie?' whispered Joseph.

'No, and you know what they say about no news being good news.'

* * *

As soon as Niall had delivered the tracker to Freddie's driver, he returned to the station and caught up with Yvonne. She was still immersed in Keel Chandler's sketchbook.

'There's something here that I ought to understand,' she said pensively. 'But for the love of Mike, I can't think what it is.'

'It will come to you, it always does. It's what you do best, sifting through information looking for connections.'

Yvonne rubbed her eyes. 'I suppose we will all be on high alert to take Carver down, but I'd really love to talk to the author of this tome.'

'There are enough troops on the ground to bring down a small country, let alone one man. I'm sure they won't miss us. Go have a word with the DI or the sarge.'

'Don't you want to be in on the action?'

'You know me, I love a good scrap, but as it's my engagement party this weekend, I rather think I should protect my boyish good looks for my bride to be.'

'You muppet! She'd love you just as much with a black eye!'

'Ah, but I really need to impress my future mother-in-law, don't I? She's coming to the engagement party and I don't think she's too happy about her daughter marrying a copper,' he added, with feeling.

'Oh right, I see.' A wide smile spread over Yvonne's face. 'So we actually get to see the sarge's ex-wife. Now that will be something, won't it?'

'She's not a patch on the DI.'

'Niall! Don't even go there!'

'Well, they are so well-suited, I just thought . . .'

'Don't think. You know how dangerous that can be in your case.' She looked around. 'Are they back from the Ash interview?'

'They are in her office, I think.'

'Then I'll see if I can organise a trip to Carter's Fen. Nothing should happen to that pretty face of yours out there.'

* * *

She was lying on the kitchen floor. She had tried to get out of the cottage, but found that the doors were locked from the outside and the keys had gone. She knew that she didn't have the strength to get back to her bedroom, and she had been so exhausted by her efforts that she simply lay on the cold tiles and closed her eyes.

The reason she had been trying to get out was to look for food.

Animals and birds ate berries and fruits. Cows ate grass. Maybe she could do the same. She had discovered some stale bread in a bin in the kitchen, and then some dry cereal, but she would need to supplement it. All she had in abundance was brackish water. And brackish or not, she knew that water would keep her alive for some time. It was just the hunger that tore at her stomach — oh yes, and the pain. She gave a short cackling laugh. But she could actually do something about that now, because she had found his stash of her tablets in the bread bin. She wasn't sure which was which, but they were all painkillers of some sort, so it didn't matter really.

As soon as she felt a little rested, she would get herself up, eat a crust of bread, then take some of the stronger pills. That would give her just enough respite to get back to her bedroom with her rations. She grimaced. And that's what they were, rations to keep her going until . . . what? There were several possibilities, but she held onto her belief that he would come back. Come back with proper food, chocolates and even flowers perhaps? He'd tell her he loved her and get her a hot water bottle for her aching back and fluff her pillows to make her comfortable. He had never meant to leave her, she was sure of that. Something had to have happened. He'd cared for her for so long, he'd never abandon her now. He would come for her. He would.

CHAPTER TWENTY-THREE

After lunch, Nikki called together an impromptu meeting of her team. She had a feeling that they were very close to finding out what had happened to Dina Jarvis. She also needed something to occupy her mind until they knew whether Freddie Carver had been apprehended.

'Has anyone got anything interesting on the three musketeers — Lyons, Kirkby and Chandler?'

'Lyons was really taken with Dina at the time, and doesn't seem to have settled with anyone else since. A few casual girlfriends, but nothing serious,' Dave said. 'I think he had his heart set on Dina and no one else has matched up to her.'

'So he would have been pretty pissed off when she was sweet-talked by Ash,' added Nikki. 'Angry enough to confront her about it, do you think?'

'He does have a temper,' said Joseph. 'I saw that when I interviewed him. He was extremely reluctant to speak to the police. He could have done as you said, and maybe lashed out and hit her too hard. I don't think he would have intentionally hurt her, but if he saw red, who knows?'

'And Kirkby?'

'He was much more laid back, almost flippant, but I got the impression that he was also deeply hurt by her.' Joseph frowned. 'This has probably got nothing to do with anything, but I don't think he liked Dominic much. Apparently Kirkby, who loved her singing voice, had been urging her to make a demo in a mate's studio. Dominic wasn't keen, and Dina turned down the offer.'

'I've found out something else about him,' volunteered Cat. 'Kirkby worked with Dominic Jarvis for a year or so, and my enquiries tell me that you are probably right, Sarge. He didn't get on with Dominic at all.'

'Where was that?'

'The psychiatric hospital at Needham Hall. They were both nurses there and both specialised in caring for the elderly. After a time, Kirkby threw in the towel and went for the job at the nursing home where he is now.'

'And Dominic?'

'He had to give up after his sister disappeared. He was off sick for ages. The Jarvis twins weren't badly off, by the way. Apart from the mortgage-free property, there was some kind of legacy a while back, they were left a considerable sum of money. He's not working anywhere at present.'

'And I suspect he won't be working for some time, if ever.' Joseph's voice was grave. 'He's in ICU and they are still saying that his chances of survival are poor.'

Nikki felt a chill of recognition at hearing those words. It was what they had said about her lovely Hannah. They had been right, it had been a very long time with a lot of heartache, until she finally gave up. She blinked and moved the conversation on. 'So, do we think Kirkby is a possible candidate?'

Joseph sounded reflective. 'I'd be surprised, but I got the feeling that I wasn't seeing the real Arthur Kirkby. It was almost as though he was putting on an act for us. Good bloke, and all that, but underneath, well, I'm not sure what was going on. I think he's deep, that one.'

'And deep can be dangerous,' added Dave.

'And then we come to Keel Chandler,' continued Nikki.

'Yvonne and I have been studying his book, and we both agree that he needs to be interviewed again. We are quite certain that this diary is telling us something, but we don't know what.' Joseph shook his head.

'Is he actually mentally ill? Could he have been so infatuated with Dina that he killed her rather than let Gibson Ash take her from him?' asked Nikki.

Joseph frowned. 'He certainly has learning difficulties and psychological problems, hence we can't rule that thought out, but my personal impression of him tells me no. I don't think he would hurt anything or anyone, especially not someone he cared about.'

'Then we should go talk to him again.'

'Can I take that one, ma'am?' asked Yvonne. 'I'd really like the chance to speak to Keel.'

'Me too,' chipped in Joseph.

'Okay. As I'm getting really jumpy about the Carver takedown and I don't want to wear my carpet out, I'll drive you. It's my old stamping ground, and I don't want you two wandering aimlessly around the fen lanes for hours on end.'

Yvonne grinned. 'That's a relief. I know this area like the back of my hand, but Rainer's Gowt and that part of Carter's Fen are still a mystery to me.'

'So, anything else?'

Cat stood up. 'One thing, ma'am. I've had a text from Derbyshire and it seems that the Met have identified something buried beneath the flooring of the garden room at Freddie Carver's old property. They are probably firing up the Kango drills as we speak.'

'If they find the remains of his first wife, he'll be looking at life.' Nikki smiled grimly.

'Apart from all the other crimes that his men are fessing up to,' chuckled Dave, rubbing his hands together.

'Don't want to put a downer on proceedings, folks, but we haven't caught him yet,' Cat said.

'A mere formality,' said Dave. 'This time that villain is ours! And he can kiss goodbye to his sunshine home on the Costa del Crime.'

* * *

Nikki parked the Land Rover outside the Chandlers' cottage and looked around. A strong wind was blowing salty ozone in across the marsh. She sighed. She had always loved this desolate spot. Once upon a time the Chandler family had been her great aunt's nearest neighbours. She wondered if old lady Chandler would recognise her.

'Well, well. Little Nikki Reed! My, how you've grown, duck!'

That answered her question. 'Mrs Chandler, how are you?'

'Good enough, all things considered.'

'Is Keel around? We have returned his notebook and we'd like a quick word, if it's no trouble?'

'No trouble at all. He'll be back any minute. I'll get the kettle on.' She looked at Joseph and Yvonne. 'Three of you? You're not planning on taking him away, are you?' She cocked her head and smiled.

'You'd probably like us to — give you a break.'

'Oh aye! But the lad's got a good heart and he does his best, even if he sometimes drives me to distraction.' Mrs Chandler poured water from a big jug into the kettle and placed it on the range. 'I'm guessing it's about the missing lass?'

Nikki nodded. 'We have to find her, Mrs C. It's a mystery that has gone on for too long now, and her brother is beside himself.'

'It's not good when you are left with no answers. One of my sons got washed out to sea, and the sea took a very long while to give him back to me. We dint know what had happened to him. He just dint come home one night. It was a bad time and no mistake.'

'I don't remember that.'

The old woman sighed. 'Long before your time, lass. And I nivver said owt after. No point, was there? No amount of talking would bring him back.'

But I need to talk about my girl, thought Nikki. *I want her memory to live on forever and you can't do that if you bury it.*

'Hello.' Keel pushed the door open and smiled warmly at them. 'I saw your car. I like Land Rovers.'

'Me too,' said Nikki with an even bigger smile. 'I'm Nikki. My aunt used to live near here.'

'In the empty cottage down on Carter's Fen?'

'That's the one.'

'I hope you don't mind, I searched it once, to look for Dina, but she wasn't there.'

'I don't mind at all, it was very thoughtful of you to look for her'

'I've searched everywhere, Nikki.' He shrugged and frowned. 'So why do I think she's still here somewhere?'

'Can my two friends ask you about your book, please, Keel?'

'Oh yes, they are the police so they can ask anything they want.' He looked over his shoulder towards the door. 'And you may want to check your car. The radio in it was making funny noises.'

Nikki frowned. 'Okay, I'll do that.'

Outside, a gust of wind almost took her breath away. She opened the car door and slipped into the driver's seat. It wasn't her car radio, it was her police radio that was crackling loudly.

She listened intently, but the static made it impossible to make anything out. Then she heard one word — Carver.

Nikki gulped and wondered what on earth was going down. She had to know! Then she remembered that you could get a signal about a quarter of a mile back down the lane. It would take too long to go inside and ask to use the landline.

Nikki leapt out of the car and ran to the cottage. 'Stay put, Joseph! I'll be back, okay?'

Without waiting for a reply, she jumped back into the 4x4 and accelerated away. After three minutes, she picked up patchy radio contact. 'Nikki Galena approaching Carter's Fen. What is occurring? Over.'

The signal was breaking up but just about intelligible. 'Carver swapped cars. He is a passenger in the back of a black Lexus. The driver is the only other occupant, and the vehicle is suspected to be making for Salter's Quay. We believe he has a boat waiting on the river.'

'I can get there on the back lanes. Show me in pursuit.'

'DI Galena! Wait for back up. We believe he is armed. Repeat, he is armed.'

'Sorry, I'm losing you.' Nikki switched off the radio and put her foot down. She glanced at the clock. The tide would be high now, and on the turn. The perfect time to take a boat downriver and out into the Wash. Then into the North Sea, and speeding towards Holland and freedom.

If you made it to the boat.

Nikki set her jaw. Like so many places on the fen, Salter's Quay was a bastard to find, unless you knew the way. There was a good chance that any pursuing police cars would have one hell of a time finding the right road in. She had a head start, she knew precisely which route the Lexus driver would have to take to get there, and she was approaching from the other direction. If the gods were in her favour, there was something she could do to put a big fat full stop to Freddie's escape plan.

She gritted her teeth and took a deep breath. All she needed was perfect timing, excellent driving skills, nerves of steel, and a skip-load of luck! She grinned darkly. Sounded good to her!

As she flew around the lanes, churning up mud and scattering grit in her wake, she reminded herself of all the evil things Freddie had done. She saw Jessie, tears streaming down her face and condemned to years of living in purgatory. She thought about Graham receiving severed fingers, knowing that young women were being terrorised and probably killed, and unless he sentenced the woman he loved to the same fate, he could do nothing about it. She thought about the killers that Carver had introduced into her beloved Fenlands. Heartless, murdering assassins like Fabian and Venables.

It was time to put a stop to all of it.

It was time to draw the line.

A few minutes later, Nikki slowed down. She was on the road to Salter's Quay. It was a long, gently winding byroad with two narrow lanes. The turn off to the Quay was about halfway along, and Carver would be coming towards her from the opposite direction.

She stopped the car and took a pair of birdwatcher's binoculars from the glove compartment. In the distance she could see a single vehicle, travelling like the wind. Her eyes narrowed. It was black, a big saloon.

A lone 4x4 was a commonplace sight on the Fens. Farmers used them, land workers used them, waterway maintenance operatives used them, the world and his wife used them. Nikki eased forward, carefully judging the speed of the approaching vehicle and the exact position of the turn-off for the quay.

For the first time, a frisson of fear tingled and skittered along her shoulder blades. She had a plan. It was a good one — if it worked. She would have one chance.

With a muttered prayer to Joseph's God, she jammed her foot down. The oncoming car slowed very slightly. A tad nervous, maybe?

So he should be.

Nikki gripped the wheel tightly and sped past the Lexus. At just the right moment, she gave the steering wheel a wrench, then corrected it again immediately. The rear of the heavy Land Rover slewed across the road. With a crash and a scream of tearing metal, it impacted with the back end of the Lexus. Nikki controlled her skid and brought the vehicle to a halt.

As she released her seat belt she could see the black car spin like a top, and nosedive down into the steep irrigation ditch that ran along the side of the lane.

'Hole in one!' she yelped, and opened the door. 'Got you, you bastard!'

She ran over to the ditch and saw the driver struggling to get out of the crashed car. He had got his window down and she heard him call for help.

'Climb out of the window. I'll help you!' Nikki slithered into the cold water of the ditch.

'Can't. I think my ankle's broken.'

'Have you turned the engine off?'

'Yes.'

'Okay, then sit tight. This car is going nowhere. Help will be here shortly.' *Well, it will if any of my colleagues have managed to find the road to Salter's Quay.*

All she wanted to know was what state Freddie Carver was in.

The words, "We think he's armed!" drifted into her head.

She looked through the back window at a crumpled heap of a man, jammed fast against the far door and unable to right himself.

She would have laughed if he hadn't been pointing a handgun directly at her.

'It's not loaded!' the driver called from the front of the car. 'He keeps it hidden in the back for emergencies, but I took the ammunition out before he got in.'

Nikki watched the fat man pull the trigger, over and over and over. And then he threw the gun at her and let rip a string of obscenities.

242

Nikki gave an exaggerated sigh. 'Oh dear, what a greeting! Now it's my turn. Where shall I start? Ah yes . . . Frederick Carver, I am arresting you on suspicion of the kidnapping and blackmail of Police Constable Graham Hildred. You do not have to say anything. But it may harm your defence if you do not mention when questioned something which you later rely on in court. Anything you do say may be given in evidence.'

Nikki had never been happier to repeat the words. The sound of approaching blues and twos made her feel even better.

'Thank you for disarming his gun,' she said to the driver. 'I will make sure it is recorded that your actions probably saved my life.'

'Lucky really, because he was supposed to stick with the first car.' He gave her a grin, and then winced. 'Something must have spooked him because he ditched it and I was called for a switch.'

Something or someone, thought Nikki, thinking of the mole in the station. 'Well, thanks anyway.'

'You're welcome, lady. I've had enough of this man. Just lock him up and melt the bleeding key.' He grinned again. 'Where did you learn to drive like that?'

'Sorry? Don't know what you mean. That was an accident, wasn't it?'

'Oh yeah! Happens all the time on these lanes. Just our bad luck, I guess.'

* * *

Nikki made sure that Carver had been removed from the ditch and was wearing handcuffs, and that his driver was being cared for prior to the ambulance arriving. Then she drove back across the Fens to where she had left Joseph and Yvonne. She had managed to get Control to phone the Chandlers' cottage, so at least they would not be worrying about her.

As she climbed out of the damaged Land Rover, they were waiting for her.

'I don't know whether to hug you or give you a right telling off,' grumbled Joseph.

'Both seem appropriate,' added Yvonne. 'But I'd go for the hug. Our boss has actually taken out the Fat Man, single-handed!'

'That's why I'd go for the telling off.' Joseph glowered at Nikki. 'There was no need to go off alone like that. We were right here with you.'

Nikki tried to look contrite, but it was tough when you felt so elated. 'I'm sorry, really I am. The fact is I had no idea what had happened or where he was until I was half a mile away. Then I didn't have the time to get back here and collect you. It would have been too late to catch him.'

Joseph looked at her dented and scraped vehicle. 'That looks expensive.'

'Worth every penny! And I must say my new car was perfect for it. I don't think it would have worked in a lighter, less well-built model.'

'Bit of luck you weren't driving a police vehicle, you'd be well popular.'

'I'd still have done it.'

'Me too.' Joseph gave in and hugged her. 'Well done! Now if we can only find Dina Jarvis, it will be just about perfect, won't it?'

'What did Keel tell you while I was away?'

'Let's get back to the station, and we'll fill you in there.' He gave her a big grin. 'I just can't wait to see that evil bastard sitting in a cell! I'm thinking of taking photographs and emailing them to every copper in the country.'

'I'm not sure that would be a good move for your career prospects, although I do understand the sentiment,' Nikki said.

CHAPTER TWENTY-FOUR

Nikki had never before seen such celebrations at Greenborough police station. It was as if a war had ended. Superintendent Greg Woodhall had even conveyed congratulations from the Met, which had to be a first. But Nikki's delight at having Carver finally banged up was overshadowed by a feeling of unease. This was mainly to do with Dina Jarvis, but also with the fact that no one had heard anything of Fabian. Venables was confirmed to be on his way to the Netherlands, but Fabian had dropped off the radar, and that meant that Jessie Nightingale could not share in the festivities.

'Ben is travelling over from Derby.' Cat was elated at the arrest and hadn't been able to wait to tell him. 'He is *really* impressed with you, ma'am.'

'Well, after all the work he did on the Fern case, he of all people deserves to see Carver in a cell. He's a good copper — Ben.'

'Actually I'm not sure he wants to stay in the job, ma'am.' Cat shook her head. 'He's disillusioned with things in his area. He reckons the guys and gals are a good bunch but the way things are going, well, he can't see a future in policing.'

'That's sad. He's the kind of policeman the force cannot afford to lose.'

'Would you talk to him, ma'am? He respects you. I'm sure he'd listen.'

'Yes, Cat. I will, if you think it would help.'

'If you can't change his mind, then no one can. Thank you.'

'No problem. Now, much as I regret being a party pooper, could we have a catch-up regarding what Keel Chandler had to say? Cat, gather up the others and come to my office. We all need to talk.'

* * *

'I'm worried on two counts.' Nikki sat at her desk, looking nothing like a person who had just apprehended the county's most wanted.

Joseph watched her carefully. He knew that when she said she was worried, she meant it.

'The men Carver would have chosen to go after Jessie and Graham would be Mr Fabian and Mr Venables. Venables has been seen boarding a plane to Schiphol Airport, so we know that, for a while at least, he is of no concern to us, but Fabian is a different matter entirely. We do not know his whereabouts, and he is a very dangerous man indeed.'

'Will he still want to complete whatever Carver had in mind, knowing that Freddie's plans have been scuppered?' asked Dave. 'Especially if Carver isn't around to pay him.'

'I should think that if Carver activated Fabian, the money would have changed hands immediately,' Joseph said. 'Fabian is lethal. Carver would believe that if he paid that man to do a job, it would be done, no question.'

'I agree.' Nikki lowered her voice. 'By the way, I have just been speaking to Greg Woodhall, and Carver has to be moved to another station, out of the area. We cannot risk him being held here if we've been infiltrated by one of his men. Right now he is being watched by a small team of designated trusted officers, but even so we cannot risk anything getting in, or being smuggled out for him. So, Cat, maybe Ben Radley will have to travel a bit further unless he gets here soon.'

Cat just nodded. Joseph secretly thought that maybe the aim of Ben's trip was more to visit a certain detective than a prisoner.

'Joseph, give Mickey a bell and ask him about Fabian. Any news would be gratefully received.'

Joseph stood up and went to his office.

'Mickey? Sergeant Joe here.'

'Good to hear you, Joe. Give our warmest wishes to Inspector Nik, won't you? Even Raymond is well impressed. Tell her, from the whole Leonard family, nice one!'

'Does news travel at the speed of light around the Carborough?'

'It does when you listen to a police radio. Er, forget I said that. How can I help?'

'Fabian.'

'Gone to ground. And Raymond says he has something planned, or he would have joined the rush to leave.'

'If you hear anything, anything at all, can you ring me?'

'If I do, he's all yours, Joe, and you're welcome to him. Just don't get within touching distance of him. Be careful, Joe, won't you?'

'And you, kiddo. Just keep away from those really bad men, okay?'

Mickey laughed. 'I do — other than my uncle. See you!'

Back in Nikki's office, Joseph had little to offer. 'As we suspected, Fabian is still around and evidently planning something.'

'Blast it! Well, there's little we can do other than make sure every available officer on the streets is keeping their eyes peeled.'

'The Leonards will keep us informed too. He's the kind of man that even *they* don't want contaminating their manor.'

'So, on to Dina Jarvis.' She looked at Joseph. 'How is Dominic?'

'No change, but he's still holding on.'

'I'd like to be able to give him some good news, wouldn't you?'

Joseph nodded. He knew that Nikki had always been certain that even though Hannah had been in a vegetative state, she could hear and understand what was being said to her. 'Yes, I'd like to tell him that we'd found her.'

'We can do nothing until Fabian shows his ugly face, so we concentrate on Dina, okay?'

They all murmured their agreement.

'Yvonne? Joseph? Tell us about your afternoon with Keel Chandler.'

'He has a butterfly brain,' said Yvonne. 'It jumps from one thing to another, that's why his notebook is so jumbled.'

Joseph joined in. 'What we did ascertain was that he certainly did see Gibson and Dina together on several occasions, hence the drawing of the Audi.'

'But because of the way he doesn't make connections, that didn't mean that the Audi was ever anywhere near Ruddick's Farm.' Yvonne leafed through her pocket book. 'It seems that he was writing about at least three different occurrences that all involved Dina, but at different times and possibly with different people, not just Gibson Ash.'

'And the potato shed at Ruddick's Farm is one of those occurrences?' asked Nikki.

Yvonne nodded at Joseph.

'Yes, for sure,' he continued. 'We think that whatever happened to Dina either started or ended in something that happened there. And Keel witnessed some or all of it, but—'

'He has blocked it out,' Yvonne finished for him. 'He tried to tell us, but whether it was because of his grandmother's presence, or maybe because he just can't face it, Keel couldn't tell us what he saw.'

'Couldn't or wouldn't?' asked Cat.

'Absolutely *couldn't*,' Joseph confirmed. 'He really struggled. We were wondering whether, if we got him away from the cottage and into a neutral situation, perhaps he might be able to remember.'

'I thought,' said Yvonne, 'That he might like a guided tour of a working police station? I think it would delight his kaleidoscope mind.'

'Then if he turns out to be the abductor, we could just keep him here.' Cat grinned.

'If he turns out to be that, I'll buy you all Danish pastries for a year,' Joseph returned.

'And now, you lot, back to the potato shed,' Nikki said quietly. 'I find it very disconcerting that it was the place where we discovered Lilli's body. We have a confirmed connection now between Lilli and Freddie Carver's men, so we have to consider that the use of that shed was deliberate, not random. Which means that Carver's men could have taken Dina there, does it not?'

Joseph's thoughts had followed a very similar track. 'We think that as some of Carver's men are local or have been based here for a while, they could have got talking to the Ruddick boys.'

'And in conversation over a pint in the Leather Bottle, a pub they all frequent, one of them might have mentioned that they have a nice new selection shed at the farm,' Yvonne joined in. 'Meaning that the old one was out of use.'

'And Ruddick's Farm is about as isolated as you can get.'

Cat frowned. 'You don't think the Ruddick brothers could have been involved with Carver?'

Nikki shook her head. 'Very doubtful. They are not criminals. Not one of them has a record. They are hardworking farm boys, maybe not too bright, but nevertheless, Carver would scare the pants off them.'

Joseph felt a tiny niggle of concern. He wasn't sure why, but he didn't like the thought of that potato selection shed being connected in some way to Dina Jarvis. He picked up a small file of papers from the table in front of him. 'I photocopied Keel's artwork.' He handed them all a copy of one particular page. Ruddick's Barn and Keel's "night creatures."

Yvonne stared at the picture. 'This bothered me at first. But now I believe it is simpler than we thought. Those creatures do not represent Gibson Ash or the bad thing that happened to her, they are just the people that took Dina to the barn. The three figures are most likely Carver's men. Whatever Keel saw them do, it traumatised him so badly that he no longer knows what he saw.'

Nikki groaned. 'After two years of constant use, until recently anyway, it would be useless to search a filthy shed for trace elements or DNA.'

'But would it?' asked Cat. 'Forensics has moved on in the last few years.'

'But not in the Fens, Cat, and add to that the fact that our budgets have been slashed to ribbons. And as I don't have buddies in CSI to jump in and help us, we're stuffed as far as hi-tech equipment is concerned.'

'You have Professor Wilkinson.'

'I love him to bits, but he's not a miracle worker. He has budgets too.'

Joseph saw where Cat was going and nodded excitedly. 'He also has friends in the Fenland University, who have lots of gizmos and huge enthusiasm. I have even heard that they have their own body farm, somewhere discreet and very hush-hush. Forensics studies are big over there.'

Nikki looked miffed. 'Why don't I know about this?'

Dave chuckled. 'Probably because you never read memos that have nothing to do with the cases you are working on.'

'Fair cop, Harris. You think it's worth asking him?'

'Definitely.'

Yvonne was staring at the photocopied diary, apparently in a world of her own.

'Hello? Where have you gone?' Niall asked her. He turned to the others. 'I've seen this look before, folks. It could be something momentous.'

'Or it could be wind,' suggested Cat, and smirked.

'It could be nothing,' said Yvonne dreamily, 'but I need to get it off my chest, or it will drive me mad.'

Nikki leaned forward. 'We're all ears.'

'Two things. Niall, you saw Dina in a clinch with a man. You have now met Gibson Ash. Was it him?'

Niall sucked on his bottom lip and shut his eyes tightly. 'I hardly looked, but . . .' His eyes opened wide. 'No, I don't think it was Ash. The man she was with had sandy-coloured hair. Gibson Ash is dark. And what I saw was no chaste kiss, judging by where his hands were going. Hers too for that matter, that's why I looked away.'

Yvonne took a breath. 'Second: how many Ruddick boys are there?'

'Three,' answered Nikki immediately.

Yvonne stretched out her finger and hovered over the three night creatures in the picture. 'Three men. It was their father's barn. They might not be criminals, but did they take the gregarious Dina there to party? What colour hair do they have?'

'Two are light brown, one is sandy-coloured. Ryan Ruddick has sandy hair.'

* * *

Eve Anderson was in the kitchen, enjoying having company and someone to cook for.

Jessie was perched on a stool, watching her. 'I'm always impressed by confident cooks.' She tilted her head to one side as Eve deftly cut fresh ginger into wafer thin strips. 'I'm a kind of "Give it a try, but don't expect too much" sort of chef. I'm always disappointed in how my dishes turn out. They never look like the pictures in the recipe book.'

'My grandmother was a cook in a big manor house in Hampshire. I grew up watching her make marvellous concoctions from practically nothing. She said it came from trying to produce nourishing meals in wartime. Whatever, her love of cooking was certainly passed down to her grandchild.'

'It looks amazing. The ginger smells wonderful, doesn't it?'

Eve nodded. 'Does Graham cook?'

Jessie burst out laughing. 'He has trouble toasting bread! No, my Graham is a microwave salesman's dream. He uses it so often that he has to replace them on a regular basis. I don't think he's used a conventional oven in his life.'

'I'm sure he has lots of other worthy attributes.'

'In abundance, Eve. He's a good man, and I love him so much.'

'Then he'll come back from this. If you have love, you do.'

'That sounded like it came from the heart.'

'It came from personal experience, my dear, trust me.'

Jessie smiled and looked down. 'I do trust you. And thank you for what you are doing for me. It's a big thing, and neither of us will forget it, I promise you.'

'It's nothing. When this is all over, you must put it behind you and forget this awful time.'

'I might forget some things, Eve, but not you.'

'Oh, go on with you! You'll have us both in tears in a minute. Now pass me that jar of Chinese spices. I think those lads out there deserve a treat tonight.'

Jessie smiled broadly. 'I've never known anyone get the "workmen" to actually do any decorating! They are well into stripping the wallpaper.'

'Authenticity is the key to good deception.'

'Is that what you told them?'

Eve looked up to the ceiling, all innocence. 'I might have said something along those lines. But I can tell they are well trained. They are constantly on the alert, one-hundred-per-cent professional.'

'I just wish this were over.'

'I'm sure you do, child.' Eve felt a rush of affection for the young woman. 'I'm sure you do.'

CHAPTER TWENTY-FIVE

Once again, Nikki was leading the way out to Carter's Fen. This time they were returning to Ruddick's Farm, for a little chat with the three brothers. She and Joseph were in her Land Rover, which had sustained no serious damage, and Yvonne and Niall followed in a squad car. When they arrived at the farm, Joseph and Nikki went in alone.

They found Stan and Betty in the kitchen. Stan was reading the paper and Betty was chopping vegetables.

'The boys are upstairs getting changed. Denis and Clive are going into town after their dinner, and I expect Ryan will be going to the local for a pint.' Betty still looked tired and drawn, and Nikki wondered if all was well in the Ruddick household.

'I take it this is to do with that poor lass we found out here?' Stan folded up his paper and put it aside.

'In a way,' Nikki answered. 'Although we actually need to speak to them about an old case that might be connected in some way.'

Betty ran her hand through her hair. 'What would my sons know about anything? They are good boys, they've nivver been a scrap of trouble.' Her face was creased with worry.

Joseph's voice was calm and even. 'It's alright, Mrs Ruddick. They are local lads, and we need to know about someone the same age as them, who they might have known.'

Mrs Ruddick's face relaxed. 'Oh, I see. Of course.'

Stan looked at Nikki and raised his eyebrows. He nodded towards his wife. 'Worries about everything, that one.'

'And you don't, I suppose?' Betty's tone was sharp, leaving Nikki in no doubt that there was a distinct lack of domestic bliss in the Ruddick kitchen. Last time she had been here they had come close to arguing over something too. Oh, yes, Stan wanted to sell up, even though Betty had spent a great deal of money on the farmhouse. It seemed the boys weren't keen to continue with the family business. Now why would that be, I wonder? A steady income, hard work, but the Ruddicks had never shied away from that. They had a lovely home with every convenience and meals cooked for them. Surely that was every young man's dream, until he married and got some other poor soul to shoulder the burden of looking after him. Odd, she thought, very odd.

'Here they come now.' Betty looked towards the hallway. 'Stan, take the officers into the front room. They will be comfier there.'

'Hey, Mum! There's a cop car outside!' Clive almost ran into the kitchen.

'I know, son, and there are two police officers in the other room, waiting to talk to you. They need your help with something.'

The three young men walked slowly into the "best" room and looked suspiciously at Nikki and Joseph.

'You two were here when the girl was found,' Ryan stated flatly.

Nikki nodded. 'Sit down, lads. This shouldn't take too long.'

Denis and Clive took the sofa, and Ryan sat on a hard chair apart from them. Nikki noted his body language. He clearly had no wish to be close to his brothers, nor was he joining them for a night on the town. Alarm bells rang in her head. A family feud, no less.

'Were any of you ever friendly with a girl called Dina Jarvis?'

If alarm bells had rung earlier, an almighty great klaxon went off now.

Ryan had tensed. Nikki could see his hands tighten on the chair arms. The other two gasped.

'I'll assume you were friends, shall I?'

The silence was palpable.

'Would one of you three stooges like to add anything? Or even answer the question?' She looked at Joseph, and he shrugged.

'It's not a trick, boys. It's actually quite simple, or shall I offer you multiple choice answers?'

Still no one spoke.

'Okay. Clearly that one was too difficult. Try this for size. What happened in the defunct selection shed on that night two years ago when you brought Dina Jarvis here?'

The reaction to that was nothing less than bizarre.

Clive doubled forward, head in his hands, and began to cry.

Denis stared at Ryan, then began screaming obscenities at him. Ryan himself went white, his face a death mask.

'Okay, you three. I think we need to start from the beginning, don't you? And I need the truth, understand?' Her eyes narrowed to slits. 'I want some straight answers, and cut the hysterics. It's time to grow up. You first, Ryan, and the whole story, please.'

* * *

Eve didn't like the twilight. She found it eerie. The shadows were long and illusory, light came and went before fading into darkness, and she didn't always trust what her eyes were telling her.

She was working in her garden studio, although not producing a great deal. They had agreed that for the sake of the neighbours, she should keep to her normal routine. She had spoken with the nearest of them and sprinkled her conversation liberally with comments about her lovely niece, Michelle, and how delighted she was that the girl would want to spend time with her.

'You might call it a bit of a recuperation holiday really. Poor girl had glandular fever for ages, so she's staying with me for a while to get her strength back before returning to work.'

That had gone down easily, along with the fact that she had casually mentioned using Michelle's brother's decorating business to carry out the work on her new property. 'Keeping it in the family, you know. I'm so lucky that they had a cancellation *and* another job in this area. They are not local, you see. Michelle's family live in Loughborough. The boys are fitting me in in sort of shifts.' She had laughed conspiratorially. 'Mates' rates if I feed them and put John and his foreman up for a few nights. Not that I mind, dear, the more the merrier as far as I'm concerned, and I get my decorating done too! Win, win, I'd say, wouldn't you?'

She was a good liar, although she preferred to think of it as being a talented actress. She'd had a lot of practice in the old days. Eve sighed. She missed the excitement of her job. She missed a lot of things, as well as a few special people — one in particular.

She stretched. *Enough of that!* There was no use getting lost in a reverie, she needed to keep her wits about her. The men who were looking out for the young policewoman were perfectly competent professionals, but Eve had been in the business a lot longer than they had.

Eve put away her pastels and wiped her hands on a damp towel. It was time to go back inside and finish preparing dinner. She moved towards the door, then stopped in her tracks. Something was wrong. She had no idea what it was, but she never doubted her gut instinct.

Her stomach muscles had tightened, and all her senses were on alert, trying to source the cause of her discomfort.

Nothing was immediately apparent, but she went back to her artist's table and opened the big wooden storage box that she used for her pastels and painting materials. From the bottom drawer she carefully removed an object shrouded in a duster. Then she left the studio, leaving the lights on.

She moved to a shadowy spot in the garden and checked the gun. She had practised blindfolded, and could do it quickly and efficiently in the dark. She hoped that the gun would not be needed, but if it was, she had no doubt of her abilities. Proficiency in small arms is of course mandatory for all military organisations, but Eve had also been a long-serving member of the RAF Small Arms Association, and had more trophies stashed in her cupboards than most people had pairs of socks.

The gun she now held was a 9mm Browning Hi-power semi-automatic pistol. It was an L9A1 service pistol, loaded, well looked after and cleaned regularly. It made her feel a whole lot better about whatever it was that was worrying her.

After carefully watching the garden for several minutes, Eve moved stealthily into a border of shrubs that flanked the neighbour's fence. She made her way through the bushes until she had a clear view through the French windows into the house. Jessie was watching television in the lounge, and one of her guards could just be seen moving about in the dining room.

The side gate that connected to the front garden was unlocked and clipped back. Looking down the passageway, Eve could see the white van still parked on the drive. Nothing seemed anything other than normal, but she knew, in every part of her body and mind, that something was not right.

Then it came to her.

Smoke! She could smell smoke.

And then she saw it. Tiny tendrils of pale smoke were drifting out from the "builders'" works van.

Eve knew a diversionary tactic when she saw one, and she pulled out her phone and tapped the send button. She had already written the text message, *Fancy a pizza tonight? Love Eve* x. Nikki would receive it immediately.

That done, she took a deep breath. Eve had an intruder to deal with.

* * *

Ryan Ruddick was now a sickly shade of grey, but at least his brother had stopped swearing at him.

'I've been waiting for this since she went.'

'Why is that, Ryan?' Nikki asked.

'Because I knew you'd think I had something to do with her disappearance.'

'And didn't you? I mean, she disappeared the very next day after you and your brothers . . . What exactly did you and your brothers do to her? Did you kill her?' Nikki probed.

'No!' Denis shouted. 'Of course we didn't kill her!'

'So where *is* Dina Jarvis?'

'We have no idea, I swear.' Clive had finally found his voice.

Joseph shook his head. 'Okay. Ryan? You and Dina were an item, yes?'

Ryan nodded. 'Yes, we had been seeing each other for about six months.'

'As girlfriend, boyfriend? Or lovers?'

'Lovers,' he muttered.

Nikki frowned. 'Ah, now here I have a problem, Ryan. Because all her friends and everyone else we have spoken to, say that Dina was a virgin. So could you explain?'

Ryan sighed. 'She told everyone that so no one would suspect we were seeing each other.' He glowered at Nikki. '*And* to keep one or two local letches from trying to get into her knickers.'

'What would be so terrible about admitting that you were in a relationship? I suppose you were both really fond of each other?' asked Joseph.

The glower deepened. 'Have you met her brother? He'd have killed us both. Dina was his precious little twin sister, no one was good enough for her. He didn't mind her going out and having a bit of fun, but the thought of her sleeping with someone . . .'

'What about the talent scout, Gibson Ash?'

Ryan pulled a face. 'She said he was really kind to her and honestly believed that she could make it big time, in London maybe. But although she went along with it for a while, she didn't really want to go.'

'Why not? It was a huge opportunity for her.'

'She liked what she already had. She didn't want to spoil it.'

'And what did you have that was so special?'

'Sex,' growled Denis. 'She was addicted to my brother's di—'

'Shut up, arsehole! You've never done anything to help with the problem. You were just so jealous of Dina and me!'

'As if!'

Nikki held up a hand. 'What problem?'

Ryan turned a sad face in Clive's direction. 'I have to tell them, bro. I'm sorry, but it's over. We need to tell them everything.'

'I know we do, but could we do this someplace else?' Clive looked towards the door, where Nikki knew his mother and father were hovering impatiently. 'Somewhere private?'

'The station sounds like a good place to me,' said Joseph quietly. 'Just for a chat, if that's okay with you boys?'

Ryan stood up. 'Perfect. It's time this mess came out into the open, then maybe we can be a family again.'

Nikki looked at Denis's belligerent expression and thought that Ryan probably shouldn't hold his breath.

As Clive and Denis climbed into the back of Yvonne and Niall's squad car, and Joseph held the door for Ryan, Nikki's spare mobile made a chirruping noise.

'Eve!' Nikki grabbed the phone from her pocket and read the text message — one word stood out: *Pizza*.

In seconds she had alerted the station and the superintendent. She knew that an armed unit had been dispatched, but she needed to be there too.

'Hold on, Ryan! This could be the ride of your life!'

CHAPTER TWENTY-SIX

One thing that Eve was planning on changing in her new home was the conservatory. It was old and hadn't been constructed particularly well, she suspected it had been a DIY project. It was long and narrow and had single-glazed doors and windows, something the man with the glass cutter had probably been extremely happy to discover. The cutter was a standard piece of old-style house-breaking equipment and consisted of a circular cutter and a suction pad. A ring of glass was carefully cut out and removed silently, leaving a neat hole big enough to slip an arm through to unlock the door from the inside. Simple!

Eve observed him from beside her garden shed, and decided that he was definitely not an amateur. He worked fast. She had heard the front door open, and shouts coming from the front of the house. His fire had been noticed, and no doubt one of the two police officers had gone to try to either stem the blaze, or get the van off the drive and away from the house. And that left Jessie with only one man to watch over her.

The man who was just about to enter her house evidently thought that a single opponent would prove no problem. It made him either very good or overconfident.

Eve opted for "very good." It was safer that way. Never underestimate your enemy.

She felt in the pocket of her artist's apron. The gun was right there, and so were a couple of other useful items, just in case. She looked through the conservatory and saw that the sliding doors to the lounge were wide open. She had not left them like that. Maybe Jessie had gone out there and then forgotten to close them again. Whatever, it did not make things easier. If the man was armed, and she was sure that he was, he could kill Jessie's minder before the man even knew he was a target. Eve needed to sort this, and fast.

The man was now opening the door and silently entering the conservatory.

'Can I help you?'

She saw him jump. He glanced back at her, and she smiled sweetly at him. An older lady in slippers, wearing an artist's smock and sporting dabs of indigo blue pastel on her ageing face was not exactly a threat to a six foot, muscular man, but the gun did seem to bother him.

Eve had kept far enough away to prevent him reaching her with a blow. And he obviously realised that she was watching him like a hawk in case he went for his own weapon.

Her voice was as steady as the hand that held the pistol. 'If you make the slightest move, I will take you down. This gun, as you probably know, has a 13-round magazine, and I don't need to tell you the effect that it would have on human flesh at this close range.'

The corner of his mouth lifted ever so slightly. 'Oh yes. I know very well.'

'I see you do. And I also see that you are considering your next move. Please don't make one. I have killed men before, and I *will* kill you, make no mistake.'

In the background, Eve saw Jessie's minder bundle her unceremoniously from the lounge. Then she saw him making a call. Just so long as no one decided to play the hero and butt in on her.

'So, dangerous lady, what do we do now?'

'We do nothing.'

'Can I sit down?'

'No, you cannot. You can breathe, but I'd even do that with extreme caution.'

'You will not be able to hold that gun like that for long, you know. Your arm will tire, and if you make the slightest adjustment to your grip, I will be the one issuing the threats.'

Eve knew he was right, but wasn't about to tell him so. 'I disagree, but let's not argue.'

The man laughed. Eve thought it was the coldest sound she had ever heard.

And then he called her bluff and lunged.

Eve stepped back through the open door and shot him in the elbow.

His screams echoed through the shadowy back gardens of the leafy residential lane. He was still screaming when the armed response team arrived.

* * *

Nikki looked at the tableau before her and wasn't sure if she should laugh or cry.

The house was lit up like Blackpool Tower. Uniformed policemen were stationed all around it and the gardens. A van was smouldering quietly in the road, two paramedics were trying to tend to a profusely bleeding man under the close surveillance of several sharpshooters from SCO19, and her mother was standing, centre stage, lowering a wicked-looking semi-automatic pistol into an evidence bag.

'Shame, ma'am, you missed the big finale.' Jessie was white, but smiling. 'Eve was incredible.'

Nikki stared at her mother. 'Was she indeed?'

'And now I suppose I have to be taken down to the station and held for questioning.'

'Yes, you probably do. It's customary when you've just shot someone.'

'Just saved my life, more like,' said Jessie shakily.

'And in front of some very reliable witnesses,' added the policeman who had taken Jessie out of the room. 'It was the most clear-cut case of self-defence I've ever seen. He came in with intent, ma'am. A hand gun and a knife were taken off him.'

Nikki looked at her mother. 'Are you alright?'

'Is he as bad as I believe he is, Nikki?' She nodded towards the conservatory.

'Probably worse. He's an assassin and a terrorist. He's wanted right across the continent, and I have never met a more ruthless man in all my years on the job.'

'Then maybe I should have killed the bastard.' For a second a sparkle danced in Eve's eyes, and Nikki wasn't sure if she meant what she had just said or was joking.

'Can I go home now?' Jessie looked like a small schoolgirl who had been kept in for detention.

Nikki sighed. 'Not just yet, Jess, although you certainly can't stay here. We still have the matter of finding the mole.'

Joseph laid a hand on her shoulder. 'I'm sure one of our many new grasses can be convinced to drop whoever it is in the doo-doo, don't you?'

'I hope so.'

'And, Nikki?' Joseph whispered in her ear, so that no one else could hear, 'Why don't I ring Cat and ask her to take Jessie back with her for the night? I'm sure the threat ended when Eve turned Annie Oakley.'

'Good idea. Get her minders to look after her until you've arranged that.' Nikki rubbed her temples and groaned. 'And we still have Ryan Ruddick in the back of my car. We *have* to deal with those boys tonight.'

'The night is yet young.' Joseph pulled a face, 'To be honest, I'm dying to know what the hell those young men got up to with Dina Jarvis, aren't you?'

'Too right. I just need to make sure that our wailing assassin gets the very best treatment, prior to being locked up.' Nikki turned to one of the armed officers. 'This man is probably the most devious and deadly criminal you'll ever have the misfortune to meet. Treat him accordingly. Don't be fooled by the fact that he has just been apprehended by a senior citizen in fluffy slippers, okay? He needs the highest level of maximum security. Are we clear on that?'

'Ma'am, we've already had a heads-up from Interpol about him. Be assured, Mr Fabian won't be able to look anywhere without seeing a gun trained on him.'

Nikki went back to where Eve was talking to Joseph. 'I'm so sorry it came to this, Eve. I never believed that anyone would make the connection with you.'

Joseph shook his head. 'Well, I certainly didn't. It had to have been our damned insider, didn't it?'

'We need to find him, or her, and fast.' Nikki turned to Eve. 'Do you want the medics to check you over? That must have been one hell of a scary moment.'

'I'm fine, honestly. A stiff drink would be good, but I guess we'd better get the formalities over with first.' She smiled. 'And before you ask, the gun is completely official, so don't worry about that.'

'I'm glad to hear it.' Nikki squeezed her mother's arm, and whispered, 'Thank you. You really were amazing.'

CHAPTER TWENTY-SEVEN

An hour later, Nikki and Joseph sat opposite Ryan Ruddick in the only free interview room. Greenborough was stretched to capacity, but at least Freddie Carver had been transferred to another station with larger custody facilities.

'I'm tired, Ryan, and I really want to go home at some point tonight. Do you think you could explain, clearly and succinctly, what the hell happened with Dina Jarvis?'

Ryan sat forward. 'It all happened because of my younger brother, Clive. He had problems. Well, er, one very embarrassing problem really.'

Nikki had to sit on her hands to stop herself shaking him. 'Just *say* it, Ryan. It's simpler in the long run.'

'He couldn't . . . do it.' Ryan shifted around in his chair then finally sighed and told them the story.

'He saw the doctor and had tests, but they all came back okay, so the doc said it was probably just nerves. He needed to relax and chill and not worry. But the kid did worry. He'd got a girlfriend, but she started to come on too strong, and he finished up ditching her. He was almost twenty years old and he was getting ill over it.'

Joseph nodded. 'I'm sure the pressure was pretty intolerable for a lad of that age.'

'And girls can be quite cruel in that department. I wanted to help him because I thought if anyone else took the piss out of him, he'd really crack up.' Ryan exhaled. 'I went with him to the doc, and he said that maybe some stimulation might help, so I bought him some really dirty magazines. But they didn't help. The only one who finished up with them under his bed was Denis.'

Nikki had a nasty idea of where this was going, but decided to wait to be told.

'I told Dina, and she knew how worried I was, so . . .' He raised his eyes to the ceiling. 'She wondered if it would get him going if we let him watch us, kind of, making out, you know?'

'I get the picture, thank you.'

'Well, two years back, the old barn was not in the state it is now. Dad had only just built the new one and got all the new grading equipment, so my brothers and I dragged a couple of old sofas in there, and we had a beat-up old billiard table, so we took that in too, and we'd go there after work and play some music and have a few beers. Basically get out from under Mum's feet.'

'And you took Dina there too?'

'Several times. It wasn't exactly luxury, but we did get some privacy. Anyway, as the doc had said Clive needed sort of "encouraging," Dina said we should try something a bit, well, a bit more . . .'

'Naughty? Raunchy?'

Ryan looked really embarrassed now. 'I sent for some stuff from the Internet. Leather face masks with eye holes, and some other kinky stuff. I think they call it bondage gear? Dina thought it was great and couldn't wait to try it. I wasn't so sure, but if it helped . . . it was only meant to be a bit of fun, and a kind of therapy for Clive.'

If you believe that, my boy, you'd believe anything, thought Nikki.

'But we all had too much to drink and Dina, well, I don't know if it was because most of her life she had been so sheltered, but she really got into it.' He stared at the table. 'It all got a bit wild. She said that she could take us all, and she meant it.'

'And this is the sweet girl that everyone believed was a virgin?'

'The silly thing is, she *was* that sweet girl. She was kind and caring and wonderful to be with, but she had another side to her. She loved sex and she was almost insatiable.'

Joseph reached into his pocket and drew out the photocopy of Keel's diary. He flattened it out on the table in front of them. He pointed to the night creatures. 'Three men wearing black leather face masks with only the eyes showing. Our young voyeur was watching sex games! Only he didn't understand. He thought something terrible was happening to her. Did you know you were being watched?'

'We heard something, and Denis ran out. As he was buck naked he couldn't exactly give chase, but he was pretty sure it was Keel Chandler.'

'It was, and we believe he was so traumatised by what he thought he had witnessed, that he can't even speak about it two years on.'

'Oh shit.' Ryan slowly shook his head from side to side.

'Indeed. So what happened then?'

'We got dressed, and I drove her to where I always left her, a little way off from her home, and she walked the rest of the way.'

'You drove when you'd been drinking?'

'I know, but I had to get her home or her brother would have gone apeshit.'

'How did she seem?'

'She was on an all-time high. She told me that I had to keep the masks and the kinky stuff, because she couldn't wait to do it again.'

'And that was the last time you saw her?' asked Joseph.

'Yes, although she rang me later that night and said she had some exciting news for me. She had made a decision about something but didn't want to tell me over the phone. But I never saw or heard from her again.'

'Did you have any idea what she meant?'

Ryan clasped his hands tightly together. 'It could have been to do with the offer of an audition?'

'I sense an "or?"'

'Or, there was a chance she was pregnant.' He looked crestfallen. 'I told you how demanding she was? Well, I didn't always get the chance to take precautions.'

Nikki glanced at Joseph. That opened up all sorts of possibilities.

'No one else knows that, and I'd be obliged if you could keep it just between us?' Ryan asked solemnly. 'As to the rest, my brothers will confirm everything. Denis's version might be a bit more colourful, and probably overegged, but he was always jealous of what Dina and I had together.'

'As would quite a few other suitors, if they'd known what she was really like,' muttered Nikki.

'Maybe one of them did, and he didn't like it.' Ryan's voice was full of emotion. 'All I know is, Dina would never have run away. Someone took her. And maybe they took my baby too, but I'm beginning to think I'll never know the truth about that.'

'Don't be so sure. We are learning more every day.' Nikki looked at the young man long and hard. 'And I do not give up easily.'

Ryan nodded. 'I'd like you to believe that I am deeply ashamed of what I have told you, and I wish I'd had the courage to tell you about her a whole lot earlier.'

'So do I, but better late than never. Now stay put while we check a few details with your brothers, and then we'll get you home. Your parents will be beside themselves.'

'Oh dear, what do I tell them?'

'I'd advise the truth, but maybe a slightly sanitised version? Personally, I'd skip the masks and the gangbang, so as to save your mother from having a heart attack.' Nikki stood up and walked to the door. After Joseph had left, she turned back and whispered, 'And Clive's problem? Did your cure work?'

'Oh, um, yes, it did.'

'Well, I never!'

* * *

Nikki found her mother in a different interview room and clad in a paper suit.

'Not exactly Chanel, is it?'

Nikki smiled at the tall, upright woman who had kept her long, lustrous brunette hair well into her late sixties. 'You cut a pretty good figure in anything, Eve, even a disposable paper suit.'

'I didn't look too good earlier though.' She gave a half smile. 'Your villain must have wondered what the hell was going on, being threatened by a harridan with paint on her face.' The grin widened. 'But he underestimated me, didn't he?'

'Big mistake. I bet he's now seen the error of his ways.' Nikki sat down. 'They are almost through with you, but you can't go back there tonight, so come home with me. I've got some clothes that will fit you, although the trousers might be a bit half-mast.'

'Then I can pretend they are fashionable cut-offs.'

'If we are lucky, Joseph might rustle up something for us to eat too.'

'I'd like that. Oh, and I've left a telephone number with your superintendent. He can call it if he needs to, regarding my ownership of the gun. The party concerned will also confirm that I still have a certain "status" within my old department.'

Nikki tilted her head to one side. Every day another little snippet of information surfaced about her mysterious mother. She wondered what else was hidden behind that rather beautiful face. 'Considering you were essentially running a safe house, with two protection officers in-situ twenty-four seven, *and* you apprehended an armed intruder, whatever transpires here will just be routine paperwork. I doubt the super will be making any calls to your shadowy men in dark suits. And you only shot to disable, not to kill.' Nikki stood up. 'I have some loose ends to tie up, then as soon as you are free to go, we'll head home.'

'What a day!'

Nikki laughed. 'We don't make a bad team, do we? I chuck Fat Man Carver in a ditch, and you shoot his hired assassin!'

'Must run in the blood.'

'You could be right.'

Nikki caught up with Joseph in the CID room. 'I'm taking Eve home to Cloud Fen tonight.'

'Excellent. I was going to suggest that too. And luckily, I took a homemade chilli con carne out of the freezer this morning. There will be plenty for three. Stop at my place on your way home.'

'My hero.'

'I think you and your mother deserve that accolade today, don't you? I'm just the catering corps.'

'An army marches on its stomach, doesn't it?'

'Yours certainly does,' Joseph chuckled. 'Now what's left to do tonight?'

'Have you checked with the hospital regarding Dominic?'

He nodded. 'Mmm. Just done it. Still no change, I'm afraid.'

'Well, he's hanging on, I suppose.' Nikki sniffed. 'So tomorrow we have two jobs to do. Find a grass who is willing to free this station of its bloody mole, *and* start all over again with the men who lusted after Dina Jarvis.' Nikki suddenly laughed. 'I suppose we had better not tell them what their pure and chaste little maiden really got up to?'

'Absolutely not!

'Shame, I'd love to have seen their faces.'

* * *

In the lonely cottage close to the marsh, the shadows had eaten all the light. She recalled a poem that her mother used to read to her, and it was not one that warmed or soothed. It had scared her as a child, and it was scaring her now. It was about wicked shadows marching up the stairs to consume the terrified child lying in its narrow bed. She wondered what her mother could have been thinking of to read her such a thing.

Could she hear that tramp, tramp, tramp, now?

Her heart beat faster. There was definitely something.

Was it his voice calling to her? It was! Very faintly, close to her ear she heard him whispering. He was telling her that they would be together again soon.

Tears filled her eyes and she looked around hopefully, but she was still alone. It must have been the wind, or those insidious, gathering shadows.

At least she was no longer hungry. Food no longer mattered. As she had crawled under the filthy cover that evening, she had come to a decision. Tomorrow she would take all of the tablets that she had found, and then she would finally fall asleep and never wake again.

Then the wicked shadows could do whatever they wanted, because she would never be frightened again.

CHAPTER TWENTY-EIGHT

Joseph was already in his office when Nikki and Eve arrived.

'What time did you get in?'

'Not sure. Early. Couldn't sleep.'

Nikki thought he looked tired and preoccupied, but there was also something about him that made her ask, 'Have you come up with something on Dina?'

Joseph gathered up some paperwork from his desk. 'I think I have.'

'And?' she almost shouted.

'Give me a few more minutes, and as soon as the team is in, I'll explain. I could use their input to tie up the loose ends in my supposition.'

Nikki nodded. 'Right, that just gives me time to sort out Eve and get someone to take her home.'

'How was last night after you two left Knot Cottage?'

Nikki gave him a rather sad smile. 'I think it was quite hard for her. I mean she knew it was my father's home, but she had never seen it before. They were incredibly disciplined about what was acceptable in their relationship, and Eve never encroached into Dad's home life. Up until yesterday, she has always found an excuse not to visit me at Cloud Cottage Farm.'

'Life does deal out some painful situations.'

'Still, she seems fine today. At least that first trip is done with, now I feel I can invite her whenever I want, and I think she'll say yes.'

'It's another big step forward, isn't it?' Joseph smiled at her warmly.

'She's an amazing woman.'

'So is her daughter. Now, if you'd just leave me to finish this.'

* * *

Thirty minutes later the whole team had gathered in the CID office.

'Ma'am? DC Ben Radley is still here. Can he sit in on this with us?' Cat asked.

'More the merrier. He's welcome.' Nikki stood up and told them what had transpired the night before. She did not mention Jessie Nightingale, or the fact that she was at present ensconced in Cat's flat with her two protection officers. 'As you all know, we are unlucky enough to have someone among us who is, or was, on Freddie Carver's payroll. If it makes you feel any better, so does Fenchester nick, and a couple of other stations in the area. I want him found. There will be no more secrecy about what we know. I *want* him or her to know that we are actively trying to hunt them down. If any of you has a snout, or knows anyone connected to Carver who might be coaxed into revealing our mole, then lean on them hard. This situation has to be resolved, and quickly.' She drew in a long breath. 'Now I'm going to hand over to Joseph who, due to an attack of insomnia, has apparently singlehandedly cracked the Dina Jarvis mystery.' She threw him a smile and sat down.

'Thanks.' Joseph stood up and walked to the front of the room. 'Last night, after talking with the Ruddick brothers, I realised that our whole idea of Dina was flawed. She was far from what we believed. She had fooled everyone around her with a simple lie — that she was a virgin. For six months she had been having a steamy affair with Ryan Ruddick, and who is to say that he was her first? Two other people knew about their relationship, and that was Ryan's brothers, Clive and Denis. Clive would never have mentioned it to anyone, but I'm not so sure about Denis. He was eaten up with jealousy because, like so many other men around Dina, he fancied her too.'

'Deliberately or not, he could well have let it slip while having a few drinks in the pub, couldn't he?' said Dave.

'Quite possibly. But would he be believed? Denis doesn't have a warm and friendly personality, and although we know he has a lot of drinking buddies, he has very few real friends. I think it would have been generally considered that he had tried it on with her, been rejected, and was getting his own back by badmouthing her.' He paused. 'But going back to Dina herself. If Ryan is to be believed, and I think he is telling the truth, she was on very good form the day before she disappeared, and this was confirmed by other people we'd spoken to earlier. She told Ryan on the telephone that she had come to a decision about something, and that she had some very exciting news for him. The next day, she was gone.'

'Gibson Ash and his promise of X-Factor stardom?' offered Cat.

'I don't think so,' Joseph said carefully. 'I think her "exciting" news, and her decision about it, was what sealed her fate. Last night, when I couldn't sleep, I kept hearing over and over again, two chance comments. One was Niall talking about Dominic Jarvis, and saying something along the lines of "We think that deep down, he knows what happened to his sister, and sadly he couldn't admit that she would move on and make a life away from him. Hence he makes waves every so often because it's expected of him, but *he* knows, Sarge, he knows." The second comment was from Dominic Jarvis himself, just before he collapsed. He said, "You *really* should have found her by now." He wasn't just accusing us of not investigating her disappearance properly. The implication was that it was right under our noses, but we had failed to see it. Oh, yes, and he also said, "I can't do this anymore." I had the feeling he meant he couldn't keep living a lie.'

Nikki stared at him. 'You are saying that Dominic really does know what happened to his sister?'

Joseph nodded. 'I think so. And there is something else. When I visited Dominic's house and saw Dina's room, I told you that it was as if she had just stepped out for a moment. There were fresh flowers and women's magazines, and I've only just realised that the copies of *Heat*, and *Bella*, were current. Why buy up-to-date magazines for someone who was not there? It doesn't make sense.'

'He could do it out of habit,' said Ben. 'Like if he stopped buying them, he would have to admit that she was gone forever.'

'Or is she still there?' Nikki said slowly. 'Does that house have a basement?'

'No, ma'am,' Yvonne stated. 'None of the houses in Woolpack Lane have cellars, because of the silty soil.'

'What about the rest of the house, Joseph? How much of it did you see?'

'Only the lounge and Dina's bedroom. And it was a fairly big property. There could certainly be an attic or a box room.'

Nikki stood up. 'Okay, let's run with this. Dave, ring first, then get yourself over to the hospital and see if there is any change in Dominic's condition. We *really* need to talk to him. Joseph, we have to search that property. Forget a warrant, we're suspecting a person in jeopardy, so take the bloody door off if you have to. Take Yvonne and Niall with you.' She turned to Ben. 'You want to assist?'

'Absolutely.'

'Then help Cat to go through anything and everything you can dig up on Dominic Jarvis. Check his credit cards, bank statements, see if he has been buying women's things. Even look at his Tesco lists — food for one, or for two, you know the sort of thing.' She punched one fist into a cupped hand. 'Health and employment records too. I want to know everything there is to know about that man.'

'You got it, ma'am,' Cat said excitedly. 'Come on, Ben. Take this spare desk and computer and let's get digging.'

'Everyone keep in touch, and I want to know every piece of information that corroborates Joseph's theory. I'm off to talk to Greg Woodhall. Let's aim to regroup at midday, okay?'

* * *

Joseph, Yvonne and Niall were back first.

Joseph looked despondent. 'No damage done on entrance. Luckily there was a window left on a latch. But no sign of Dina, I'm afraid, and indeed no sense that anyone other than Dominic had been there for a very long while.'

'The place was like an old people's home,' said Niall. 'Really naff furnishings and a patterned carpet.'

'I thought when I went there before that it didn't suit a young unmarried guy,' agreed Joseph.

Nikki narrowed her eyes. 'That doesn't mean that he didn't do something else to her.'

'Like kill her?'

'Been known, hasn't it? "Threaten to leave me and I'll kill you." What's the garden like?'

'Rather overgrown, with an unkempt feel to it but it is fairly small and overlooked by the neighbours. I can't see Dominic burying her there,' Yvonne added.

Nikki closed her eyes then gently rubbed the lids with her thumb and forefinger.

'If only we knew what that *exciting* news was. It would give us a big clue as to what happened.'

'I can't help but think that as those words were spoken privately to Ryan Ruddick, they actually concerned him, which would indicate that maybe she *was* pregnant,' Joseph said thoughtfully. 'After all, it could be classed as exciting, and certainly something to make a decision about.'

'And it would be exactly the sort of thing that would send her overprotective twin brother Dominic right off the rails.' Nikki glanced at the clock. It was almost midday. 'Let's go and see if Cat and Ben have come up with anything useful.'

As they walked into the CID room, Dave was entering by the other door. His face was sombre. 'Dominic died earlier this morning, ma'am. I'm sorry I couldn't let you know straightaway but there was some sort of crisis going on in ICU and I couldn't get a straight answer from anyone.'

Nikki uttered a loud groan. 'Damn! Damn!'

Niall looked calmly at her. 'Ma'am? Don't sweat over it. He would never have told us anything anyway. He had plenty of opportunity to help when the sarge said he would re-investigate his sister's disappearance.'

Nikki flopped down into a chair. 'You are probably right. So . . . let's assume Dominic *was* responsible for her disappearance. Did he kill her? If so, what did he do with the body? Or did he send her away or imprison her? If so, where?'

'Ma'am? This might be nothing . . .' Ben called over from his new desk. 'I've been looking at his grocery purchases over the last few months and he seems to have bought several boxes of very expensive hand-made dark chocolates.'

'And?'

'He's severely allergic to chocolate. His medical records show that it brings on vomiting and migraine attacks.'

'Maybe they were gifts?'

'Who for? He's your original Billy No-Mates and he has no family close by,' Yvonne chipped in. 'So were they for his sister, do you think?'

Joseph suddenly said, 'Ben! When was the last purchase made?'

'A week ago. Ah . . .'

'So if they were for her, she's still alive,' whispered Nikki. 'But where?'

'Can I make a suggestion, ma'am?' Yvonne asked.

Everyone looked at her.

'I've been thinking about Keel Chandler. He was right about what he saw in Ruddick's Barn, even if he did misinterpret it. Well, he said that she had never gone away, didn't he? That he used to hear her out on the marsh. What if he really did?'

'He also said that he'd searched high and low for her. He even went into your great aunt's deserted cottage.' Joseph looked at Nikki.

'Hey! Got something!' Cat almost jumped from her chair. 'That daft kid could be right! You know I said the Jarvis twins had been left a wad of dosh? Well, that wasn't all. The old uncle who left them his estate had a cottage too, and I bet you can't guess where?'

'Carter's Fen!'

'What was the uncle's name?' demanded Nikki.

'Jude. Jude Dutton.'

'Bloody hell! He owned a big chunk of land and a farmhouse. It was closer to the marsh than Ruddick's place, and he used to keep cattle down there. Then he got hit with foot-and-mouth disease and the whole place was quarantined. He had to destroy his herd and he threw in the towel, I remember that clearly.'

'This will doesn't mention a farmhouse. It just says a small farm cottage.'

Nikki screwed up her face in concentration. 'There was something . . .' She exhaled. 'Yes, you are right, there was a cottage! But it was a wreck, as I remember.'

'Could you find it?'

She puffed out her cheeks. 'I suppose so.' Then she stood up. 'Yes! Of course I can find it! Joseph, Niall and Yvonne, let's go back to Carter's Fen.'

'I can hardly wait,' muttered Joseph. 'Bloody miserable hole!'

CHAPTER TWENTY-NINE

'Go past the farm on the drove road, then take the track that leads off to the left. It looks as if it ends with an old rotting caravan and a pile of pallets, but we go around that and there's a sort of copse. A bit beyond there, there's an inlet that comes in from the marsh itself. The cottage is between the trees and the water.'

Nikki's mind raced. People never went further than the farmhouse. She was sure about that. If she herself hardly knew of the cottage's existence, then she was sure no one else did. Maybe not even Keel Chandler.

She felt a flutter of excitement. The location was perfect for a hideout. If it was where she believed it to be, it could only be seen from the sea or the farthest reaches of the marsh. The only people who might have been near there in recent months were illegal migrants, and they were hardly likely to approach the authorities if they saw anything out of the ordinary.

Yvonne drove carefully, picked up speed on the straight drove, then slowed almost to a standstill on the sharp left-hand turn. 'There's the caravan, ma'am.'

'Park up, Yvonne. We need to go the rest of the way on foot.'

Behind the rusty carcass of the abandoned caravan, a narrow path could just be seen. It was half covered by nettles and overgrowth and difficult to follow.

Niall forged ahead, trying to clear the way for the others.

'Straight on. It opens out a bit as we get closer to the cottage.' Nikki winced and tried to pull away from a bramble that had snagged itself in her skin. Ahead of them was a dense patch of scrubby, wind-distorted trees, and she heard Joseph mumble a curse about the desolate bloody place.

They made their way through the cluster of stunted trees and down a slight incline that led to the marsh. 'The sarge is right, this is a dreadful place!' muttered Niall as he slipped on some loose shale. 'Let's hope we've got this wrong. If that girl has been kept out here for all that time I dread to think what state she's in.'

Nikki felt ice cold hands touch her heart. There seemed very little chance of finding anyone alive in this desolate spot.

Then the cottage came into view, a tumbledown, ramshackle hovel, dark and forbidding.

They made their way through a shattered wooden gate, and found a dilapidated shed door. Niall yanked it open and stared inside. Leaning against a wall that gleamed and glistened with droplets of damp, was an old-fashioned black sit-up-and-beg bicycle.

'That's no junk! There's not a spot of rust on that. Is that how he came and went without making any noise?' asked Yvonne.

'Maybe. He could also leave a car hidden somewhere, then ride in, I suppose.'

'Do you really think anyone is here?' Niall whispered.

'I think that bike indicates recent usage, so I'm guessing yes, but if she is here, we must not frighten her. If she's been held against her will for two years, well, who knows how she will react. And we'll need to call in specialist officers who understand hostage care.' Nikki shivered at the thought. 'We'll find a way in, and conduct a thorough search, room by room. Are we all agreed?'

They nodded.

'Okay, it's a long shot, but let's check the doors and see if any of them are open. You and Yvonne take the front, Joseph. Niall? We take the back, and don't go in alone anyone. We will do this together.'

In a few moments, Niall located a weak spot. 'Kitchen window is bowed with age. I can pop the latch.'

'Okay, I'll get the others.' Nikki hurried around the old building and returned with Joseph and Yvonne, by which time Niall was already raising the old sash window.

One by one they climbed inside.

The deserted kitchen was dark and dingy.

'I should think this is much the same as it was two generations ago.' Yvonne switched on her torch and the beam picked out a deep old Belfast sink, a ridged wooden drainer, bleached white with years of use, a quarry tiled floor and a battered table with two straight-backed chairs. In a recess was a black, wood-burning range, which appeared to be the only method of cooking or heating water.

Niall whistled softly. 'Look at the state of it!'

The ceiling was draped with great tangles of filthy cobwebs, and the whitewash on the walls was patchy and mouldering in places. He moved silently into the room, then stopped abruptly. 'Ah, but this is worrying. Look.'

Nikki and Joseph looked down at the thick greasy layer of dust on the surface of the kitchen table, and saw a small clear patch, free of dirt. Something had very recently been removed. There were heaps of fluffy ashes in the grate, and the hob of the ancient oven had been meticulously cleaned.

They stood and listened.

There was no noise, other than the distant sound of trickling water from the marsh. The fen was unnaturally quiet. No birds cried out, no water rats scurried through the dry reedy grass. No breeze whispered across the acres of sea lavender and tall black grass.

'I don't like this,' muttered Niall.

Nikki coughed to break the tension. 'Right, this won't get the baby a new bonnet. Let's see what's through here.' She took hold of the round, brass door handle, and looking braver than she felt, went into the living room.

They stepped straight into the Victorian era.

Joseph stared. 'What *is* all this?'

The room was decorated with heavy, flocked wallpaper. Pictures hung on the walls, ornately framed, and the furniture consisted of a bulky sofa, two wing-backed armchairs and a mahogany table. There were books, oil lamps and marble statuettes.

Yvonne lifted the corner of one of the heavy drapes that hung at the window. 'Clever! Look, ma'am. This window faces out of the back of the house, but just in case any nosey parker did happen to look in, he's lined these fine curtains with old bits of rag. No one would dream this place was inhabited.'

Nikki was looking into a velvet-covered, brocade-fringed waste bin at the empty wrappers from expensive Belgian chocolates.

Joseph was examining the books. There were textbooks on psychiatry, surgical procedures, and the identification and usage of drugs. 'What on earth was he doing here? I mean, I know he was a psychiatric nurse, but why all these?'

There was a panelled door to the right of the fireplace, and a staircase disappearing upwards at the other end of the room.

'You and Yvonne look through there, Joseph, and check any other rooms downstairs.' Nikki pointed to the door. 'Niall and I will check upstairs. I'd say there are two bedrooms. We'll take them one at a time, okay, Niall?'

'Right.' The young man edged his way carefully up the steep, narrow treads, with Nikki close behind him. On the tiny landing, they saw two closed doors. The rooms behind them were silent, nothing stirred. The first door opened at a touch.

The room was small and plain with no decoration, just distempered walls, floorboards and a single iron frame bed with a chest with three deep drawers beside it. The bed was neatly made up with white linen sheets, worn, but clean, Nikki noticed, and faded, threadbare blue blankets. There was nowhere to conceal anything, no cupboards, no doors, nothing. It was like a monk's cell.

Without a word, they moved back to the landing, and again, stood motionless, straining to hear the slightest sound from inside the second room.

As Niall leant closer to the thick oak panels, Nikki was seized with a powerful sense of dread. She knew this was where they would find Dina Jarvis.

'Ready, Niall?'

'Ready, ma'am.' He put his shoulder to the door, but it did not budge.

He tried again, but the stout oak held fast. Then Niall stepped back as far as he could on the tiny landing, and kicked hard. The lock shattered and he stumbled into the room, Nikki close on his heels.

The air in the room was foul, it smelled of a mix of excrement, urine and the staleness of a long-closed room. Nikki retched, and put a hand over her mouth. The curtains were pulled tight and there was very little light.

They carefully scanned every part of the big room, which was dark and full of shadows. It was quiet. Too quiet.

The bed was situated under the grimy panes of a barred dormer window. The dark, unmoving shape that lay upon it told them they had finally found Dina Jarvis.

Nikki wanted to call for Joseph to join them, but she could hear him still moving through the downstairs rooms and decided to let him complete his check.

She approached the stinking bedclothes, and cautiously pulled back the soiled covers.

Suddenly she was struck from the side with a blow that knocked the breath from her body and sent her sprawling across the filthy floor. As she struggled to get up, another heavier, almost crushing weight took her back to the boards, where she lay, half stunned and fighting for breath. Pinned down, she heard a throaty, gurgling cry, followed by the sound of someone scrabbling and stumbling on the staircase. Desperately fighting to drag herself from beneath whatever was holding her down, she gasped out for Niall or Joseph to help her.

Above the rattle of her laboured breath, she heard a commotion coming from the ground floor of the cottage. A manic, high-pitched scream, a thud and a groan, and then more sounds of someone blundering around and sending furniture crashing.

Then there was silence.

Nikki tried to get a grip on the iron bed leg to pull herself up from whatever was pressing on her ribcage. She had partially extricated herself and begun to wriggle free, when she heard a low moan, and realised that she had been immobilised by the full weight of Niall Farrow's body.

'Niall! Oh God! Niall!' She pushed herself to her knees and carefully turned him over, to see the dull gleam of a metal knife handle sticking from his upper arm. A great dark patch of blood had already oozed through his clothes, and in the pale light, she saw his eyes roll up, showing only the whites, and then he began to shake.

She eased herself behind him, supporting him and holding him to her, as if she were comforting a child. Gently she laid him down and pushed her rolled up jacket beneath his head and screamed for Joseph.

Instead of Joseph, Yvonne appeared in the doorway, and with a cry, she threw herself down beside her crew-mate.

'Shock more than anything, I think,' breathed Nikki. 'Although that wound is bleeding like hell. We'd better not remove the knife, but can you pack it with something?'

Without hesitating, Yvonne tore off her jacket and then her uniform blouse. She balled the white shirt up and wrapped it around the blade, gripping it tightly. 'I'm not using anything from this foul dump on my boy,' she muttered.

Nikki pulled her radio from her pocket. Thankfully it had not been damaged in the scuffle. For once in this remote area, there actually was a signal, so she immediately radioed urgent assistance required and told them their exact location. Then she knelt down again and checked Niall's pulse.

After what seemed forever, his eyes began to focus, and then he gasped loudly with pain and shock. 'What . . . ?'

Yvonne gripped his hand. 'Relax, muppet. Paramedics are on their way.'

'If they can find this cesspit of a place,' he croaked. 'And why do you have to call me "muppet?"'

'They'll find it.' Nikki assured him. 'Our vehicle is up on the lane, so they'll not miss it.'

'And you are "muppet" because you are the Most Useless Police Person Ever Trained,' Yvonne said smiling at him. 'And don't try to deny it.'

'Nikki, are you alright!' Joseph lurched into the room, one hand held tightly against his forehead.

'I'm okay, it's Niall who is hurt. She was waiting for us, Joseph, she stabbed him.'

Joseph fell on his knees and ran his hand gently through Niall's hair. 'How the hell am I going to explain this to my daughter?'

'Very carefully, I should think.' Niall managed a weak smile. 'Hell, this hurts!'

Nikki touched Joseph's arm and beckoned him away. 'Did you get her, Joseph? She went straight down the stairs.'

He shook his head. 'No. We heard the noise, but we were checking an old outhouse attached to the cottage. By the time we got back to the living room, she was behind the door. She pushed it into my face and knocked me off my feet.' He removed his hand to reveal an ugly purplish lump, 'She was like a mad thing. It was bizarre. She half ran, half hobbled outside. As soon as I'd stopped seeing stars I chased her, but then we heard you calling. I sent Yvonne to you, but when I looked for the girl, she had disappeared. I think she's hiding somewhere. Will you be okay here if I go back out there to look for her?'

'Yvonne will look after Niall. I'll come with you. She's completely deranged, so we'll stand a better chance together.'

Yvonne nodded. 'We're fine. And don't worry, I'm not going to lose the best sidekick I ever had, especially when he's engaged to the sarge's daughter. I'd get drummed out of the force.'

By the time Nikki and Joseph had got outside, a wind had got up and dark thunder clouds were gathering. The marsh looked cold, grey and desolate.

'Where could she hide in this place? Surely we'd see her.'

Joseph scanned the bleak marshland. 'She was heading towards the inlet. She could easily lie down in one of the drainage ditches below the reed line. Let's go that way.'

Nikki ran across the uneven boggy ground beside Joseph. 'Dina! Dina! We are here to help you!' She knew it would do no good, but she felt better for trying.

They were almost at the water's edge when Joseph touched Nikki's arm and held his finger to his lips. He pointed.

Nikki could see a scrap of pale material lying between some clumps of sedge.

'If she runs,' whispered Joseph, 'our best chance is a pincer move and we just bundle her down to the ground. We know she's unarmed and she must be tiring. She's definitely injured, or something is wrong with her. The way she was running — she was scuttling along, it was really odd.'

'Okay, let's go then.'

They split up, one to the right and one to the left, and ran towards what was lying in the reeds.

Dina Jarvis rose up and with a blood-curdling scream, ran straight for the water.

'The tide is coming in, Joseph! Don't let her get too far ahead or we'll lose her!'

Nikki plunged on after her. The wind carried Dina's voice back to them. She was calling to her mother to wait for her. Nikki shivered as she ran.

'Dina! Wait! We can help you!' The water was already above her ankles, and Nikki knew how easy it was to get caught by the undercurrents.

Then Joseph hurtled past her and threw himself on the wild and unkempt figure. They crashed into the water and for a moment Nikki couldn't see what was happening. Fear gripped her. Then the dark waters broke, and Joseph was staggering towards her with a figure limp in his arms.

'I've got her! Let's get her back to the cottage and find some blankets. She won't last long if we don't get some warmth into these cold bones. There is nothing of her.'

As they fought their way through the wind, across the marshy terrain, the rain started to lash down.

'Oh, marvellous!' cursed Nikki. 'As if we weren't bloody wet enough! I think we could do with some divine intervention, don't you, Joseph? Come on, you're the one with connections.' She pointed skyward.

'Prayers already answered,' he gasped. 'Look.'

As Nikki looked up she saw a line of blue lights making their way across the lane towards them. 'Oh, thank God for that!'

'Don't worry, I already have.'

CHAPTER THIRTY

That night, tired and weary, Nikki and Joseph waited for news of Dina Jarvis.

Niall was being kept in overnight for observation after an operation to remove the knife from his arm. He had been lucky, the wicked old blade had missed severing his brachial artery by millimetres, although it had nicked the cephalic vein. He had been pumped full of antibiotics, stitched up and told that although he couldn't work for some time and would need physio, he would definitely be fit enough to enjoy his engagement party at the weekend.

Nikki yawned. 'He denies it emphatically, but I've been going over and over what happened in the godawful room. It was Niall who pushed me, not Dina, as he claims. He pushed me out of the way and got between me and that knife. He saved my life, Joseph, as sure as eggs is eggs.'

'Which makes my future son-in-law, a bone fide hero, I guess?'

'It does, and his commanding officer is going to hear about it first thing tomorrow.' She yawned again. 'Tamsin looked distraught.'

Joseph nodded, 'Didn't she! I hoped it wouldn't make her think twice about marrying a copper, but,' he laughed softly, 'I underestimated her. She told me that it really brought home to her how important our work is, and how necessary our presence is when things go wrong.'

'That lass has changed beyond all recognition.'

'She has grown up, Nikki. She's a strong woman now, and I think she's going to make a damned good policeman's wife.'

'And you will stop fretting over her?'

'Never.'

'Good. But nevertheless I hated to see you so affected by Lilli and those other poor girls.'

'Some cases really get to you. It's unavoidable, isn't it?' Joseph looked at her.

'If you have a heart and are still capable of compassion, yes, they do.'

'And that poor kid, Dina. When I lifted her from the water she was soaked through, but she still weighed nothing. She was so emaciated it was like picking up a bundle of clothes with no body inside them.'

'After what she's suffered, I'm not actually sure if I want her to survive. Is it cruel to think that way?'

'Of course not. You just don't want her to suffer even more.'

Nikki's phone buzzed in her pocket. 'DI Galena.' She listened for a few moments then thanked the caller and punched the air. 'Yes! They've identified the mole!'

Joseph heaved a sigh. 'So our Jessie can come home!' Then, 'But who was it?'

'A young PC, sadly. He didn't show up for work today, but the desk sergeant had an anonymous call giving his name. They went round to his place, but he'd already gone.'

'That's really bad news.'

'Apparently the kid had a lot of problems, some of them financial. Maybe Carver's boys caught him at a low point.'

'Why are you making excuses for a rogue cop, Nikki Galena?'

'Because I'm getting older, and things don't seem as black and white as they used to.'

A tall thin man with dark-rimmed glasses walked in and held out his hand. 'DI Galena? I'm Dr Levin and I'm looking after Miss Jarvis. I've been given a little background information, but could you tell me any more about how she came to be in this condition?'

Nikki explained as much as she felt was appropriate, and the doctor sighed. 'As soon as we had stabilised her, we needed to operate, I'm afraid. She had a massive infection and she is still in a critical condition.'

'What happened to her, Doctor, to make her so . . .' Joseph wasn't sure how to explain the odd gait and the fact that Dina had been almost bent double when she tried to run. 'Her body so twisted in that way?'

'She has undergone what I can only describe as butchery. It was apparently an attempt at aborting a foetus. The abominably inept "operation" caused severe haemorrhaging and infection, and later, massive and agonising adhesions formed.' The doctor stared at their shocked faces. 'Sorry to put it so bluntly, but there it is. And she still has a weird cocktail of drugs in her blood. Analgesics, anti-inflammatory drugs, hallucinogens and a few other things that we haven't yet identified. From her general condition, and from what you've just told me about her incarceration, I suspect she had regularly been given a variety of drugs for her pain as well as to keep her docile.'

'Poor little devil,' whispered Joseph. 'And to think she once had a chance of singing and dancing professionally.'

Nikki shuddered. *Her own brother! Her twin brother! How could he?* 'And the operation?'

'We've really just done what we can to make her more comfortable. She had severe sepsis, so we had to remove infected tissue and try to reduce the bacterial load.' He frowned. 'If she survives, she should consider more radical surgery sometime in the future.'

'And her chances of surviving?'

'Impossible to guess at this point.' His pager began to bleep. 'Sorry, got to go.' He paused. 'I'd say she'll recover from the physical injuries. As to her mental state, that's not mine to call.' He hurried away, then called back, 'Mind you, if they can get her safely through coming off the drugs, the whole event might seem to her like a really bad trip. Believe it or not, people have survived worse than this.'

'Not convinced,' said Nikki to the man's retreating back. 'I can't think of too much worse than what she's gone through.'

'Me neither. Shall we go home?'

'Yes.' Nikki linked her arm through Joseph's. 'Oh yes!'

CHAPTER THIRTY-ONE

Greg Woodhall's room no longer looked like a lost property office. Even his desk was tidy. Nikki and Joseph sat opposite the superintendent.

'Hired a daily help?' asked Nikki lightly.

He rubbed his hands together. 'More or less. New office manager actually, and he enjoys a challenge.'

'He must,' murmured Joseph. 'Or maybe he's just a masochist.'

'Now, now, Joseph, it wasn't that bad.'

Nikki raised her eyebrows.

The conversation stalled. There was serious business to attend to and none of them really wanted to deal with it.

'You've been back to the place where Dina Jarvis was confined?' Greg asked.

'Yes, sir, forensics are working the scene now. It has been photographed and evidence has been collected, but it does seem as if no one else was involved. It was Dominic Jarvis alone who abducted her.'

'We found a series of notebooks, sir, not diaries exactly, but he was an inveterate note maker. There were memos everywhere. I'm sure when we piece them together they will answer some of our questions about his state of mind.'

'What about the drugs he fed her?'

'We spoke to his GP. Dominic had convinced him that he suffered from a condition called CRPS, or complex regional pain syndrome. Its symptoms are excruciating pain in certain areas following a simple knock or bruise. The intensity of the pain bears no relation to the injury. It is a difficult condition to prove or disprove, and the GP issued a repeat prescription for very strong painkillers. We think he gave them to Dina.'

'He stole others from the psychiatric hospital, but mainly he bought whatever he could from dealers,' added Joseph. 'We found ketamine, barbiturates, PCP, LSD in the form of microdots, and roofies, sorry, benzodiazepines, bit like rohypnol.'

'All of which I suppose can cause hallucinations, altered states of reality, nightmares, memory loss and paranoia.'

'She's lived for two years in a drug-induced hell, all because her brother was either a control freak or eaten up with jealousy. I think prior to that, he subjected her to years of psychological manipulation.' Nikki shuddered.

'And she found an outlet for all her pent-up emotions in Ryan Ruddick and their sex games,' Joseph said. 'Which should have caused no harm really, but we believe she made the mistake of telling her brother that she was pregnant.'

'I saw some marginal notes in one of his medical books. They referred to the fact that he was only doing it, *because he loved her and would stand by her even though she had done something so terrible that everyone would shun her, everyone except him*. It made me feel sick.' Nikki shifted uncomfortably in her chair. 'The bastard.'

Woodhall frowned. 'I know that some of the time she was drugged and locked in her room, but couldn't she have found a way to escape?'

'We also found restraints attached to her bed, sir. I think he took no chances whenever he was away. And we are thinking, from what we have seen, that he led a double life. Partly in the comfortable town house, and partly with her on the marsh.'

'And we would never have opened a new investigation if you hadn't been hunting down Freddie Carver.'

Nikki nodded. 'The connection was tenuous, wasn't it? Linking her to Freddie's talent scout, Gibson Ash, but we got there, didn't we?'

'And now Jessie and Graham can come out of protection?' asked Joseph.

'It's being arranged as we speak. Oh yes, and the Met have found the remains of Carver's first wife, so along with all the other charges, here, in Derbyshire, and down south, I'm certain that Freddie Carver won't ever taste freedom again.'

'Bet the Spanish villa that he hated so much doesn't look so bad to him now,' laughed Joseph.

'Let's take bets on where he goes, shall we?'

'I'll put a fiver on Wakefield,' said the super. 'Biggest Cat A in Western Europe.'

'I'd prefer Belmarsh,' mused Joseph. 'It holds the most dangerous men in the country and has that infamous "prison within a prison" facility.'

'I'd put my money on Frankland.' Nikki sighed. 'I'd love to think of him sharing the good life with Huntley and Sutcliffe and the rest.' She sat back and looked at her two colleagues. 'Does this mean we can actually afford to relax again for a while?'

'Once you've cleared the mountain of paperwork that these cases have generated, I'd suggest some leave. How does that sound?'

Nikki sat up. 'Do you know, that sounds absolutely great!'

Greg and Joseph stared at each other, wide-eyed. Had they heard right? Was Nikki Galena actually agreeing to take a break?

'I think Eve deserves a treat after what she did for Jessie Nightingale. I'm going to suggest a holiday. My treat.' She grinned at Joseph. 'I could probably just stretch to taking you too, if you fancy it?'

'Oh dear, it's a lovely thought, but *someone* will have to stay and hold the fort.'

Joseph clasped his hands together, looking pathetic. 'Greenborough has never had to manage without you before. I'm not sure how we will cope.'

'Oh bollocks, Joseph. Just bugger off and arrest someone, will you?'

* * *

Graham Hildred stepped into the house that had once been his happy home with Jessie.

'It's not changed a bit, Jess.' He wandered around, running his hand over familiar objects, picking up ornaments and carefully putting them down again. 'You know, all the time I was away, I remembered the smell of our home. Wood smoke, those smelly dried flowers of yours, and the herbs you hang in the kitchen to dry.' His voice faded. 'I never thought, although I always hoped . . .' He walked over to the fireplace. 'What's this?' He looked at the birthday card. 'But your birthday isn't until summer!' He picked it up and read it. Tears filled his eyes. 'You bought this for me? Even though I could have been dead? Or run off? My poor Jess, you had no idea what had happened, had you? Yet you still clung on.'

She gave a helpless shrug. 'It's like you just said, I always hoped.'

He held his arms out to her, and she fell into them with a sob. In that instant, he knew that he'd been right to hold on, to put up with the terrible suffering. It would take time, he knew, he was no fool, but surely, if they could each pull through alone, then they would damn well pull through together.

EPILOGUE

Joseph looked around. The gathering for the engagement was verging on the surreal.

Niall and Tamsin had said it was to be a casual drop-in/drop-out affair, to accommodate their colleagues working shifts, but it seemed that everyone had stayed. The room was full of guests, all drinking, eating, talking and laughing.

The surreal part was the mix of people.

Eve Anderson was laughing with the pathologist, Rory Wilkinson. Niall's sister, who worked at a seal sanctuary, was in deep conversation with Superintendent Greg Woodhall. Mickey Leonard was happily chatting to the custody sergeant, and that was *really* weird. Dave was having a friendly joke with a friend of Tamsin's, who looked more like an eco-warrior than a party guest. And Nikki had been cornered by a couple of probationer constables, eager to hear what sort of advanced technique she had used to run the Lexus off the road.

The only two who were glued together were Cat Cullen and Ben Radley, and Joseph wondered if they might be the next ones to be celebrating.

Tamsin swept up to him and clung onto his arm. 'No Jessie?'

'They sent their love, but it's a bit too soon for Graham to be in a crowd like this.' Joseph looked around. 'Where did all these people come from? The nick must be empty!'

'Search me, Dad. I sent out ten invites — methinks my husband-to-be is a popular man.'

'He is.' Joseph smiled at his daughter. 'I am so very pleased for you, sweetheart.'

'It's going to be okay, you know that, don't you?'

'I do now. You make a wonderful couple.' He took her arm and steered her to a couple of empty chairs. 'I haven't mentioned this before, but as an engagement present, I'd like to help you with the deposit on your new home. I'm telling you this first, because I want to make sure that I'm not doing the wrong thing. I know Niall is a proud lad and he wants to provide the best for you, and the last thing I want to do is upset him.'

Tamsin hugged him, and kissed him on the cheek. 'Dad, that's wonderful! And you won't offend Niall, I promise you, he'll consider it a huge compliment that you want to help us.'

'Good, then keep it quiet for now, and I'll tell you both together.'

'And I'll act *so* surprised!' She looked at him. 'Speaking of being surprised, someone who obviously wanted to remain anonymous has put a large sum of money behind the bar. You wouldn't have anything to do with that as well, would you?'

'No, Tam, sorry. Not me this time.'

'Mmm, then I need to do some sleuthing. Although I do have my suspicions.' She kissed him again and ran off to join Niall and his brothers.

'She looks so beautiful, and so happy.'

He turned to find Nikki staring after his daughter. Her eyes were misty, and he knew that she was thinking of

302

Hannah. He slipped his arm around her waist. 'Yes, yes, she does. I never dared to believe this day would come.'

'But it has, and I can't tell you how pleased I am for you. It must feel like it's taken forever, but you really do have your daughter back.'

Now it was his turn to wipe a tear from his eye.

'Joseph? It's been a very long time, hasn't it?'

He turned to see his tall, elegantly dressed ex-wife watching them.

'Well, introduce me, Joseph. This has to be the famous Nikki Galena!'

Joseph stared from one to the other and coughed. 'Of course, sorry, Laura, meet Nikki, and Nikki,' He gave a small shrug, 'I think you probably guess that this is Laura.'

They shook hands, all smiles and pleasantries, but the tension hummed between them. Joseph felt the chilly draft. Until this moment the party had been so relaxed, but now he wished he was out on the marsh somewhere.

'Would you mind, Nikki? I'm terribly sorry, but I really need to interrupt. Joseph and I have a lot to talk about, and some arrangements to sort out, as it seems *our* daughter is about to marry.'

'Of course. Take all the time you need.' Nikki gave him a strange look. He was sure it meant, 'Good luck, mate, looks like you're going to need it.'

* * *

Yvonne Collins sipped her glass of wine and moved closer to Dave. He looked like he needed rescuing before he went off to join Greenpeace.

'I was talking to Jessie earlier,' Dave said, helping himself to a sausage roll. 'She is taking extended leave to be with Graham.'

'That's good. They need some time together.'

'I don't think she'll come back, Yvonne. Graham knows that he couldn't do this job any more, not after what he's been through, and I get the feeling they will move a long way away from here.'

'Can you blame them? I would, if I had someone I loved like that. I'd go at the drop of a hat.'

'Me too, but I'll miss the kid. She's not been with us long, but I really liked her.'

'That's life, my friend. But on a more serious note, what do you make of that?'

She nodded her head to where Joseph and Nikki were talking to a tall, rather austere looking woman.

'Ah, the ex has arrived.' Dave stared, unabashed. 'She's beautiful, isn't she?'

Yvonne took another mouthful of wine and looked over her glass at the trio. 'Sure, she's beautiful on the outside, but . . . damn, I was really looking forward to this bit, but not anymore.'

Dave stood beside her in silence.

As they watched, Nikki walked away towards Eve Anderson. Just before she reached Eve, she glanced back at Joseph, and Yvonne and Dave both saw the look on her face.

'Oh dear,' said Dave.

Yvonne merely sighed loudly. Then she said, 'I could be wrong, but this does not bode well.'

* * *

Nikki and Eve walked together to the back of the room and found a quiet spot away from the hubbub.

'I've just met Joseph's ex-wife, Laura.'

'And from that stony expression, I gather you were none too impressed.'

Nikki shrugged. 'She's not what I expected, that's all. I thought she would be, well, nicer, I suppose. Joseph always said how good she was with Tamsin, and she did pull out all the stops to help when the girl was in danger a while back, but, I don't know, she doesn't seem like the same person.'

'Didn't Joseph say something about things going wrong in her life? With her job *and* with her partner leaving her?'

Nikki nodded.

'That could be the answer then. People change when bad things happen in their lives.' Eve looked at her shrewdly. 'You don't have to worry, you know. Joseph is a very astute man. He won't be doing anything silly, have no fear on that score.'

Nikki didn't reply. She had sensed something about Laura, and she didn't like it. She sometimes experienced the same feeling when working a case, and it always spelled trouble.

She took a long swallow of her wine, then looked at Eve. 'If you could go anywhere in the world for a holiday break, where would it be?'

Eve didn't hesitate, 'Santorini.'

'Greek island?'

'In the Aegean Sea, one of the Cyclades.' She smiled at the thought. 'I went to so many places while I was in the RAF, but somehow I never made it to Santorini, and I've always regretted it.' She looked enquiringly at Nikki. 'Why?'

'It should take a couple of weeks to get my desk cleared. Will you be free then?'

'As a bird, but—'

'I'll book the tickets.'

Eve stared at her. 'When was the last time you had a holiday, Nikki?'

Nikki opened her mouth and then shut it again.

'Come on, when?'

'Hannah must have been about eight, I suppose. We went to Scarborough for a week.'

'I thought as much. Work always came first, didn't it? So why now?'

'Er, because I'd really like to spend some time with my mother?'

'And that's absolutely wonderful, but is there another reason?'

Nikki gave a brief glance over to where Laura was in deep conversation with Joseph. 'Because it's time I got away from Greenborough for a little while.' She finished her wine. 'Yes, Eve, it's time for a break.'

THE END

Thank you for reading this book. If you enjoyed it please leave feedback on Amazon or Goodreads, and if there is anything we missed or you have a question about then please get in touch. The author and publishing team appreciate your feedback and time reading this book.

Our email is office@joffebooks.com

www.joffebooks.com

ALSO BY JOY ELLIS

CRIME ON THE FENS
SHADOW OVER THE FENS
HUNTED ON THE FENS
KILLER ON THE FENS
STALKER ON THE FENS
CAPTIVE ON THE FENS

THE MURDERER'S SON

Printed in Great Britain
by Amazon